SOMETHING TO DO WITH LUCK?

SEX, DRUGS & ROCK 'N' ROLL
HAS NEVER BEEN TOLD LIKE THIS BEFORE

By

Graham W.B. Smith

*As this is my debut novel, I'd like to dedicate this
to my nearest and dearest, my partner Jean,
my parents Angie and Gordon, and my brother Colin. I love you all.
But also to my grandmother Elizabeth "Betty" Hutt (nee Paul)
whom I never met.*

CONTENTS

ACKNOWLEDGEMENTS

To my partner Jean for her love, patience, encouragement, and her unshakeable belief in my ability to complete this. To my proof-readers Colin Smith, Moyz MacLeod, and Adso Broon for their time, feedback, and general words of encouragement. To William McIntyre for answering my questions and providing information on legal proceedings in Scotland, to Angie Spoto for page layout and chapter advice and last but by no means least to Tom Johnston for all his insight into the legal proceedings and terminology used in Scotland, for all his time in reviewing multiple editions of the manuscript and constantly correcting the grammar and punctuation held within and also for his words of encouragement. Thank you to you all. Your help and assistance were very much appreciated and without it this book would not have been completed.

Actually, it would have, but it would've been shite!

Mayo for Sam!

INTRODUCTION

You have in front of you a story. A story about many things. Daft things, clever things, funny things, and sad things. It's a story about friendship, respect, and betrayal. It's also about love and hate and life and death.

This story takes on many different forms and the grammar throughout, I'm guessing, will be of a poor standard. As will the punctuation. For this I make no apologies. I see it as a failing by the Scottish education system to which I dedicated 13 years of my life only to have them reward me with a half-arsed education, leaving me ill prepared for the big bad world.

The writing also takes on many styles, jumping from first-person narrative to third person, whoever and whatever that may be. It can switch between present tense, past tense, and future tense with more frequency than a Quentin Tarantino film. It also features ordinary prose, diary style, poetry, musical lyrics, and daydream ramblings.

I have written it in this way because … well, it's the only way I know how to. See above with regards to the Scottish education system.

For many years I have dreamed of becoming a writer, however, circumstances, procrastination, and general apathy kept me from fulfilling my dream.

Until now.

What's changed?

Well, I suppose circumstances. Tired of waiting for the right opportunity to present itself to me, I, along with some gentle pushing, took the crazy notion to go find one for myself. You never know what you might find if you go looking. I'd be lying if I said that this is the type of thing I saw myself writing about.

But it's a start.

Who knows what roads lie beyond this one? Perhaps many, long and winding. Perhaps none. I'll never know unless I start walking.

This story is about myself and my two childhood friends Sid and Bobby and the time we spent touring Scotland with our band Champions Of The Underdog, desperately trying to land a record deal so we wouldn't have to go back to our dead end jobs in our dead end town.

This is a story about survival, about perseverance, about pride, about destiny.

My name is Jimmy Steel, and this is my story.

This is our story.

Make of it what you will, after all, it's just a story.

CHAPTER 1

"That's a ridiculous idea, Sid," I complained as I sat opposite him in a packed, dark and dingy boozer watching the expression on his face change the way it always does when he's trying to convince me that he's right and I'm an arsehole for disagreeing with him.

Glaikit would best describe it.

"No it's no'. It'll be brilliant. Think about it, the three of us out on the open road touring Scotland, playing our tunes, visiting all the towns and places we've never seen before … "

Sid took a large gulp of his pint as if to emphasise his next point.

"… there'll be loads of boozing …"

There it is.

"… and burds and … "

Wait for it. Hold. Steady now. Here comes the pièce de résistance.

"… amazing scenery."

Voilà.

"It'll be rare fun, man. Come on, where's your sense of adventure, Jimmy?"

"Sid, we're only a kick in the arse from 40. Do you no' think that's a wee bitty too old to still be playing at rock stars? Folk'll laugh at us, it's a young person's game. Have you no' read any music magazines lately? They're full o' kids with styled hairdos and skinny jeans and all that shite. I've hardly got any hair left and Bobby dresses like he's waiting for his pension book to drop through the letter box any day now."

"Aye, well, sometimes it takes a bit o' time for folk to get their talents recognised. Look at Jarvis Cocker. He was in his 30s before Pulp made it big. Bill Withers was 32 before he even entered a recording studio and Alex Harvey was like us in his late 30s before he became sensational, so your argument is totally pish."

If Sid thought that by waving his arms in a wild sweeping motion it would give his argument that wee bit of emphasis, he was sorely mistaken.

"Bill Withers was amazing, and Alex Harvey was sensational. We're no'.

They all had something to offer, we dinnae. It's making me cringe just thinking about it. It's bad enough playing the same old pubs in town every week but touring Scotland for six months? Christ we're lucky if we get a dozen folk coming to see us play in the local and they all ken our tunes, what chance have we got of pulling in a crowd in Wick or Oban or wherever else you dream of playing?"

"Ullapool. I've never been there before; we should definitely play there. Apparently, they've got an amazing chippy, almost as good as the one in Anstruther. Look, this isnae a spur of the moment, first-thing-I-thought-of-when-I-got-up-this-morning number. I've given it some serious thought. I've been in contact with a few pubs up and doon the country and they're more than willing to put us on. The pay'll no' be that great but just think how cool it'll be – you, me, and Bobby McGee on the open road playing in all these wee trendy independent joints. Imagine the cult status we'll acquire and by the time we hit King Tut's, Brian Epstein himself will be clambering out of his grave to sign us."

"Pish. What about transport? We cannae just hitch around the place with all our gear. What about our jobs? What'll we do for money? Where are we gonnae stay? Have you spoken to Bobby about this? What about Debbie and Mel? I mean for fuck's sake, Sid. We've all got ties now. You cannae just snap your fingers and go weeeeeeeeeee, this is magic I think I'll bugger off for a wee jaunty around the country singing my songs and living off the land cause I've got magic snappy fingers and when I click them all my dreams will come true and the world will be filled with rainbows a la dee dah de dee."

"Fuck off you sarky wee shit. You see, that's your problem."

Now he's giving me the stabby finger routine. He reminds me of an irate football manager who's gesticulating wildly and constantly pointing at the player he's not best pleased with.

"It's always been your problem, nae ambition, cannae see the big picture. Well I'm being serious, I'm selling the flat—"

"You're selling the flat?" I spluttered in shock, sending a spray of beer flying across the highly polished wooden table.

"Would you let me finish?" Sid glared at me until I sank back into my seat. "I'm selling *MY* flat and with the profits I'm gonnae buy a big motor, I'm gonnae buy some new equipment, maybe pick up a new guitar and amp …"

I tutted in disgust at this ridiculous money wasting list and Sid held up his finger for silence when it looked as though I was about to interrupt him further.

"… and then I'm gonnae buy a fancy new laptop so I can email all the bars and clubs to see where we can play and keep in contact with the folks in the big smokes. You can update our Twitter and Facebook sites and even do one o' thae blogs telling a'body what we've been up to and once I figure out how to work the bloody thing properly, we can maybe record demos and gigs on it too. The rest of the profits will be for food and petrol and such likes to supplement our income for the trip. Look, I hate my job and you certainly hate your job, and Bobby … well, Bobby'll just go with the flow as usual, so I cannae see any real difficulties on that front which just leaves the girls. Maybe if I snap my magic fingers they'll disappear in a puff o' smoke and it'll be just like the good old days, eh?"

I felt the rage bubbling violently inside me.

"Jesus Christ have you lost the plot? You're seriously going to sell the flat? Where the hell am I gonnae stay? That's my home too. You cannae just sell it without giving me any warning, I've got rights as a tenant. I cannae believe this. You're seriously thinking about doing this and for what, eh? So you can massage your ego by telling anyone that'll listen that your band's gonnae be touring the country playing all the hot spots and that we're gonnae be the next big thing, next stop the Hollywood Bowl and aw that jazz."

"Calm doon. Fuck's sake. A'bodys staring at us. I dinnae want those nosy auld bastards knowing my plans," Sid whispered as he pointed over my shoulder to the inebriated mass slowly creeping towards our table hoping that they might get to hear some juicy gossip. "Listen, you ken this is all I've wanted to do since I was a kid. I'm tired of playing the same old shit houses week in week out to a bunch of pissed up wankers demanding to hear Led Zeppelin and The Who covers. I've got to do something about it. Like you say, we're no' getting any younger, this could be our last chance. I dinnae want to be sitting in a retirement home in a few years slurping soup and reeking o' foosty pish thinking 'if only I'd taken that music thing seriously, I could've been someone and done something with my life'."

"So yet again everyone's life gets mucked about for one of your stupid ideas? Look, if you're that serious about giving it one last chuck o' the dice with the band could we no' just do something like the Fence Collective? That way we could stay here and still make music? It's all the rage these days."

"Whit?! Those jumper-wearing, beardy cunts? Piss off, we want to be rock stars. If you're gonnae do it, do it right. Everyone's making music in their bedroom these days and that's why it's all shite. If we want to be big, we've got to do what the great bands did. Tour. The old-fashioned way. Put in the effort and you'll get the rewards. If I don't do this, Jimmy, then I'll regret it for the rest of my days. I've got to give it a shot. I've made my mind up, it's happening whether you and Bobby want it or no'. I'd much rather do it as a band but if you're no' up for it, well, que sera an' aw that jazz." Sid smirked as he waved his hands in an infuriating jazzy fashion.

"You're a selfish prick, you ken that?" I seethed. "I'm out of here."

I snatched my belongings from the wobbly wooden table, kicked my chair back and shoved my way past the nosey punters who were all squeezed around the puggy next to our table.

I was so pissed off with Sid's ridiculous plan that I had fled the pub with three quarters of a pint remaining.

I'm not entirely convinced with my decision to open the story like that.

I was thinking about beginning with Sid, Bobby, and myself driving off into the sunset before heading to our first gig on the tour. Then I thought about being all cultured and starting off with the ending and then meandering my way back through the story.

But what can I do about it now, eh?

I suppose it's as good a place to start the story as any other and it all took place one lazy Saturday afternoon with Sid and myself chewing the fat over a couple of pints in a decrepit pub in our hometown when he went and dropped that bombshell on me. I was absolutely livid. That boy can be such a self-indulgent twat. It amazes me that he can still find ways to make my blood boil, considering he's pulled almost every cuntish stunt on Bobby and me over the years.

I was annoyed by the way he always expects everyone to drop everything and come running, like we're his servants awaiting his beck and call.

Ding a ling a ling.

Yes master, you rang? What's that, master, drop everything and come with you? Why certainly, master, it'd be my pleasure. Would master be wanting his balls caressed too? Oh you really are the best, master.

The band is Sid's baby.

Sure, Bobby and me are a part of it, but only a small part. We mainly tag along for the ride because it's something to do, It fills a void in our otherwise

6

meaningless, pathetic lives, giving us a chance to relive our youth and deny the fact we're hurtling towards middle age with a severity and speed that we're only too keen to deny.

If Sid could do it all by himself, he'd kick us into touch without as much as a 'see you later, lads'.

We're only there because he needs a bass player and a drummer.

But the thing that angered me most of all was that I knew I'd give in.

I always do.

There's a major flaw in my system that won't let me say 'NO' to any of his crazy ideas. Even more frustrating is that he knows it too. Perhaps I need to acquire a self-help book on assertiveness.

I'll agree that on paper it does indeed sound like a great idea, really good fun you might say. A bunch of mates touring their beloved nation playing songs to all and sundry. But everything sounds good on paper, hell even Communism sounds all right. It's only when you put egocentric, power-hungry maniacs in charge of said paper that things start to go horribly wrong and in Sid we've got a gem of a leader.

It's as somebody once said though, "He's a mate, what can you do?"

Allow me to borrow a few moments of your time as I reminisce.

I've known Sid since I was three years old. We both grew up in the same sleepy town in a lovely wee part of the world known as the Kingdom of Fife, or to be more specific, the constituency known as North East Fife.

We first met at playgroup, a pre-school gathering where we bonded over our love of playing in the sand pit and the fact that we were the only two boys to greet when our mummies dropped us off in the morning. I'm not talking about the 'aw, boo hoo my mummy's gone, woe is me' kind of greetin'. I'm talking about the 'cannae even breathe cause I've been screaming that much, snotters flying everywhere, stringy slavers bungee jumping down to the floor and back up again' kind of greetin'.

Not for the faint hearted.

We spent our tranquil primary school days dreaming of playing football for our favourite team, the mighty Dundee United, but alas it wasn't to be. Despite our best efforts to do this through dedicated training and the honing of our skills with various coaches at various local teams, it took us several years of bench warming on cold, wet, miserable weekend mornings to realise that we were in fact what you might term 'pish' or 'no' guid enough'.

It still cuts like a knife when I think back to the dawning of this revelation in my head when I suddenly became aware of the thought, 'what the hell am I gonnae do with my life now? I'll need to get a proper job'.

That's how good we thought we were.

We just took it for granted that we would both get picked up by a passing scout from Dundee United F.C., who just so happened to be wandering through the town and using his instinctive abilities to suss out the next Duncan Ferguson, would stumble upon our park and find himself staring in disbelief at the amazing array of skills put on show by the two of us. The deft touches, the defence-splitting passes and the way I leapt like a salmon to head in crossed balls. Not forgetting to mention the classic goal celebration of waving team mates out of the way so we could complete our meticulously rehearsed knee slides in peace.

I'm still convinced the football scout's car broke down en route.

After our crushing disappointment in the football field, Sid turned his attention to finding something else where he could be the centre of attention.

Rock 'n' Roll.

And where Sid went, I duly followed.

I should probably mention at this point in the proceedings that Sid isn't his real name. We just got lazy and shortened his nickname. Sid was christened Ian Maxwell Hughes by his dotting parents. He came by the nickname of Sidney whilst performing work experience at high school.

For those of you who never had the pleasure of 'work experience' at high school, let me tell you that you missed out on a treat.

You take a bunch of 13- to 14-year-old kids (most of whom already have work experience by doing paper rounds, milk rounds, shop work etc.) and let them choose a job that they would like to have a brief working experience of. Preferably something that relates to the field of employment in which they see themselves slaving away at once said 13- to 14-year-old leaves school.

So far so good you say?

But wait, it gets better.

In the slight eventuality that your choice isn't available from the diverse list, the sweet folks at the education department give you another two picks to choose from as a form of consolation.

For example a kid with a high level of intellect might choose thus; 1: Doctor 2: Lawyer 3: Accountant.

Your kid of average intellect might go for 1: Architect 2: Engineer 3: Estate Agent.

And your window-licking mentalist would probably pick something like 1: Stunt performer: 2: Circus owner 3: Incredible Hulk.

Now this is the best part, the climax.

You've spent a month thinking about your pick and where you're going to be spending your two weeks' work experience. The intelligent kids are almost wetting themselves with excitement at the thought of administering prescription medication to the poor and needy. Me personally, I was dreaming of working in a sweetie factory, oh please, please, please.

No, this is the best part, the crippling impotency of the anti climax.

The highly intelligent kid will spend two weeks of work experience licking envelopes in a bank and perhaps, if lucky and has impressed the branch supervisor, being entrusted to count a couple of bags of pound coins on the second last day.

The kid of average intellect will spend two weeks sweeping the floor of a joiner's yard whilst being ribbed mercilessly by the former window lickers who now work there as apprentices and, if lucky and have impressed the yard supervisor, won't be set upon by the apprentices on the last day.

And your current crop of window lickers?

Well, they don't actually get to leave the classroom as they're deemed a menace to society and spend their two weeks throwing sharp objects at each other and teasing the supply teacher mercilessly about his/her sexual orientation. If they have been threatening enough to the supply teacher, they will be allowed to leave school early on their last day.

These examples apply for both male and female students. At least the education board is non-discriminatory.

Now Sid was a bit of an inbetweener, he was too smart to be a mentalist, but he was too anti-authority to allow the school to trust him for two weeks without adequate supervision. Therefore, he was allowed out of the classroom but not out of the school grounds.

So he spent his two weeks' work experience as a janitor's assistant. It was brilliant, we took the piss for ages. To be a janny's assistant was the lowest of the low. You weren't deemed responsible enough to carry out sweeping duties or be able to administer the piling of sand onto the puke of fellow pupils on your own, you merely had to assist.

And it was thanks to Ian's janitorial uniform of blue overcoat and cloth cap, which the head janny kindly lent him for his stint, that Ian Hughes became ...

Stars In Your Eyes, dry ice, tonight Matthew I'm going to be, entrance ...

Sidney the Tetley Tea man.

Fucking magic!

The piss taker had become the piss takee!

Sid of course denied he wore the outfit but we had it on good authority from one mentalist, so his nickname stuck.

For the record I spent my two weeks' work experience in a joiner's yard sweeping sawdust and listening to a nutter go on and on about how it would be dead funny if there was a guy with a surname called Wood who worked down the road at the steel fabricators and because my surname is Steel and I'm working in a joiners yard it would be dead funny eh?

Irony?

Fantastic.

Aye I see what you did there, pal, Wood-Steel, Steel-Wood. You're a fucking genius. How come there's never a two by four with a nail driven through it lying around when you need it most?

And in a joiner's yard too, what's the chances of that?

Right, that's enough reminiscing for now, back to the story.

I was in a right huff after my lazy Saturday afternoon fat-chewing session with Sid so I went where I always did in moments like that, to see my beloved girlfriend Debbie.

When a man's feeling troubled there's nothing like the loving affection of his lady's kind words and warm smile to cheer him up again.

"Hiya, darling," I sighed as I trudged through the back door and into her newly renovated kitchen, putting on my best doe-eyed puppy dog expression for effect.

"What's the matter with your face, have you been getting stoned again? If you're stoned you can just turn around and walk straight back out the door, you know I can't stand you when you're stoned," Debbie lectured as she continued emptying the dishwasher.

That wasn't quite the sympathetic response I had in mind.

"No, I'm not stoned, I'm pissed off. I went for a couple of pints wi' Sid earlier and … och, it doesn't matter."

I'm such an idiot. This is the last place I should have come when I'm having problems. Especially when they're with Sid.

Debbie hated Sid and the feeling was mutual.

When Debbie first moved to town a few years back, Sid made a bee line for her after one of our gigs and she spurned his sleazy advances in spectacular style in front of the whole pub. He's hated her ever since.

I fell in love with her at that exact moment.

What the fuck was I thinking coming back here and mentioning his name?

Oh shit here it comes, her expression changed the minute I mentioned his name, the gag reflex, the fury …

"What's that moron been up to now? Still swaggering around thinking he's Jim fucking Morrison? That guy is such an arrogant prick, how he's never had a good slap I'll never know."

Debbie carried on with her anti-Sid rant as she noisily placed crockery onto shelves, but my mind was already gone. I could see her lips move as her eyebrows lurched and arched and slid around her frantic face.

I threw in a few 'yes's' and 'no's' here and there for courtesy whilst she was in mid rant but I was off in my own little world.

What is Jim Morrison's middle name?

Does he even have a middle name?

I bet it's not as cool as 'fucking.'

I wish I had a middle name.

Maybe I could use 'fucking' as my middle name. Jimmy Fucking Steel? Nice. It makes me sound really hard.

'Watch out here comes Jimmy 'Fucking' Steel, he's mental.'

I'd better get in there quick and use it before Sid gets wind of this.

Ian Fucking Hughes? Sid Fucking Hughes?

Nah, that sounds shite, more like an exasperation. 'Oh no, here comes Sid Fucking Hughes.'

I'll look into it in more detail later.

"Well, have you?"

Debbie cut my middle naming session short as she paused throwing cutlery into a drawer and turned to face me.

Time to think fast Jimmy boy, she absolutely hates it when you don't listen to her and I'm not in the mood to get into a heated debate on the dangers of smoking hashish and the effect it has on your capacity to concentrate. Especially when I haven't even been smoking any weed.

Well have you indeed? Is it 'yes' or 'no'? The clock's ticking, she's looking suspicious, she might know you weren't listening. Don't make her repeat the whole thing again, she'll go mental. Well, say something then.

"Yes," I splutter. I gambled all my chips on 'yes'.

The roulette wheel's spinning, the ball is bouncing madly off the side … the wheel's slowing down, the balls hopping between numbers, is it? Is it 'yes'?

"Well, what did he say when you told him?" she replied accusingly.

I have no fucking idea what you're talking about.

Bollocks! The wheel comes to a gradual stop and the ball's nestled comfortably on 'no'. I've lost all my chips.

Why the fuck didn't you say 'no'? Always go with 'no'.

But what's this? I've found another chip stuck in my pocket; how did you get there? This is my last chance, I flick it into the air and watch it spin slowly, wherever it lands is up to the gods.

What did he say when you told him about that thing she's talking about? Hmm…

Here goes nothing.

"Eh … well nothing much really, you know, just the usual." There's no going back now. My chip is still spinning slowly through the air, it's reached the arc of its journey, it's picking up speed now and it's plummeting back to earth.

"Nothing much? I thought he would've been really hacked off. You know he loves to control you and with you moving in here now he'll not be able to do that anymore. I'm really surprised that he didn't throw a strop like usual. What did he say about me, I bet he was really slagging me off?"

My chip crash lands onto the green baize, and it bounces once and onto its side. It's rolling now, heading straight for another pile of chips. It smacks into the chip pile and is deflected off its course and starts slowly circling the table like a dying bird in flight, spiralling in ever-decreasing circles until at last it stops on a number. 'Winner' the croupier says and everyone at the table is on their fleet applauding me.

I did it, I really did it, how lucky was that? I totally got away with it and saved myself from more aggro.

I look around the table and graciously accept their praise. A man in a dinner jacket walks towards me with a shiny leather briefcase and places it directly in front of me. I can smell the leather and see myself in the reflection of the locks. The man pulls on pristine white gloves as he gets the combination to the locks in order.

Click, the first catch flies open.

Click, there goes the second.

The anticipation is at fever pitch now. Everyone has gathered round the table. No one has seen anything like this before.

What the hell is inside the case?

He opens it slowly, pausing for effect.

He sure knows how to work a crowd.

We've all held our breath as he pulls something out from the case.

"Sir it gives me great pleasure in awarding you this, the highest winning chip denomination there is. You have just won, The Spawny Bastard chip."

Everyone roars with delight; my back is slapped and my cheeks are pecked. I raise both arms in a triumphant salute.

This is truly magic.

As I clasp my chip in a clenched fist and head for the exit, I stop at the top of the stairs to look back at my awe-inspired crowd.

I hear Marilyn Monroe ask, "Who was that dashing man?"

Carey Grant replies, "Who him? Why that's Jimmy Fucking Steel."

"Eh … aye he was. I mean no, he didn't even mention you, eh … we weren't really talking about it."

Shit, don't fuck it up now, Jimmy, not in front of Marilyn.

"But you just said you *were* talking about it. Did you give him a date when you're moving out?"

Oh fuck, the finally moving out of Sid's flat thing again. I never even got a chance to talk to him about that, guess it doesn't matter now. Will it never go away? Why can't we keep things the way they are? I like things the way they are.

Debbie's relentless when she's like this though, she's like a hound who's caught the fox's scent.

"No. I mean yes. Well, no. It's not that simple, Debbie. Sid's come up with a plan for the band and it's kinda thrown everything into the air. I don't know, it's like, well, what if …?"

I'm stumbling about like Mr Magoo in a room full of bear traps.

This is going to be messy.

"Oh grow up for God's sake, Jimmy. How many years have you been arsing around in that bloody band? I'll tell you how many, too many. What about all the things we talked about, what was all that? Did I just imagine that? From what I can remember I'm pretty sure you agreed to finally move in here lock stock and barrel with a plan to starting a family. What was that, Jimmy, eh? Or did I just imagine the whole conversation we've been having for the past five bloody years? It's embarrassing telling people about us. We're supposed to be partners in a serious relationship, but you just come and go as you please like a snotty teenager."

She's digging her way down the hole, snarling and growling all the while. Her nostrils are filled with my foxy stench. She wants blood, my blood. I can hear her scraping at the earth overhead, my heart's pounding, and I'm suddenly aware of the closeness of the earthen walls in my den.

It's hot in here, really hot.

I can't breathe.

My fur's too thick, I'm sweating underneath this heavy coat, why is it so hot?

The scraping and snarling is getting louder and closer. A helpless yelp escapes from my muzzle and echoes around the wall of my den, letting me hear in surround sound just how pathetic I really am.

My claustrophobia is getting worse, why is it so damn hot in here? I need to take my coat off.

If I get out of this alive, I'm building my next den in a bloody tree.

"We did, Debs. And I do. I don't know it's just, well I don't know, I'm not sure if I'm really ready for all that just at this minute in time. I mean, what's the rush and that? I do want to, I'm sure I do, we will do it and that, I'm sure. It's this thing with the band and we've got a tour of Scotland to do. Sid's got it all sorted and that, with places to play and stay and well, it'll only be for like six months or something and …"

It's like I'm ten years old again being severely scolded by my mother and try as I might I just can't seem to find the words that are going to appease her. In fact, I seem to be going out of my way to say all the wrong words. I desperately want her to stop shouting at me. I can't think straight when I'm being shouted at and being called names isn't good for my esteem.

I just want to do the right thing and say the right thing to make her smile and make her happy again and then it'll all be okay.

Stop shouting at me, Mum, please. My stomach hurts.

"You're not ready? What the hell do you mean you're not ready, what are you waiting for, Jimmy? We've been over this a hundred times before and we agreed on it … six months?" Debbie said 'six months' in such a high-pitched shrill that I thought I was going to lay an egg.

"So while you go off gallivanting round the country I'm supposed to do what exactly, hmm?" Debbie seethed.

I can see the hound's head as it peeks around the entrance to my den.

It's loving this, the heat, the sheer panic in my eyes, the scent of my fear.

It can taste my blood already.

I've got nowhere to run.

I am well and truly fucked.

Unless, maybe if I can run out just as it's coming through the entrance.

"You could come and visit us in a few places. You'd like Ullapool, apparently they've got a chippy there that's as good as the one in Anstruther."

As I say this her eyes appear to revolve 360 degrees.

Oh Mary Mother of God and Sweet Jesus himself, save me from what I'm about to receive.

"You are a fucking … "

The hound lunges for me with raging fangs, I try to move to the side of the den.

"… useless, worthless, piece of shit …"

It's too cramped in here. I can't move and it's still so hot. I feel a searing pain on my shoulder as the hound's teeth rip through my fur coat and into my tender flesh.

"… get the fuck out of my …"

I try to shake it off but I can't move because I'm trapped against the earthen walls of my stinking hot den. I'm yelping now in desperation as the realisation that I'm going to die hits me.

"… sight you fucking hopeless …"

My life will be over in seconds.

I actually feel quite calm as I accept the inevitable.

The hound senses my lack of fight and goes straight for my throat.

I feel her jaws around my neck. It hurts like hell as her fangs pierce my skin.

I register the sensation of blood pouring down my neck and onto my chest from the puncture wounds.

It doesn't feel so warm anymore.

"… waste of a life. I hate you, you inconsiderate … "

All I can feel as I close my eyes is the crushing sensation on my throat as the hound's jaw squeezes tighter and tighter.

"BASTARD!"

"I'm sorry, I'm sorry," are the only words that escape my mouth. I repeat them over and over again like a pathetic mantra.

I stumbled out the back door as another kitchen utensil was launched. I turned just in time to see a shiny pot hurtling towards me. Unfortunately, I didn't have enough time to duck and cover. The heavy metal pan crashed into the side of my head, knocking me senseless as I fell hard onto the patio slabs. Struggling with my vision, I looked back at the menacing perpetrator.

"Aargh, fucking hell, Debs," I yelled in shock.

I was hurt and angry at myself for allowing this stupid fight to happen and as I started to shout back, she slumped to her knees put her head in her hands and started weeping. This hurt me more than the plate, pot, and throat-crushing brutality of the hound. I had just broken her heart again and the guilt and subsequent emotional pain made me feel sick.

"I'm sorry, Debs ... I'm really sorry, I'll quit the band, I'll go and tell Sid right now."

"Just leave me alone," she cried. "Leave me alone."

"Debs, I love you, come on, eh? Don't be like this." I felt the tears well up and started to sob.

I stood standing in the back garden of a busy estate in full view of the neighbours' windows whilst blood trickled down my cheek from a Tefal wound. I would normally consider this to be an extremely embarrassing moment but at that minute in time I really wouldn't have given a shit if there was a camera crew filming.

I started to walk back up the garden to where she was kneeling.

"Sorry Debs, let's just forget ..." as the words left my mouth Debbie returned to her normal fearsome self after her split second lapse of composure and rose quickly to her feet. Her eyes penetrated mine and bore deep into my soul.

I was filled with that all too familiar sense of fear again.

"You'll never change, Jimmy. NEVER," she screamed and slammed the door shut before I could reach it. I half expected the door to reopen and for her to bellow 'And you're shite in bed' just to give the voyeuristic neighbours the satisfaction of saying 'aye we thought as much.' But that didn't happen.

I was left standing there in Debbie's back garden nursing a nasty gash to my head and a badly bruised ego. If this happened in a film, there would be a crash of thunder followed by lightning. The violins would strike up and then the rain would come lashing down upon the weeping sodden man in the back garden. Perhaps the viewer might even be moved enough to feel a little bit sorry for the lone figure. But this wasn't a film and so I stood there motionless like a spare prick wondering what I was going to do.

After a big fight with Debbie, I would normally go home and bitch about it to Sid. But I couldn't go back there because this was all his fault.

Plus, I couldn't be bothered dealing with him whilst my head hurt like hell. I'd have to sit there and listen to him whilst he gave it the same old 'I dinnae ken why you're with her anyway, moody stuck up bitch' routine.

So for my next trick I took inspiration from the movies.

Where does the downtrodden guy always go when he's down on his luck?

That's right, folks, the pub.

And why does he go there?

Right again, folks, to feel sorry for himself whilst getting completely plastered.

If only I could deal with my problems in a sensible grown-up manner i.e. talking to Debbie and Sid about how I really felt. Apologise for the upset and inconvenience I'd caused then life would be just dandy. But no, I've got to play the downtrodden, whole world owes me a favour character and cover up my problems and insecurities in the only way that approximately 95%* of Scottish males know how to for fear of being labelled a Big Jessie (*actual percentage of Scottish males who indulge in this practice isn't actually known).

With my mind made up I dragged my sorry arse from her garden and headed for the nearest boozer, hell bent on drinking until I could no longer see whilst boring the pants off anyone who was unfortunate enough to be sitting in my vicinity.

In reality I sat at the bar downing whisky like a spaghetti Western villain whilst listening to the locals take the piss out of me about the pot throwing incident only hours earlier.

Just my luck that Debbie's next-door neighbour was in there telling anyone in the vicinity that I took a 'milk pan aff the napper' and 'drapped like a sack o' tatties' then 'stood there greetin' like a wee lassie' announcing to the bar in a pathetically effeminate voice 'I love you, I love you, I'm sorry, I'm sorry.'

The whole bar erupted at this or so it seemed to me and cries of 'whit a fanny' and 'stupid bastard' rang around my ears until I was forced to laugh at my own ridiculous predicament.

Any normal person would've simply left the bar at this mass ridiculing, but I was more than happy to stay whilst listening to their put downs as it gave the neurotic self-loathing part of my brain more ammunition.

And so it came to pass that I sat there getting drunker and drunker still, consoling myself with the fact that the world did indeed owe me a favour and that everyone on this planet, excluding yours truly, is a 'narrow-minded bigot' and if it wasn't for people like me 'you'd aw be fucked.'

Ah, the drunken ramblings of a self-righteous prick.

The last thing I remember was attempting to play pool.

It seemed like a simple pot.

Black ball over the middle bag, easy peasy for a man of my experience.

Not so.

It appears my judgement had been hampered somewhat by Messrs White & Mackay.

As I went to strike the ball my legs suddenly announced that they were tired of all this standing malarkey and crumpled beneath me.

The cue flew from my hands and nestled somewhere far beyond my line of focus with a clatter.

I collapsed into a heap and heard a muffled cry of 'Davy, you're up.'

I might also have been sick.

CHAPTER 2

"Jimmy? Jimmy? Come on, man, wake up."

I came to in the communal garden at the back of my flat.

Though my eyes were tightly shut I could tell that it was bright and sunny. I could also feel my face being lightly slapped.

As I struggled to wake, it slowly dawned on me that I didn't know where I was and this frightened me.

"Whit the fuck? Get aff me," I shouted anxiously as I wrestled with my aggressor.

"Relax, man. It's me." I couldn't see Sid because my brain was working at quarter speed due to last night's whisky and wasn't relaying the signals quickly enough.

"Look at the state o' you, you look like a bag o' shite. Come on, let's get you upstairs."

But through his kind words and mocking tone I knew it was him. He helped me to my feet but the sudden rush of blood to or from my head had an outstanding effect on my stomach.

"Bleurgh!" I vomited all over the good Samaritan who had come to aid me in my hour of need.

"Aw for fuck's sake, Jimmy," Sid wailed as he released his grip on me.

For the second time in days, I dropped like a sack o' tatties.

"But what about my wounds?" I moaned as I collapsed onto the velvet grass, listening to the fading retching sounds of the good Samaritan as he beat a hasty retreat.

"Save me Jesus. Help me," I pleaded for my Samaritan but to no avail.

My brain had had enough excitement for one day and decided the best course of action would be to temporarily shut down all systems and so for the second time in a matter of days I passed out in the communal garden at the back of my flat.

TAKE TWO

"Oh ma heid," I moaned as I woke up in the familiar surroundings of my own bed. I felt terrible and not just from the raging hangover. The fight with Debbie was still on my mind.

Stupid whisky, you were supposed to make that problem magically disappear, you've only made things worse.

Strange that, eh?

My throat felt like I had spent the previous night dining on sawdust whilst quaffing champagne flutes of sand.

I could taste the remains of puke.

My thirst needed quenching and pronto. To my absolute delight, and like a holy vision, I could see a pint of water staring at me from the bedside table. I greedily grabbed the glass and poured its contents down my arid throat.

Is there a better sensation in the world?

I gulped down the water and felt its effects immediately. The water descended like a cool river rushing over the falls of my throat, bringing life and salvation to the needy organs below. Droplets escaped from the side of my mouth and dribbled down my chin and onto my throat. They tickled as they slithered down my chest.

"Aaah," I gasped as I slammed the empty glass down. I was left panting by the exertions of all the gulping, but I didn't mind, that felt amazing. Like having the itchiest itch finally scratched the thirstiest thirst was quenched.

"Sid, you're a fucking legend ma man," I exclaimed and raised the empty glass in tribute to him.

For all I bemoan him, he's a good lad really. He delivered me safely to my bed and the glass of water? Well, that was just a touch of class. Like a Benedict's mint on the hotel pillow. All that after I'd called him a prick and then puked on him.

Ah shite.

I suddenly recalled the puking incident from earlier that morning.

I'd better go apologise.

Now where did I put it?

I scanned the room.

Ah there it is.

I picked up my tail and lodged it firmly between my legs and went off in search of Sid.

First things first though. I retreated to the kitchen to refill my glass of water.

"Wahaaaaaay, he's alive," Sid announced, waving his arms about like an idiot on a roller coaster as I entered the brightly lit living room.

"A'right, Jimmy?" Bobby asked, sounding genuinely concerned.

"Morning, Sid. Morning, Bobby. Aye I'm a'right. Must've got a dirty pint last night."

It's an old one but it's a classic and has been used for centuries by shame-faced drunkards to excuse their behaviour from the night before. It had nothing to do with the umpteen gallons of liquor that was thrown down my throat, oh no, it was a dodgy pint that was to blame.

I have no shame.

"Morning?!" Sid sounded incredulous. "It's nearly half past seven. You've been out of it for hours; we were starting to get worried."

"Aye I was a wee bitty messed up. Listen, Sid, sorry about puking on you, I'll get your stuff washed."

This could go two ways depending on which mood Sid was in. He'd either brush it off lightly or he'd squeeze as much out of this as he could whilst revelling in my obvious discomfort. On this occasion I would be betting on the latter.

"It's cool, dinnae worry about it we've aw been there. I've put my clothes in the wash already. We're just gonnae order some pizza, you want some?"

I didn't expect that, but I'll take it. My brain was too busy repairing its damaged cells to bother going into intricate details about the deeper meaning behind Sid's reply.

"Aye, get us a large pepperoni and a bottle of Irn-Bru."

I could feel my stomach growling in anger as it caught wind of my order. I imagined it saying 'Large pepperoni and a bottle of Irn-Bru, are you insane? You didn't feed me properly all day yesterday then allowed me to swim in cheap whisky all night and now you're expecting me to deal with this veritable feast?'

My stomach convulsed and rumbled as it shouted 'Hey Brain? You're an idiot. How the hell do you expect me to function properly if you keep telling him to get pissed and eat shite all the time, eh?'

My brain reverts to standby mode as it combats the raging hangover, allowing my mind to conjure up the inner conflict between my guts and my head.

'Relax Stomach, you're too uptight, man. If you keep shouting at me like that, you're going to get an ulcer.'

'Too uptight? Are you taking the piss, Brain? Of course I'm uptight, I'm also burning with hunger and rage at your continued stupidity. If I don't get some proper nourishment down here soon, we'll all be in trouble. Just because you're up there in your ivory tower don't think you're exempt from all of this.'

My stomach actually growled louder and louder as I continued with the little pantomime in my head.

'Ssssshhh, there there, Stomach, it'll be all right. I'll send you down some wheat grass and some tofu and perhaps some organic bee's wax to fix you good and proper, how does that sound, hmm?'

My brain is toying with my stomach. If it's not careful I could have an emergency on my hands.

'Fuck you ya cheeky piece of self-righteous matter. Me and some of the boys down here have been talking. Liver, Kidneys, Spleen, Gall bladder and we're all in agreement that your time up there is coming to an end. We're all paying the price for your inept leadership, and it's got to stop. This is your last chance, Brain, dinnae go fucking us about!'

'Yeah yeah yeah, who do you think is giving you a voice, eh? Without me, you're nothing. You hear me Liver? Kidney? Gall bladder? The whole lot of you. Without me you're all nothing aha ha ha ha ha ha.'

My brain had suddenly turned into a Bond villain.

I do admit that I find it amusing to imagine numbskull-like characters at the helm of my organs. I guess it gives me comfort to think of it in this way to save me from living up to the fact that it is I alone who is fully responsible for my inner health.

Passing the buck, one of my favourite pastimes.

I munched my way through the pizza trying to figure out how many of my five a day were contained within this Italian-American-Turkish-Scottish treat.

None.

No wait, there's a tomato sauce, surely that counts?

I knew I should have added sweetcorn.

After the continued piss taking of my appearance and drinking habits, the conversation turned its attention to the band and how two thirds of its members were in agreement to tour Scotland.

"Bobby's well up for it. Eh, Bobby?" Sid said, spraying half-chewed pizza around the room.

"Aye, man. It sounds like a great idea," replied Bobby, moving closer to the edge of his seat and looking at me excitedly.

"We'll get a chance to play some really cool places and see some fantastic sights. I'm actually really excited about it. I've no' had a holiday in ages, I know we'll be working an' that, but it'll feel like a holiday. I cannae wait to get started. Sid says you're no' that keen though, Jimmy?"

Bastard!

Sid's a bastard.

A clever bastard, I'll grant him that but a bastard nonetheless.

He's made me look like the stick in the mud, the boring one, the destroyer of dreams, well I'm not giving him that satisfaction.

"It's not that I'm not keen, Bobby, it's just that … well I've got a few things to sort out if I'm gonnae commit to this. I need to get all the loose ends tied up and that."

I was keeping my cards pretty close to my chest. I didn't want to go through last night's Debbie situation with Sid. It was bad enough listening to strangers in the pub taking the piss, but Sid would be intolerable. He'd love hearing about that and his constant 'under the thumb' remarks and general slagging ignited a primal anger within me.

"Aye that's understandable, mate. I'm sure you'll have a load of stuff to sort out," Bobby said through mouthfuls of onion rings.

"Like what?" asked Sid in that goading way of his.

He knows.

Somebody's told him about the fight with Debs.

Shite.

He's loving this, the prick.

"Eh?" I replied, trying to buy myself some time to allow my brain to plan its next stage of attack

"What things have you got to sort out like?" Sid continued with his attack.

Is that a smirk on his face?

"Well quite a few things actually, Sid."

Before I continued, I stuffed a huge slice of pizza into my mouth, momentarily rendering me speechless, allowing my brain further precious seconds to decide its full frontal counterattack.

Come on, Brain, for Christ's sake think of something, anything, the truth if you must just hurry. You weren't so shy when arguing with Mr Stomach earlier, were you?

"Dee dee dee dee dee dee dee, deedle dee … " Sid's phone rang, halting my train of thought. He gazed at the number on the screen for a couple of bars of The A-Team theme tune before answering it.

"Hello? Aye speaking. Oh hello there, how're you doing?"

Sid removed himself from his chair and accidentally booted over his glass of Irn-Bru as he departed the room with his phone pressed hard against his ear.

I was saved by those brave soldiers of fortune. That was a real film moment right there, that never happens.

"That's gonnae be a nightmare getting that stain out," Bobby said, laughing to himself as he pointed to the bubbling ginger puddle that was rapidly soaking into the cream carpet.

"He's selling the flat anyway. I cannae see that proving to be a major stumbling block. It's a lovely flat Mr Hughes and we're really interested, it's just that, well, the nasty luminous orange stain in the front room doesn't really go with our Ikea soft furnishings," I replied sarcastically.

Bobby roared with delight, sending yet more pizza and onion rings flying onto the already heavily stained carpet. If we keep going at this rate nobody will want to buy this place.

"So what stuff do you need to get sorted out, mate? Do you need a hand with anything?" Bobby asked, putting down his pizza and onion rings so he could give me his undivided attention.

"Ach just the usual, Bobby. I had a big fight with Debs yesterday. She's not too keen on the idea of me pissing off wi' the band. She gave me a nasty smack on the heid too." I turned my head and pointed to show Bobby the bruised swollen lump.

"Aye Sid was saying."

How the fuck does he know already?

Nothing's a secret in this town. You fart at the top of the street and by the time you get to the bottom the folk there are telling everyone that you shat yourself.

"I think I'd like to do this, it's just, well, the way Sid went about it. When he told me he was selling the flat it threw all my plans in the air."

"How come?"

"Well me and Debs have been talking for ages about living together permanently. You know, doing the whole proper grown-up thing like you and

Mel rather than me splitting my time between her place and here. And we've discussed, well, you know, maybe starting a family and all that."

"What? Really? Nice one, man. You guys would make great parents. Good for you. Mel and me have been giving that some thought too."

"Aye? Well I told Debs that I'd tell Sid I was moving out to go live with her, but the thing is, I didn't. I'm not really sure that's what I want, man, not at the minute anyway. Debs keeps harassing me and that makes it worse. I don't know what I want, that's my problem. Ideally, I'd like things to remain the way they are. I couldn't make a decision and when Sid told me he was selling this place it was like he'd made the decision for me and now I'll have to stay with Debs. I was pissed off with him for that, which was stupid. It's just one big fucking muddle, man, you ken? This place is my safety net. I love living here, just getting time away from Debs and now that's gonnae be taken away from me all for a stupid half-baked scheme to tour the country. I know I've got to make a decision but somebody's gonnae be left hurt. It's complicated, man. I dinnae ken what to do."

Talking to Bobby is easy. You can open up to him because he doesn't judge you or make stupid immature comments like Sid or me would make to each other.

"I hear what you're saying, mate. It isn't easy but if you ask me, it sounds as though you've already made your decision."

Bobby raised his eyebrows, hands, and shoulders all at once as if to say over to you maestro.

Bobby's like Yoda, wise as fuck. He doesn't have much to say for himself but what he does have to say is straight and to the point.

"Aye I ken, man. I'm no' ready for the whole family thing. No' just yet anyway. I'll have to speak to her. I'll go round tomorrow after work, hopefully she'll have calmed doon by then and we can sort something out. But it's no' just that. What are we gonnae do when we come back? Six or seven months down the line we'll be back here in the same shitey spot. The only difference being we'll have no jobs, no money, and nowhere to stay. What then?"

I'm thinking to myself am I the only one who's given this any serious thought? This pair are willing to give up everything for what? If we'd been starting out as a band in our late teens/twenties then aye no problem, but we're in our late 30s peddling about the same old tunes and doing the same old routine that we've done for over 20 years. Do they honestly think that by touring Scotland everyone's suddenly going to sit up and take notice and watch us hit the big time at last?

I mean, have some self-respect, boys.

"Who knows, Jimmy, who knows? But that's what makes this interesting. This is pretty much our last throw of the dice as a band. It's a gamble sure but what are you really going to lose? You've been moaning for years about your job, how you need a new challenge, something completely different. Well, here's your chance and it's being handed to you on a plate. Sid's putting his money where his mouth is, he's prepared to finance this whole trip. If we come back in a few months and nothing's changed then we'll all have to look for work and you boys will need to find a place to live, simple. You're being too negative, man. Like Sid says we've got to take a chance. We've got to go for it, imagine getting a record deal on the back of this. How amazing would that be? Our lives would change forever and you two could finally kiss goodbye to this place. Don't be confined by society's demands, life's for living, Jimmy. Reach for the stars, man." Bobby clasped his hands together as he slumped back into his chair. I guess that's all he's got to say on the matter.

"But it's really not that simple, Bobby," I replied, trying to make sense out of his speech, "what's Mel saying to it?"

I knew as soon as I'd said it that she'd be behind the idea, it's all peace and love with that pair.

"Mel's cool with the idea, she thinks it'll be great fun if nothing else. She'll come and join us when she's free, you know, take the train to meet us wherever. It's a good opportunity for her to get out and take more photos."

"I'm still not convinced. I'll talk it over with Debbie again tomorrow and see what's what. I need to get it all sorted out in my own heid as well, it's up my arse at the minute. This is all just a wee bitty too mental for my liking. I hate the idea of giving into Sid. He's always trying to control me."

I was covering old ground trying to play the lost soul.

"You pair are ridiculous. You're like a couple of bairns. If it'd been you that had come up with the idea, Sid would be doing exactly the same thing, stalling and trying to steal your thunder. Jimmy, come on, man, we need you for this, Sid needs you. He's no gonnae come out and say it, you ken what he's like but he's counting on us. It'll be brilliant, just like the old days. Who knows what could come of this. We're always saying we should see more of the country, well now is the perfect opportunity."

"It's no' about stealing his thunder, fuck's sake. I couldn't give a shit about his thunder," I whined in a raised voice.

Maybe it is about his thunder, is that the reason I'm so pissed off at all this?

"Look, I'm gonnae be straight with you. I think you're being a wee bit selfish about this. Sure, I understand the situation with Debs, it's not easy, but this could be our last chance. It's different, it's something none of the other bands around here have done. Hell, even established bands don't tour the whole country, it's a great way of attracting publicity. Sid's depending on you, I'm depending on you. We've been there for you when you needed it most now Sid's asking for your help. Give it some serious thought, mate. Let's have some fun again, eh?"

Shit I didn't expect the whole guilt trip, not from Bobby anyway, that's a Sid trick.

Why is everyone out to get me these days?

"Look, Bobby, it's no' as simple as aye, nae bother let's pack our things up and go do it, we've all got responsibilities now."

"What are you two talking about?" Sid asked as he came thundering back into the room, instantly changing the atmosphere.

"Shopping," we replied in unison.

"Well, guess who I was just talking to?"

"Santa Claus? Mother Theresa? The Prime Minister? Jim Morrison? Your Mum? Give us a clue, Sid," I asked, giving my usual response to one of the stupidest questions someone over the age of seven can ask you.

"No. Sandy Brown from Inverness."

"Sandy Brown, eh? Fuck's sake how's he getting on I've no' seen him since the 1950s?" I really need help; my sarcasm knows no bounds.

"Shut up and listen, prick."

Sid's eyebrows almost touched his nose, indicating that he's not to be messed with.

"Sandy Brown owns a couple of venues in Inverness and has a few pubs in Dornoch and Nairn. I left a brief message on his answer phone on Friday telling him about our plans, so I've just been filling him in on the details. He's well up for giving us a few slots, that's five gigs in total and he can put us in touch with a few of his mates who've got decent venues up in that neck of the woods too. Magic eh?" Sid flashed that toothy, gummy, gormless grin of his.

"Brilliant. That's tremendous, man," Bobby shouted as he leapt from his chair to slap Sid on the back.

"See, Jimmy? This isn't a half-arsed scheme. This show is on the road, man. All we need now is for your backing, so what's it gonnae be, are you in or out?" Sid asked with a look that dared anyone to defy him.

"I'll let you ken the morn, Sid. I'm tired, lads, I'm gonnae hit the sack. I've got an early start the morn. I'll see you tomorrow, a'right?"

I resorted to retreat mode; the white flag had been raised. I wasn't willing to give anything away. I'm neither for nor against, I'm just a big useless pile of nothingness. Bed is the only place where I could justify my position on all this.

"Bed?" Sid asked disgustedly "Christ you've only been up for about two hours."

"I'm no' feeling that great, hopefully a good night's sleep will sort me out," I replied, looking to Bobby for a way out.

"Aye that's maybe a good idea, mate. A good night's sleep will do you the wonder of good. It'll clear your head," Bobby nodded before giving Sid a brief glance.

"Aye probably," I agreed and made for the door.

"Jimmy?" Sid called out.

I turned to face him.

"Think about it, mate. That's all I ask, eh?" He shrugged his shoulders and did that thing with his bottom lip. I still haven't figured out what it means.

"Will do. 'Night," I croaked as I closed the door gently for effect. What effect I was going for, I'm still not entirely sure of, but I think it suited the moment perfectly.

And so, with 12 inches of pizza and approximately 1.5 litres of Irn-Bru sloshing about inside my grumbling belly, I headed for the sanctuary of my room to mull over the situation.

Perhaps if I was lucky enough, I would even get some peace from the weekend's events by escaping to the land of nod. Sleep is the eternal ally of the troubled soul. It offers temporary relief from the mind's poisoned chatter. The dream state is as comforting to the mind as the womb is to the unborn child. But as a child is born so doth the mind awake. These occurrences are equally painful to both parties as they are wrenched from their tranquil surroundings and introduced to the living realm.

A bit drastic you may say?

Sometimes hangovers can leave me feeling a little bleak.

Sleep, alas, never came that night.

I spent the evening going over the episode with Debbie again whilst trying to fathom out how best to approach her without getting another cooking device bounced off my head. I was sure that she'd be fine with me putting the moving and family thing on hold for a little while longer. If it worked out with the band and we got a deal we'd both benefit long term.

The band, the bloody band.

I thought about the tour, trying to pinpoint the exact moment in time when I lost the passion for the band.

Did I ever have the passion for it?

Do I really want to do this or am I just being a stubborn fool?

What will Sid and Bobby think of me if I say no?

What will my parents think if I say yes?

Then my attention turned to work.

I hated my job.

To millions of people the world over this will come as no great revelation.

Why am I any different to anyone else?

I'm not.

I'm like most of you out there. I live by a routine which is constantly guided by time and money (or lack of) and social and moral obligations. The days are long gone when I burned with ambition and had a lust for life. My dreams have been shoved aside by the everydayness of life. I spent my daylight hours in a large office space working for a multi-national media firm. I had been fortunate/unfortunate depending on whose side you sympathise with in all of these twilight ramblings to work for this firm for about six years.

Ample time you may say to get the hell out of dodge if you so wished?

Quite correct I'd respond.

In truth it's not that simple.

Well maybe it is, hell I don't know. I'd fallen into the classic trap of mediocrity. A nine to five bear pit where my allotted space at work is defined by a couple of partition walls.

The job wasn't challenging, far from it. There are many ways to earn a poorer living from working a lot harder. This fact alone got me through the tough times. It's just not *ME*. Aside from making a living playing professional football I had no career aspirations. I just went with the flow. Guidance teachers at School would ask me the same thing and I'd shrug my shoulders and say 'Dunno.'

'We've been looking at your grades and we see you're getting excellent marks in the social sciences. Perhaps you should think of studying Geography or History at university?'

'Eh, okay then.'

When Sid announced his dream of being a rock and roll star, I was more than happy to jump on his bandwagon and tag along for the ride, hell it would beat working for a living.

I peered at my alarm clock again.

4:34 a.m., it shone in bright red calculator writing.

I'm sure Bobby said these digital display alarm clocks are bad for you.

I'll have to get rid of it.

I was trapped in the old circle of can't sleep, won't sleep, and I pictured Ainsley Harriott waltzing into my room talking loudly and excitedly about why I should sleep.

I fucking know why I should sleep Ainsley. To save me from listening to your shite patter.

'Is it going to be Wide Eyes or Big Zeds?' he shouted to a non-existent audience. To my surprise an audience appeared from the darkest depths of my mind to hold aloft placards, some with an open eye complete with eyelashes and others with a big Z. There appeared to my eyes anyway to be far more Zs than eyeballs, but Ainsley saw otherwise.

"The Wide Eyes have it. No sleep for you, son," he announced in a stupid voice before completing an unnecessary shuffle/dance.

"Aw come on, Ainsley, there were clearly more Zeds than Wide Eyes, just let me sleep, eh?"

He couldn't hear me though cause he'd already shuffled from the room.

I made a mental note that if I ever met Ainsley Harriott I was going to punch his smiley puss.

It was a long night.

One of those crazy old nights where I thought of and came up with an answer to all of life's mysteries.

Except one.

Why is it when you really need to sleep your mind wont drift off until approximately 10 minutes before your assigned wake up time, leaving you feeling as if you've spent the entire night smoking opium when the alarm shrieks in your ear?

I fucking hate my job!

CHAPTER 3

What a week

DAY 1

It was a long week. A long and depressing, angst-filled week.
I can laugh about it now but at the time it was terrible.

As per usual I had the Monday morning blues. Unfortunately for me the blues decided that they rather enjoyed Monday and would therefore be hanging around until Friday.

I couldn't get my arse in gear on Monday morning, so I arrived at work half an hour late, much to the disgust of the office manager, a snivelling rat of a man called Frank Harrison who had the social skills of an autistic chimpanzee and despite being five foot two charged around the office barking out orders as if he was a muscled giant.

A classic example of small man syndrome you might say.

After a brief heated altercation whereby he threatened to cut my bonus and I threatened to cut his throat it was back to work.

I couldn't concentrate though.

I'd planned to see Debs that night and the thought of this made my stomach lurch. I'm hopeless at apologies and grovelling and admitting that I'm useless. Plus, I knew she'd still be flaming mad but a man's got to do what a man's got to do. Besides, I was needing a shag. I thought about the time-honoured favourite of a bunch of flowers and then a candle-lit dinner.

Was that too clichéd?

I toyed with the idea for most of the day before deciding to book a table at the swankiest restaurant in town.

After work I picked up a classy-looking bouquet of flowers and swaggered round to Deb's flat feeling pretty darn good about myself.

This would be the last time I felt good about myself for a considerable length of time.

I arrived at Debbie's flat and the atmosphere was the wrong side of chilly. I handed her the bunch of flowers and apologised in the only way I knew how.

"Eh sorry about the other day an' that, darlin'. I wasn't thinking straight and I'm really sorry if I hurt you. I've spoken to Sid and he's cool with everything so I'm gonnae move in here as soon as ..." I tailed off in mid sentence as I noticed Debs was motioning me with a come hither gesture. She did this from time to time as a playful build up to a spontaneous shagging session.

Ho ho ya beauty!

I could feel the uncomfortable tightening of my underpants as my erection fought to break free. My throat went dry as I stepped nearer and looked into her eyes.

God you're one sexy lady. I'm gonnae fuck you like I haven't fucked you in a long time.

She flung the flowers nonchalantly onto the kitchen table and turned towards the living room, still motioning me over her shoulders. I quickly followed, unzipping my fly as I went through, unleashing my full erection.

I'm gonnae bend you over the couch and fuck you senseless.

As I walked into the living room with my cock jutting from my trousers like a barber's flagpole (minus the red and white stripes obviously) I noticed that Debbie's mother Anne was sitting on the couch alongside Debbie's work colleague whose name escaped me.

"See all this stuff here ..." Debbie motioned as she turned around to face me.

All six eyes looked at me then looked down to my raging hard-on then looked back at me in unison in a kind of synchronised gawking way.

"Jimmy, what the hell are you doing?" Debbie gasped.

All of this happened in the space of about two seconds, and I was left with the arduous task of stuffing a fully fledged stiff one back into the confined space of my underpants.

It was a bit like trying to shove a Jack back into its box.

"Eh I think I've got the wrong end of the stick, Debs. Sorry, Anne," I replied as I tucked my throbbing member under my belt out of harm's way.

"You've certainly got the wrong end of something, Jimmy. You're a bloody fool. I've packed all your stuff into boxes and black bags, pick it up and then get out of my sight, you're an embarrassment," Debbie shouted.

"What do you mean? All my stuff?" I whined in bemusement.

"I mean pick up all your crap and get out of my sight, Jimmy. It's over, we're finished. I'm not playing games anymore."

"Games? It's *over*? Come on. What are you talking about, you're not fucking serious?"

"Oh I'm serious all right. Get your stuff and then get the hell out of here and don't swear in front of my mum."

"But this is ridiculous, Debs. I've booked us a table at Lorenzo's. Can we no' at least discuss this like two adults in private. I mean for fuck's sake, this cannae be happening. Sorry, Anne."

"Look, Jimmy, it's over. I'm not discussing this with you anymore. I've got nothing to say to you, stop making this harder than it already is."

"Seven years, Debs. Seven years? You're throwing that all away?"

Tears were starting to well up in my eyes as it slowly dawned on me that she wasn't mucking about. My mind reeled in confusion and embarrassment at being dumped in front of an audience.

"Can we not talk about this? I love you; I need you," I pleaded.

The tears started to roll down my face as I looked at her cold hard stare.

This woman's not for turning.

"Yeah, you're right, Jimmy, seven years. Seven years I've been hanging on, waiting for you to show some serious commitment to this relationship. Well, I'm not hanging around for another seven years. You've had ample time to prove how serious you were but when it comes to the crunch it's the same old story. I need someone who wants what I want and you're clearly not that person, Jimmy. You're just a waste of my time."

Debbie threw a bag of belongings at me.

"Get your stuff and go. In case you hadn't noticed I've got guests."

"I cannae believe this," I whimpered as I picked up another couple of bin bags containing my stuff.

"I cannae carry all of this in the one go, I'll have to come back for the rest of it. Can we no' sit down and talk about it then, once everyone's gone?" I pleaded, sniffling back a load of snotters.

Debbie's mother and friend continued to stare at the carpet.

Man, this is fucked up.

"JUST GO, JIMMY!" Debs bellowed as I grappled with the bags of stuff and made a hasty tearful exit. I lugged my disconsolate frame and as many bin bags as I could carry back to Sid's place.

In my head the theme tune to the *The Littlest Hobo* accompanied my walk.

'There's a voice that keeps on calling me, down the road that's where I'll always be'

Sometimes it's comforting to wallow in your own self pity.

After chucking the bin bags in my room I decided against going back to Deb's for the rest of my gear, I couldn't handle all that emotion right now.

I mean, what the fuck?

What just happened there?

She's dumping me?

It was too surreal for my fragile eggshell mind to take. Instead, I went and paid Bobby and Mel a visit. I managed to scrounge enough weed off them for a couple of joints and spent the evening locked in my room getting drunk and stoned and attempted to nurse my aching broken heart.

I sifted through old photographs of the two of us.

Happy, smiling, in love.

I reread old text messages she'd sent me.

It was too much for me to take.

I put some Otis Redding on the record player and cried myself to sleep as he sang 'These Arms of Mine.'

DAY 2

The alarm clock read 09:04 a.m. and it was a few seconds before my eyes slowly registered its meaning.

"Oh for fuck's sake," I groaned.

I started work four minutes ago. Or rather, I was supposed to.

Frankie boy's gonnae be one cheery chappy this fine morning.

I was in no mood or hurry to get to the office, so I went about my usual routine.

The clock in the foyer read 10:37 when I finally arrived.

"Right where are you, Francis?"

Francois clocked my entrance from the other side of the office and came charging over like Benny Hill minus the theme music.

Man, I would love to slap his stupid wee face.

"Jimmy, that's two days in a row now, do you think it's amusing to let your team down like this?"

My back was already up at his mention of the word 'team.'

This isn't Man Utd we're playing for, you stupid cunt.

"Look, Frank, I ken I'm late just dinnae start a'right? I'm having a few personal problems at the moment, okay?"

He had forced me to play my joker card. Any mention of 'personal problems' took this to a more understanding level.

"Right I see, well … this isn't acceptable behaviour, Jimmy. Come and see me in my office after hours and we'll discuss this matter further. I'll get Jane from HR to drop in, you know, what with it being a personal problem."

I knew he didn't believe the personal problems bullshit, but he couldn't afford to take that gamble. With all the laws and human rights guff, you could sit at your desk and inject heroin into your eyeball and the bosses still couldn't sack you for fear of being sued for not following the correct dismissal protocol.

"Aye whatever," I replied, and I gave him my best Sid Vicious style sneer as I shoved past him.

The rest of the morning was spent playing solitaire and thinking about Debs and life in general and what a mess I was making of mine.

Woe is me.

I made the reckless decision to go for a couple of lunchtime pints at the bar around the corner with a view to pouring my heart out to the cute wee Latvian barmaid.

Perhaps get lined up with a sympathy shag.

Apparently, she only works evenings.

Bollocks.

Instead, I knocked back a couple of pints and a couple of Jim Beam chasers whilst listening to Gus, the not-so-cute Scottish barman telling me about his adventures in the Territorial Army. I must've enjoyed his tales though because it was after another couple of pints and Jim Beam chasers that I decided to go back to work. Approximately one hour later than scheduled.

I didn't realise I was drunk until the office air hit me.

I must've made a pretty memorable entrance though as everyone was staring at me as I negotiated my way around the open plan feng shui layout.

"JIMMY?!" Franny shrieked on my reappearance as he bounded over to me. "You're just taking the piss now, son," he shouted, thrusting his finger at my face.

Oh how I hate you, you little bastard.

"Who the fuck are you calling 'son', you wee prick? I'm ten years older than you, have some fucking respect," I shouted back, and I swatted his finger out of my face.

"You reek of alcohol. You're drunk."

"And you are a wee fanny."

"Get into my office now." He grabbed me by my tie and attempted to pull me into his office. It was at this gesture that I acted completely out of character.

"Get your fucking hands off of me. Who the fuck do you think you're pushing about, eh?"

The whole office was by now completely silent as everyone stared in amazement. Some people had even risen from their seats so they could get a better view of the crazy proceedings.

"Look, Jimmy, don't bloody push it. Get into my office, NOW."

His finger was back in my face again, shaking with rage.

"Or what?"

I batted his finger away again as his pupils dilated. His face was a contortion of embarrassment, rage, and pure resentment.

He's going to hit me.

How humiliating, getting knocked out by this wee tool.

Hit him first then!

Everyone was watching. Somebody was even filming this on their phone. Their glares clouded my judgement.

Are they willing me to do it? They ARE willing me to do it.

'Go on, Jimmy, do it for us,' they were all thinking. Everybody hates him, you'd be doing us all a favour. DO IT.

AYE, FUCKING DO IT!

As he came forward to manhandle me once more, I grabbed his collar and stuck the head on him.

"Aargh fuck," I cried as my nose smashed into the top of his head. I hadn't judged the height difference between us very well. Through the resulting tears I could just make out the look on Frank's face as he realised what had just happened. His shock turned to cold amusement as he looked at my bloodied nose. Cold amusement swiftly turned to rage. He shifted his foot and turned his shoulders in preparation to strike me. Through anger, alcohol, and the sheer embarrassment of delivering the world's worst Glasgow kiss, I made a fist and hit Frank Harrison as hard as I could.

His nose exploded as it made contact.

He flew backwards.

Everything seemed to happen in slow motion.

At first his fall was graceful, beautiful even as he pirouetted to the floor. However, he landed heavily in a crumpled heap after banging into Sally's desk, sending piles of stationary soaring into the air.

I stood and looked at the miserable wee shite with a sense of awe. I had never punched anyone in the face before.

It felt tremendous. No, it felt better than that. It felt amazing.

Bursting with testosterone and macho pride I turned to receive the appreciation of the crowd.

"For goodness sake, Jimmy. What are you doing?" shouted Mark as he rushed to Frank's aid.

"Call an ambulance. Jesus Christ, Jimmy. Think you're a hard man?" seethed Amy.

"Aye, he's only wee. You're such an arsehole," Sally moaned as she pushed past me to attend her stricken hero.

I stood there staring at the crazy scene trying to rationalise in my head what had just happened.

I'd knocked my boss out.

Fucking hell!

As the sense of guilt slowly crept up to wrap me in its sickly sensation, Frank, whose face had turned a ghostly white, opened his eyes. They darted rapidly over his helpful colleagues before coming to rest on my own. The colour quickly returned to his cheeks as he yelled.

"You hit me, Steel?"

He pushed himself up from the floor using the arms of Mark and Amy as crutches.

"You hit me? You're fucking fired."

Spittle flew from his mouth as he pushed his aides aside and marched his way towards me. My initial feeling of guilt was instantly replaced by a fear for my own safety. Although only a small man his eyes had that psychotic look that said they were ready to kill the person responsible for this unholy scene.

Shit!

I quickly scanned the office for a possible escape route.

I'll never make it.

When Frank was approximately a metre from where I stood my primal instincts kicked in again.

Literally.

As he approached me with that psycho killer glare, I pulled back my right leg and volleyed him square in the testicles.

I felt the squidgy soft contact through the leather uppers of my hush puppies and knew by the silent squeak he softly omitted that he wouldn't be getting up from that horrible assault for quite some time.

He crumpled to the floor with his hands clasped firmly around his manhood.

I removed my photo ID and threw it onto his chest. It bounced and then landed on the floor next to his head.

My smiling photograph juxtaposed his painful expression.

"You cannae fire me. I quit," I bellowed into his crushed face.

I stepped over his foetal-like frame and headed for the door. I couldn't bring myself to look at anyone as I left but I could feel my colleague's glares burning into the back of my head.

Once I was out the main entrance, I ran down the steps that led to the landscaped garden and promptly puked into a privet hedge.

Spitting the last few chunks from my mouth, I wiped the tears from my eyes and the blood from my nose with my sleeve and turned to look at the grey brutalist building where I had spent the last six years of my working life. I felt a warm feeling of comfort at the thought of not having to return there to slave over a desk beside people I knew nothing about or had anything in common with.

But as my mind replayed the scenes from the last few minutes I bowed back to the bush and vomited again.

You stupid cunt!

DAY 3

"What the hell are you still doing here, Jimmy?"

I was rudely awakened by Sid's presence in my room.

"What are you wanting? I'm trying to sleep," I moaned and pulled the duvet over my head.

"You need to get up, I've got the estate agent coming round to take pictures of the house and I dinnae want the one for this room to have your bare arse hinging oot the bed. Are you no' working the day?"

"No, I'll just have another hour and then I'll get up."

"No you'll no', the lassie's coming in half an hour, so come on, move it."

Sid ripped the duvet from my warm embrace and threw it onto the floor.

"Piss off," I yelled as I turned to confront him.

"Jesus Christ what happened to your puss? Who hammered you?"

"Eh?"

"Your puss? It's a right state, did somebody hook you?"

"Oh that. Och it's nothing, you should've seen the other guy though." I cockily grinned as I remembered Frank Harrison's stricken pose.

"Why? Did he break his hand?" Sid chuckled in response.

I sat up and put my feet to the floor and rubbed my eyes and promptly winced from the pain. My face was agony to touch. I gingerly walked over to the dusty mirror on the wall.

Who is the fairest of them all eh?

"Fucking hell," I gasped as the view Sid had seen stared back at me.

No' you anyway!

My nose was bruised and swollen and the skin under my eyes was a colourful mixture of black, blue, and purple. I looked like I had been well and truly battered.

"What happened?"

Shite. How am I going to explain this one without making myself look like a complete tosser?

It was too early and I was in too much pain to listen to Sid's repertoire of humiliating jokes.

"Eh, I had a wee barney at work and it kinda got out of hand."

"A wee barney? You look like you stepped in front of a bus. Who hit you?" Sid enquired.

"Nobody hit me. Well, it was me and Frank. We were arguing and one thing led to another. I knocked him out, pure smacked him square in the puss, sent him flying, blood everywhere. We must've clashed heads in the fracas. I left him sprawled on the office floor and walked out."

"Clashed heads? With Frank Harrison? *WEE* Frank Harrison? Piss off! He knocked you out more like, look at the state of you."

"Fuck off. There was a bit of grappling going on, he must've hit me with his head as I was picking him up. I'm telling you I laid him out. The whole office was rushing to his aid as I walked out. I quit."

"Hoo hoo, I didn't know you had in you, Jimmy."

Sid threw mock punches at me and was ducking and diving like a boxer.

"Better no' get on your wrong side, eh champ?"

"Aye well, he had it coming to him."

I was now sparring with Sid and returning mock punches of my own.

"Frank Harrison, eh? Aye he's a wee fanny. Good for you, man."

I felt like a world champion getting praise from my trainer. My chest swelled with pride.

"Aye well I needed to quit my job to tour with the band so I thought I might as well go out in style, eh?"

"Aye? And what about Debbie, what's she saying to it?"

"I dumped her. She was holding me back, didn't want me to go on this tour."

"No fucking way? Are you serious?" Sid beamed.

"Aye, man. She's really cut up about it. If I'm being honest, I'm pretty cut up about it too, I mean, we were together for ages you know?"

"You'll get over it, it's about time you dumped that moody bitch. You were under her thumb. Welcome back to the real world, ma man."

Sid grabbed me in a bear hug, and we danced around my bedroom laughing.

"It'll be brilliant, Champions Of The Underdog on tour. You'll no' regret this, Jimmy."

Sid's eyes were filled with excitement as we danced and whooped around the room, shouting, "Champions Champions." Sid's excitement was contagious, and it was hard not to get caught up in the whole idea of it all.

This might actually be really good fun.

My thoughts were interrupted by Sid putting me in a head lock and knuckle rubbing my head, shouting, "Who's a legend, who's a legend?"

"Aargh, not so tight, Sid. You're hurting my nose."

The doorbell rang, forcing Sid to release his vice-like grip on my fragile face.

"Shit. That'll be the estate agent. Right get this room tidied up and hurry."

I was furiously throwing clothes in drawers and flinging books into wardrobes when Sid came back into my room.

"Eh, Jimmy. It's for you. It's the polis."

"The polis? What do they want?"

I made my way to the front door in a panic.

Who could've died?

Images of stricken family members raced through my mind's eye. I couldn't breathe, my heart thumped the inside of my chest as absolute terror gripped me.

Oh please God, not my dad.

As I reached the front door, I could feel the familiar welling of tears as I waited for the dreadful news.

"James Steel?" the taller of the two officers asked.

"Yes," I whimpered in response, "who is it? Is it my dad? Just tell me what's happened."

The two officers looked at each other and then back to me with a puzzled look etched on their faces.

"James Steel, we are arresting you for the assault of Francis Harrison which took place yesterday afternoon. You do not have to say anything, however anything you do say may be used against you in a court of law. If you could accompany us to the station for questioning."

I don't know how long I stood staring open mouthed at the two officers of the law. My mind was racing.

What did they say?

Who died?

Nobody died.

Oh that's good. That's very good. Thank Christ for that.

I'm getting arrested?

Frank Harrison?

Questioning?

What the fuck?

He grassed on me?

What the fuck?

"What the fuck?" I spluttered.

"Watch your mouth, son. Get your clothes on, you're going to the station. We're not here to piss about."

I got dressed in a daze whilst Sid bobbed about me, saying "keep your mouth shut, say fuck all" and "be cool, it'll be fine."

I'd never been arrested before. In fact, I'd never had any dealings with the police before, apart from that one time I got a speeding ticket. Suddenly images of H.M. Barlinnie crept into my mind and thoughts of brutal beatings and gang rape quickly followed.

"What's gonnae happen, Sid? What'll happen to me? I cannae go to prison," I snivelled as I pulled on a jumper and pair of jeans.

"Prison? Shut up, you wee fanny. You slapped a boy in the puss. Plead self defence. Look at the state of your face. He hit you first right? Right?"

"Eh? Aye, aye, right. He hit me first," I nodded lamely in agreement.

As the police escorted me from the flat, we met Jenny, a friend of Debbie (who apparently is an estate agent) coming up the stairwell.

"Tell them fuck all, Jimmy. Self defence, man," Sid bellowed over the balcony for the whole building to hear.

Down at the station I was given a cup of tea. I tried to play it cool but noticed my hands were trembling uncontrollably as I gripped the polystyrene cup.

Shit, keep it together, Jimmy. Show no emotion. Play it cool.

"Just tell us your side of the story, son, and we can get this all over and done with," said PC Apathy.

I sat there trying to make sense of Sid's conflicting information "say fuck all, keep it shut and plead self defence."

Unlike my good self, Sid had had more than a few brushes with the law in his time. I ran through episodes of *The Bill* in my mind, thinking of the cool and witty things the bad guy would say to the cops. I was just about to unleash 'you've got nothing on me pigs,' when PC Empathy spoke.

"Look, do yourself a favour and tell us what happened. We've checked on you and there's nothing in the system, not even an unpaid parking fine. You're not a bad guy, you've just been a bit silly, you've dropped the ball for a minute, and you've made a mistake. You'll be out of here in no time if you just give us a true statement. Besides, we've got a lot of witnesses."

He even smiled a reassuring smile at me.

Maybe it was the kind words. Maybe it was the smile. Maybe it was my break up with Debs or maybe it was a combination of all the events of the past week that broke me. Whatever it was I broke easier than anyone they had ever broken before.

I'm ashamed to say I spilled my guts. I was like a guilty Catholic schoolboy at confession. I wailed through floods of tears and snot, telling the two stunned officers about my breakup with Debs and the resulting afternoon binge I embarked on which led to me momentarily 'dropping the ball' and assaulting Frank.

They had to stifle sniggers as I explained how I received the swelling and bruising to my face.

They both nodded in agreement that it looked nasty and that I should get it checked out.

PC Apathy brought me in another cup of tea and as I shakily reached for it, he patted me on the shoulder as if to say 'you pathetic excuse for a man, go home and grow some balls.'

I admitted my guilt and was able to leave shortly after. I was told a report would be sent to the Procurator Fiscal and I'd have to attend a court hearing whereby I'd most probably be fined and have to pay that wee prick Harrison compensation.

I would also have a criminal record.

Outside the police station I stepped into a shrubbery and puked.

I made my way home and stopped into the Dog and Whistle for a stiff drink to steady my nerves after my brush with the law. The stench of my violent crime clung to me as I downed a couple of whiskies.

I sat alone in the wood-panelled pub except for a couple of older punters who were studying the racing form. The Bell's quickly rushed into my bloodstream, calming my nerves and dulling the pain from my face.

I decided to act on the officer's advice and stopped off at A&E on the way home to get my nose looked at. I wished I hadn't bothered. I spent three and a half hours in a stuffy, smelly waiting room with a bunch of sour-looking people all suffering different states of emergency. It was only then that the pain began to kick in.

I'm sure there is a direct link between surroundings and pain relief. I can't imagine my face hurting quite as much if I was, say, in a nicely lit, well-ventilated room surrounded by cooing naked women whilst listening to some mellow jazz.

My thoughts were dramatically halted as a young woman burst through the doors shrieking and screaming. She dragged behind her a small, wailing child who had one hand clasped to her mouth trying inadequately to stem what could only be described as a flood of blood pouring from her mouth. It was truly horrifying to see. Everyone that was able to stand did so as we all rushed about ignoring our own injuries to help this poor wee lassie. Thankfully a doctor was at hand and escorted the pair of them into an adjacent room. I thought to myself that I should take a first aid course so I could spring into action in a situation like that instead of just standing there like a wet lettuce. I felt momentarily good about myself and my intended selfless actions, but the feeling quickly passed as I remembered my addiction to procrastination.

The waiting room was alive with anticipation as to what could have happened to that poor wee girl. Was she stabbed? Did a dog bite her? Did another child hit her? I'd never seen that much blood streaming from a body before and it put my own self-inflicted pain into perspective.

The time ticked slowly by as I looked at all the other pathetic cases. You couldn't actually tell what was wrong with any of them. There was no one with a bucket stuck on their head. Nobody had a knife protruding from them. Nobody with any limbs dangling at precarious angles. It was all rather dull.

It was a Wednesday afternoon after all, maybe the good stuff only happened at the weekend. I was eventually called in and had my face x-rayed. It turned out I had broken my nose and was prescribed extra strong painkillers. As I walked out of the waiting room with my broken nose, I made a few enquiries as to the well-being of the wee girl. Nobody had stabbed her or hit her, she'd bitten clean through her tongue whilst mucking around with her sister and had to receive stitches.

On her tongue?

Ouchy!

That evening, having collected and taken my super duper strength painkillers, I sat and had a few drinks with Sid and Bobby whilst they laughed and made jokes about my deformed appearance. I didn't care though, I felt at peace with myself and the world. Even thinking about Debbie didn't hurt as much. We talked long into the night about our upcoming tour with great excitement and camaraderie and I went to bed wishing we were starting the tour in the morning.

Prescription painkillers are fucking magic.

DAY 4

I could hear my phone ringing. But I was trapped at the bottom of an old-fashioned well. The phone was at the top, inside the bucket. The constant ringing echoed softly from the tin bucket and then down the side of the damp, mossy, stone walls before penetrating my ears. I was quite comfortable down the well even though I had no idea of how I came to be there. The thought didn't really trouble me. I stretched my arm up the cold, slimy wall of the well and fumbled around in the bucket for the phone. Its constant ringing was now starting to annoy me.

"James? James? Are you there? James it's Mum" my mum sounded upset, as if she'd been crying. Perhaps it was because I was down a well?

"Helloooooo, Muuuuuuuuum, I'm down here it's okay."

"James, are you blinking drunk? It's Dad, he's been rushed to hospital, he's had a heart attack, get round here now … James? James?"

As my mother's words bounced around my brain, I opened my eyes and threw off my duvet.

"Dad's what?"

"He's had a heart attack, oh you should have seen him, it was terrible, he looked awful."

My mum was sobbing down the phone as I tried to make sense of what was going on.

"Fucking hell. He's gonnae be okay though, eh? He'll be a'right though, Mum?"

"He's in with the doctors now. Oh I don't know what I'll do without him, James."

"Fuck, this is too much. I'll be there as quick as I can."

I hung up the phone, picked up yesterday's clothes from the floor and threw them on in a panic.

On route to the hospital, the same hospital that I had visited only the day before, I thought about my dad's mortality and what we would do if the worst was to happen.

The thoughts terrified me, and I prayed all the way to the hospital.

Not being of a religious disposition, I still found myself praying to God, a God that for me didn't exist. I prayed to the God that was imposed upon me at primary school.

The Presbyterian version.

Jesus' old man.

I prayed to this God for my own father's safety.

It didn't feel wrong or weird or hypocritical. At that moment in time it felt right, it felt comforting, and I hoped to hell that the big man was listening.

I rushed through the hospital doors and into the stuffy, smelly waiting room. My mother burst into tears as soon as she saw me.

"Where is he? Where's Dad?"

"What happened to your face?" she asked between sobs.

"Oh that? That's nothing, eh I fell. Where's Dad? How is he?"

"He's in theatre now. I told him he was working too hard at his age, he should have retired years ago, I told him to slow down but would he listen? Oh no, he knows best. Bloody pig-headed man. I can't lose him, James, I can't."

"He'll be okay, I'm sure of it. You know Dad, he's a fighter."

My words were meant to provide comfort, but they just sounded feeble and hollow. I hadn't the faintest idea if he would be okay. The truth was my dad wasn't a fighter, he'd throw in the towel at the first sign of trouble or unrest and my mum knew it. She was the fighter, the strong one. I tried to imagine him walking through the doors with a big smile on his face but every time I did so intrusive images of the surgeons frantically fighting to save him would appear in my mind's eye.

I could even hear the beep beep beeeeeeeeeeeeeeeep of the life support machine.

The walls of the waiting room were closing in on me. I was finding it hard to breathe and the constant beeeeeeeeeeeep of the useless life support machine hurt my ears.

"I need to get out of here, Mum. I need some air."

As I stood up, blackness engulfed me, black, black, blacker still.

Until I couldn't see.

I think I called out as I felt myself falling.

"James? James? Can you hear me, James?"

I was strolling alongside a burn. A burn I recognised yet couldn't recall from when or where. The burn was close to bursting its banks as the dirty brown water surged past. It had obviously been raining heavily because the water normally ambled past like it had all the time in the world.

It probably did.

I needed to get to the other side of the burn but there was no bridge. If I tried to wade across, I'd be swept away for sure.

I can't swim against that current.

The noise of the water gushing past was starting to alarm me, and I noticed its volume had increased. It was starting to spill over the sides. The path I was on was narrow due to overhanging branches, so I had to scramble up a grassy embankment to a copse of trees to avoid being dragged in by the burn. I was starting to panic as the water was still rising as I scrambled free of the trees and into the adjacent field. I was now a good 20 metres above the water level but still the dirty liquid kept coming. I started to jog across the newly ploughed field, moving further away from the burn, but I could feel the water lapping at my ankles all the while like an angry terrier.

This is impossible.

This can't be happening.

But still the water kept on coming. I jumped a barbed wire fence and into another field.

I looked round and to my horror the water still kept on coming, following me like a crazed stalker. It was carrying a pile of debris it had picked up en-route.

Up ahead there was a drystane dyke and I sprinted towards it as fast as I could. After vaulting it I sat with my back against the mossy grey stones trying to catch my breath.

This is ridiculous.

I was surely about a mile from the burn's normal course. The water couldn't possibly reach this far. It wasn't even raining.

How could the water keep rising? It's not possible.

I had been sitting with my back against the stone dyke for about ten minutes and decided I'd head for home. As I stood up and looked back over the wall from whence I'd came, I was met by the sight of a giant dirty brown wave of water about three metres high.

The sky went black as the wave devoured everything in sight. It was heading for me. I closed my eyes and curled into a ball. I could hear the giant wave crashing down upon me with its thunderous roar, I stiffened in anticipation of the dirty cold blast … "Aaaaarrghhhh!"

"Aaaaarrrghhhh!" I winced as I felt a sharp pain penetrating my forehead.

"It's all right, James, we're just putting a few stitches in your head. You're okay, gave yourself a bit of a dunt on the head on the way down though."

I lay on a bed being looked down upon by a woman with a serious expression on her face as she apparently sewed my head together. She told me the gory details of my fainting and subsequent crash headfirst into a door as it was being opened from the other side.

I pictured my delicate forehead connecting with the sharp wooden corner of the door frame and it made my stomach lurch.

Shortly after I was patched up and given the all-clear and we were allowed in to see my dad.

He was still weak from the surgery and had the look of a wee boy on his first day at school, all nervous and terrified and just wanting a cuddle from his mammy.

He looked grim and he looked a lot older than he did the last time I saw him, but he was alive. We checked out our respective wounds with mutual admiration and skirted around the issue of mortality as best we could despite Mum's best efforts to make this the main topic of conversation.

That and how I came to have a broken nose.

As soon as I was comfortable enough with a level of guilt I thought I could cope with about leaving my parents in their fragile emotional state, I made my excuses and left.

I've never been the best at dealing with situations that require deep emotional discussions for reasons that I have yet to properly explore. All I know is that I don't like the emotions they evoke in me, so I find it's best to ignore these difficult situations and emotions till they disappear.

On leaving the hospital I met Bobby at his local, had a few pints, and explained the growing number of cuts and bruises to my face then I walked home through the local park to gather my thoughts.

My dad had been lucky today.

Or had he?

He was born in this town, educated in this town, worked in this town, married in this town, raised a family in this town, and although he'd survived a heart attack today, he'd more than likely die in this town.

That thought depressed me. Actually, the thought that concerned me was that I was walking the same path as him and that depressed me more than the thought of my dad dying.

I've got to get out of this town. I've got to make something of my life.

DAY 5

I awoke with a new sense of being. Today was the start of a new era in my life. After last night's walk home, I now had a purpose in life, well perhaps not a purpose but I was certain of one thing, I had to give this tour my best shot. It looked like the only way I'd be able to get out of this town for good. Maybe we *could* make it with the band? Hell, nothing ventured nothing gained as they say. What did we have to lose?

I was getting more and more excited at the prospect of touring Scotland and this excitement made me feel much happier within myself.

Buoyed by my new self confidence, I phoned Debbie to arrange to pick up the rest of my belongings. We had an amicable grown-up chat and so I duly headed off in the direction of her house intent on showing her what she was missing. I added a cheeky wee spray of her favourite scent, Jean Paul Gaultier here and there just in case.

Well, you never know …

She answered the door in just a towel which wreaked havoc with my emotions, but I tried not to let them show.

"What happened to your face? It's a mess," she asked sullenly.

"Good to see you too, Debs. Long story with the face, got into a couple of scraps, nothing I couldn't handle though," I added nonchalantly, hoping that I sounded tough.

"Jenny told me she'd seen you looking a mess being led away by the police. You been a naughty boy?"

Fuck I forgot about that. Just play it cool, Jimmy, don't give too much away, you want to sound mysterious.

"Ha ha," I gave my best nonchalant laugh. "Yeah, something like that."

"Don't be getting any ideas, Jimmy," she said whilst pointing to my bulging groin.

"Don't get any ideas? Don't answer the door wearing nothing but a bloody towel then. I can't help it if I still find you attractive, you're standing there practically naked."

"I'm in the middle of getting ready actually." And she turned and walked back into the hall.

I adjusted myself before walking through the front door.

I have never been good at reading or listening to signals from the opposite sex and so my mind was now a hotbed of activity.

Why the fuck did she answer the door in just a towel?

Why did she call me a naughty boy?

She knew I was coming round. If she didn't want me getting any ideas, then why didn't she get dressed or wait till I'd gone to have a shower?

This doesn't make sense, maybe she's testing me to see exactly how attractive I find her.

Maybe she wants me back?

Debbie went upstairs to her room, and I followed, staring at her beautifully sculpted arse as it swung hypnotically beneath the clinging towel leaving little to my imagination.

I adjusted myself once more as I entered the bedroom.

"What are you doing, Jimmy? I need to get dressed, get out."

"What? I've seen you naked millions of times, I know your body inside out."

"That was as my partner. You gave up the right to see me naked when you chose your childish games with your friends over me. Now get out."

"Oh dinnae bring all that up again … all right, all right, I'm going. I just thought there might be some of my stuff in there that was all. Anyway, it wasn't me who ended this. If I had my way, I would be standing naked beside you right now. As your partner."

"Piss off, don't try and pin this on me. You ended this with your stupid ideas. You knew how serious I was about us; it was you who couldn't commit. You can't have your cake and eat it. Anyway, I'm not discussing this."

"You started it … look, I still love you, Debs, I guess a part of me always will."

It was corny and it was shallow, but it was true, I did still love her and want to be with her but the reason I told her how I felt was because she was standing in front of me wearing only a towel and all I wanted to do was rip it from her, throw her on the bed, fuck her brains out, and then shoot my load inside her.

My plan didn't work.

She strolled over to me and flicked me in the balls.

"Now get out."

"Aargh!" I slumped out of her room clutching my broken sack and went in search of the last of my meagre possessions.

As I flicked through her CD collection, making sure she hadn't purposely kept a few of mine, Debbie came into the living room.

Looking amazing.

And I mean STUNNINGLY amazing.

She stood before me wearing a figure-hugging black dress with just the right amount of cleavage on show and her hair was tied up to accentuate the slender long neck that I loved to kiss.

FUCK!

Curiosity instantly flared in me only to be extinguished seconds later by a flood of acute jealousy.

There could only be one reason she was dressed up like that.

To impress someone.

I was pretty sure it wasn't me judging by the damage she'd just inflicted on my testicles, rendering them useless for the best part of a lifetime.

"You look nice, going somewhere special?" I asked, trying to sound disinterested.

"Nowhere special. I'm just meeting someone for a drink." It was now her turn to play the mysterious card and I was absolutely hating it.

"You're dressed like that just to meet someone for a drink? Come on," I whined, sounding desperately more pathetic than I had intended.

"Why should you care what I'm dressed like or where I'm going and with whom? Unless you're jealous?" She was loving this, the power, the secrecy, and the fact that I was melting inside under my own steam.

"I am not jealous," I snapped, a little too angrily for it to be mistaken for anything else but jealousy. "I've just never seen you dressed up like that before … you never dressed like that when we went out for drinks … even at the start."

"Well maybe this is the new me. Maybe I've been hiding in the shadows for too long. Maybe you were holding me back all these years and it's only now that I'm fulfilling my true potential."

To say I was shocked by her last statement was an understatement. I was utterly flabbergasted.

Was that how she really felt about me?

I held her back?

"What are you talking about? Holding you back? I've never held you back, Debs."

"Emotionally you did. Emotionally you kept me hanging onto something that was never there or was ever going to be there. I always came second to whatever latest fad had your attention. Well now I've met someone who has opened doors in me that have been locked for too long."

What the hell is she talking about?

I loved her with all my heart and gave her all I had emotionally. Granted, it wasn't much but I gave her all I had.

Why is she saying these things?

Locked doors?

What the fuck is that?

"You've met someone else?" I shouted, startling myself with the ferocity and pitch of the blast. "You only dumped me on Monday. Christ, you don't hang about, do you? Fuck's sake, did the last seven years mean nothing to you? Obviously not if four days later you're off swanning about with Johnny come fucking lately."

"You are jealous," she screamed back at me, "and yes the last seven years meant a lot to me but they're over, gone. What would you have me do, Jimmy? Sit indoors bored and alone waiting for what's deemed in your eyes a reasonable amount of time to mourn a failed relationship?"

Her crippling honesty hurt me as much as the fact that she'd already moved on and I hadn't. Maybe it was my pride that hurt more than anything.

"Of course I'm jealous, I'm hurting," I tailed off, I couldn't think of anything else to add. "But four days, Debs? Four days?"

I sat on the edge of the sofa rubbing my temples like a demented psychiatric patient.

"Well what's acceptable to you, Jimmy? Four weeks? Four months? FOUR FUCKING YEARS?"

She almost removed the skin from my ears as she unleashed her latest retort. I knew she was right though, there is no specific time for when it's right to move on. I was just hurting that she was dealing with this more responsibly and sensibly than me. That and the fact that I clearly needed her and wanted her a lot more than she wanted or needed me.

Or was that just self-indulgent bullshit too?

My head was a mess, I needed to get out of there. To get away from Debs. To get away from the truth. I needed a drink.

"Aye whatever," I sighed. "Four days is as good as four years I suppose. It's just, ach, I don't know, Debs, this is all just a bit too much. I've got emotions flying all the place. I'm gonnae go now, I've got the last of my stuff. I'll call you later. We can still keep in touch, eh?"

"Of course, this town's too small to be strangers." She gave me a wink and my heart sank.

"Well good luck with your drinks tonight, I hope it all goes well. Who's the lucky guy by the way?"

"It's … It's …" she fumbled.

"Sorry, look you don't have to tell me, it's a'right," I lied, desperately hoping she would tell me the bastard's name.

"No it's just that I'm not sure you'll know him, he moved away from the area years ago when he joined the army and he's only just returned. His name's Daniel."

Daniel? Daniel? Daniel?

The name rattled around my brain as it released mugshots of all the Daniels I knew.

I used to work with a Dan Balfour.

"Not Dan Balfour?" I asked, praying that it wasn't him.

"No, it's Daniel, not Dan …"

Phew. Dan's all right, big Rangers fan but decent enough. Glad it's not him.

"… Daniel Foster."

Daniel Foster?

Daniel Foster?

Nope.

A disturbing sensation slowly crept from the back of my brain and twisted its way down my spinal chord before smashing into my stomach.

Danny Foster?

Surely not?

"Danny Foster? Got a big brother called Stevie?"

"I'm not sure, why, do you know him?" she answered whilst giving her gorgeous neck and cleavage another spray of the expensive perfume I bought her last Christmas.

Holy Mary Mother of God.

Suppressed images came flooding back to me with feelings of terror that had remained locked away for years.

"If it's the same moron who left to join the army then yeah, I know him. We were at school together and he was the biggest cunt that roamed the corridors, a fucking brute who made our lives hell, all muscle with no brains. We all breathed a sigh of relief when he left the area. Nice choice, Debs."

"You're just jealous. Daniel's charming, polite, and a very funny guy actually."

"Aye? Try telling that to Bobby next time you see him. I cannae believe that bastard came back here. He's trouble, Debs, you should stay away from him." And I pointed a stern finger in her face.

"I'm old enough to look after myself, Jimmy, but thanks for your concern."

She patted my left cheek in a piss off and mind your own business kind of way.

"Look, I really need to go, is there anything else?" she asked whilst ushering me through the front door.

"Naw. Eh enjoy your night with Danny. I'm sure it'll be intellectually stimulating," I sneered sarcastically.

"Thank you, now run off home to Sid like a good little boy." Her dimples looked cuter than ever as her shiny pink lips broke into a beaming smile thanks to her witty comeback.

Deflated and with no witty retort of my own, I turned and left her, looking back as she skipped off in the opposite direction.

Man, she looks amazing.

She smelled amazing.

It was in that instant I knew I had done the wrong thing by choosing the band. Choosing to live with Sid all these years when I had this amazing woman ready to give up her life for me. Choosing to put her second over everything I did and never thinking about the consequences and choosing to act like I was still 16 years old.

Fuck, fuck, fuck, fuck, fuck.

To make matters worse she was walking off to meet the biggest bastard that ever walked this earth looking and smelling amazing.

FUCK, FUCK, FUCK, FUCK, FUCK!

I hawked and spat onto the ground in disgust and headed for home.

Suddenly an image of Danny Foster cradling a naked Debbie in his arms entered my head.

He smiled and then winked at me as his hand moved lower, lower still …

"AW PISS OFF," I roared into the evening sky, causing something to take flight from the nearby trees.

I didn't go home. After the week I'd had I deserved a drink. The mother of all fucking drinks. A drink that would banish the memory of that week forever.

CHAPTER 4

I awoke in a strange bed in a foul mood. My eyes strained as I scanned the dimly lit room looking for clues as to my whereabouts.

No joy. I could be anywhere.

My head ached and my mouth tasted of stale booze and a million cigarettes.

I slowly turned my head.

Fuck!

There was a body lying next to mine. As my eyes adjusted to the gloom, I lifted the sheets for further inspection. There was a BIG, naked body lying next to mine. Peering down to my own body I was naked too. Except for one sock. Despite the big body being turned on its side facing away from me I could tell by its bulk and by the hideous black roots of her nicotine-coloured hair that it was Susan, one of the barmaids from The Crown.

My mood deteriorated further.

I couldn't recall how I came to be here but that didn't matter.

What mattered was did we have intercourse?

I looked under the duvet again. There was no sign of any condoms used or otherwise. I scanned the floor looking for torn wrappers.

None.

Ah shite, it'd be just my luck to shag the fat ugly burd and get her pregnant.

I started to panic.

In my mind I could see us raising a child together. A stupid, ugly, fat child. All of us dependent on benefits and getting fatter by the day.

My life ruined by one drunken mistake.

"It's all Danny Foster's fault," I gasped, causing Susan to stir.

"Morning, lover boy," she croaked as she turned to face me.

Jesus Christ!

She looks bad enough with her make-up on but without …

"You dinnae look so hot yersell, Romeo," she muttered as my face must've evoked what my mind was thinking.

"Eh, all right, Susan? Look, eh, about last night …"

"Whit? That you're shite in bed? Cannae even get it up? Well how's about we try again, eh?"

She scooped up my balls in her large clammy hands and squeezed them like she was extracting juice from a lemon, making me recoil with a whimper. Unperturbed she moved in to kiss me, but the smell of her morning breath mixed with her body odour made me sick. I threw up where I cowered. Yellow stinking vomit shot from my mouth with such a force that my head actually rocked backwards. Susan unfortunately didn't have time to cover herself from the deluge. My puke sprayed into her face and into her mouth and down her chin onto her big flabby tits before nestling in a disgusting puddle on the bed.

"Aargh, ya dirty bastard!" she screamed whilst spitting out my lumpy bile. She threw back the duvet and leapt over me and into the bathroom.

Due to the force at which the puke blasted from my mouth I didn't have a drop on me. There was a half-drunk bottle of beer on the bedside table and I grabbed it, gulped a mouthful, gargled it, then spat the lot into the puddle of puke on the bed.

Just as good as Listerine!

I was so relieved at not impregnating Susan that I didn't care about my current predicament or the fact that my stud-like reputation would be in tatters once this little mishap hit the gossip pages.

I got dressed as quickly as I could while listening to Susan throwing up next door. I couldn't find my shoe to go with the sock that I had lost and, in my haste to get the fuck out of there, I decided it was a small price to pay for my stupid drunken behaviour and that I should consider myself lucky I hadn't produced a child with that hideous creature. I stuck my head around the door of the bog to find Susan clutching the toilet bowl as if it were about to take off for outer space.

For some inexplicable reason I'm ashamed to say I found the sight of her lying there with her big naked arse stuck in the air a bit of a turn on. I shook my head in disgust at my useless loins.

"Eh I'll see you later, Susan. Sorry about the sickness and that. Eh, I've got to go grab some fresh air, I think I'm gonnae be sick again. I'll call you later though, eh?"

She didn't even remove her head from the white porcelain bowl, she just threw her hand at me in a 'get the fuck out of here, you disgusting scum bag' motion.

That little adventure had distracted my mind from the 'Danny Foster back in town' situation but as I walked home it wrestled its way to the front of my mind. I changed course and headed for Bobby's place instead, he had to know Danny Foster was back.

After walking ten minutes in the direction of Bobby's house I thought it would probably be in everyone's best interest if I didn't show up there still half pissed, wearing only one shoe with breath that would melt steel and a face that would curdle milk.

I turned around and headed for home again.

I'll go see Bobby this evening.

I think it's time for another stroll down memory lane, bear with me please as this wee stroll is important.

Sid and I met Bobby McGee at high school. He wasn't in the same class as us in the first couple of years, but he came to our attention and that of everyone else's because of his appearance. First up he was almost 6 foot tall and still growing at 12 years of age. Secondly, he wasn't white. The fact that I even mention this gives you a little insight into the demographics and mindset of the area's population. Bobby's father was Fijian, and his mother is Scottish. I say *was* Fijian because his father (who was an RAF pilot) died tragically in a training exercise when Bobby was only eight years old. And thirdly none of Bobby's clothes seemed to be from this planet. My earliest memory of Bobby and the one that always makes me shudder is seeing Danny Foster aided by two of his goons gathered around Bobby jabbing him with sticks calling him a 'smelly wog' and a 'black bastard'. Bobby didn't react to any of this vile goading, he just stood there and stared at Foster. This seemed to rile Foster as next it was 'What the fuck are you staring at, you monkey?' before the stick whipped across Bobby's face. knocking him to the ground. Foster and his two accomplices bore down on Bobby like a pack of dogs on a kill, kicking, punching, stamping. Sid and me and dozens more stood and watched this terrible scene in sheer horror.

Still, nobody did anything to help Bobby.

I wanted to go over and do something to help but I couldn't move. I was frozen. Scared shitless by the ferocity of the attacker's hatred.

Better that lad there than me.

So I stood, along with 20 or more other kids and watched the whole bloody scene. The kicking, the punching, the stamping, the shouting, 'take that you dirty coon. Fucking black bastard.'

Through his hands I could see Bobby's eyes. They looked straight into mine. They didn't show anger, they didn't even show fear. They just stared into mine with a kind of cold resignation as if to say, 'here we go again.'

After five minutes of the brutal assault Foster and his comrades got bored and simply walked off laughing, but not before sniffing up a load of phlegm and gobbing it all over Bobby. Sid and me just looked at each other. We had never seen anything this barbaric in our lives.

"Fucking bastards," was all we muttered as if that somehow made up for our lack of assistance in the brutal slaughter we had just witnessed.

After waiting till his attackers were out of sight, Bobby simply got up, looked at his wounds, rubbed the spit from his jacket. and walked away.

There walked the bravest man I had ever seen.

The constant violence and bullying continued to various degrees throughout high school. Well, until Danny Foster left at the end of fourth year to start a career in the Army. God help us if that's the kind of persons responsible for the defence of this United Kingdom

Uneducated, bigoted, racist, violent arseholes.

On second thoughts it's probably in our vested interests to use these ignorant fuckers as cannon fodder.

Gets rid of them without the guilt I suppose.

Bobby was in a couple of my classes in third and fourth year and he was a good guy to talk to, but I never let our relationship develop into a solid friendship due to the fact that I was terrified I would get the same treatment as him if Danny Foster thought I was pals with him.

Years later. I still feel a sense of shame and anger at my actions or lack of them and go over the 'what if' scenarios in my mind.

Throughout high school I fantasised about walking up to Danny Foster whilst he was busy beating up Bobby, tapping him on the shoulder then smacking him in the face as hard as I could, knocking the bastard out cold.

That never happened though. It would never happen because I was a coward.

I still am a coward.

In fifth year, Bobby, Sid and I were in a lot of classes together and with Danny Foster gone we were free from the fear of assault and so became good friends. We bonded over our love of football and music and marijuana.

I asked Bobby when I got to know him better why he didn't fight back?

After all, he was almost twice the size of his tormentor.

His reply cleared things up.

"Because he would've killed me. He hated me, really hated me. I saw it in his eyes every time he came near me and, if I had fought back, he would've seen that as a threat and would have gone to any length to get me back. It happened once at primary school, a guy took the piss out of me for years and the insults gradually got worse until they turned to violence. One day he jumped me after school and beat me up. I couldn't go home and tell my mum, that would just make matters worse cause she'd be straight down the school berating the headmaster. Instead, I told my uncle who told me to 'fight back, to get stuck into the kid, he'll no' come near you after that.'

"So that's what I did, the next time he started taking the piss I got stuck in. I broke his jaw. Everything went crazy after that. A week later I was walking down the street when a car screeched to a halt. The kid's dad and two older brothers jumped out. 'There's the black bastard there,' one of them shouted and they all started running for me. I turned and ran as fast as I could. They were throwing stones and anything they could lay their hands on. Something hit me on the back of the head, and I went down. As I scrambled to my feet I was kicked in the head and back and then they were on me. The kid's dad grabbed me, he was shouting and swearing at me, spraying my face with his saliva. He let go my jumper and punched me in the stomach. I collapsed in agony, I couldn't breathe, all the air had been punched from my body. I gasped for air, and he picked me up by my hair. He was still screaming and shouting and pointing his finger in my face. I thought I was going to die. Before he could hit me again a couple of old ladies who happened to be walking by scared him off. I lay on the ground in agony. As soon as my breath returned one of the old ladies tried to console me, but I pushed her away and ran home in tears. I always knew I was different despite Mum telling me otherwise and I could handle the name calling and the piss taking. But this was different. I was ten years old, and I'd just been assaulted by a grown man, all because of the colour of my skin. This didn't happen in a run-down scheme in Glasgow or Dundee. This happened in a quiet middle-class village in Fife. The kid's dad wasn't an unemployed junkie, he was a civil servant, a so-called educated man. So, if I'd fought back with Danny Foster whose family members are a cross between The Addams family and The Krays, I probably wouldn't be here now."

So for fear of his own life Bobby took the brave decision to do nothing and was subjected to four years of horrific, violent, humiliating abuse at the hands of Danny Foster. The same Danny Foster who was now out on a date with my Debbie.

CHAPTER 5

"Hiya, Jimmy, you all right? Come in," Mel beamed the way she always does as she opened the front door to their cosy cottage.

"Aye doing good, Mel. How's tricks?"

"All good here, we're just having a quiet night in. Your face is starting to heal up. I've got some cream you can put on it if you want? It's made with Aloe vera, it'll speed up the healing process."

"Eh thanks, aye I'll take some." My face still resembled a burst couch, but I appreciated Mel's positive spin on things. She was always trying to hand out lotions and potions of some sort to anyone who would take them. Like mine was going to, I was sure the potions she gave to everyone else would sit in a drawer and never see the light of day. I appreciated her kindness none the less.

As I walked down the long narrow hallway lined with Mel's photographs and Bobby's paintings, I could smell the familiar sickly-sweet scent of weed emanating from the living room.

Good, it's probably for the best that Bobby's been anaesthetised before he hears what I've come to say.

"Hey, Jimmy. How's it going, man?" Bobby mumbled whilst inhaling.

"I'm good, mate. I still look like the elephant man, but these pain killers are ace. I feel like I'm walking on clouds."

"Well you'll no' be wanting any of this then, eh? Fresh batch, just off the radiator." Bobby replied by waving a massive spliff in my direction.

"I didn't say that my green-fingered friend, it would be extremely rude of me to turn down the opporchancity of smoking a fresh batch of your infamous home-grown weed. Come on, don't be shy." I took the joint from Bobby, sat on the couch, then inhaled deeply myself.

"Aaaah, that's nice, man."

Bobby had been growing weed for years and was considered to be quite the expert on horticultural matters. He stopped growing it a few years back when a young student who was smoking Bobby's produce jumped from his bedroom window in the halls of residence wearing nothing but his

61

underpants. Luckily, he was on the ground floor, so no lasting damage was done. It was only when he started smashing up his stereo and set it alight that passers-by started to show signs of concern. And when he smashed the windows of parked cars to attack their radios by swearing and screaming at them, the entire population of the street was present to see him being carted off to the local nut house by two confused-looking paramedics. The poor guy was later diagnosed as a paranoid schizophrenic, and it was reluctantly accepted that the smoking of Bobby's weed had triggered something in his brain, giving rise to his mental illness. Bobby was devastated and promptly set about destroying his prized possessions, blaming himself for the lad's demise.

It was only after months of pleading from the townsfolk who, sick of smoking cheap soap bar and realising that they actually hated everything about themselves, their jobs, their town, the weather, and each other whilst straight that Bobby felt it was his moral duty to restore some normality to the place and started growing weed again.

Six months after the schizophrenic incident general apathy was once again the mood of the townsfolk and they all lived happily ever after.

I myself am what you would call a part-time toker. I enjoy the odd doobie now and again purely for medicinal purposes. If I smoked weed at the rate Bobby did, I'd never leave my armchair never mind the house.

I stick to the booze as my drug of choice. I can handle it better, although I have noticed the hangovers are starting to last a wee bit longer than they used to.

"You a'right, Jimmy?" Bobby asked.

"Eh?"

"Are you all right? You've been sitting there for five minutes and haven't said a word. And you're hogging that joint, come on, share the love," Bobby teased.

"Oh aye sorry, man. Here," I passed the spliff onto Mel and melted back into the suffocating embrace of the couch. Smoking weed on these painkillers wasn't such a smart move.

"Aye I'm fine, Bobby, it's just that, well I've got something to tell you and I dinnae ken how best to approach the subject. I mean do I just blurt it out all blunt and that or do I try and you know sort of soften it around the edges like?"

"Just give it to me straight, man. I'm a big boy."

I was a wee bitty worried how Bobby might react to the news, after all it had been over twenty peaceful years since we had last heard of Danny Foster and his name had seldom been mentioned since. I was worried that all the old feelings of fear and terror might rumble up in his mind like they had done in mine when Debbie told me she was dating the vile prick.

I hadn't even been subjected to a tenth of the abuse Bobby had but I still reacted with silent revulsion when I heard his name mentioned. The mere mention of his name brought back the old familiar gnawing sensation in my guts, just like it used to when I sat at my desk and worried whether he'd seen me talking to Bobby.

Will he be waiting for me outside class?

I now had a picture in my mind of Bobby upon hearing the news of Danny's return, jumping out of the window wearing nothing but his Y-fronts before running screaming down the road hotly pursued by two confused-looking paramedics.

"DannyFoster'sbackintown," I spluttered. My thinking was that if I said it really fast it would lessen the blow.

Mel let out a horrified gasp and said, "Say that again," before looking straight at Bobby.

I looked at Mel and then at Bobby and took in a deep breath before replying slowly.

"Danny Foster is back in town."

"I know," Bobby replied nonchalantly.

"What? How?" Both Mel and I shouted in unison.

"I know. I spoke with Whitey the other day and he said he'd seen him coming out of Scot-mid."

"The fucking bastard," I spat, struggling to keep my hatred in check.

"There's not a law against him going into Scot-mid, Jimmy," Bobby chuckled.

"Aye I know, it's just, what the fuck did he come back here for?" I moaned.

"Why didn't you mention this to me, honey?" Mel asked.

"I don't know, I suppose I didn't want to go over old ground."

"I can't believe he's come back after all the trouble he caused. How are you feeling about it, baby?" Mel asked. She got up and walked across the room and kissed Bobby on the forehead before cuddling into his arms. "What are we going to do?"

"Let's put this into perspective here, we're not kids any more. He's probably got a wife and family now. I don't think he'll be all that interested in hunting me down to shout a few insults at me and throw a few punches. I'd like to think that he's grown up," Bobby replied a little too calmly for my liking.

"What the fuck? Bobby, this guy made our life hell, yours especially. We should get him back, strike first. You'll make mince meat out of him."

"Jimmy, I'm not going to get him back, like I said that was years ago, it's all water under the bridge as far as I'm concerned. Life goes on."

"Are you sure you're feeling okay about this, honey? He did do terrible things to you, it's natural to feel angry," Mel asked, handing the joint back to Bobby.

"I'm fine, baby. Honest. You know I'd tell you otherwise. Look, the guy was a bastard to me and plenty others too but I don't hold any grudges, what's the point? You only make yourself sick. What goes around comes around, eh? I'm sure Karma will take care of him. Chances are he's only back visiting his mum; she's not had it easy either remember. I'll probably not even see him."

"Aye but what if you do, Bobby, what then? We cannae let the bastard get away with what he did. He's not just visiting either, he was out on a date with Debs the other night. He plans on sticking around for a while."

"What?" Bobby and Mel shouted in unison with eyes wide and mouths pursed, making them look like caricatures of what a shocked person looks like.

"He went out with Debs the other night. I went round to hers to get the last of my stuff and she was all dressed up to the nines looking gorgeous. I've never seen her dressed up like that before, she smelt amazing. Anyway, she tells me that she's going out on a date, only four days after we'd split up by the way, with a new guy in town called Daniel Foster. Well my heart almost fell out my arse when she mentioned his name. Of all the guys to pick though, fucking Fanny Foster. If he's making romantic moves on my lady then he must be planning on staying put. Even after all these years he's still trying to humiliate me."

"Calm down, man. And stop pacing up and down, you're like a caged animal. Look, Debbie's a sensible girl and Danny wouldn't have a clue she was your ex. If he's moved back, well, there's nothing much I can do about it, eh?" Bobby said then took a long drag of his joint before passing it on.

"Aye there is. You're built like a fucking Sherman tank; we could go and boot the shite out of him. See how he fucking likes it. Cunt."

"Get off your high horse, Jimmy. If Bobby's fine with it, and it was him who had it hardest of all remember, then we all should be too. Here, have this back. I'm going to put the kettle on, who wants tea?"

Mel handed me the joint and went off to make a soothing brew.

Is there any problem a cup of tea can't solve?

I took a long puff of the joint and inhaled deeply, sooking in every last drop of smoke and held it in my lungs till they were fit to burst before exhaling.

"Seems to me you're more upset about Debbie going out on a date with Danny than you are about the whole playground stuff," Bobby stated.

"Hey, that's not true and you know it. I've told you what it was like having to stand and watch you take those beatings and I've had to deal with the feelings of guilt ever since so don't tell me I don't care about the playground stuff."

"That's not what I'm saying, man, calm down. Anyway, it was me who took the beatings, not you, so what are you getting upset for? If anyone should be gunning for revenge, it's me. But I'm not and you shouldn't be either so just leave it. It's not that big a deal. Besides, we'll soon be gone on our world tour of Scotland woohoo, come on."

Bobby leapt off his seat, punching the air, then dived on top of me ruffling my hair and punching my arm, shouting "champions, champions."

"Aargh get aff me, you big lump, watch my face, it's still fragile."

"Hey you pair, stop mucking about, here's your tea," Mel scolded.

"Thanks, Mel. Is it Scottish Blend?" I asked once Bobby had seen fit to remove his sixteen-stone frame from on top of mine.

"No, it's not Scottish blend, we only drink Sid's tea in this house."

"Ah Tetley." We all raised our mugs in mock salute to our dear friend Sidney.

"So, are we still on the topic of Danny Foster or can we change it please 'cause I don't really want to spend my evening strolling down memory lane?" Mel asked, blowing on her hot cuppa.

"Yeah we can change the topic. I just think it's unfair that he gets to saunter back into town like nothing ever happened. But I suppose as Bobby says it's water under the bridge, eh?"

"Aye. Anyway, we've got more important things to think about. CHAMPIONS ON TOUR," Bobby shouted into his non-existent megaphone.

"Aye true, it will be good to get away from here," I agreed.

We sat and toked and talked and supped cups of tea into the wee small hours until Bobby decided it was time for bed.

"Some of us have got to get up early in the morning, we cannae all stay in bed till midday creaming money off the government like you, Jimmy."

"Piss off. I'm getting nothing from the government, the bastards won't give me any money for weeks because I had the cheek to quit my job. I'm living off my savings at the minute. I'm gonnae have to get a temporary job till we go on tour, I'm bloody skint."

"Well good luck with the job hunting. I'll see you this weekend though, I think Sid mentioned something about us playing at The Crown."

"Whit?! The Crown? Ah fuck," I groaned as my head slumped into my hands.

"What's the matter, you got something else planned?" Bobby asked curiously.

"What? Eh no, it's cool, I'll see you for the gig then, 'night, man. Goodnight, Mel."

"Goodnight, Jimmy," they cooed together.

As I walked home through deserted streets with a cold breeze bouncing off my face, I thought about Bobby's reaction to Danny Foster's return. He was taking it far too calmly for my liking and after everything Foster put him through. Well, if he wasn't keen on getting Foster back, I certainly was. Whilst walking through the close and up the stairwell to the front door of the flat, I thought about our upcoming gig at The Crown.

I hadn't planned on showing my face in there so soon. Actually, I had planned on never setting foot in The Crown ever again after my performance with Susan. The more I thought about it the more I was convinced that Sid had set this gig up as a direct result of hearing about my antics or lack of them with her.

"You bastard," I muttered as I walked past his bedroom door. I reached my bedroom and as I was closing the door I'm sure I could hear a low chuckling sound escaping from Sid's room.

"You fucking bastard, Sid."

CHAPTER 6

After watching daytime television for four days solid, and still resisting the urge to stick my head in the oven, I decided that it would be in the best interest of my mental wellbeing to get a job. Any job. Why these programmes are on television and why somebody felt it necessary to make them in the first place is anyone's guess.

They left me feeling depressed and disillusioned with the state of our once great, proud nation. They did however have the positive effect of getting me off my lazy arse to go look for work. Having had time to reflect I now think that it's the government who is responsible for making these life-draining, soul-sapping, brain-numbing programmes. They were made as a means to deter unemployed people from remaining unemployed. The Government's aim being to bore the unemployed into submission. 'We'd be better off working than watching this shite everyday,' they expected to hear.

I can only imagine the head scratching and shoulder shrugging that went on at Government HQ as they realised the opposite was happening.

Desperate cries of 'they weren't supposed to enjoy this tripe' and 'what's wrong with these people? It's not scientifically possible to watch more than three days of the stuff. We carried out tests,' echoing down the corridors of power.

And it was with these thoughts in my head that I wandered the streets of my hometown handing my Curriculum Vitae into shops, pubs, clubs, sites, yards, and the library in my quest for employment.

I was offered a couple of evening shifts at The Legion so old Fred Cruickshank could have a couple of nights off. The first since 1976 by the look of him.

I was promised £50 cash in hand for two five-hour shifts. Plus, I'd be able to help myself to a few nips here and there. Better than a poke in the eye with a sharp stick as the saying goes.

Mind you, a punch in the face is probably better than a poke in the eye with a sharp stick.

I applied for a night-shift position with Tesco and was rightfully rewarded with an interview on the forthcoming Monday morning. Satisfied with my triumphant quest of employment seeking, I headed off down the pub on Friday evening to meet Sid and Bobby to discuss our gig the following evening at The Crown.

"There you go, boys," Sid said, handing Bobby and me our respective pints of Belhaven Best.

"Cheers!" we replied in chorus.

"To Champions Of The Underdog and our tour of this fine nation," Sid announced misty eyed.

"Aye. I'll drink to that," Bobby responded proudly.

"Aye, too right," I added, trying my best to get into the spirit of things.

"Right, are we all set for tomorrow night? If we meet at The Crown about half six that'll give us an hour to get set up, sound check, and have a pint beforehand," Sid instructed as leader of the band.

"Sounds good to me, man," Bobby replied before tucking into his pint.

"Why The Crown? I mean, we haven't played there for years. I thought they'd stopped putting on band nights?" I asked nervously, looking for any indication from Sid that he knew about my disaster with Susan. How he could have known was anybody's guess. There were only two people who knew what happened and I for one would happily go to the grave not mentioning that whole incident to anyone and I'm sure Susan would rather keep it quiet too.

Sid let out a snort followed by a cheeky smirk that didn't give much away.

"Aye they dinnae normally put on bands anymore but they're hosting an evening for the rugby club after their match. So they asked us along. We'll get £300 for the evening but they only want covers played, bit of rock, some of the old classics, maybe a request or two."

"Sounds good to me, man," Bobby said again before draining his pint. "Same again, lads?"

Sid and me both nodded and watched Bobby go to the bar.

"Okay smart arse what's going on?" I seethed, trying to keep my anger in check. It was just too big a coincidence for us to play The Crown right after 'The Sooz crisis', especially as we never played there.

"What are you talking about? What's got into you these days, man? You're awfy touchy," Sid replied in mock shock and outrage.

Shite, he's got me right where he wants me now.

I knew he knew that I knew he knew. But he wouldn't admit he knew because he'd rather sit there and watch me squirm with embarrassment and shame as I retold the story. And I sure as hell wasn't about to admit to him what happened because he always did the same old 'you did what? With whom?' In an exaggerated mocking tone as he waited, arms folded whilst sporting a beaming grin for the juicy facts. Facts that he already knew anyway thanks to this town's obsession with playing Chinese fucking whispers.

So we went about things in the usual manner whereby I'd pretend that he didn't know anything and try and act as normal as possible and he'd pretend he didn't know anything but would drop inappropriate comments about the said incident that would start the whole stupid charade off again until the horrible truth finally came out.

A vicious circle you might say.

"Aye I know, it's just everything that's happened over the last few weeks what with Debs and me and my dad being no' well. It's been a lot to take in. It's been pretty tough, man."

I played the sympathy card in the vain hope that it would distract him from the inevitable.

"Yeah I know but chin up, we've got the tour coming up. That'll do you the world of good. It'll do us all the world of good to get away from this shite hole."

Bobby returned from the bar and plonked three fresh pints down and chucked a couple of bags of peanuts on the table.

"The Crown, eh? Mind that was where we played our first ever gig outside of the school assembly hall," Bobby reminisced.

"Oh aye so it was. Fuck, that was ages ago," Sid said whilst tearing into the peanuts. "They were good days though, eh?"

"Aye," we all sighed, "those were the days."

We all sat back in our seats and supped our pints in silence, retreating to the annals of our individual minds to replay scenes from long ago.

It was around about the springtime of 1994 when grunge was on the way out that Sid announced we should start a band. He had received a guitar for his 15th birthday the year before and I, after seeing the attention he was attracting from certain female pupils, asked for the same gift from Santa that Christmas.

The big, bearded man didn't fail me.

It wasn't exactly the summer of '69 but I still played till my fingers bled. Actually, that's not true. I practised till my fingers got really sore and developed blisters on the tips of them and then I put the guitar down for a few days till they had recovered.

But no matter how hard I practised I still couldn't catch up to Sid's level. By the time I had mastered the gentle strumming and quite frankly boring chord structures of Yellow Submarine he was belting out the solo parts to Guns N' Roses numbers.

Oasis were the new kids on the block that year and it was this band more than any other that got Sid thinking it was about time he got some of that same attention.

I personally couldn't stand Oasis. They were responsible for thousands of Sid-like teenage boys thinking that by walking with an exaggerated swagger whilst sporting a ridiculous haircut it would made them look cool.

It didn't.

In my humble opinion, just like the lead singer did it made them look a bit simple.

But I went along with the plan regardless, mainly because of the attention I hoped to get from the girls and the respect I'd demand from the boys.

"Right, I've been thinking. We're going to start a band," the young Sidney announced as we went two's on a cigarette behind the janitor's hut before Geography class.

"Cool, man … what, just the two of us?" I asked whilst watching him puff way past his half of the cigarette.

"Dinnae be daft. There's been no good bands with only two folk in them."

"What about Simon and Garfunkel?" I queried, genuinely having a soft spot for their melodic harmonies.

"Nah, they're shite, American Chas and Dave," Sidney disagreed, "there's gonnae be three in my band. That's the magic number, so we need a drummer. I'll do the singing and be on lead guitar obviously, and you'll be on bass so we need to get a drummer."

"Bass?" I asked in a confused tone, "I cannae play the bass."

"Aye and you cannae play the guitar either, so you're on the bass. It's easy, there's only four strings, that's two less for you to fuck it up with."

I mumbled something in resignation before finishing off the much smaller half of the cigarette and pinging it onto the roof of the janitor's hut.

And so it was in that instant that my bass guitar career was born.

"What about asking Keith Pearson to be the drummer? I offered. "He plays in the school orchestra and I'm sure he plays for his dad when he plays the box."

"Keith Pearson?" Sid replied in disgust. "I'm no' having that spotty wanker in my band, we want to be cool."

"Well he's the only drummer I can think of. Who are we gonnae get?"

"I'm gonnae ask big Bobby McGee."

"Bobby McGee?" I panicked. "What the hell are you gonnae ask him for? Can he even play the drums? Do you want us to get the Fanny Foster treatment?"

"Fuck Danny Foster. Anyway, he's leaving soon so he'll no' be able to touch us. I've started speaking to Bobby recently, he's a'right. He's staying on next year to do higher art, wants to go to art college to do … whatever," Sid stated, a plan already formulated in his mind.

"And can he play the drums?" I asked, already knowing the answer.

"No he cannae, but he'll learn. Black guys are renowned for their natural rhythm."

"Well would he no' be better on the bass then? I could play the drums. I'd be like Keith Moon. Cool," I enthused whilst lighting our next cigarette.

"No, you wouldn't. You'd be shite. You need more rhythm for the drums and you've got about as much rhythm as an epileptic fit. Bobby's got the right character for the job, the tragic outcast figure finally finding solace through music. Plus, I heard his mum grows her own weed and there's an old outhouse next to their farm cottage where we could practice," Sid concluded.

"So you're just using him cause he's got a place to practice and we can scrounge some cheap weed? Come on, Sid, there's got to be somebody else. Bobby's a weirdo and he's always attracting trouble."

"Look I need him, and he needs me. I'll be able to turn him around, make him popular and stop all the hassle he gets. Plus, it'll do him good to hang around with some normal folk instead of those freaks he hangs about with, fucking moshers. Depressing bunch of bastards if you ask me. Here come on, that's way passed the two's line, gie's that fag."

And so it was in that instant that Bobby's drumming career was born. Handpicked by Sid thanks to his ability to provide weed and a practice venue.

Bobby eventually and reluctantly agreed to Sid's constant asking, pleading, and hounding and became the third point of our musical triangle.

We rehearsed all summer long and after initially sounding like a massive pile up, Bobby and myself gradually got to grips with our respective instruments, resulting in us sounding not brilliant but ultimately not too bad either. We were of course encouraged all the way by the ever-empathetic Sid.

"For fuck's sake it doesn't go like that. It's one, two, three, four beats and then you come in, Jimmy. It's not fucking difficult, stop pissing about and let's start again. We'll be here all fucking night at this rate. You're fucking hopeless."

I loved the thrill of learning a new skill and being part of something creative. Not just a part of but actually contributing.

The fantasies I'd have about our band and how we'd be huge rock and roll stars led to me ignoring homework and devoting all my energies to mastering my bass. I used to rush home from school and get changed quickly before cycling the six or seven miles to Bobby's house in preparation for practice. Bobby's mum would always make us a sandwich or some chips to eat. She loved Sid and me. She had nothing but praise and encouragement for all our efforts.

We thought she was a bit weird.

We rehearsed songs from the Definitely Maybe album and despite my contempt for Oasis we gradually started to sound pretty damn good.

At first I thought it was my imaginaysheeyun but clearly it wasn't.

Sid was singing in a Mancunian accent and he sounded exactly like his hero at the time, much to the embarrassment of Bobby and myself but being the reluctant and unskilled musicians that we were we didn't dare question Sid's authority or the fact that he sung like a Northern twat who needed to blow his nose.

That summer and the following couple of years were probably the happiest period of my life. The three of us worked hard on the band and when we weren't practising, we were sitting shooting the shit and listening to music and getting stoned. We laughed and fought and argued and consoled each other until the bond had been sealed and the band had been formed … 'Cigarettes and Alcohol.'

It was Sid's band, so it was only democratic that he named us. I'm ashamed to admit that I actually thought it was a cool name at the time. We were basically an Oasis tribute band but after a lot more practice we managed to throw in a few songs by The Stone Roses and The Charlatans into our routine. Requests for songs by Sonic Youth and Rage Against The Machine from Bobby and myself which we thought should be included in our repertoire were constantly turned down by our front man for no apparent reason other than them not being 'what this band is about.'

We finally learned months later why they weren't included. It turned out Sid could only sing with a Mancunian accent.

Back at school for the new term we put on our first gig during lunch break and played 'Cigarettes and Alcohol' and 'Live Forever' by Oasis, 'The Only One I Know' by The Charlatans and 'Sugar Spun Sister' by The Stone Roses.

It was FUCKING AMAZING!

All the months spent slaving away at our craft paid off as we drank in the applause and soaked up the cheers at the end of our set. It wasn't the biggest crowd but that didn't matter. All three of us came off that assembly hall stage feeling like super stars.

The effect it had on our high school reputation was instantaneous and ridiculous. From the minute we walked off that stage we were treated differently, almost like kings. We could have ruled the school if we so wished. Sid and me no longer had to go two's on our cigarette break, fellow pupils were only too happy to provide a smoke and a light for us and the hot girls we were able to snog was utterly outrageous. All because we played a few songs.

Sid was in his prime. He swaggered around school like he was a rock icon. Even the teachers, who all hated him, started showing him a bit of respect, and as he was the front man he got the first pick of the girls. I had never had a girlfriend before, though not for the want of trying. In fact, I'd only had my first snog the previous year with a rather plump girl who shall remain nameless.

Previously I had set my sights way too high for the status I had and was rebuffed many a time in humiliating circumstances. But after that gig, girls who would previously not have been seen dead in my company were suddenly fighting for my attention.

Amazing what a wee bit of positive exposure can do eh?

Overnight I had turned into The Fonz "AAAY!"

Her name was Katie Richardson.

My first love.

Now as I have previously stated, ordinarily there would have been no way in hell she would have considered going out with me. She was pretty and popular and therefore only dated the high school hard men. Of which I was not one. But unlike the high school hard men I was now in a band. She approached me during lunch break. I was standing outside the canteen with

Sid and Bobby generally just loving being me at that moment in time. I watched her as she approached, her dark silky hair flowing behind her as she gracefully marched over to our group. I was positive she was about to ask to be another of Sid's conquests so was dumbfounded and speechless when she asked me if I would like to go out with her. Sid naturally stood there and took the piss and asked her why it was me she was asking out and not him. I mumbled something along the lines of 'yes please' and she took me by the hand and led me out onto the playing fields where we had our first kiss.

I almost came in my pants.

It was fucking fantastic.

My head swirled with thoughts of 'I cannae believe I'm getting off with Katie Richardson,' as the testosterone and hormones swooshed through my veins.

Over the weeks my confidence grew as we spent more and more time together and I gradually stopped feeling unworthy of being in her presence.

This was due to me being a horny little virgin.

I had to fuck her.

No, I *needed* to fuck her.

My balls were an aching sack of uselessness.

Until now.

It was hard in those days to get the appropriate alone time together to actually do the deed. Both our parents were of the conservative nature and wouldn't agree to us sleeping over at each other's house so we couldn't do it in the sanctuary of a comfortable bed. I wasn't old enough to drive so that ruled out any romantic trysts in the back of a clapped-out motor and Katie wasn't willing to let me shag her up against a tree in the woods next to the school playing fields so our options were what you might call limited.

Limited specifically to a 'free hoose.'

A free hoose was my saviour.

To the ignorant I must explain that a free hoose is one that has been vacated by the owners of said hoose. Vacated for reasons that normally included a holiday during school term. The parents had finally deemed their darling little kids old enough and responsible enough to be left home alone and in charge of the house and pets whilst they, the parents, caught up with some serious shagging of their own in a room where they wouldn't have to mute their efforts for fear of corrupting their darling little kid's minds through the paper-thin walls.

God bless the free hoose.

On this occasion it was a classmate of mine, Eddie Soutar (God bless you Eddie), who held it. This was a guy so low down the political corridors of high school power that few even knew of his existence. He was a nice guy who kept himself to himself for obvious reasons. When you are a very intelligent person who excels in the world of academia and actually enjoyed the thought of bettering oneself, it was wiser to keep this viewpoint hidden because it could sometimes be frowned upon by the knuckle dragging masses who roamed the corridors.

Having seen the turnaround in my own fortunes in the political playground and with the ladies, Eddie, being a smart guy, naturally wanted a piece of this action for himself and so hoping this would be the case he hosted a free hoose which was the next best thing for popularity behind being in a band, being hard as fuck, or being the top striker in the football team.

Eddie had asked me to organise it mainly because I was suddenly one of the coolest kids in school and knew a lot more cool people than he did.

I didn't actually know these people, but they were keen to be associated with me.

So, I agreed.

Everybody wins.

Eddie's folks had a really nice house, too nice a house to be holding a free one in. I didn't care about that though. As payment for organising the free hoose I got to sleep in his parent's bedroom. Which had a door that locked.

Peace at last for Katie and me.

I'm finally going to lose it.

When the night came, I was a bundle of energy and excitement. Katie looked stunning in her tight beige Levi jeans and lacy white blouse. We spent the first few hours of the party drinking cheap wine and socialising with mates, but I couldn't concentrate. All I could think about was getting my end away for the first time. After what seemed like an eternity and much secretive nodding from myself in the direction of upstairs we managed to sneak away to Eddie's parent's bedroom. My heart was pounding as was the erection in my boxer shorts. We stood at the bottom of the bed and kissed. Softly at first but I was eager to get things moving so I rammed my tongue down her throat and squeezed her breasts. She, obviously being much more experienced in this department than myself, promptly took over and pushed me away. She threw me on the bed and then straddled me, pinning my arms to either side of my shaking body. She gently unbuttoned her blouse, deliberately lingering on each button.

Oh fuck, oh fuck, oh fuck I think I'm gonnae cum.

She threw off her blouse, revealing a purple bra. She cupped her breasts then slid her hands down her slim stomach and into her jeans.

Holy fucking shit, dinnae cum, dinnae cum, dinnae cum.

She unbuttoned her Levi's to reveal matching purple knickers and promptly put her hands inside them. At this point it was unclear to myself what she was doing but she appeared to be rummaging around for something in her underwear.

Maybe that's where she keeps the condom for safekeeping?

She groaned with pleasure then slipped her slimy fingers from inside her underpants and popped them into my mouth.

Fucking hell, am I eating pussy juice?

I slurped and sucked on her fingers as she moved them in and out of my stunned mouth.

I am, I am eating pussy juice. Hey, this doesnae taste like fish at all, it's actually pretty good, and she seems to be enjoying it too.

She took her fingers out of my mouth and went back to pleasuring herself.

Eh? what the fuck? What about me? Two can play this game.

I shifted my position and threw her off me and pinned her to the bed. Katie squealed in delight. I pulled her jeans off and threw them over my head.

"Okay I won't be a minute, I'm just gonnae take my clothes off."

I got up and unlaced my new CAT boots. I'd managed to get a knot stuck in one of them and the harder I struggled to free the laces the tighter I pulled the knot. I bent my leg towards me with all the grace of an angry yoga student and attempted to bite the knot.

By the time I had finished fannying about with my boots and then removed my clothes, Katie had got bored and finished undressing herself and was lying seductively on the bed.

I stood for what must've been an eternity simply staring at her naked body. This was my first close encounter with a naked woman, and I could not stop staring at her gorgeous pert tits and hairy bush.

Sure, I'd built up a nice little collection of wank mags as a horny teen, but nothing prepares you for your first sight of an actual naked woman. This was apparent as Katie laughed, "Well are you going to stare at me or shag me?"

We ducked under the floral covers and immediately got down to business. She grabbed my erection firmly at first just to see my reaction, then she slowly started working it up and down. Firmly aware of the impending explosion I told her we should skip the foreplay and get on with the deed. It took me a little bit of time to get the condom on the right way round.

Who would've known you could put it on inside out?

But after some directions from Katie, I was finally off and running.

Ho ho ya beauty!

I'm finally inside a girl.

This feels much better than my hand, it's all warm and moist.

I'm fucking, I'm really fucking.

It was way better than I had hoped it would be. In all my excitement I came in about two minutes but after a ten-minute break of discussing where I had gone wrong and how I could improve my performance, my youthful enthusiasm shone through. The second time was much better, and I think Katie may have come too.

I felt like a stallion.

Katie lay in my arms, our sweaty torsos stuck together, and I had finally gotten that monkey off my back.

I wanted to do it a third time, but I'd only been able to scrounge two condoms and Katie wasn't willing to do it bare back.

Despite this I was more than satisfied with my fill.

I'm a man, yes I am, and I can't help but love you so.

The Spencer Davis Group sang in my mind, and it was truly fucking awesome.

The rest of the night, however, didn't go so well for poor Eddie, his house got trashed. Windows were smashed, ornaments were broken, cigarettes were stubbed out on shag piles.

Nasty.

My lasting memory of Eddie is seeing him bawling completely out of character at some hard cunt who'd just put in another pain of glass in his front room.

"I'm out of booze," mumbled the guy incoherently in response to being asked what he was doing.

"You're out of booze? I'm out of fucking windaes," shrieked Eddie.

But I didn't care about poor Eddie.

I'd just had my first shag.

Bobby too was getting in on the act. Like myself he had had limited success with the girls until our newfound fame. By limited I of course mean NO success.

It was during this crazy brilliant time that Bobby started a relationship with Mel. She was *THE* prettiest and most popular girl in school. Suddenly the clothes you wore or the group of friends you hung about with didn't matter. Having the ability to play a few songs by popular bands of the time instantly catapulted your credibility from the bottom of the pecking order straight to the top.

The three of us were unstoppable.

Our last two years at high school carried on in this vein and as a band we got better and better as our confidence grew and our set list improved. Whereas before going to school was a complete chore it was now a delight to attend.

We had been given a little sample of what being in a band had to offer and we fucking loved it.

About a year after our début appearance at school we were offered a gig at The Crown.

In 1995 that was the best pub in town for live music, so we were delighted, nae, delirious to be given a spot there.

As far as we were concerned, we had made it.

Sid had been pestering the management there for months to give us a gig but due to the fact we were all only 17 years old (and Sid and me looked it) we had to wait for our fake ID to arrive before we could play. Bobby didn't have this problem as he could've walked into a bar at 13 years of age and been served without hesitation.

It was the talk of the school for weeks leading up to the gig. For the rest of the pupils the mediocrity of swatting for exams and the continued effort of having to find their place within the political spectrum of high school power were issues which were pushed to one side.

We were a band of the people for the people regardless of gender, race, age, or popularity.

Everybody wanted a piece of us.

Bobby had made up some really smart flyers and we'd been busy handing them out to not only our fellow pupils but teachers and anybody who would take them. We were a bit like those chuggers that ruin your stroll down the street, only we weren't after your hard-earned cash. We just wanted your commitment to our growing cause.

Our fellow pupils had been busy making up their own fake ID to varying levels of authenticity so they could attend.

As far as they were concerned, we'd made it too.

As our musical skills developed, so did our tastes and we started writing our own songs. The first few sounded like a couple of Oasis songs badly welded together.

Gradually we weaned Sid off his Manchester fixation with lashings of Pink Floyd, The Doors and Radiohead and he started to find his own voice, minus the Mancunian drawl. Bobby and I were suitably impressed and Sid's song writing improved dramatically. My own song writing efforts which I thought were fairly decent at best were slapped down by Sid.

There would be no room for a Lennon/McCartney relationship in this band.

I never questioned his judgement.

Come the night of the gig at The Crown, Sid, Bobby, and myself were climbing the walls with nerves and excitement. We couldn't wait to get out onto that tiny stage and shake the foundations with our tunes. The stage in those days was housed in the back room of the pub and once the pool table had been removed you could expect crowds of up to 50 or 60 people if they didn't object to being crammed in like sheep on the way to market.

Minus the faeces obviously.

We walked out the door that led to the cellar and onto the wee slightly raised stage to hear the biggest roar we'd ever heard. Our girlfriends at the time were there and most of our school friends had made it through the vigorous ID screening process of a quick glance at the card and if you vaguely resembled the person in the photo or had memorised the date of birth on the paper driving licence your big sister or brother had given you then you were in.

Our relatives were all there too. My mother who had previously been in a pub once before in her entire life (for her wedding reception) put aside her old-fashioned belief that 'pubs were for the menfolk only' and that 'women had no business being there' to show her support for her wayward son. I could see her obvious discomfort as folk pushed and pressed against her. My dad appeared to be enjoying himself, but he was careful not to let it show.

There were a few of the regular genuine music fans crammed into their regular spot right next to the speakers. A melting pot of long hair, beards, tattoos, and piercings stared at us in expectation, as if to say, 'you'd better be good, you wee fannies.'

It was by far the biggest crowd we'd played to, and we had to wait a few minutes longer before we could get started as it was announced by one of the door staff that there was a back log of folk in the bar waiting to get through to see us. Eventually they were all shoehorned in. I could see the discomfort growing on my mother's face. Health and safety, although having come a long way from the days when people died from asphyxiation in this sort of instance, still had a long way to go.

Lives before profit was still a few years away.

With claustrophobia setting in I didn't want to be a rock 'n' roll star anymore. The hundred or so eyes all staring at me with eager anticipation was too much. This was nothing like our previous gigs. Back then we played to our contemporaries, our friends, and it had been performed in the sanctuary of the assembly hall.

The large, tranquil assembly hall.

Where you could actually breathe.

This?

Well this was a hodgepodge of hardened drinkers, delinquents, and my parents all wedged so closely together that my mother looked as if she had some rocker's finger shoved up her arse.

They were begging to be entertained too.

I'm not ashamed to admit that I was shiteing myself. I turned to look at Bobby who was slumped against his drum kit, but he just shook his head, shrugged his shoulders, and gulped for air.

That didn't fill me with confidence.

Shite, we're going to blow this!

Sid turned around from his mic and gave me a wink and a cheeky smile. At least he was loving this.

"Good evening everyone," he bellowed, resulting in ecstatic cheering from the crowd and feedback from the microphone. Thankfully, due to the continued jostling of the crowd, my parents had been squeezed from my eye line or perhaps they had just fled the sweaty mob in disgust. Whichever it was it left me feeling a little more relaxed.

"YEEEAAAHHH!" the horde chanted back.

They were so close. I felt the warm alcohol scented blast from their collective breath smash into my face as they bellowed.

"Are you ready to rooooooooooooooooooooooooooock? One, two, three, four."

As I stood and stared in child-like wonder at the crowds energetic moshing response, Sid had already ripped past the opening chords of our first song 'Night Nurse', catching me off guard and off pace. I struggled to keep up and find my rhythm which in turn put Bobby off his time keeping, making the song sound like a drunken rabble. Just as we were starting to catch up with Sid's thunderous pace the song finished to a lukewarm response.

The bearded nut jobs down the front did not look impressed.

Sid turned to Bobby and me.

"What the fuck was that? We've been waiting ages for this, and you fuck it up on the first song. Get a fucking hold of yersells."

Due to our nerves/incompetence, we changed our planned set list and quickly threw in a cover song so that Bobby and myself could get to grips with Sid's adrenaline-induced pace.

It worked.

After that the rest of our set went shooting by in a blur of excitement, adrenalin, and sweat.

We even did our first encore. This hadn't been expected but owing to crowd demand we returned to the stage bursting with pride. We only had a limited number of songs and we'd exhausted those already but not wanting to disappoint the merry horde we repeated our opening four songs.

I didn't want to leave the stage. My ego had been well and truly fluffed. I surveyed the crowd and drank in their applause.

My mum would surely be proud, but she was nowhere to be seen.

Man, this is the life for me.

As I looked to Sid and Bobby who were laughing and whooping in delight, I knew they were thinking the same thing too.

"Come on, Jimmy, get the pints in, it's your round," Sid demanded, interrupting me from my daydreaming.

I walked up to the bar and ordered.

As I stood patiently waiting for our pints to pour, I wondered if the tour would invoke the feelings of old in me. The excitement, the nerves, the sheer ecstasy of performing live to an absorbent crowd. For the past 15 or so years I had felt nothing. I just went through the routine; it was almost like a job. Turn up, play gig, get paid and go home feeling empty. Nobody cared about us, we were as much a part of the fabric of the town as the historic buildings. But like them we were also overlooked and passed our best.

The adulation had long gone as our childhood friends moved on to pastures new to live their lives and the next generation simply viewed us with mild trepidation. We'd almost become a caricature of ourselves trying in vain to find popularity in a world that had moved with the times.

We hadn't.

Maybe I still wasn't over the crushing disappointment of not getting signed. Back in the good old days we were great, and I mean really great. The talk of the town. We had just taken it for granted that we would become rich and famous.

Or maybe it was due to the fact that we played the same old venues week in week out. Like my playing they were stale and better years ago.

The fact that I might start to feel something again was an exciting prospect. I was looking forward to the tour, the chance to escape this place, my family, and all my problems as well as all the negative bullshit that seemed to surround me in this town.

It would be amazing if this was finally our time.

We sat and drank our last pints of the evening whilst discussing the tour. I had spent the last few days updating our Twitter, Instagram, and Facebook pages to brief all of our 'friends' about the infamous tour with a list of upcoming gigs and events. I'd also set up a link to a blog that I would be updating frequently as we toured the country, advising the world of our exploits in a no-holds-barred way whilst allowing them to see that we were in fact a lovely bunch of guys that played really good songs that just had to be heard.

All we needed now was for Sid's flat to sell so we had the money to put this show on the road.

Bobby had come up with a brilliant design for the flyers and posters that we would distribute before and after our upcoming shows.

Slowly but surely things were starting to take shape.

CHAPTER 7

The next day (the day of the gig at The Crown) I sneaked off to The Crown around midday, intent on fumbling about with some sort of apology to Susan. The intention being that by the time we got there that night the whole situation would have been somewhat diffused.

That would wipe the stupid grin from Sid's face.

I got there to be told that Susan wasn't working today. She had the night off.

Thank fuck for that.

Somebody must be looking out for me up there.

I skipped home smiling, safe in the knowledge that Sid would be denied his aim of embarrassing me in front of the masses.

We turned up that evening to find The Crown's clientele in good spirits.

As we were finishing our sound check, the doors burst open with what seemed like a hundred stocky guys barging through shouting and laughing and punching each other in the friendly way that rugby players are found wanting to do.

I hate rugby.

I hate fans of rugby and I especially hate players of rugby.

There is absolutely no skill to the game. It's just a bunch of middle-class wankers throwing a ridiculously shaped object (balls by definition are round) about a field whilst feeling each other up at every opportunity.

A game for wankers played by wankers.

It was bad enough in my day when the game had amateur status. At school it was the sons of farmers, lawyers, and bankers as well as anybody else who couldn't play football that came together to form a clique who would provide the main body of muscle for the Howe of Fife Rugby Club.

Talentless losers that were ridiculed and harassed on the football pitch (a good old-fashioned working man's sport of tenacity and gamesmanship) found themselves to be champions on the rugger pitch.

A game that substituted skill for brute force.

Nowadays the game has become professional for whatever reason, resulting in players dropping their day jobs in the city to bulk up in the gym so they resemble body builders on steroids.

This colossal mob were no different.

Not a neck in sight between them.

To say I was intimidated by their appearance would be an understatement. How it pained me that I could no longer hurl taunts and abuse them for their participation in a sport I found worthless.

Well, without having my skull cracked.

However, despite my fears, the evening progressed peacefully and the gig was going well. The brutes were responding enthusiastically to our choice of tunes and the drunker they were becoming the more boisterous and carefree their dancing became. (Think of American professional wrestlers on ecstasy.)

I was actually enjoying myself.

We all were.

That was about to change.

As we brought 'All Right Now' by Free to a close, the doors crashed open for a second time.

Not so much a crowd but still a burly mass.

Susan.

A clearly intoxicated Susan.

"Ah shit," I muttered to myself as I dropped to the floor and pretended to fix the leads on the amp. My plan failed. I could already hear the commotion as Susan barged her way past the rugby players to the front of the small stage.

"1, 2, 3, 4," I quickly shouted in the hope that by starting the next song I could delay the messy scene that was about to unfold. I started the first few riffs on my bass but noticed that Sid had opted not to join in. He was standing there wide eyed like a delinquent who had just thrown an aerosol can onto a fire and was eagerly awaiting the impending explosion.

"You, ya bastard!" Susan bellowed at me as she overcame the small rise up to the stage. "What have you been saying about me?"

"Get your tits out," a voice from the crowd shouted, bringing roars of approval and laughter from the rest of the pack.

"Nothing, nothing, wh … wh … what are you talking about?" I stammered, bewildered by her question. The last thing I would've done was tell a soul about what happened the other night.

"He said you were telling everyone that you puked on me when you saw me naked," Susan responded, thrusting a shaky finger at Sid.

The rugby crowd started cheering and clapping and wolf whistling.

I knew that bastard had planned something and as I cast him a daggered stare, he burst out laughing, raising his arms in defence. I don't know why but I burst out laughing too. Perhaps it was the shock of the moment or my pathetic attempt to diffuse the ridiculously embarrassing situation, but I simply couldn't help it. We both doubled over in a fit of the giggles.

Susan however viewed my laughter as further insult and lashed out with a firm right hook to my jaw. Caught unawares by the blow I was sent crashing into Bobby's drum kit. Through the ensuing crashing of cymbals, banging of drums, cheering and roaring of laughter, I could just here Susan announce to the baying crowd that I had a tiny cock and couldn't get it up.

I lay there entwined amongst the dismantled kit as the laughter and roaring intensified. I wanted to stay amidst the carnage and hide forever. Sid and Bobby unfortunately pulled me free from the wreckage.

"You bastard," I growled at Sid as he brought me to my feet.

"What? Come on, Jimmy, that had to be done," Sid replied, laughing.

"No, it didn't. Who the fuck told you anyway? You've humiliated me in front of all these people. Susan too. I'm out of here, fuck you." I attempted to take off my bass strap but as I did Sid grabbed me.

"Oh come on, man. It was just a joke, stop being such a big pussy. Suck it up and let's get on with the rest of the gig."

The crowd were still laughing and shouting, and I could see Susan was being felt up by a few of the rugby players as she made her way through the crowd to the bar.

Poor lassie.

I hung my head in shame, but she appeared to be enjoying the attention as she wrapped her arm around the neck of one lucky punter.

"All right calm down," Sid announced to the drunken crowd, regaining his position at the microphone.

"It's hardly ground-breaking news, is it? We already knew what Susan has just graciously confirmed."

He turned and grinned at me as the crowd cheered in appreciation.

"Now, who's for some Creedence Clearwater Revival?"

And just like that, as if the whole sorry business had never even happened, we carried on with the rest of our set. During which I had to listen to heckles of 'hey tiny cock gie's a shot of your guitar, you'll not be used to playing with something that big in your hands,' and such like.

Hilarious.

I fucking hate rugby players.

We took a short break whilst the heathens set about the buffet which had been lovingly prepared for them.

I was subjected to some more 'good humoured' abuse during the interval, much to Sidney's delight.

Some of the Neanderthals even took to throwing food at me. As the cocktail sausages and half eaten Vol-au-vents continued to bounce off my frame, I looked around the pub to find Sid chuckling away to himself. Bobby was sitting quietly in a corner with Mel and Susan was sat at the bar being harshly groped by a mean-looking guy with a pair of ears that looked like they'd been scraped off the butchers floor and stapled to the side of his head.

Drunken rugger buggers would take it in turns to slap my back and say 'cannae get it up, eh? Fucking poof.' They then pointed to Susan and declared in no uncertain terms that they would 'shag the fuck out of that, she's a game big bird.'

Fuck this for a game of soldiers.

I predict a riot

After the mob had been suitably fed and watered Sid, Bobby and myself returned to the pathetic stage to play out the last of our set. I took to the microphone, much to the delight of the drunken, cheering crowd.

"Gie's a song, limp dick," some pumped-up moron shouted.

"I have a request here," I said as I dug out a piece of paper from my pocket.

"It's from Mike from the Academicals." A huge cheer went up from the winning Accies players to a few boos from the home side.

"Mike would like to dedicate this next song to, and I quote, 'The Dragons rugby team who are about as much use on a rugby field as I am in bed'."

Cries of 'easy, easy, easy,' sprinkled with laughter and cheers went up from the Academicals players as they pointed and taunted the disgruntled opposition.

"He also says he hopes the women of this town like to lie down and take a good fucking like the Dragons did today." I crumpled the blank sheet of paper into my pocket and watched with a smile on my face as nature took its course.

I love it when a plan comes together.

I couldn't see through the scrum to witness the first punch being thrown but after the initial spark, The Crown went up like an inferno. At first it was just the players slugging it out, standing on the spot trading drunken swings. But slowly weapons were introduced. Bobby fled the stage to grab Mel and dragged her back to the relative safety of the drum kit.

Within minutes the floor was a mass of writhing, punching, scraping, kicking, screaming bodies. Bottles and glasses flew back and forth from one end of the pub to the other. Most of them smashed innocently into the surrounding walls but occasionally a wail would go out as someone took a bottle to the face. Sid, Bobby, Mel and myself cowered in the corner behind the drums. We barricaded ourselves in with the amps and used our guitars as shields to protect us from the stray glasses. I watched through a crack in the amps as drunken men tried to obliterate each other. Fists the size of my head were launched with full force into brutish faces. The resultant crunch of bones and teeth added to the concerto of smashing glass, groans of agony and shrieks of rage.

It was like a hellish opera.

"What the hell did you read that out for?" Bobby whispered harshly as if talking normally would alert the crowd to our existence.

I just shrugged my shoulders and looked at Sid. "It had to be done," I replied.

The police entered the equation shortly afterwards. They waded in with batons swinging, mace spraying, and handcuffs locking. The four of us popped up from our defensive fort with arms raised as the local constabulary cleared out the last of the offenders.

"What the hell happened here?" asked PC Overenthusiastic.

Johnny the bar manager peeked his head up from behind the bar.

"The teams went mental after that idiot read out a request," he replied, pointing his nicotine-stained finger at me.

The officers followed the line of point until their eyes met with mine.

"Hey don't shoot the messenger," I protested with my hands in the air.

"You again," PC Apathy said to me, "right you lot we're going to need statements from you before you leave here tonight."

After the initial high of the riot, I was brought straight back down to earth with an almighty crash as I gave my statement.

PC Thick As Shit listened and wrote in his wee black book as I told him about the request I read out.

"Who asked for this request?"

Bollocks.

As nobody had actually asked for a request I hadn't a clue which name I had used. I frantically raked through my memory bank for a name but came up with nothing.

"Eh, I can't actually remember the name of the guy. He was a big fellow though and his ears were all misshapen."

"And where were you standing when this all took place?" he queried besides asking a bunch of other pointless questions with maximum suspicion that I had no answer to.

As the night wore on it became clear to me that I could be in a wee spot of bother over this.

PC Big Boss Man approached me.

"Where is this piece of paper you read out the request from?"

"I, I don't know. I threw it on the floor after I'd finished reading it."

"And who wrote the request?" he asked, looking down at this wee black book and then back at me with an accusing stare.

"I don't know, it could've been the guy that handed me the bit of paper, but it could've been one of his teammates. I didn't ask," I lied convincingly, surprising myself with the ease which I had done so.

You've got nothing on me pig.

After an hour or so of questioning we were told by PC Big Boss Man that we could go with the promise that 'he'd be back in touch soon as this was a serious matter. A very serious matter.'

"What about our money, Johnny?" Sid shouted across the devastated room.

"Money? What money?" replied the visibly shaken bar manager in disbelief.

"The £300 we're owed for tonight," Sid moaned as if it wasn't obvious.

"You can take a run and jump, sunshine. Look at the state of this place. This is going to cost me a fortune and it's all your fault," Johnny replied, exasperated, pointing his yellowy finger at the three of us.

"What? How's it our fault? It's no' our fault these idiots wrecked the joint. You should've stopped selling them alcohol the state they were in. That's illegal you know?" Sid emphasised, hoping he would get the police on our side.

"You're getting nothing," Johnny screamed dismissively.

"You cannae do this. Officer, he cannae do this, he owes us money," Sid whined, appealing to the officers that were present.

"Look, you can clear this up between yourselves later. Now come on, off you go," Big Boss Man said.

Like scolded children we gathered up our instruments and amps and left the scene of the crime.

The Crown was in a terrible state.

There were smashed tables and chairs lying at various angles strewn about the bar.

The paintings and mirrors depicting days gone by and breweries of old which once hung proudly on the walls were broken in pieces on the floor amongst cocktail sausages and trodden egg sandwiches. Curtains had been ripped from the windows, one of which had been smashed.

I noticed a shoe and what appeared to be a pair of false teeth lying on the blood-stained carpet which crunched with glass underfoot as we exited through the side door and into Mel's car.

"Fucking nice one, Jimmy," Sid bellowed as Mel drove us home.

"What are you on about?" I shouted back.

"Come on guys, shut up, it's been a hectic night, let's just go home and talk about this in the morning when we've all calmed down," Mel pleaded into the reaview mirror.

"Aye, I can't be dealing with you numpties going at it after all that," Bobby agreed.

"Well, he's just cost us £300 for Christ's sake," Sid continued.

"Did I fuck. I didn't ask them to turn the place into a boxing ring. Anyway, I didn't want to play there in the first place. It was your stupid idea just so you could make me look like a prick on stage," I argued back.

"Aye what's this about you and Susan?" Bobby pitched in, chuckling from the front seat.

"Now is not the time, Bobby," I shouted, immediately changing the atmosphere in the car. Even Sid took note of my mood for once and we all travelled home in silence, bringing an end to a crazy evening.

That was the last time we ever played The Crown.

I suppose it's better to burn out than fade away.

CHAPTER 8

The next couple of months melted by in a state of nocturnal confusion. I was offered and gratefully accepted the job of stock replenishment executive (shelf stacker to you and me) with Tesco.

I was on the night shift rota starting at 10 p.m. and finishing at 6 a.m. It took me a few weeks to get my head around eating lunch at 2 a.m. but once I'd conquered that, the job actually wasn't too bad.

There were ten other staff members on my shift ranging from normal human beings to raging insomniacs. I kept myself to myself seeing as this was only a means to an end. No point in going to the trouble of forming acquaintances when I'd be leaving soon.

Sid's flat still hadn't sold. There had been a few parties showing interest, none with a confirmed offer but the signs were improving apparently.

Sid and myself hadn't spoken since the night at The Crown. He was still in the huff about the £300 we never received despite himself, Bobby, and me all going up to see Johnny on separate occasions and pleading for the cash.

So we lost £100 each? Big deal, no need to keep greetin' about it.

He still held me responsible for the loss of income though, conveniently forgetting that if he hadn't kicked the whole thing off by fabricating lies to Susan none of the ensuing mess would have happened.

I had only planned on stopping the insulting banter aimed at myself. I hadn't planned on the two teams going at it hammer and tong trashing everything that stood in their wake.

I tried to put a positive spin on the evening by writing about it on our pre tour blog.

"Champions Of The Underdog gig ends in full scale riot!" It produced little impact though as we weren't actually involved in the aforementioned riot.

Stacking shelves all night with tuna and beans gave me plenty of time to ponder life's meaning.

I was free to think about the upcoming tour.

But it also gave me too much time to think about Debs and how much I missed her.

Why the hell is she still with that arsehole Foster?

Was I that bad a boyfriend that she prefers his company to mine?

Maybe it's the sex.

Oh fuck off!

I was also thinking about Sid and how to approach the subject of talking to him again. I sure as hell wasn't going to apologise because I wasn't in the wrong and he wouldn't do it because he's a stubborn prick.

As I packed aisle 23 with various breakfast cereals my mind drifted back to the time we fell out and didn't speak for over a year.

It was 1996 and we had just finished our last exams. School was out for summer; in fact it was out for ever.

Bobby had been accepted to study art at Duncan of Jordanstone College in Dundee.

Sid had been accepted to do sound engineering at some college in Glasgow and I, depending on how my exam results went, would either be going to Glasgow or Aberdeen to study history. I chose to study history as I was fairly good at it without having to actually try very hard.

My preferred choice was Glasgow because Sid and myself had planned on getting a flat together if I was accepted but I needed to gain better exam results.

The few months we had left before we went to college were spent fine tuning our songs and writing new ones for the band.

'Cigarettes and Alcohol' had burned out as Sid's fixation with Liam Gallagher faded to be replaced by a new obsession with Jim Morrison.

'The Lizard Kings' was our latest incarnation.

In the couple of years since we started the band, we had all grown our hair to varying lengths of ridiculousness and had flirted with different styles of clothing as we tried to look the part that we acted so well.

Sid had even taken to wearing leather trousers.

It takes a certain type of person to pull off wearing leather trousers.

Certain females, with their long legs and amazing arses can certainly do it. I'll admit that Jim Morrison did look very cool in his. Sid, however, just looked like an arsehole.

He unfortunately didn't think so and continued wearing them for some time despite drawing comparisons to an overweight Michael Hutchence.

At this time, we were listening to a lot of Pink Floyd, The Thirteenth

Floor Elevators, The Doors and The Byrds etc. etc. Psychedelic music mainly. We were also smoking a lot of weed. Sid, upon hearing Jim Morrison was an advocate, suggested we try some LSD so that we could open the doors of perception in our mind, man.

Bobby and I reluctantly agreed.

Finally, after months of false alarms and dawn raids at various dealers houses, the LSD arrived. Sid opened his palm to reveal three tiny pills of acid in a plastic bag.

"Microdots," he enthused, "meant to be brilliant."

We made arrangements to take our first trips at Bobby's house. His mum was kind of a hippy so she wouldn't mind us tripping out in the comfort and safety of her home.

We planned it like a military operation.

Up in Bobby's room we had lit candles, turned on his lava lamp, and the albums we were going to turn on, tune in, and drop out to were methodically laid out in order of trippyness.

The ambience was perfect.

Sid opened out his palm again and we each picked up a tiny pill and popped it into our mouths. We stuck our tongues out to show each other that the pills were still there and that nobody had chickened out at the last minute before we swallowed them and again showed each other our gaping mouths to prove that we'd actually taken the pill.

Half an hour of nervous anticipation passed, and nothing had happened.

"How long did you say this stuff takes to kick in?" Bobby asked in trepidation.

"Andy said it takes about twenty minutes to get into your blood stream and then everything goes mental. Good mental though," Sid replied, and we all laughed nervously.

There was no turning back now.

"Let's have a joint while we wait," Bobby said and sparked up a pre-rolled spliff.

After taking a few tokes each, everything did indeed go mental.

"Can you see that, man? Look at the carpet!" I giggled, then laughed again and again as the floral carpet on Bobby's bedroom floor came to life. It resembled a corn field in the breeze. The ears of corn billowing gently back and forth in hypnotic rhythm. I stared at it for minutes, but it could have been hours so lost was I in the trance.

Everywhere I looked there was a new adventure for my eyes and brain to feast on.

It was absolutely beyond my wildest dreams. There were swirling patterns dripping, then sliding up and down the wallpaper. The ceiling rippled and glistened like a silken bed sheet on the drying line. As I stared in amazement at the beautiful colours emanating from the candles, angels flew from the haze to rest at my feet. I couldn't stop smiling and the feeling of love I had coursing through my veins for my two tripping companions, my best friends, was unconditional.

"Pass me the guitar," Sid slurred, and he started to strum soft, sweet chords. Bright flashes of light burst from every string he plucked and then floated into the air in colourful bubbles.

"Fucking hell, man, this is amazing," Bobby laughed and went in search of his bongos. I picked up my guitar and the three of us sat cross legged lost in our little trippy cocoons playing our individual tunes.

The three separate tunes intertwined to create a symphonic melody of the likes I'd never heard before or since. Tears of joy rolled down my face as I sat and strummed and listened to the beautiful sounds we were creating.

If there's a heaven, I hope it feels like this.

I could hear the music, but I could also feel it. I mean really feel it, right down in the pit of my stomach as if it was a lost emotion being reawakened after centuries of hibernation. I could see the music too in different colours as the chords and mood and tempo changed. I could also taste it and touch it as the sounds engulfed my hallucinating brain.

That was an unbelievable evening and an experience I'll never forget.

It was also an experience we were keen to recreate as soon as possible. The general consensus was that tripping was 'fucking amazing.' The three of us raved about the drug to anyone who would listen with Sid declaring that 'LSD is my new drug of choice.'

We had been getting a good number of gigs up in Dundee and had started to achieve a bit of a following thanks to our self-penned songs and energetic sets. Our next gig was back in Dundee at the Westport Bar, and we'd heard from a member of staff in Groucho's (legendary record shop) that there was a guy from an independent record label coming to see us perform that night. Apparently, he'd been in the shop saying he'd heard good things about us and was enquiring to the whereabouts of our next gig as he was keen to hear us.

When we heard this, we went mental.

Good mental though.

We tried not to get too carried away with the news as nothing had happened.

Yet.

We convinced ourselves that this was the break we had been waiting for, the big time was about to be bestowed upon us.

I pictured the trappings of fame and fortune, the whole sex and drugs and rock 'n' roll scene. We were all on a high and all we needed to do to achieve our ambition of rock stardom was to put on one hell of a gig and leave the record label begging us to sign for them.

We didn't disappoint.

The record label executive did indeed get one hell of a show.

"We should do it on acid, lads," I enthused to Sid and Bobby, "think how amazing we'd sound, we'd play out of our skins. He'd definitely sign us."

"I'm no' sure, I dinnae want anything going wrong you know. This is our big chance. This is it; this is what we've been working for. Our shot at the big time. We dinnae want to fuck this up," Sid pondered.

"We'll no' fuck it up, it'll be amazing. It'll give us that edge we need, that wee creative boost that'll have your man begging to sign us. There's three other bands on that night and we want to stand head and shoulders above them all, we need to be different. I'd be gutted if he came to see us and ended up signing one of the other bands," I concluded.

"Aye you're right, we do want to stand out from the crowd," Bobby agreed.

"Hmm, I'm no' sure. I suppose we could maybe take half a trip. Maybe we should wear something different too, like you said we want to stand out and get noticed," Sid responded.

And so the night of the biggest gig of our lives was upon us. We'd brought a big crowd made up of friends, girlfriends, and family to support us.

It would dramatically improve our chances of being signed if we had a big crowd cheering and screaming when we went on.

I had eventually talked Sid round to the idea of taking acid whilst performing and so each of us consumed one tab prior to taking the stage. The acid wasn't in pill form like before. This time there was a picture of some sort of alien on a wee piece of paper. We were reassured they were just as good as the microdots if not better.

This gig was going to be the start of the rest of our lives.

We'd dressed up for the occasion too. Sid had his usual leather trousers and white shirt a la Jim Morrison and he'd decided that Bobby and myself should go down a similar route to keep in with our band name and beliefs. What beliefs he meant I will never know so Bobby and myself were dressed up like extras from a dodgy cowboy film.

Bobby, thanks to the darker shade of his skin, got lumbered with wearing a make shift feather head dress and wore dream catchers around his neck. He also sported a leather waistcoat on top of his bare torso. I was wearing cheap looking cowboy boots that were a size too small with a gingham shirt and tweed waistcoat combo. My efforts to find a Stetson hat in the charity shops proved futile and so I had to make do with a kind of bowler come panama hat instead. We certainly stood out from the rest of the bands. They were mostly post grunge indie kids who took to the stage in ripped jeans and trainers.

When it was our turn, we took to the stage looking like the losers in a Village People tribute act competition. However, the roar from the packed crowd was deafening as we assembled on stage. That was exactly the kind of reception that would impress a record label executive.

We were the last band to go on and none of the previous bands had received anything like that response.

The LSD trip kicked in about a minute into our second song 'Lost Along the Highway', when Sid suddenly flinched to his left and stopped playing his guitar.

I wasn't feeling the effects, so immediately went up and whispered in his ear.

"What the fuck are you doing, get it together."

He turned to look anxiously at me, and his face was ghostly white. Beads of sweat had formed at the top of his brow as his eyes continuously shifted from side to side for something to focus on.

"Tell that idiot to get off the stage then, he's freaking me out," and he nodded his head to indicate the guilty party.

I looked over his shoulder. There was nobody there.

"It's cool, Sid, relax, it's the acid. Keep calm, this is big our night, remember?" I said, trying to focus his tripping mind on the job at hand.

We started the song again from the top.

My trip kicked in.

Whereas our first trip was a vision of heaven and all the delights it hopefully beholds, our second trip was a vision of hell.

Ying and Yang man.

I too was starting to sweat, and my body tingled and itched. I was convinced my clothes were trying to gnaw their way into my body.

I tried to relax, tried to calm myself down.

It's just the acid, man, no harm will come to me. I'm gonnae be okay, I'm gonnae be okay.

That didn't work.

Harvey Keitel had started singing to me.

You're gonnae be okay, you're gonnae be okay

SAY IT, SAY THE GOD DAMN FUCKING WORDS …

AAAAARRRGHHHHHH!!!!

We played the song by instinct alone, but it must've sounded horrendous. The once angelic melodies we concocted on our previous trip had been replaced by demonic screeching and wailing. Sid mumbled and half sobbed undecipherable lyrics to a bemused and startled audience. Bobby had kicked away his drum stool in the fear that it was trying to burrow its way up his arsehole and now stood pounding the snare drum and cymbal simultaneously as if they were an attacking beast. My guitar strap had by now turned into the snake from *The Jungle Book*, complete with hypnotic eyes as it tightened its grip around my neck. I'd completely given up trying to play the bloody thing and put all my energies into wrestling this snake to the ground. The fret board sprouted fangs that were trying to snap at my face. I was interrupted from my wrestling bout with the snake by an ear-piercing scream as Sid sprinted from the stage screeching at the top of his lungs.

I looked up to find the audience staring at us wildly whilst the walls around them licked with flames.

"FIRE, FIRE!" I shouted, pointing hysterically to the increasing inferno. People at the back were starting to burn but still the audience stared at me in shock.

I launched my guitar into the wings and tried to flee the stage.

Bobby grabbed me. "What the hell's going on, man?" he whimpered with terror in his voice and shock in his eyes.

"LET'S GET THE FUCK OUT OF HERE BEFORE WE ALL BURN!" I roared as we both jumped from the stage and burst through the crowd and out into the cold dark night. We ran for a couple of streets until I could run no longer. I sat between two parked cars with the rain pouring down as I struggled for breath.

"It's the acid, it's all messed up. We just need to ride it out," I said as Bobby hunkered down beside me.

"But it shouldn't be like this, man, not like this. I don't feel like … me. Where's Sid?" Bobby ranted in a state of turmoil.

"I dunno, we'll find him. Everything will be back to normal in a couple of hours," I replied, trying to convince myself more than Bobby.

"I hope so, man, 'cause I don't think I can take this much longer. Is that acid rain? I think it's burning through my clothes. Jimmy, I'm melting, look my skin's smoking."

I don't know how long we spent hiding between those parked cars or how they even found us. Perhaps it was Bobby rolling about the road trying to stop the acid rain from burning his skin, but we were thankfully rescued by Mel and Bobby's mum. They bundled us into the back of Mel's Fiesta where Sid was already cowering. The three of us sat there crammed into the back of that tiny car whilst we were interrogated by the two women. The radio was playing strange sounds which amplified my panic. The interrogation carried on even when we were back in the relative safety of Bobby's house. We alternated between glasses of water and cups of coffee in an attempt to speed up the tripping process, but this proved futile. This endless process of caffeine, water, and ranting accusations carried on for hours until eventually as the sun was starting to rise the acid finally wore off.

The call never came from the record company.

Hell for all I know he/she never came in the first instance. That didn't matter to Sid though. He held me fully responsible for ruining his rock 'n' roll star career.

"If it wasn't for you and your fucking 'let's take some acid, man' we'd have been signed up by now. Stupid cunt," he spat.

One angry word led to another, and it wasn't long before angry words turned into angry pushing and shoving. Angry pushing and shoving soon made way for angry punching and kicking and biting and scratching and gouging of eyes.

Bobby eventually stepped in and hauled Sid off me before I was permanently blinded.

To make matters worse, when we returned to the bar the next day to pick up the equipment we had left behind in our haste to flee the 'burning bar', the only thing left was my shitey bass. Apparently there had been a break in and all our gear had been nicked.

Aye fucking right.

That was the last contact I had with Sid for over a year.

It was me who made the effort to patch things up back then. It's always me who makes the effort to smooth things out.

Not this time though.

Fuck you, Sid.

CHAPTER 9

"Jimmy-boy get your arse round here pronto, Sidney's got some good news for you lads."

And with those jolly words uttered down a mobile phone, Sid and myself were back on speaking terms again.

I met up with Bobby and we walked round to the flat to hear his good news. By method of deduction, we'd worked out that the only reason he could be in a such a jovial mood was because he'd sold the flat and our long-awaited tour could finally begin to take shape.

"Guess what?" Sid said excitedly whilst dancing about like a child in desperate need of the toilet.

"What?" we flatly replied, not daring to hazard a guess in case we burst his bubble.

"I've sold the flat. £80,000 profit, get in there, yeehaa!" Sid punched the air in victorious fashion.

"Fucking hell! £80,000?" Bobby and I replied in genuine shock.

"Aye eighty grand in ma hipper, boys. How's about that then?" said Sid in a Jimmy Saville accent. Sid's never been one to let a minor issue like paedophilia get in the way of a decent impression.

"That's tremendous, mate, what a result." Bobby congratulated Sid by slapping him on the back and grinning like it was him who had inherited the vast fortune.

"Aye. Sweet, man," I responded.

I tried to show enthusiasm but what I was really thinking was …

£80,000?

You lucky, lucky bastard.

How the hell does he do it?

That boy could land in a pile of shite and still come out smelling of roses.

Sid's Grandmother had left him a rather large sum of money in her will which he wisely used as a deposit on a flat and now nine years later the little property entrepreneur had been rewarded with eighty thousand big ones to play with.

My jealousy was almost choking me.

Wish I'd had a rich Granny who'd left me money when she croaked it. All I got was a smack on the back of the head from my dad and a stern talking to from my mum for having the cheek to ask them how much she'd left me. There really is no justice in the world. I used to visit my granny at least once a week enduring her mundane ramblings on various meaningless topics which she interspersed with casual racism and compulsive bigotry and ended up getting hee haw when she died.

Sid, on the other hand, who generally couldn't stand the sight of his grandmother, would only visit her twice a year, on his birthday and at Christmas when he was guaranteed of receiving a gift from his dotting gran. Despite his lack of care or attention to his dear old granny, he still received thousands of pounds when she snuffed it. I shook my head in bewilderment at this sad state of affairs.

"Right let's head doon to the boozer to celebrate. The drinks are on me," Sid announced whilst brandishing a pile of ten-pound notes.

"I cannae," I replied sadly. "I'm working the night."

"To hell with work, 'mon let's go."

So we headed off to the pub to revel in Sid's newfound wealth and to put our plans into action for the tour

"Cheers lads!" Sid raised his glass, took a large gulp, and wiped the foam from his top lip. "Right, the money goes into my account when the keys get handed over in two months, so we want to be ready to make tracks by then. I'm putting in my notice at work in the next couple of days so that still gives me a month to put the finishing touches on things. Right, Jimmy, here's a pen and paper, write down all that we've got to do in between then and now."

Sid passed me the paper and threw the pen as we set about our drink-induced brainstorming session. We all shouted out what we thought we should do and organise and bring with us before we set off on our tour and I sat and wrote it all down in between umpteen rounds of beers and whiskies.

You would think it would be quite a quick and straight forward exercise making a list of things to be done and items that we needed to bring. It was nearly six hours later and too many pints and whiskies to count that we were finally happy with our list/plan of action.

LIST O' HINGS TO BE DONE AND BRUNG

(In no specific order)

- Buy a van – best kinds would be old Volkswagen Combi or Ford Transit.
- Get a tent and fishing rods and camping gear.
- Bring the air rifle.
- Get new guitars and amps, leads, pedals etc. etc. etc.
- Buy new drum kit with 'Champions Of The Underdog' on Bass Drum.
- Buy loads of booze and fags and skins.
- Hand notice into work and tell banks etc. of change of address.
- Move belongings from Sid's into respective parent's abode.
- Draw up location tour map.
- Phone more bars and clubs to get gigs.
- Bring playing cards.
- Phone hostels in towns to find out costs of rooms.
- Speak to The Skinny and other music mags advising them of our tour.
- Pack clothes.
- Buy new all singing, all dancing laptop.
- Organise a 'so long a'body/start of tour' gig in toun.
- Buy AA road map, nae need for one o' thae sat nav things. Old Skool is best.
- Make a list of all the rare places in Scotland we want to visit.
- Get insurance, van/contents/personnel, any other kind they offer.
- Speak to local radio/newspapers for advertising.
- Get quotes for 'Champions On Tour' to be put on van. Painted or vinyl?
- Find out the local bands in various towns – contact them to support us.
- Get t-shirts printed and other merchandise to sell at gigs. CDs etc. etc.
- Hae oorsells a rare old time!!

We ran through the list excitedly, talking up the tour and wishing we were starting it in the morning. As Sid dipped into his pocket once more for another round, I noticed his watch read 8:55 p.m.

"Shite I'm gonnae have to go, lads, I start work at ten," I moaned.

"Fuck work. Stay and celebrate wi' us," Sid slurred as his head flopped about on top of his neck.

"I cannae, man, I need the money," I slurred back. I was pretty drunk myself.

"You want money? I've got loads a money," Sid declared and he jumped to his feet and waved a sticky looking fiver in my face in Harry Enfield character style.

"You're steam … oats, man. Ye cannae go t' wor' lie tha'," Bobby stammered in between hiccups "stay an drin' wi' ussssss. We're you're … pals."

"I'm pissed but I'm no' steamboats. It's cool, the supervisor's a big stoner he'll no' gie a flying fuck. As long as the work gets done it'll be fine. It might actually be fun packing shelves wi' a drink in me."

"Ma arse. Whit are ye daein stacking shelves for anyway? That's a shite job. Ha ha ha LOADS A MONEY!" Sid laughed at his own shite joke and continued to smack the five-pound note against my face.

"Piss off," I shoved his hand from my face, sending the fiver floating to the ground and Sid scampering after it. "I'm away hame to get ready. I'll see youse later. I'll take the list with me."

I turned and left the bar to two solitary shouts of 'Champions, Champions,' then 'Loads a money,' followed by cackling laughter.

I walked out into the cool evening air and headed for home. I could smell the alcohol on my breathe, it smelt sweet and tasted good. I should have stayed and helped Sid spend his money, after all it's not everyday he gets the rounds in. He's definitely a man with short arms and long pockets. But I really needed the money, a small sacrifice to pay you might say.

As I drunkenly shuffled along the path of the main street, I could see a couple up ahead hunched together walking my way. They were silhouetted against the streetlights but as we approached each other I could make the figures out. I stopped in my tracks in panic. It was Debs and she was nuzzling into Danny Foster.

Fuck.

They hadn't seen me yet, so I was faced with a couple of options. Turn around and flee or cross the road and ignore them. I spent time fretting over my predicament but could think of no logical outcome. My hesitation was costly as they were now only yards from me.

Fuck, what do I do?

I quickly decided on a third option of acting drunk and pretending not to notice them.

"Jimmy?" I heard Debs call as I stumbled passed them staring at the pavement "Jimmy?"

"Eh?" I mumbled as I swung around dramatically for effect to where they stood.

"You been celebrating?" she laughed.

That beautiful laugh. Those perfect teeth. Her wide gleaming eyes.

"Eh? Oh … It's you, Debs … a'right?" I turned to face my ex-girlfriend of seven years whose arm was linked through Danny Foster's.

Cunt!

I hadn't seen him in over 20 years, but he hadn't lost his ability to instil fear in me.

"Yeah not bad thanks, we're just away into town for a drink. You know Daniel, eh?" She looked up into his eyes, smiled a happy fucking smile then patted his arm.

I squinted at him, pretending not to recognise him, but he couldn't be mistaken for anybody else. He was older. We all were but he hadn't changed. His eyes were still the same. Those mocking, hateful, challenging eyes.

"Aye I know him," I mumbled, keeping my hands firmly clamped in my jacket pockets.

"How are you, Jimmy? Long time no see, eh?" And he held his hand out to be shook, never taking his eyes from mine. I stared at him and then down at his outstretched hand.

Did he really want to shake my hand or was this just a show for Debbie?

I dinnae want to shake your fucking hand, you miserable prick.

I could feel Debbie's glare so reluctantly grasped his hand and shook.

"I'm a'right," I replied, freeing myself from his tight grip.

You might have got me to shake your hand, you cunt, but I'm not about to ask you how YOU are.

Got to take the small victories.

"Debbie tells me you and your band are doing a tour soon?" Same cold eyes.

"Aye," I replied with as much disdain as I could muster.

"Guid," he nodded. "Guid luck wi' that." Then he turned to Debs. My Debs, patted her hand, and said, "Well I suppose we should be making a move then, darlin'. Guid seeing you, Jimmy. Take care."

"Aye," I said.

"See you, Jimmy. Come and see me before you go," she said and smiled as I nodded.

They turned and she pushed her head against his chest as he wrapped his arm around her slender shoulder then pulled her tightly into his embrace and kissed the top of her head.

As I watched her skip off in another man's embrace, *that* man's embrace, my heart exploded into a million tiny useless pieces. I watched them walk down the street until they were nothing more than silhouettes again and then they vanished. It was only then that I allowed myself to break down.

I booted a nearby bin with such force that I caved its plastic side in.

Then I punched it a number of times until my fists ached.

I wept silently at first then the racking great sobs overcame me, and I was forced to seek refuge in the doorway of a shoe shop. I fell to my knees and, with my face pressed against the glass announcing '50% off already reduced items', I cried.

Images of Debbie floated through my mind. Her smell engulfed my nostrils and her laughter echoed in my ears. I called her name as I sobbed to myself. Each time I called it aloud it hurt a little more.

The women that I loved more than anything was no longer mine and the pain of this was slowly killing me.

I cried until I had nothing left inside me.

I felt slightly better after releasing all those tears, but I still felt numb, angry, and hurt.

Eventually I got back to my feet, wiped my face with the back of my sleeve and headed for home to get changed for work.

I've heard it said that some people would rather feel pain than feel nothing at all. Whoever these people are I don't think they could possibly have ever felt real pain.

The walk home in the fresh air combined with the bursting release of pent-up emotions had sobered me up completely.

Now all I felt was sad and alone with aching knuckles as an added bonus.

All I wanted to do was curl up in bed and never wake up.

Instead, donning my Tesco-issue work clothes I stepped back into the cool night air and headed for an action-packed evening stocking shelves so the greedy bastards of this town could get their fill and allow me to do the same thing, same time, same place tomorrow night.

Know your place in the world, Jimmy.

Smoking a joint with my two colleagues, Simon and Jill, at break time allowed me to feel thankful that I wasn't the only sad looser in this town. Listening to their tales of woe and comparing them with my own allowed me to slip comfortably into a nice big blanket of depression.

"What's the point, eh? You're born, go to school, go to work, get drunk, get high, get shat on then die," Simon forlornly philosophised.

"Aye and some bastard breaks your heart along the way. This has to be a test. I mean, this cannae be all there is, eh?" Jill added insightfully.

"Aye you're spot on there, Jill. This *is* all bullshit. This is hell and up there that's heaven," Simon ranted wide eyed, pointing to the cloudy night sky before handing me the joint.

"What do you think, Jimmy? There has to be more than this, eh?" Jill asked. The sense of deflation in her voice made me shudder.

"I dunno. I don't think I really care. Maybe we're not as important as we think we are. Maybe it's an alien experiment, maybe Armageddon will happen at 5.45 p.m. a week on Tuesday. Maybe I was your lover in a past life who then brutally murdered you and I'm now trying to atone for that crime by stacking cans of beans in the next aisle from you in this life. Or maybe it's just a load of old bollocks."

Simon and Jill stared at me in stoned amazement, slightly fearful of my Confucius-like wisdom.

"Here," I said, passing the joint to Jill. "I'm away in for a coffee, who wants one?"

So that was how I passed my time on the night shift for the remaining weeks that I spent there.

I'd drink four cans of beer before I left the house to give me a wee glow and then spent the evening philosophising and theologising with Jill and Simon whilst smoking a good number of joints of varying blends and strengths of cannabis.

I almost forgot that Debbie even existed.

Almost.

CHAPTER 10

Time seemed to drag from the minute Sid received his money till the time we actually left for our tour. All the loose ends and wee niggly bits had to be tied up before we went.

I had another visit from my good friends the 'polis', advising that after further investigations my good self along with several thuggish rugby players would be charged with breach of the peace for the riot at the crown. I would receive a citation in due course to appear at the local sheriff court. I was still awaiting a date for my original charge of assault for punching Frank Harrison. I was racking up quite a record. I still had to sort out a lawyer but that could wait till the shit hit the fan.

I had more important things to do.

I had to move from Sid's flat back to my parent's house on the other side of town. My old bedroom, which now acted as an office (for what I'm not entirely sure of), had ample space in which to dump my meagre possessions and I had to make do with the old spare room which currently looked like it had been decorated by Lawrence Llewellyn Bowen whilst drunk on Absinthe.

Nearly 40 years on this planet and all I've managed to acquire in that time is a half decent collection of vinyl records and CDs complete with average sound system, a shitey telly, some books, and a bundle of old clothes. I was in a state of mild depression at the thought of moving back home after all these years but, after realising that my worldly possessions amounted to nothing more than an accumulation of worthless shit, I wanted to cry.

In some religions it is said that material possessions cause attachment and that attachment is the origin or root of all suffering.

If that was true, then I should be a deliriously happy Guru.

I was not.

My dad was still recovering from the sudden heart attack he suffered a few months previously and he was a shadow of his former self. He seemed resigned to the fact that he's going to die and there's fuck all he can do about it. It might not happen today or even next week but it's going to happen and he's shitting himself.

Normally when people have been faced with a near-death experience they come out of said experience with a renewed vigour and a lust for life they had never known existed. My dad, however, had gone in the opposite direction. I felt sorry for him. He just sat there in his chair all day watching the usual guff on television. He was at the 'what's the point stage.' There was some serious soul searching going on in that head of his. He doesn't give much away, my dad, but I could tell he was really hurting. My mother fussed around him like a mother does a child. I don't think this helped his predicament.

By the time I left my parent's house to meet the lads I wanted to jump off a bridge.

Sid was still buzzing about town with his pile of cash, buying all the things we needed for our tour and many things we didn't.

"Check it out, telescopic sights," Sid boasted as he handed me the spanking new air rifle he had just purchased.

"What the hell do you need this for? You've already got one," I griped whilst giving the gun the once over.

"Aye but this one's more powerful. You could kill someone with this, and it's got telescopic sights," Sid grinned, snatching the rifle back to inspect the sights again.

"You could not kill somebody, it's an air rifle."

"If you hit them in the right spot you could. You could definitely blind somebody."

"So you plan on doing a bit of sniping on this tour, eh?" I smirked.

"Naw. It's for shooting rabbits and stuff. To eat. We might be faced with some tough times ahead. We could be stuck out in the highlands wi' nae food so it's better to be safe than sorry."

"Who do you think you are? Bear Grylls? We'll be in Scotland no' the bloody outback. If, God forbid, we ever did by some tragic twist of fate face some tough times we could use our phones to call for help."

"What happens if there was nae signal, eh? You'll no' be taking the piss when this air gun saves our life," Sid hissed, griping his new purchase closer to him.

"Okay, man. If you say so," I sighed.

Sid was schizophrenic when it came to making purchases with his newfound wealth. He wouldn't bat an eyelid at forking out nearly a grand on an air rifle, an air rifle which he didn't need, but he would baulk at the thought of paying two grand on a van that was going to be our mode of transport for the foreseeable future.

Myself, Bobby, and Mel were sat in the beer garden of The Archers partaking in a few beverages as the unusually hot May weather scorched me and Mel's pasty skin to a salmon pink when Bobby took the call from Sid to say he'd bought 'the wheels' and that he'd see us in five minutes.

We heard the screech of tyres and overindulgent revs as a motor turned the corner into the street. We shot each other a worried glance and collectively squirmed in our seats.

Thoughts of 'please let it have four wheels' and 'I hope it has seat belts' floated off to nowhere in particular.

We heard a vehicle pull to a halt.

Then a door creaked open and slammed shut.

Nobody moved a muscle, hoping that by doing so we'd be spared the inevitable.

"A'right you bunch o' fannies?" Sid shouted as he popped his head over the wall of the beer garden.

The three of us looked up and replied our greetings in apathy.

"Well what are you sitting doon there for? Come on and see the van," Sid enthused.

We left our drinks on the shoogly table to the mercy of the million flying insects that whizzed and buzzed about our heads and trudged up the uneven path that led out onto the street to see what type of contraption Sid had entrusted to carry us around Scotland in.

"Ta-Daa!" Sid gleamed with arms spread wide like the model on the Wheel of Fortune presenting the sought-after star prize.

"It's … It's … nice, Sid," Mel replied, trying harder than anyone to show praise.

"Aye … aye. It'll do …" Bobby offered, nodding his head slowly.

"What do you mean 'it'll do'? It's perfect. It's got low mileage, there's plenty of room in the back and wait till you hear the horn," Sid grinned.

"It's a fucking fish van," I blurted out.

"No it's no'. It's our *TOUR* van," Sid grumbled defensively.

"It's got McCall's Fresh Fish plastered across the side of it," I continued, pointing to the prominent signage that was indeed plastered across the side of the van.

"Aye but we'll get it sprayed, smart arse. Champions Of The Underdog right along the side there." Sid now pointed to show where the new signage would be housed.

"Where did you get it, Sid?" Mel quizzed.

"It was a stroke of luck really. I was speaking to Wattie Munro who was telling me about Bob McCall, the fishmonger. Turns out Bob's missus, you ken that hot wee Polish burd? Aye? Well it turns out she's left the country, gone back to Poland. She's taken the two kids, the BMW, and everything that was in Bob's bank account. She cleaned him out and done a runner. Poor bugger, eh?"

"So how come you've got his van?" Bobby asked reluctantly whilst rubbing his chin.

"I bought it off him. I'm actually helping the guy out; I mean, he's got nae money so I offered to take this off his hands for a very reasonable price. Now he's got money to get a plane ticket to Poland to hunt down his missus and we've got a van. Everybody wins."

The fish van resembled something between an old ambulance and an ice cream van. It looked ridiculous.

"We can rip out these two counters here," Sid said as he creaked opened the back doors, "and there'll be plenty room for all our gear, it's perfect. It's even got one of thae wee side hatches, look. We can sell our merchandise from there after gigs. Cool, eh?"

I climbed into the back of our new tour van to closer inspect the surroundings.

"Pooh, it reeks of fish in here," I gagged.

"Aye, it'll need a bit of an airing. A few Magic Trees stuck here and there, and you'll never know. Stop being such a moany bastard, Jimmy. When it's you who's putting up the money for this then you can comment. Until then shut your moaning wee puss a'right?" Sid seethed.

"Aye I was only saying likes," I pleaded, raising my arms in defence.

"You've got no vision, Jimmy, that's your problem. That's always been your problem."

"A'right calm the beans, eh? The van will be *tremendous* once it's all sorted out," I tried to appease him whilst silently raging at his spiteful words.

"Too fucking right it will. Here, check this out," Sid skipped past us and dived into the driver's seat and pressed the horn. A high pitched shrill emitted from the air horn.

"Ha ha cool, eh? It's still got the fish horn."

As we gave the van the once over a second time an elderly lady approached the back of the van.

"He's early this week, is he no'?" she asked us in confusion. "I normally don't get ma lemon sole till Friday. I was just saying to ma George I fancy a wee bit sole for ma tea the night, but we'll just have to wait till Friday and here he shows up on a Tuesday, he must've read ma mind."

We all stared at the old lady in bemusement as we listened to her fishy tale, neither of us wanting to be the one who had to break it to her that this van was no longer a working fish van and that she would have to wait a lot longer than Friday for her lemon sole. Bobby, Mel, and myself turned to look at the proud new owner.

"Eh sorry hen, this isnae a fish van any mair. I bought it fae Bob tae carry ma guitars and amps when we do our tour of Scotland," Sid replied, pointing at us to form the collective 'we'. The old lady looked over her glasses that were perched on the end of her nose and stared at Sid then looked at me and Bobby and Mel and then back to Sid.

"What do you mean it's no' a fish van? I heard the horn that's why I've come out here. What guitars?" she asked, completely baffled.

"Sorry about that, dear I was just letting my pals hear the horn on my new van. I've no' got any fish tae sell."

"You silly wee bugger you shouldn't be pressing that horn if you've no' got any fish. Half the street will be out in a minute wanting their tea. How come you've no fish? Where's Bob?" she demanded whilst wringing her wrinkly hands.

We turned to go back into the beer garden. "We'll get you a pint, Sid," and left Sid to defend himself and explain to angry would-be purchasers why they wouldn't be getting their fish early this week.

Sid eventually arrived at the sanctuary of the beer garden and the comfort of a nice cool pint.

"Fucking mental pensioners giving me grief aboot Bob. It's no' my fault his missus pissed aff and left him," Sid moaned and then promptly got stuck into his pint.

"It is a cool van though, Sid, once you get over the initial shock. I think it's got character."

"Well thank you, Mel. I'm glad someone is showing enthusiasm. You want to come on tour and take over from one of these two muppets?"

"Aye once it's been sprayed I think it'll look pretty cool eh, Jimmy?"

Bobby said, trying to get us back on side of a huffy Sid.

"Eh aye, and once all the fishy stuff has been removed from the back it'll be even better. The side hatch is a nice touch by the way," I lied.

"There you go then, everybody's happy. Now that's pretty much everything sorted. I've checked the list and there's just a few minor bits that I've still got to pick up but other than that all we need is a start date and then we can get this show on the road, woohoo!" Sid cheered, raising his glass, encouraging us all to do the same.

And so over a good number of pints, and then chasers, we eventually set a date for the start of our tour. It was unanimously agreed that we'd do a kind of 'see you later' gig at the local on the night before and have a good knees up with everyone before we left the next day to begin the tour officially. I scratched the date on a beer mat with an old match using the burnt charcoal head to fill in the lines. I held it up to the sunlight and stared at the inscription like it was some form of ancient text.

This was our date with destiny, this was our new beginning.

Was this finally going to be our chance to break the monotony of our dull lives?

The date was the 25th of June.

I felt a shiver go down my spine as I whispered it to myself.

It was just over four weeks away.

For the first time in a long time, I was beginning to feel alive.

CHAPTER 11

Sid and I were on our way round to Bobby's. It was a beautiful day for a walk, the sun was high in the sky, making all the leaves on the trees shimmer, and the birds sang cheerfully. You could hear kids in neighbouring gardens screaming shrieks of delight as they ran through sprinklers and jumped into paddling pools to relieve their skins from the sweltering heat. There was a heat haze reflecting off the road like the kind you see on American films. Even some of the tar on the roads had started to melt. When we were kids, we used to poke the melted tar with sticks, watching in fascination as it clung to our small branches like stretched bubble gum. Somehow it would always end up on our clothes which would result in us getting a skelp round the head from our disgruntled mothers who would cry in despair that it was 'a nightmare to get off' and that it would 'ruin the washing machine.'

But instead of taking a nice wee stroll round to Bobby's we were cooped up in our newly painted tour van.

Our newly painted, still reeking of fish, tour van.

"Could we no' have just walked roond? I'm melting in here and it still stinks of fish," I moaned.

"Do you no' get tired of moaning? You're like a bairn, 'Can we no' walk? I'm tired, I need a wee wee'," Sid replied in a childlike mocking tone.

"Well look at it," I moaned again, pointing out the window, "it's gorgeous out there and we're stuck in here."

"Would you shut the fuck up? I'm wanting Bobby to see the van now it's all finished. We'll be there in a minute then you can walk about smelling the flowers till your wee moany heart's content, a'right?"

I had to admit the van did look pretty cool now that it had all been resprayed. Gone was the original off white and yellow from Bob McCall's fish van. In its place was a navy blue or a dark blue, depending on which colour chart you went with. To me, it was the same colour of blue as an old Scotland football strip. Set on top of that in blinding white adhesive vinyl it stated 'Champions Of The Underdog'. It really looked the part. I reluctantly had to admire Sid's vision, there was no way I could have seen it looking this good. The insides had all been ripped out and replaced with wooden panelling with hooks allowing us to hang our guitars and leads, leaving the floor space free for the amps and Bobby's drum kit. The only problem I had was that it still stunk of fish. It wasn't as bad as before, but you could definitely smell it. Sid denied this of course and ignored the subject when I brought it up as he was obviously hurting at the truth, so he responded with insults linking the smell of fish to my association with Debbie.

Prick.

We pulled up outside Bobby's house to find him sitting on a large deck chair in his overgrowing front garden smoking a large joint, as per usual.

"You shouldn't smoke that shit so much, Bobby. It's no' guid for you," Sid shouted as we opened the gate.

"So's not minding your own bloody business," Bobby replied with just the right amount of venom to know he wasn't joking.

"Touché my good man," said Sid and left it at that, "come and see the van, it looks the part now."

Bobby took a large toke, stood up from his cushioned seat, exhaled, and then handed me the joint. Like a substitute coming onto the park, I enthusiastically grabbed the chalice and replaced him in the seat.

I could faintly hear Sid and Bobby behind the beach hedge. I could just imagine Sid giving him the spiel on the new van.

I wonder if Bobby will mention the fishy smell.

Ah this is the life.

I truly hadn't felt this happy or content in ages. I think it was because everything was finally falling into place. The tour date had been set and we were finally going to do this. No band had ever embarked on a journey like this before, if this fails to drum up support then nothing will. I had no worries at the fore of my mind. Even my face was back to normal after all the injuries I had inflicted on it. Well almost, I still had a bit of a scar where the stitches had been and my nose was slightly crooked on the bridge, but I think it added character, gave a bit of mystery to my psyche.

As I delved deeper into my conscience though, I discovered there were still a few concerns niggling away.

I was still upset about the whole Debbie thing. I missed her terribly.

Am I just missing the sex?

No, I genuinely missed her.

I still loved her.

As for Danny Foster, I still felt the rage and hatred inside me whenever I thought of him.

Change the subject.

My dad came into view, and I was concerned for him. Not about him dying necessarily, I wasn't too concerned about his physical wellbeing, he'd recover. I was concerned about his state of mind. Since I moved back home, he seemed distant, broken almost. Like somebody who had enjoyed horse riding, not just enjoyed it but lived for it. Lived for the thrill of the wind rushing past their body, the risk of taking on a jump. But like a rider who had never experienced a fall when it eventually came it hit him really hard. It had terrified him. What was the point of getting back on the horse if you're only going to fall off again?

Life for my father hadn't been exciting but it hadn't been dull. It hadn't been easy but it hadn't been hard. He just seemed to coast by never really questioning anything, merely accepting his fate. Until now. I really hoped he got back on that horse soon, not just for his sake but for my mother's too.

Man this sun is hot.

If the weather was like this all summer long, I think Scotland could just about be the most perfect country in the world.

I'm thirsty, I need a drink.

A Coke would be nice.

Wonder what Bobby's got in his fridge?

"Here wait till you see what I've got," Bobby said as Sid and him walked back through the wrought iron gate and into the garden.

"Any juice, Bobby? I'm parched," I croaked.

"Dunno, see what's in the fridge. There's water in the tap though," Bobby replied as he marched past us like a man on a mission.

"You want anything?" I asked Sid who swiftly declined as I set off in search of rehydration

The fridge was devoid of all kinds of liquid except a pint of skimmed milk.

No chance.

And a pineapple Breezer.

At least it's cold and it tastes like juice.

I raked around Bobby's cupboards for some orange squash to disguise the taste of the tap water. In this part of town, the tap water tastes like the smell of chlorine, fuck knows what's in the water these days.

Probably better not to know.

The cupboard searching proved fruitless, except for blackcurrant squash but I hate that stuff.

I stepped back out into the dazzling sunlight clutching the ice-cold Breezer just in time to see Bobby revealing his newly designed tour flyers. He laid them out flat on the plastic patio table and smoothed down the edges.

"Fucking nice one, Bobby. They're brilliant. Bloody brilliant," Sid drooled and congratulated Bobby with some hard slaps to his back.

"Tremendous, mate. They really look the part, excellent job," I enthused.

We were starting to look like a professional outfit what with our official tour van and now soon-to-be posters and flyers.

"I'll take them down the printers next week. I'll put the dates of our gigs on the back of the postcard flyers once we've got them all sorted. How's that coming along anyway, Sid?" Bobby queried.

"Pretty much sorted for the first month, I mean it's all subject to change after that but that's why we've got the social media sites. These are perfect to hand out to folk when we get to a new town and to put into pubs and clubs. They're really cool, I love the colours, man," Sid cooed.

"So how many should I get printed then?"

"I'm no' sure, you're in charge of the arts department, Bobby. I'll leave it up to you," Sid replied.

"Well it'll no' be cheap there's a lot of coloured ink to use," Bobby reasoned.

"Can we get them done in black and white instead then?" Sid retorted.

"You just said you liked the colours?" I offered my ten pence worth, stoking the fires of anger within Sidney.

"I ken that, I do. It's no' you that's paying for this though, is it?" Sid seethed.

"Look I'll get a few of the posters done in colour and maybe a few flyers the rest I'll get done in black and white. I'll give you a shout when I know how much it's going to cost," soothed Bobby.

"Aye, aye good idea, I'll leave it with you then. Right, if you boys will excuse me, I'm popping over to Dundee to look at a few guitars," Sid said, rubbing his hands together.

"When am I getting my new bass?" I asked.

"Eh, there's been a change o' plan on that one," Sid replied with a guilty glint in his eye. "Money's pretty tight what with buying the van and getting it resprayed and kitted out and now I've got to fork out a load of money for the flyers and stuff. You've already got two bass guitars, they'll do fine. I cannae afford to buy you a new one."

"Aye one of them I've had for over 20 years and doesn't hold its tune for any longer than one song and the other one's purple," I raged, "you said you were getting us new instruments."

"Aye I ken but things change, Jimmy. If you want a new bass, you'll have to buy it yourself, I'm no' made of money," Sid concluded.

"You're no' made of money but you'll think nothing of paying a grand for an air rifle when you've already got one?" I spat through clenched teeth.

"It's my money, I can spend it on whatever the fuck I like, it's none of your business. End of story," Sid fumed then turned and headed for the gate.

"I'm no' stopping you spending your money on anything, all I'm saying is I think you're being selfish with your distribution of the wealth, you're moving the goalposts all the time, promising us this and that and then changing it when it suits you. Where does it stop? 'Oh sorry boys I've no' got any money to pay you this week cause I spent our earnings on a stripey catsuit and some furry dice for the van'," I mocked.

"Fuck you, you jealous wee prick," Sid spun around and came charging towards me, "any money we make from the gigs will be getting split three ways. You're way out of order by the way," Sid raged, jabbing his finger into my chest "I'll see you later." And off he trudged again, shaking his head as he pulled open the gate.

"Ooooooh somebody needs to chill out," I mocked wide eyed to Bobby.

"Knock it off, man. You ken what he's like, stop taking the piss. He is spending a lot of money on this."

"Why are you always taking his side? He said he would buy us the stuff and now we're gonnae be left with our old shitty stuff whilst he prances about on stage looking the bollocks with his shiny new guitar, selfish prick."

"I'm no' taking sides, dinnae go over that one again, I'm just trying to make you see it from the other side, I'd do the same with him. I know what he said but in all honesty I didn't expect anything anyway."

"No I know, neither did I. He's a greedy bastard though, all that money and he cannae even spare us a few quid for new gear. He's full of shit. What about the new drum kit with Champions Of The Underdog on it that he promised?" I asked.

"Slight change of plan, due to the current financial climate certain cuts had to be made so he's getting the guy that did the adhesive vinyl for the van to come round and do it. Probably cost about twenty quid," Bobby laughed.

"Miserable bastard," I replied, genuinely angry at Sid's tight fistedness and Bobby's nonchalant acceptance of this.

"Fancy a bong?" Bobby asked, ending the discussion and changing the subject in one fell swoop.

He's a crafty one is Mr McGee.

"Aye why no', it's a braw day for it. Got any more Breezers?"

CHAPTER 12

The next two and a half weeks came and went in a ganja-filled blur. The three of us retreated to Bobby's mother's house to stay so we could rehearse in the bothy.

The bothy was an old stone building that would've been used to store feed for the cattle on the farm back in the old days but it was now unused and came with the cottage when Bobby's mum and dad bought the place. Bobby had painted the stone walls and stuck up his paintings and some of Mel's photographs to decorate it and laid a few of his mother's old carpets on the flagstones for comfort. It was like a den for adults. Once the couches were in place and the stereo was hooked up it gave the place a perfect relaxed atmosphere. It felt just like the early days and the three of us were getting on like the proverbial smouldering house.

Sid had his swanky newly purchased Les Paul '54 in tow. It was a beautiful example of craftsmanship, and we were gently breaking in the new amps and sound equipment he had bought. Fair play to the man, when it came to splashing his cash on making us sound good he didn't scrimp, it was all the best of gear he had bought. I was too scared to ask him how much this little collection had set him back.

There wasn't a lot to rehearse really, we'd been playing together for over 20 years and knew each other's style inside out. It was a bit like putting on an old jumper, it might look scruffy and past its best whilst smelling slightly strange, but it felt comfortable. Better than that, it felt right.

Even if I do say so myself, we were still the tightest band I had heard in a long time. We could find our groove without even trying and when we played in this sort of compact surrounding there genuinely was a loving bond between the three of us, a sort of musical, spiritual triangle.

I am very aware that that sounds totally ridiculous, but you'll just have to trust me on that one.

During breaks we would sit and go over our set lists and put in suggestions for cover songs we thought would be suitable for the different towns. We ran through everything on our to do list. Amazingly everything had been completed. We had interviews with local papers and music magazines and even a few radio station interviews and performances lined up.

I was starting to feel like a kid playing at being a rock star again.

The only thing that was slightly annoying me was my purple bass. I couldn't have Sid walking out on stage all cool with his Les Paul and me with my camp purple bass.

I'd inexcusably bought it on a whim several years ago because I bizarrely thought it was cool.

What the hell was I thinking?

Like the clothing and footwear trends we subjected our bodies to in our younger years, it most definitely was not cool.

I hadn't managed to save much money from my night shifts at Tesco so I'd have to tap my parents for the loan. I'm sure they'd be obliging.

"It's here at last boys, I cannae fucking wait," Sid whooped as he danced around the bothy with his Les Paul still strapped to his chest.

"Aye it's been a long time coming, man. I'm bursting to go," I concurred, my purple bass having been discarded on the floor.

"Me too, I'm like a coiled spring," Bobby chirped in from behind his drum kit.

Analogies of who was the most excited went on for some time.

"Tomorrow night's the big send off, the pub's gonnae be jumping. We'll do our usual set, but I was thinking for a bit of fun we could have like a suggestion box on the bar and folk could put their requests in and if we know it we play it, what do you think?" Sid asked.

"Aye that'll do for me, sounds cool," Bobby and I replied, nodding along with the general feeling of enthusiasm.

For the past week we had been sticking up black and white posters and handing out black and white flyers for our farewell/start of tour gig. We had completed an interview with the local paper basically describing the whys and whats of this tour but also giving Sid a platform to launch a scathing attack on X-factor style programmes and the mass promotion of mediocrity through Simon Cowell's soulless corporations.

The article was published the week before and despite only having a circulation of approximately fifty people (with forty-five of those said fifty readers being over 70 years of age) we somehow managed to drum up interest and excitement in the town from which the likes it hadn't seen since our football team managed to get through to the Amateur Scottish Cup

Final in 1999.

People stopped us in the streets and were genuinely interested in what we were doing and wished us all the best. Cries of 'good luck' and 'remember us when you're famous' echoed through the town. We even seemed to muster some respect from the local indifferent youths who normally couldn't give a flying fuck about our 'shitey middle aged music.'

I'm sure several of the young ladies were giving me the eye as I strolled past the bus shelter they were cowering in whilst sharing their vodka and coke as underage drinkers are found wanting to do.

It's amazing what a good bit of publicity can do, we had raised our profile tenfold and I was doing all within my powers to contain the ego that was silently growing larger and larger inside me every day.

"What about meeting up here tomorrow afternoon for a barbecue and a few beers before heading into town?"

"Good idea, Bobby. I haven't had a barbecue in years," I enthusiastically replied.

"Aye that'll do nicely, man. We can have our scran and then head into town to soak up the adulation. Then we'll put on the best goddamn gig this place has seen for a long time," Sid triumphantly stated.

"Right, I'll get the burgers in, do you want to invite your folks round, Jimmy?" Bobby asked.

"I'll ask them but I'm no' really sure they'll be up for it," I replied, "we should get something for your maw as a wee thank you for putting us up again. Should I pick up a card and some flowers or something?"

"Aye she'll appreciate that," Bobby smiled.

We drank and toked the rest of the night away before slipping into our sleeping bags in the wee small hours.

Three excited lads awaiting their big adventure.

In true Scottish fashion we awoke the next morning to a heavy down pour which scuppered our barbecue plans.

"Fucking typical. You cannae plan anything in this shitey country. This is supposed to be summer, so much for global warming … fuck's sake," Sid ranted to no one.

But we didn't let the weather or Sid's foul mood deter us and we carried on regardless with our going away party, although our burgers were electrically grilled rather than char-grilled.

A few of Mel's friends joined us as well as a couple of locals from the pub. I didn't bother asking my parents, but I did ask Debs to join us. She declined, saying that she and Danny were busy but that she'd definitely be there to see us perform that evening. I tried my hardest not to think about what 'busy' meant but my brain had other ideas and deliberately ruined my day by projecting horrifically graphic images of its definition of the word.

The party was a flat affair and not the mood I'd expected to find in the run up to our big gig.

Perhaps it was down to the weather or maybe it was due to our nervousness which just left the sparse crowd feeling uncomfortable?

Bobby's mother, however, was determined to enjoy herself and was knocking back the drinks as if the bar had just rang the bell for last orders.

She's a very cool lady, Bobby's mother. Not unattractive and you could imagine that in her younger years she would've been a bit of a stunner. I was wary of her when we were in our teens because she dressed strangely and dabbled in the ancient arts of witchcraft. She was highly regarded as a fortune teller, and some said she could speak to the dead. Apparently she did a mean Janis Joplin impression which is how Bobby came by the nickname Bobby McGee. Bobby told us that she would always sing this to him at his birthday parties when he was younger, much to his friend's delight and his horror.

The nickname stuck.

It wasn't until a few months after I'd gotten to know Bobby that I found out his real name was actually Joseph Serevi.

Sid and myself had never heard her sing her party piece before because by the time we became friends with Bobby, he'd put a halt to her singing.

"Come on, Sandy, gie us a song," I shouted. Bobby quickly shot me a stare that could kill, but one of Mel's friends backed me up.

"Yeah come on, Sandy."

That was all the encouragement Sandy needed. She floated over to the record collection and quickly found the one she was after. She slipped the vinyl from its sleeve, carefully inspected both sides then blew some dust from it and gently placed the black plastic on the record player.

There was silence in the room as the needle landed on the uneven surface.

As the first hisses and crackles emitted from the speakers, Bobby left the room, unnoticed by anyone except me.

The jangly sound of an acoustic guitar started to play and Bobby's mother Sandy, Mrs Serevi, began to sing.

"Busted flat in Baton Rouge, waiting for a train. And I's feeling nearly as faded as my jeans …"

I can honestly say I have never experienced anything like that in my life. I watched hypnotised as she sang that song. She did indeed sound like Janis Joplin, but it wasn't her voice that captivated me. Her whole persona appeared to change as she was lost to the song and the lyrics and what they meant to her.

"… But I'd trade all of my tomorrows for just one yesterday, to be holding Bobby's body next to mine."

A single tear welled and then rolled from her closed eyes as she swayed backwards and forwards in time to the melody. I too felt the well of tears in my eyes as I watched the performance in front of me.

I can't express properly in words what it felt like, only that I'd never felt so moved by a piece of music before.

(Well apart from the time I heard a busker in Spain singing 'Caledonia' and I burst out greetin' as I clutched my San Miguel on a Benidorm street. In my defence I was very drunk and was feeling slightly homesick even though it was only a two-week holiday.)

Perhaps it was Sandy's performance that moved me more than the music or lyrics. As the song played out its last few bars, she opened her eyes which were fixed on her feet, wiped the moisture away from her cheek then looked up and smiled sadly at the remaining voyeurs standing awkwardly in the room. We stood in silence for far too long before Sid broke the tension with some over-exuberant clapping.

"Any time you want to join us on tour, Sandy, you just say the word, hen," Sid beamed, still clapping. "That was brilliant."

Sandy smiled and patted Sid on the cheek with her right hand. As she left the room the tension lifted.

"That was a bit fucking weird," Sid whispered to me through gritted teeth, "nae wonder Bobby doesnae like her singing that, she shouldn't be singing those lyrics to her bairn. Great voice though, she sounds just like her, eh?"

"Eh aye, aye, great voice," I repeated, turning to wipe the salty liquid from my own eyes.

Bobby came out of hiding with another beer for Sid and me.

"A'right my Bobby McGee?" Sid sang into his non-existent microphone and laughed. "Man, your maw can fairly sing."

"Aye, she can that," he replied sighing. Jiiiiiy, do as a furaw pol, never ask her to sing that again, eh?"

"Sorry, man. I didn't mean to upset you or anything or your mum. I just thought it would be good to hear her voice you know?"

"I know ... it's, just complicated ... she's no' had it easy ... lots of memories and stuff ... " Bobby mumbled, looking at Mel for support.

"RIGHT, WHO'S FOR COCKTAILS?" Bobby's mum bellowed as she burst through the stringed beads covering the kitchen door clutching a bottle of tequila in one hand and a bottle of Cointreau in the other.

"We've got a gig in a couple of hours, Mum, we don't want to be wrecked for it. In fact, we'd best be making a move, we need to sound check," Bobby said angrily, quickly bringing proceedings to an end.

We all gathered our thoughts and possessions in a confused manner like when the lights come on in a club at closing time and the bouncers start hustling you out the door before you've had a chance to register what the fuck is going on.

As we all piled out the front door whilst saying our goodbyes to Sandy, she grabbed Bobby by the arm and called Sid and me over.

"Enjoy yourselves, boys. I mean it, what you're doing is really great. Enjoy every last minute of it. Your lives are going to change forever after this, this is just the start." She smiled at us all with maternal pride and drunken eyes.

"And look after him for me," she asked delicately, cupping her only child's chin in her hands.

"Nae bother, Mrs S," Sid said boldly, "see you when I'm famous."

"I've no doubt I will, Sid," Sandy whispered.

After our goodbyes we headed back to Bobby's house to get changed and ready for our gig in a couple of hours. Sid was bounding about the place with renewed excitement.

"Did you hear what she said? 'Our lives are going to change after this', she'll see me when I'm famous? She knows stuff, your maw. This is it, boys, this is the start, after this it's gonnae take off big style for us."

"I thought you didn't believe in all that fortune telling stuff and talking with the dead?" I asked, confused.

"No way, man. Sandy kens what she's on about, she knows her stuff. Who am I to argue with her?" Sid replied, checking himself out in the mirror and smiling.

"You said it was all shite," I concluded.

"No I didnae. It's just misunderstood. Eh, Bobby? What are you on about anyway? Shut up and get ready, we're leaving in a minute."

When the predictions suited him, Sid believed in what he otherwise described as 'made up shite.'

"Aye she's got something," Bobby defended, "she's told me plenty stuff that's come true, but I prefer not to know so I don't ask her."

"There you go, Jimmy, proof of the pudding. Oh I just know that something good is gonnae happen," Sid beamed.

"Settle doon, Kate Bush," I laughed.

"Eh?" Sid uttered in confusion.

"Kate Bush? Cloudbusting? I just know that something good is gonna happen?" I sang.

"Whit?! Shut up, prick!" Sid growled, still confused by my statement.

If the singer didn't have a cock and two balls, then Sid didn't deem it music.

"We're gonnae hit the big time, boys. Are you ready for it?" Sid announced triumphantly.

"Oh aye, too right we are. It's been a long time coming," Bobby replied whilst straightening his tie and checking his teeth for embedded food particles.

We arrived at the pub to a party atmosphere. Everyone was in good humour and Les the bar man came over with a tray of drinks for us as we set up our gear.

"Here's to you, lads," he said as he raised his nip of Auchentoshan. "I hope you get what you deserve. Mind us all back here when you're famous, eh?"

"We'll be too busy for that, Les," Sid replied, lifting his pint and grinning, "we'll be playing in decent places to decent people."

"Cheers, Les. Here's to us." We laughed and clinked glasses.

That was the first of many free rounds and toasts throughout the evening.

Debbie walked in the door as we were chatting to a group of young lads who were keen to tell us about their own band. I caught her eye over their shoulders and my heart melted.

Be strong, Jimmy.

Danny Foster walked in the door 20 seconds behind her, allowing waves of repulsion to swell within me, tossing aside all feelings of melting hearts. She waved and smiled then came over, leaving her wretch of a boyfriend to get the drinks in at the bar.

"Excuse me, lads," I said, pushing past the young wannabes to greet Debbie.

"Hi Jimmy," she said, beaming a fresh-faced smile and looking just divine.

"Hey, Debs. How's it going?"

Play it cool, son, play it cool.

I leaned in and planted a soft kiss on her cheek.

Fuck. It's hard though when she's smelling so good.

"Really good thanks. You all set for your big night? Quite a crowd in here."

"Yeah it should be a good night. Play a few songs, have a laugh. The real fun will start tomorrow when we hit the road. I cannae wait it's gonnae be brilliant."

"Where are you going first?" She tilted her head slightly and her eyes sparkled as she listened to my reply. I had never found her as attractive as she was right then. She had a glow about her. I just wanted to gather her up in my arms and pull her close to me, hold her tightly, smell her, feel her, kiss her …

Fuck, here comes that prick Foster.

"A'right, Jimmy?" he boomed, grabbing Debbie round the waist and kissing her neck "You want a drink?"

Want a drink?

Aye I'll tak' a drink.

Gies a bottle o' beer so I can smash it over your thick fucking skull you gormless looking cunt!

"No thanks," I replied, doing my best to keep my jealousy under control.

"Jimmy's just saying he's off down to Dumfries tomorrow to start the tour," Debs said, smiling at Foster.

"Oh aye? Guid luck wi' that, hope it all goes well."

No you dinnae you lying bastard, you hope we'll fail miserably.

Man I'd love to break every bone in your body.

"Thanks. Eh, I'd better go we're on soon, I'll speak to you after though, Debs?" I asked, hoping I didn't sound too desperate.

"Yeah of course." She patted my arm as Foster dragged her back to the bar.

This tour better be worth it.

The set went well, we played for an hour and a half then left the stage to great lasting applause, forcing us to do an encore.

"Thanks for coming tonight," Sid shouted as he grabbed hold of the microphone stand, "this is the start of a new chapter in the band's long history. We're trying something a bit different, but we think it'll pay off …" Sid turned to Bobby and me and smiled and he made the three of us link arms. I felt a bit uncomfortable standing there staring at the crowd not knowing who to look at as he rambled on with his clearly rehearsed speech.

When the fuck did he plan this?

"… you can all tell your children that you were here tonight, before we made it big …"

Hurry up, Sid, this is torture.

Foster is staring at me with a sarcastic smile on his puss.

He's loving this, the cunt.

"… you can follow our progress on our social media sites …"

You're losing the crowd, Sid, wrap it up.

"… we'll see you all again I'm sure, we won't be strangers. Thanks for coming, good night and God bless."

God bless?

What the fuck?

Sid grabbed our arms by the wrists and held them aloft before forcing us into several theatrical bows to meagre applause.

I wrenched my arm free from his grip.

"Take it easy, Bono. It's no' Wembley we're playing," I snipped.

"Whit's the matter wi' you, you huffy wee cunt? These folk have all come out to see us off, the least you can do is show them some respect."

"What, with a cheesy speech and a couple of bows?"

"You can be an ungrateful bastard at times, Jimmy. You better sort that attitude out." Sid pushed past me off the stage into the embrace of some drunken locals.

"What's up wi' you?" Bobby asked, sounding angrier than his usual concerned self.

"It's that arsehole," I replied, nodding in the direction of Debbie and Foster, "he's put me in a bad mood. Look at him, kissing her and stroking her. He's only doing it 'cause he kens I'm watching."

"Dinnae do this to yourself, man. Come on, move on, you'll have to get over this," Bobby said, patting my shoulder. "Come on, let's go get a drink, this is our party, remember?"

We drank the rest of the evening away and I didn't buy a single round.

Tremendous.

This lifestyle is definitely for me.

I felt a light tap on my shoulder as I was discussing the finer points of touring to the two unfortunates who happened to be at the bar at that particular moment in time.

I turned around to see Debbie smiling at me

"You're having a good time. We're going to go now, it's getting late," she said whilst examining her watch.

"No no no no noooooo. Don't go, Debs," I pleaded, laying my hands on either side of her shoulders.

Oh shit that feels so good.

"We haven't had a chance to catch up yet."

"That's 'cause you've been too busy playing at rock stars as per usual," she chuckled.

"Stay for one more, look there's a table over there we can sit and have a wee chat. For old times sake, eh? Come on, Debs. Just the one?" I was now rubbing her shoulders soothingly.

Fuck I'm giving myself a hard on here.

"Oh all right but just one. I'll go and tell Daniel." She freed herself from my drunken grasp and I ordered two drinks.

Even rock and roll stars eventually have to buy a round.

I shimmied my way through the bustling crowd and plonked the two drinks on the empty table, spilling some of Debbie's wine over my hand. As I sooked it off she pulled out a chair and I sat down.

"Are they only serving half measures in here now?" she chuckled, pointing to the volume in her wine glass.

"Yeah, I thought you'd had enough so I just ordered a wee glass."

"You can talk."

"So where's Daniel?" I mocked in a childish tone. "I'm surprised he's not sitting with us; he can't seem to leave you alone for five seconds."

"Don't, Jimmy. If this is why you've got me here then you can forget it, I'd rather leave than go over this again."

You're so sexy when you're pissed off.

"Sorry, sorry. I didn't mean it in that way, it's just, well … I still love you, Debs. I'm having a hard time getting over you. I didn't think I would be like this but I am. There's not one day that's gone by since you … since *we* split up that I haven't thought about you. And seeing you tonight looking … well, looking just bloody gorgeous, you're breaking my heart …" I took a large gulp of my pint more to stop my wandering tongue than to slake my already slaked thirst.

"Stop it. You can't do this, I've moved on. I still care for you but I've got a new life to lead now."

"With that arsehole? I hear he's got two teenage kids too, Christ, when you said you wanted to start a family I didn't know you'd be happy with a ready-made one."

"Piss off, I'm not listening to this," Debs made to stand up.

"Sorry, sorry sorry. I'm really sorry, Debs. I didn't mean that. I'm out of order, my jealousy is getting the better of me." I ushered her back into a seated position and stared at her with pathetic puppy dog eyes.

"Look, you'll meet somebody else and soon forget about me."

"I don't want somebody else." I took Debbie's hand in mine and squeezed it. I could feel tears coming to the fore as I looked pathetically into her eyes. From the other side of the room, I could see Danny Foster making his way over to the table. I sniffed back my tears and released Debbie's hand. He stood behind her and put his hands on her shoulders and, when she looked up, they both smiled at each other.

Puke.

"Are we gonnae make a move soon, darlin'?" Foster cooed.

"Can you no' leave us alone for two fucking minutes?" The anger inside me ignited and exploded through my veins at a frightening speed.

"Jimmy!" Debbie hissed.

"What are you on about?" Foster asked, bemused by my outburst.

"You," I said through gritted teeth, "you cannae bare to see me and Debbie talking alone, she's no' your fucking lapdog."

Oh shit where am I going with this one?

"Right, we're leaving, Jimmy," Debbie hissed, clearly embarrassed at the situation that was unfolding.

"What's your problem, pal?" Foster said in a mocking tone with his arms raised in defence.

I pushed my chair back and it screeched along the old wooden floorboards as I staggered to my full height.

"What's ma problem? What's ma problem?" I was rambling now. "I'll tell you what ma problem is. You're ma fucking problem. Think you're still the big man, eh?" I was now shouting and pointing at Foster. People in the pub had left their conversations to turn and see what all the commotion was about.

"Come on, Daniel," Debbie seethed, tugging at his arm, but Foster didn't budge.

"I dinnae think I'm the big man but if you've got a problem wi' me we can always sort it out elsewhere?"

I was now 15 years old again staring down the school bully who tormented so many lives. I wanted to make up for all those lost years of helplessness and fear. Looking into his cold stare I knew I could do it.

Go on, do it.

DO IT!

FUCKING HIT HIM!

"Any time, Foster. Let's go," I spat.

"Daniel, don't do this to me. Jimmy, just piss off and leave us alone," Debbie said, still pulling at Foster's arm but his glare never left mine.

I felt a touch on my shoulder, and I flinched. I actually nearly shat myself due to the intensity of staring Foster down.

"Leave it, Jimmy. He's no' worth it." It was Bobby, doing what he does best, defusing difficult situations.

"Remember him, do you, Foster?" I nodded to the big man who kept a grip on me. "Remember how you used to torment him, eh? Well look at him now. He'd rip your arm off and smack you aboot the heid with the soggy end." Not my best fighting talk but I was a slave to the testosterone.

"That was a long time ago, I was different then," Foster growled as his eyes left mine to look into Bobby's. On seeing Bobby and his considerable bulk he gave into Debbie's pleading and arm tugging and the two of them walked to the door.

"Aye fucking run, Foster. I'll see you around though. Watch your back, sunshine," I shouted as Debbie dragged Foster through the door.

"Nicely done. Who do you think you are, Charles Bronson?" Sid sneered sarcastically from the bar, slow hand clapping all the while. "He'd knock you out with a miss, you silly wee fanny. You go on aboot me no' growing up? You're worse, acting like a bloody 12-year-old. Nice way to end the night."

"You can just fuck off, Sid," I shouted, shrugging Bobby's hand from the grip he still had on my shoulder.

"Or what?" Sid replied wild eyed, making his way over to where I was standing. "What the fuck are you gonnae dae aboot it, eh?"

"Settle down, girls. We've had enough excitement for one night," Bobby intervened, standing between us.

"Don't push me, man." I didn't want to fight Sid. I didn't even want to argue with him, but I couldn't back down now.

"Ha ha don't push me, aye nae bother, Rambo, get away home out of my sight."

"One of these days you'll push me too far," I whimpered, heading towards the door.

"Ooh I'm shaking in my boots."

I didn't rise to Sid's taunting and walked out the door, leaving my equipment for the others to take care of.

The cold air hit me like a fresh slap in the face. My head started to spin, and my guts joined in. I walked a couple of paces and then vomited in the gutter. Wiping away spit and tears I walked back to my parent's house, all the while thinking …

What the fuck just happened in there?

Foster? Fair enough, but Sid?

Now I've got to go and spend the next six months cooped up with that prick.

Suddenly the idea of the band on tour didn't seem too appealing.

But tomorrow is another day as they say.

CHAPTER 13

I sat down to breakfast with a belter of a hangover accompanied by the nauseating feeling of guilt due to my actions the previous evening.

To complete the set, I was also treated to a scolding lecture from my parents about not acting my age and wasting my life etcetera etcetera. It was familiar boggy ground they were wading through and yet they still wondered why I didn't spend time with them.

I say 'parents', but it was my mother who did all the talking whilst my dad sat with his arms folded across his chest and nodded frequently in agreement to her military-style rant.

"I mean, why the blinking heck did you pack in your job? That was a good job you had there, respectable. You got to wear a shirt and tie … do you not think it's about time you were settled down?"

I chewed and chewed my scrambled eggs, adding another forkful into my already overloaded mouth. A big ball of egg and bread rattled around my gob like a pile of damp clothes in a tumble dryer.

Still the bugger wouldn't go down.

Lack of saliva.

The wholegrain bread didn't help matters. It's like gargling with birdseed. I took a large gulp of my tea and promptly choked, coughing egg, birdseed, and Tetley all over the table.

"For goodness sake, James. Chew your food …"

It's fucking Jimmy you stupid cow.

J-I-M-M-Y. JIMMY!

She never listens to a thing I say.

"… why the blinking heck you're still mucking about in that band is beyond me, still acting like a teenager. Everything was going so well for you until this band thing came along, you're making a fool of yourself and your dad and me. Thank God your granny's not alive to see this …"

Ah there's nothing like parental words of encouragement to raise your deflated spirits.

My mother and father hated me.

I'm not looking for any sympathy, it's a fact and I'm now used to it.

My parents were perfectly happy with their lot in life. My father had a decent job whilst my mother played the good housewife and raised my darling sister. That was how they wanted it.

Fair enough.

Now for whatever reason, I'm guessing alcohol had something to do with it, my parents decided to get frisky one night and the result of their unromantic copulation was me. The shitey little bit of sperm that my dad still had rattling about his balls had somehow managed to penetrate my mum's rotten egg.

Ghastly.

My parents were both in their early twenties when they had my sister so imagine their shock and that of the whole townsfolk when they discovered my mother was pregnant again when she was in her early thirties.

Scandalous.

Dirty auld tramp.

They had thought their days of shitty nappies and sleepless nights were long gone. But I showed up and they hated me for it. I think they hated each other for it too. I've never seen them be affectionate towards each other in my entire life. Perhaps they're both terrified that they'll be landed with another child. Curse their terrible luck. They had sex twice and both times it resulted in a child.

Nightmare.

When it was made clear to them through school reports that I wasn't a super brain like my big sister, they showed me about as much affection as one would a well-used handkerchief and they constantly asked me why I wasn't 'like' my sister or why I wasn't 'as smart as her' or 'as well behaved as her'.

If they couldn't answer the questions why the fuck did they think a failure like I could?

I was never able to understand their resentment towards me till I was old enough to understand life. I didn't hate them or my sister for that matter, despite the way they all used to stare at me like I was the missing link. I saw them more as a problem that had to be endured.

They were a bit like hemorrhoids. A pain in the arse but they were a part of me.

I finished breakfast with a couple of paracetamols and gathered my stuff. After hearing the familiar abusive breakfast ramblings of my parents, I was filled with an urgency to prove to them more than myself that we'd make a success of this.

Fuck them, what do they know?

I said my goodbyes and hefted my rucksack onto my shoulder and gripped my purple bass guitar firmly in my hand. I walked out onto the street and turned back to see my parents faces at the front door.

"See you when I'm famous," I shouted.

My mother sighed, shook her head and stared at her feet as my father put a comforting arm around her meek frame and pulled her inside, closing the door behind him.

Suit yourself then.

By the time I made it to Sid's parent's house all the packing had been done.

One, two, three awwwww!

"What time do you call this?" Sid shouted, tapping an imaginary watch on his wrist.

"Sorry lads I couldn't get away from my folks. They kept making sure I had everything and wouldn't let me leave till we'd had a family breakfast."

"Aye right, lazy bastard. Sling your shit in the back and let's get out of here."

"You're in the middle, Jimmy," Bobby exclaimed, pointing to the square inch of cushion that would house my arse for the next few hours whilst Sid rammed the gear stick into my right knee every four minutes.

"Excellent," I declared.

As Sid revved the engine his parents came alongside the window, waving enthusiastically like proud parents seeing off their only child on his first day of school.

"See you later, folks," Sid enthusiastically waved back in between rolling up the window, "and we're off. This is it, boys. Page one in the new chapter. I hope you're writing all this down, Jimmy."

"Writing what down?" I quizzed.

"All this," Sid waved his arm around the van. "I want you to capture the emotions, the feelings. It's your job to write the blog so come on, get on with it."

"We're no' even out your parent's street yet. It's a blog I'm writing, no' a minute-by-minute account."

"Aye well … just remember what's being said and what's going on. We want this to be the best blog there's ever been."

"It's all being noted up here," I replied, tapping my head. "I've no' got enough room to scratch my arse sitting here let alone wield a notepad and pencil."

And so it was on that glorious day of the 25th of June, three best friends set off in search of their destiny of fortune and fame.

All that had gone before was irrelevant.

It was all in the past and was firmly rooted there.

This was our chance.

A new beginning.

This was our time.

A time for triumph and be damned anyone who stood in our way.

"Sid?" Bobby asked nonchalantly whilst his head gazed out onto the surrounding countryside that hurtled by. "I thought this tour was going to give us a chance to see parts of Scotland that we wouldn't normally see?"

"Aye it is," Sid replied as his eyes gazed grimly onto the grey tarmac that stretched ahead for miles.

"It's just that so far all I've seen is motorway embankments strewn with litter and discarded car parts. Can we no' take the scenic route to Dumfries?"

"There's plenty time for all that shit later on. I want to get down there as soon as we can and get settled. Christ we've only been on the road for an hour and you're already moaning."

"I'm no moaning I was only saying …" Bobby protested.

The conversation died and we sat in stony silence listening to the radio.

"Can we stop soon? I cannae feel my arse anymore and I'm bursting for a piss," I chipped in.

"For fuck's sake …"

CHAPTER 14

We rolled into Dumfries, the Queen of the South, several hours after starting our journey. A tedious journey which took in some of Scotland's main attractions such as the M8 and the M74.

Bobby and myself were suitably impressed at the accommodation Sid had booked as we pulled into its orange chip driveway overlooking the River Nith. I had been expecting hostels and Travelodges, but this was the kind of place your parents would go to.

"Nice choice man," I approved.

"Aye well if we're gonnae do this we're gonnae do it in style. It's no' cheap though so you two will be sharing a room."

"Aye that's fine," Bobby and me agreed as we grabbed our bags and went to check in.

After unpacking and checking out the freebies our room had to offer, we met at the hotel bar for a 'tour meeting.'

"Right, lads, you all settled in okay?" Sid asked in an extremely serious manner.

"Eh, aye?" we replied, wondering to ourselves how 'settled in' we could possibly be whilst staying in a hotel.

"Everything all right with your room?"

"Eh, aye."

"Good, good. Just you let me know if there's anything you need and I'll get it sorted for you, a'right?"

"Eh, aye we will do."

What the fuck is up with him?

He thinks he's a cross between the Godfather and an AA hotel inspector.

Get on with this stupid meeting, you twat.

"Right, lads. Here's the plans," Sid unfolded a pad of paper and thumbed through a few leafs before tapping his pen on the page he was after. "We've got the rest of today off then it's down to the serious stuff tomorrow. Midday till one we're playing in a wee coffee shop in the High Street. It'll be a nice way to start off the tour properly, an informal relaxing acoustic afternoon before we rip up the town at night."

"Sounds … eh, good. So how long will be staying here for?" Bobby asked.

Sid stared at him then looked down at his A4 pad of paper and turned over a few more sheets.

"What, in this hotel? Or in Dumfries?"

"Eh, both I suppose."

Sid looked at Bobby and then at me and then back at Bobby. He turned a few more pages of his notebook and then stared at his pad.

"Looking at the itinerary we'll probably be in Dumfries for about two to three weeks. It'll be our base whilst we play the surrounding areas. We need to have a base with a highly populated area to boost our profile. We'll play all the wee surrounding towns and villages so everyone gets to appreciate the Champions, but we'll always retreat to a large town as our base. For example, next we'll go to Edinburgh and that'll be our base for the southeast. We'll stay in Dundee, Aberdeen, Inverness, and Glasgow and so on and so on okay?"

"Seems to me like you've got it all worked out, captain," I said, giving Sid the big thumbs up whilst trying my hardest not to look like I was taking the piss, which I clearly was. "Any chance that me and Bobby could get a wee looksy at that itinerary sometime?"

"Aye, aye it's just that it's not finished, it's still very much a work in progress and is subject to change but once it's done you'll be the first to see it."

"Cool, cool," I nodded.

"Okay if you're both happy with everything I'm going up to my room to work on some stuff, I'll see you for dinner," Sid said, pointing at his A4 notepad and raising his eyebrows to emphasise that he would be really really busy working on stuff and that we should be really really grateful to him for doing all that stuff.

"Nae bother, we're gonnae take a walk around town, you want to meet us there later?"

"I'll see how I get on with all this stuff." Again, more raising of the eyebrows, cheek blowing, and exaggerated pointing to the holy pad of A4.

Bobby and myself grabbed our cameras and headed out into the afternoon sunshine of Dumfries like excited tourists.

"What do you make of all that then?" Bobby asked as I posed for a photo next to the Rabbie Burns statue outside Greyfriars church.

Click.

"Who knows, man. He's certainly acting strange. But I suppose it cannae be easy organising all this stuff. Right it's your turn, come on, say cheese," I replied, trying to form some sort of defence for Sid's behaviour.

"Cheese."

Click.

"Aye but does he have to act like a schoolteacher? It's just weird, I cannae take him seriously. I prefer it when he's treating us like a pair of numpties, you know slagging us off and having a laugh?" Bobby puzzled.

"I'm sure it'll no' be long before he's slagging us off and bossing us around again, in the meantime let's just enjoy the peace."

Bobby and I spent the rest of the day wandering around town snapping away at various landmarks like the Devorgilla Bridge, one of the oldest bridges in Scotland by the way, and sampling the hospitality at The Globe Inn, a pub frequented by the great bard himself prompting him to write 'The Globe Tavern here which for many years has been my howff.'

Fair braw!

We popped into a few pubs to hand out flyers announcing our world-famous tour but left embarrassed as we couldn't actually tell them when and where we'd be playing other than the two gigs tomorrow, prompting us to head back to the hotel to quiz Sid on his masonic abilities to keep this tour a big fucking secret.

CHAPTER 15

26ᵗʰ JUNE

Bobby and I called another meeting last night to demand more input into the tour only for Sid to triumphantly announce he'd finalised the tour dates till the end of July and had posted them on our social networking sites.

Leafing through his A4 pad I noticed he'd certainly been a busy boy. Suddenly realising how much effort and hassle it took to organise something of this great magnitude, Bobby and I shut our collective pusses and let Sid get on with it.

Time: 12 p.m.
Venue: Café Continental
Capacity: 24 seats, plus two staff behind counter

As we carried our guitars and Cajon through the doors, we knew Sid had made a bit of a faux pass.

We had been led to believe it was owned by the same people who had a smart music venue of the same name in Kirkcaldy.

The name was the only thing the venues had in common.

This was an old-fashioned tea room run by old-fashioned people for the benefit of old-fashioned people to drink their tea having just collected their pensions. You couldn't move for all the doilies.

After our first song it was only a matter of time before we would have to leave. A table of three elderly ladies got up and left halfway through the first song, tutting and muttering loudly to themselves.

The owner of this fine establishment then came over for a word.

"I thought you were going to play Scottish tunes?"

"We are playing Scottish tunes. I wrote them in Scotland and I'm Scottish," Sid sneered.

"Yes, yes. I was thinking more of the traditional kind you know? Like the Corries or The Alexander Brothers?"

Sid was silently raging with embarrassment. His venue booking skills had been called into question at the first gig.

Oh dear.

"Let's just treat this as a warm-up for tonight, eh?" he sighed.

Despite the owner's request for traditional music, she instead received a speedy little number from the Champions back catalogue.

Before we had even entered the last verse the place had emptied, and the owner was marching her way over to us, waving her hands above her head.

"No, no, no, no, this'll not do."

And by 12:14 on day one of our tour of Scotland we had been kicked out of our first gig.

"Should I leave this part out of the blog, Sid?" I asked.

"Fuck off."

TAKE TWO

Time: 7.30 p.m.
Venue: Chasers Bar
Capacity: 60

Our second gig of the day and tour was a considerable triumph compared to the first. Nobody left and we finished our set. The pub wasn't full, but it was good to receive mildly positive reviews from a few of the locals who seemed genuinely interested in what we were doing with the tour.

We finished the night drinking with a few of them, Sid holding the floor with his vision for the future.

At closing time Bobby and I headed back to the hotel. Sid disappeared with a lovely young local.

Lucky bastard.

For the next two weeks we played gigs to varying degrees of success. We usually played two gigs a day, one around 7 p.m. and again at 9 p.m. We would try to play the gigs in separate venues if it was possible.

Spread the love and all that.

We ditched the noon starts completely after the first day. As you would expect weekends were a much greater success than say a Monday night in Dalbeattie (nae offence Dalbeattie).

The good times as far as staying in our nice cosy hotel didn't last long either. After the third night we were packed off to the Travelodge on the outskirts of town. Sadly, this wasn't due to trashed hotel rooms and rock 'n' roll excessive behaviour. Our tour manager and band leader decided it wasn't good for the budget so the three of us all crammed into a £39 double room taking turns between sleeping on the couch and sharing the bed and arguing over who's turn it was to sleep in the bed.

I was enjoying myself though. Being away from home was allowing me to clear my head and forget about all the negative bullshit that had gone on there in recent times, plus seeing a part of Scotland that I hadn't spent much time in before was new and interesting. Bobby and I would venture out each day and take the van to do a bit of exploring. Sid would usually stay in the room working on stuff or romancing his latest conquest.

Mel joined us for a weekend, much to Sid's disgust.

"It's supposed to be the boys on tour," he whined over lunch when Mel had returned home.

"You've never spent a minute with us, so dinnae gie me that pish," retorted Bobby.

"Aye well, I've been up to my eyes trying to get gigs and sorting out accommodation and stuff. It's no' an easy task. I'd like to see either of you two take on a challenge of this magnitude. Anyway, we've only been on the road a matter of weeks and you're already moaning about missing Mel. Fucking hell, man, she must be one fantastic ride for you to keep rattling on about her the way you do."

"Watch what you're saying, Sid," Bobby threatened.

"Well for Christ's sake, you've only ever fucked the one lassie. How do you know if she's any good if you haven't tried anything else?"

"Shut the fuck up, you don't know what you're talking about. You wouldn't understand," Bobby snapped and glared at Sid.

"I understand enough to know it wouldn't be me licking the same pussy week in week out, year after year. That's just crazy when you've got a world full of pussies out there just begging to be eaten."

I laughed out loud as an image of Sid running about town trying to catch and lick stray cats entered my mind.

"I don't know what you're laughing at," Sid continued with his tirade, "you're just as bad as him greetin' and moaning about how much you miss Debbie. Get a grip, we're supposed to be rock stars, start acting like them instead of pussy whipped wee laddies."

Sid got up and stormed off in the huff before Bobby could grab hold of him and slap him about the head.

See you later then, Sid.

Seeing Bobby and Mel together however did make images of Debbie enter my mind. I'd been coping pretty well lately. Up until then I hadn't really thought of her much but being around a happy couple made me feel jealous and bloody miserable.

I need to get a woman soon.

Sandwiched between lazy lonely afternoons on the beaches overlooking the Solway Firth we played gigs at:

Dalbeattie
Castle Douglas
Kirkcudbright
Gatehouse of Fleet
Sanquhar
Newton Stewart
Wigtown
Whithorn
Stranraer
Girvan
Portpatrick
New Galloway
Lochmaben
Lockerbie
Annan
Gretna

I was also photographed next to such luminaries as:

Robert "Rabbie" Burns
Robert The Bruce
Reverend William Graham
and a Ram

CHAPTER 16

On the 11th of July we played two rousing gigs in Moffat and after drinking with a boisterous bunch of locals we piled into the newly renovated tour van and set off for 'base' back in Dumfries.

It was whilst driving on the A701, however, that disaster struck.

"Man, that was a rare night. The crowd were loving us," Sid laughed.

"Aye I only bought one round all night, wish all the gigs were like that," I replied.

"What about that old guy asking for our autographs?"

"The man knows talent when he sees it, Bobby. Here, stop hogging that joint."

As Bobby passed the spliff to Sid, Sid fumbled the pass and dropped it onto his crotch. He 'Oohed' and 'Aaahed' as he hastily attempted to pick it up and stop his balls from burning.

Sid recovered well though and was just about to take his first puff when …

"BLAM!"

Something smashed off the bonnet and into the windscreen of the van which cracked with the impact. Sid hammered on the brakes, and we swerved across the road and skidded to a halt after bouncing off the grass verge.

"What the fuck was that?!" screamed Sid. "Did you see anything?"

"No, I was too busy laughing at you burning yourself," I gasped, my heart racing from the fright.

"Jesus Christ, Sid. We've run someone over … oh bloody hell, bloody hell," Bobby panicked.

We gingerly climbed out of the van and peered back down the road. It was well after midnight but there was just enough light left in the Scottish summer to vaguely make out 30 yards of the tarmac surface in the distance.

There was no sign of anyone.

"Oh fuck," Sid groaned through fingers that were rubbing frantically at his face. "I've had a few pints, I'm fucked. I cannae go to jail, man. This cannae be happening to me."

Bobby and I anxiously made our way around the front of the van, fearing the worst. It was completely destroyed. The windscreen looked far worse from the outside and there was a dark liquid splattered across the crumpled remains of the bonnet which we took to be blood. But there was no body to be seen.

"Shit," Bobby gasped as we surveyed the brutal damage to the vehicle and came to the same conclusion.

"Come on, we've got to go and find them," I said, pulling Sid by his arm.

"I'll go get the torch," Bobby replied and went in search of our recently purchased million candlepower beacon.

"Oh fuck, oh fucking hell … I've killed someone," Sid sobbed as I dragged him along the road.

After traipsing a couple of hundred yards back towards the scene of the crime we heard a low guttural groaning noise.

"Oh shit," I whispered.

"Oh fucking hell, fucking hell," Sid mumbled in a state of shock.

"Are you alright?" Bobby cupped his hands to his mouth and shouted into the open air for signs of hope.

We could hear a shuffling sound coming from a field on the opposite side of the road and turned in unison to see if we could see the injured party.

The glare from the torch showed no signs of life as it wove backwards and forth like the searchlight in a dodgy prison film.

At least they sounded alive.

Just.

"Come on," urged Bobby as he vaulted the rickety wire fence with ease and ran into the field in search of our victim.

"I cannae do it, man. I cannae do it. I cannae go in there," Sid blubbered.

"It'll be cool," I lied, trying to calm him.

"Oh no," Bobby shouted, and I could hear him retching in the distance.

A terrible feeling of despair hit me as I pictured the worst possible outcome. But I had to see for myself, after all it wasn't me who knocked them down. I wouldn't be going to prison.

"What is it, what's wrong?" I shouted as I eventually untangled my legs from the fence and jogged to where Bobby was regaining his composure.

Then I saw it as the carnage was illuminated by the unnecessarily powerful beam of light.

"Oh God," I gasped as I controlled the urge to vomit when I saw the broken body of a once majestic stag lying writhing in agony. Its hind legs were smashed and trailed limply behind the beast. Its side had been ripped open, allowing entrails to spill out but despite this it valiantly tried to stand by shuffling its front legs amongst the tufted grass, looking for a foothold.

"Can you see them, Jimmy? Is it really bad?" Sid shouted from the roadside.

"Aye it's bad. But he's no' deid. We'll have to put him out of his misery though."

"Whit?!" Sid wailed.

Bobby had crept to the body and was silently weeping as he stroked the animal's antlered head. It glared back at him through wide fearful eyes as it groaned and panted and struggled to rise.

"Stay still, my friend, it'll be okay," he whimpered.

Sid came creeping over the grassy field to reluctantly view the scene.

"It's a deer. You hit a stag," I informed him.

"Whit?!" Sid exclaimed as he peered over my shoulder to see the broken beastie. "Oh thank fuck for that," he sighed and wiped the tears from his eyes. Sid then burst out laughing and he laughed and then laughed some more but this time with pure relief. "Jesus Christ. I thought I'd killed a hitch hiker. Fucking hell, a deer?"

"Aye a deer but it's no' deid. I mean look at it, it's really messed up. Poor bugger must be in agony. We're gonnae have to kill it."

"Nae bother," Sid exclaimed, clicking his fingers. He turned and ran back towards the road.

I pulled my eyes from the horrific sight and looked at Bobby who was still visibly upset.

"You a'right, mate?"

"This is terrible. The poor thing," he snivelled but his eyes never left the diminishing stare of the stag.

"We'll have to kill it, Bobby, put it out of its misery. Come on, let's look for a boulder or something hard to hit it over the head with."

Bobby eventually sighed and arose from his haunches.

"Right, stand back," Sid proudly announced whilst cocking his virginal air rifle.

"What in the name of hell are you gonnae do with that?" I asked.

"Put it out its misery. What do you think I'm gonnae do, let it admire the telescopic sights?"

"Sid, that's the Monarch of the Glen lying there, no' a bloody budgie."

"Aye, I know that. I'll shoot it in the head point blank, end of story, goodnight Bambi."

"You are a fucking remedial. You cannae kill a fully grown stag with an air gun, we're trying to put it out of its misery no' add to it," I argued.

"Out my way." Sid tried to push past me, but I grabbed his arms and attempted to wrestle the gun from his grasp.

"What're you doing? Get off me, you dick," he shouted.

"NO. Give me the gun, you're not shooting *that* thing with *this* thing," I spat through gritted teeth.

We both pushed and shoved and fell to the ground but neither of us relinquished control of the weapon. As we rolled around amongst the thistles and sheep shit, we heard a voice calling from the road.

"Need any help in there, chaps?"

"Get off me, you prick," I seethed as I released my grip on the gun and sprung up, slightly startled to see who was shouting.

"Eh, yes please, pal," Bobby replied. And so, brushing the grass and countryside matter from our clothes, we sheepishly wandered over to see the man standing by the road.

"I take it that's your van blocking the road up there?" he asked.

"Eh, aye, aye it will be. Sorry about that, we hit a deer and it's in a bad way, really hurt and, well we think we need to put it out of its misery."

"I think your van is in a worse way, pal. I'll go and get my gun."

The countrified gentleman disappeared to his Jeep and came back with a rifle of his own.

"Where is it?" he asked us.

"Over there." Bobby and I pointed.

"Bang!"

"Mooooooooooooooooooooooaaaargh!"

The deer was flailing its front legs in anger and increased pain as we approached it.

Elmer the Fud had decided to shoot it with his spud gun.

"Stand back, lads." The farmer pushed us aside, aimed once down the barrel, then pulled the trigger.

"BANG!"

The deer ceased moving.

"You'd be there all night trying to kill it with that thing, son," the farmer chap said, nodding at Sid's piece.

"See," I smugly replied.

"Right, I'll go and get my stuff. If you boys can give me a hand putting this thing into the back of the Jeep, I'll give you a lift to where you're going because your van is not going anywhere in a hurry."

Having played a really enjoyable gig earlier that evening I would never have expected to receive a butchery lesson on the way home but that is indeed what happened. We all watched in open-mouthed horror as Robin the farmer violently removed the remaining insides of the stag to much gagging and spitting from the three of us whilst Sid moaned, "I bet Neil Young never had to do this."

The farmer then swiftly snapped the already broken hind legs and pulled them so they met in the middle of the stag's body where they were tied together with the front legs. We wrapped the beast in a tarpaulin sheet and dragged it over the uneven ground before heaving it into the back of Robin's Jeep which already resembled a countryside alliance mobile shop.

We pushed our crumpled van to the side of the road and locked it up for the night and jumped into the Jeep.

"There's only room for two of you up here so one of you will have to sit in the back."

After a short stalemate I decided I'd do the decent thing and sit in the back so we could at least get home before morning.

The back of the Jeep stunk like a Moroccan meat market in summertime thanks to the decaying corpses of at least four different species. Alongside the newly disembowelled stag there were a couple of foxes, some rabbits or hares and a few pigeons and pheasants hung by the neck with twine attached to the side panels.

Robin (who had been out lamping* that evening) kindly dropped us off at the Travelodge and I immediately headed for the shower to remove the stink of death from my being. As I scrubbed my body clean with the complimentary toiletries and let the warm water cascade over my scalp, I thought to myself, what a ridiculous end to the day.

*Lamping – for all the townies out there – is apparently a means of pest control or meat acquisition or both in which the hunter ventures out into the fields at night to shine a bright torch or lamp (hence the name) into the eyes of unsuspecting animals, rendering them momentarily motionless so that the said hunter can shoot them easily because the animals have been making a nuisance of themselves (eating cooped up chickens in a foxes case or digging up manicured lawns in a rabbits) or because the hunter prefers a more natural way to obtain protein than the way in which it is currently offered in the supermarkets, or ideally both, therefore killing two birds with one stone.

Or more realistically one rabbit or fox with one bullet.

I'm not entirely sure you can eat a fox but these rural residing people are absolutely mental so they probably would before draping the fur of the deceased animal around their necks in a fashionable fashion.

Who am I to judge?

CHAPTER 17

The van was a write off.

It was towed to a garage in Dumfries where the mechanic gave us the good news in layman terms

"Aye it's fucked, complete write off."

"That's just brilliant," Sid fumed, "we're stuck in Dumfries with no bloody transport. We're humped."

Once he'd finished ranting and raving and cursing Bambi, we decided the best thing we could do was cancel the next two weeks worth of gigs and hire a van to transport us and all our equipment to Edinburgh. We had planned to spend the month of August in Edinburgh anyway gigging throughout the Festival. In the meantime, we'd just have to sort out digs and wait for the insurance money to come through so we could buy a new van and continue with the rest of the tour at the end of August.

"Get writing that blog, Jimmy. I want you to express our deepest regret at having to cancel these gigs but let the fans know we'll definitely reschedule at a later date. You'd better make it sound dramatic too, mention that I was seriously injured in the collision with the giant stag, but I'll be fit enough to perform during the festival. That should keep them all interested," Sid dictated.

"Aye nae bother, what will it be, a broken neck or ruptured spleen?" I asked.

"Be serious, eh? I couldn't recover from a broken neck in a fortnight could I, you fanny? Tell them I got concussion and had to get stitches in my arm or something."

"You're the boss."

Sid contacted his old college acquaintance Eleanor who kindly agreed to let us stay with her whilst we were in Edinburgh.

"That's very generous of her, Sid. We should get her something to say thanks," Bobby said.

"Aye and I think we should chip in and give her money for gas and electric," I offered.

"Nah it's cool, Eleanor's minted. She comes from some noble family up north and doesn't need the money, besides it'll be good for her. She doesn't have much of a social life, bit of an introverted book nerd, so we'll be doing her a favour. She should be paying us."

Eleanor, or at least her noble family were indeed 'minted.' She owned a large three-bedroomed tenement flat in Bruntsfield decked out with beautiful antique furniture. The flat also offered stunning views overlooking the meadows and you could see the ancient volcano that is Arthur's Seat peaking out from behind some flats in the distance. There was more than enough room to house us and all our equipment. Eleanor was a really cool lassie.

There was just one teeny weeny problem.

She was the dirtiest woman I had ever met.

In a hygienic sense.

Not in a personal way either.

The lassie was well groomed and had an array of expensive fragrances dotted about the once majestic bathroom that I could never justify purchasing. It was just domestically she was a tad, how shall I put it? Carefree?

The kitchen sink was piled high with crusty dishes. The worktops were covered in all sorts of solidified foodstuffs and liquids and the fridge held the cure to diseases that hadn't been invented yet. Cobwebs hung from the corner of every room and lampshade and dust sat on the Georgian mantelpiece like a treasured heirloom.

I am by no stretch of the imagination a domestic goddess, we all get a little bit lazy from time to time but this was ridiculous. I had lived in a similar state myself whilst at university, but there were four of us in the flat and we were just kids. This was a well-educated woman approaching forty.

"Nae wonder Eleanor's an introvert. Have you seen the state o' this place?" I whispered as Eleanor showed us to our rooms.

"Shut up. What do you expect, the lassie's in a position of power, she's a distant relation of the Queen. This is a sign of true class, she's no' got time to get a duster out. Anyway, it's no' costing us anything so stop being ungrateful," Sid replied sternly as we entered another large bedroom filled with timeworn brown furniture.

"We're no' being ungrateful, man, it is pretty dirty though. Could she no' employ a cleaner? This is a breeding ground for vermin," Bobby pitched in as we were guided back into the living room.

"Eh thanks very much for letting us stay, Eleanor, you're a star, we'd be snookered without you," I chirped in as we finished the tour.

"Not a problem, any time. Just remember me when you're famous ha ha," Eleanor laughed.

"Nae bother, you'll get a mention on the sleeve note of our new album," Sid grinned. "Right I've got a load of phone calls and emails to get through so if you don't mind I'll crack on with that," Sid said, excusing himself from the uncomfortable small talk, leaving Bobby and myself to nod and shrug at Eleanor like a couple of dafties as she smiled back.

As we patiently waited for the festival to start and the gigs to commence, Bobby and myself made ourselves useful by putting up posters and handing out flyers directing people to our various websites. I updated the blog and was surprised to see we were attaining a little bit of a following on Facebook ...

"Looking forward to the gig at Bannerman's, should be great."

"Hope you boys sound better than you look!!"

"Fife's finest in Embra, rock on!"

Sid busied himself organising gigs and chasing up the insurance people.

"Right the festival starts the morn, so I want us up the Royal Mile early doors to get a good spot for playing. Our first proper gigs no' for a couple of days so I figure two days up the Mile drawing the crowds in will do us the world of good," Sid announced.

"What? We're gonnae be busking?"

"No. We'll be playing a mini open-air gig, like a preview. It's advertising, Jimmy. You've got to speculate to accumulate. There's no end of things to see at the festival so we've got to stand out from the rest of them," Sid countered.

"Should I bring a cap to put down just in case?"

Time: 9 a.m.

Venue: Royal Mile, opposite some whisky shop

Capacity: Thousands!

At first the crowds were a little sparse but by the early afternoon we were raking the cash in. It was like super busking. Not just coins either, some Japanese lady even threw a tenner in. We played for forty-five minutes then handed out our flyers then played some more. We had only intended on doing two days till the gigs in the pubs and clubs kicked off but because it was such a nice little earner, we carried on into a seventh day. That was when an official from the festival came along and asked to see our receipt for the slot we had. There was a brief heated exchange between the official and Sidney which looked like it could have been a festival act in itself.

"You snobby bastard I can come up here and play any other time of the year withoot a fucking licence. Just cause the Yanks are here throwing their cash aboot you're kicking us oot? Capitalist pig!"

The festival official gave back as good as she got from Sid, but upon realising we weren't going to budge, she told us she was going away to fetch the police.

"Oh no, dinnae get the police, please, please, not the poleeeeeeeessssss," Sid sarcastically wailed back at her as she departed through the mass of bodies crammed onto the cobbled thoroughfare.

We were only three bars into our next song when Sid stopped singing and he turned to Bobby and me and nodded to indicate the two unmistakable hats of the local constabulary bobbing their way through the busy crowd. That was our cue to say our thank yous and goodbyes as we quickly gathered up our equipment and sped a hasty retreat down the Royal Mile.

Trying to negotiate your way down the Royal Mile (or anywhere in the city for that matter) during the festival is a bit like arriving at a boozer stone cold sober with only five minutes till last orders. The place is jam packed with loud, obnoxious, overconfident arseholes, it takes you ages to get to your destination and just when you think you're getting to grips with the noise and the hustle and bustle it's over.

Oh, and everyone thinks they're a fucking comedian.

Take my advice, arrive early and get as many drinks down you as possible. People are less annoying when you're drunk.

The gigs we played during the festival were great fun. Even on a Wednesday afternoon in a dark tiny cellar. Due to the influx of people to the city you were guaranteed a decent crowd who more often than not were in extremely high spirits. This enabled us to flog loads of our EP's and a good number of T-Shirts to ignorant tourists who definitely thought we were an already famous Scottish band. We must've played in every pub that hosted live music.

Bobby moved back to Fife for the remainder of the month after he awoke to find a dead/dying mouse on his bed at Eleanor's. Despite much pleading from Sid that it would ruin the tour, Bobby went home and got the bus over every morning for the start of play.

Through guilt I too went back to Fife to spend a night at my folk's house to see how they were both doing after my dad's heart attack. He still looked pretty grim but assured me he was getting stronger. They both continued to hassle me on the topic of the band even though I told them we were getting great reviews and had made a lot of money.

Parents can see straight though lies though.

We even played one of our strangest gigs to date at a flat in Stockbridge. We had just finished our set at The Cabaret Voltaire and were packing our stuff into Eleanor's car when a young man approached us.

"Hi guys, great set tonight, really dug it. I was wondering if you'd be interested in playing at my flat later. I'm having a party and it'd be really cool to have a live band play?"

"Not tonight Cliff, we're no' Franz Ferdinand," Sid mocked as he squeezed the guitars past the drums onto the back seat of Eleanor's car.

"Oh, I'd pay you. There'd be drinks for you too," the posh boy retorted.

"You couldnae afford us, son. Anyway, we're no' really intae that arty farty shite. Playing in people's front rooms, it's a bit wanky, ken?" I piped up, feeling the need to sound extra Scottish for intimidation purposes.

I hate these middle-class wankers.

"Not even for £500?" posh boy said as if he were haggling with some Egyptian stall owner.

Fuck off back to Eton, you snivelling little prick.

"£500? Cash? Deal," Sid came out the car and enthusiastically shook Tory boy's hand. "Where's the party?"

Sid sorted out the details and got the cash up front. Bobby argued that he'd made plans with Mel that night so he wouldn't be playing but after a rousing pep talk from Sid and with the promise of £150 to put in his top pocket he reluctantly agreed.

The flat was massive. It was like walking into one of those museums where they recreate how a posh Victorian living room would've looked like. It had a massive fireplace with fancy tiles around it, a crystal chandelier hung from an intricate ceiling rose which was about thirty feet from the ground. The walls were adorned with huge portraits and still life from a bygone era which hung in frames that were as big as the pictures themselves and the old teak bookshelf creaked with leather-cased volumes on every imaginable subject likely to bore the arse off you.

How the hell do you get a place like this?

Anthony (the posh-sounding twat) was apparently a doctor. He looked like he was 15 years old, so fuck knows what he was a doctor of. The party was filled with all of his beautiful successful friends with their clear skin and white teeth.

They quaffed champagne whilst having a jolly good time.

I felt very uncomfortable.

I've never liked being around these kinds of people. It's an inferiority complex pure and simple. They think they're better than me and I hate them for it. I retreat into Fife ned mode when confronted with their sorts. This normally puts their gas at a peep for a little time until they retreat into a collective huddle and whisper about my uncouthness.

We played the gig and they all clapped, and we drank their champagne and shared their recreational drugs. But by playing the Fife ned I had to drink *all* their champagne and take *all* their drugs.

Aye how do you like me now, eh?

Your performing monkey.

Throw us a coin and we'll fucking dance for you nae bother.

As the three of us stood in the large bay window belting out our tunes, I could feel the blackness coming over me.

The hatred. The jealousy. The anger.

Look at them with their happy wee lives, they've got it made. Beautiful partners and beautiful houses and beautiful jobs and beautiful cars.

Bastards.

What have I got?

Fuck all.

The bitterness flowed through me with every swig of the acrid champagne.

Cunts!

During a break I went to get acquainted with a lovely-looking lady who had been quietly staring at me from behind her champagne flute as we played. As I scanned the room for girls from behind my bass, I noticed she was the only one who appeared single so I made a bee line straight for her.

I was like the hungry lion scouring the plain for prey and she just so happened to be the antelope with the gammie leg.

I recalled Sid telling me years earlier after an encounter he had with an older lady at a horse racing event that posh lassies were 'dirty as fuck' and as I hadn't had sex in several months I was keen to put his theory to the test.

However, as I introduced myself and started to give her the chat, this gammie legged antelope turned out to be a hunter in disguise and quickly sent me scurrying for the safety of my pack with a couple of verbal shots.

I snapped up more champagne and whatever else was at hand. Bursting for a piss I want in search of the lavatory. I turned the door handle, but it was locked, and I could hear giggling from behind the frosted curtained glass.

"Needing in there, folks," I shouted as I rattled the glass. I stood there for about five minutes listening to the giggling and groans of pleasure coming from within.

I'm really bursting and some lucky bastard's in there shagging?

"Come on, I'm desperate," I banged the door loudly and shook the handle, but the fornicating occupants took no notice of my internal discomfort.

I hopped into the kitchen to see if the sink was free, thinking I could piss in there. It was free from people and dishes, but the sink was directly underneath a massive window that looked out onto a shared garden and other Georgian tenements across the way. I get stage fright at the best of times so slapping out my member to piss into a kitchen sink whilst dozens of windows stared back at me was a big no go.

By now the seal was almost breaking, my bladder was starting to ache. I hammered on the bathroom door once more to no avail.

Housed in an alcove within the hall I spied a plant and through sheer desperation and a large amount of pain I took it upon myself to empty my bladder into the large plant pot housing some exotic looking foliage.

AAAAAAAAAAAHHHHHHH, that feels magic!

"Excuse me, Jimmy? Jimmy? You can't do that here, bloody hell, Anthony …?" One of Anthony's friends had clocked me and went in search of the master of the house.

"Jimmy, what do you think you are doing? There are plenty of toilets in this house," Anthony shrieked as he arrived at the scene.

"Just takin' a cheeky piss, Tony," I replied in ecstasy as I zipped up my fly. "Aw the bogs were fu', man, an' ah was bursting, sorry eh?"

"Yes, that may be, but you can't pee in my bloody plant pot, that's an African Violet, it requires very careful watering," Anthony moaned.

"Ah wiz careful, ah hardly touched the leaves and ah didnae spill a drop on your carpet. Anyway, you wanted rock 'n' roll, my friend, you got it. Just be grateful I've no' launched your plasma oot the windae and shagged your wife."

"Right, Sid, Sidney?" Tony went off in search of my master.

"An' whit are you looking at, you arsehole?" I sneered as I launched into a tirade at one of Tony's pal who promptly told me to fuck off.

"You're telling me tae fuck off? You fuck off, you snobby cunt, this country's fu' o' pricks like you, calling yourself Scottish but talking wi' an English accent thinking you're better than us. Go on, you fuck off," Tony's pal fled so I sent a Bollinger bottle whistling past his head. It crashed against the wall, spewing glass and champagne everywhere. People burst out of the living room to check on the commotion.

Anthony returned in a hurry, having been briefed on events, shouting, "What the hell do you think you're playing at, Jimmy?"

The bathroom door crashed open as Sid and a lovely young lady tumbled out in a fit of laughter.

"Sophie?" a suited man yelped at the sight.

Sid tucked his shirt into his jeans and flattened the creases as the lassie looked on nervously.

"A'right?" Sid asked the gathered onlookers.

"Sophie, what the hell's going on?" The guy burst through the crowd and grabbed the guilty Sophie by the wrist.

"Right, I think you should all leave now, you've done enough harm for one evening," Anthony seethed.

"Whit's going on like?" Sid asked.

"Oh just the small matter of your friend pissing in my hallway and trying his best to trash the place and you shagging Brett's wife in the bathroom. Other than that, nothing much," Anthony snipped with blazing eyes.

"I didnae shag her, it was only a blow job," Sid laughed then looked at me in confusion. "What have you been up to?"

"Get out. Come on, get your things and leave. I want my money back too."

"Eh haud on the noo, Anthony. We played for well over an hour in there, you'll no' be getting your money back," Sid replied flatly.

"Well I want half the money back then, you've not completed your set, that was our agreement."

"We're no' jumping ship, pal, you're kicking us out so there'll be no refund, I'm afraid."

"But … but, you've been getting up to God knows what in there whilst he threw a bottle of champagne at my guest and violated a very expensive plant. I don't know what sort of parties you normally attend but I certainly do not tolerate that kind of behaviour at any of mine. Now, if you don't mind, I'll have my money back please."

Sid pushed past Tony and we gathered up our equipment to feeble taunts from the other guests. When we returned to the front door, we were confronted by the Eton Rifles. Tony and three of his chums blocked the exit.

"You're not leaving till Anthony's received his money," said one.

"Is that right, pal?" Sid said, laying his guitar down. "We can do this the easy way or the hard way, it's up to you?"

The four musketeers sized up the three amigos.

"You're quite correct, we can do it the easy way or the hard way. You give me back my money or we keep your instruments," Tony snorted.

Fuck, maybe these guys aren't as wet around the ears as we first thought.

"Whit?! Get oot the road you bunch o' fannies," Sid picked up his guitar and made for the door but one of Tony's friends made a lunge for his guitar and tried to pull it from Sid's grasp. This was the cue for the other lads to make a grab for my guitar and Bobby's drums. In the fracas Sid's guitar was thrown to the ground and in the rammy somebody else stood on it.

A muffled cracking noise omitted from the canvas case.

Sid turned white.

Then red.

Then really red.

He'd had this guitar since he was a kid, and somebody had just snapped its neck like a twig.

Somebody would pay.

In a raging fury Sid grabbed the person who had been stupid enough to try and take his guitar and butted him to the floor. At the same time Bobby hurled his foe against the wall and booted him in the stomach when he landed. Sid gave Tony a mean right hook and sent him sprawling through the living room door with a burst nose, prompting more attackers to spill into the hall. Bobby had picked up his snare drum and charged the cavalry. Like a human-sized bowling ball, he made light work of the pins.

I was still grappling with my pursuer on the floor. Legs and arms were sprawled everywhere as I tried to get some sort of purchase but he kept poking his fingers in my eye so I couldn't see. I was just getting the better of him when Sid grabbed him by the hair.

"Right you fucker, you're coming wi' us," Sid held his limp guitar in one hand and this poor squealing guy by the hair in the other. "Okay here's how this is gonnae work. I'm taking your wee pal here hostage until we get all our stuff safely down to the car. Once we've done that you get 'Nigel' here delivered back safely. A'right? A'RIGHT?" Sid screamed, shaking Nigel by the hair to emphasise his point, resulting in Nigel howling like a kicked dog.

"All right all right, you've made your point. Just let Melvin go and you can get your belongings and go back to which ever rock it was you came from," Tony sighed, exhausted, all the while dabbing at his burst nose with a cotton handkerchief.

"Right, boy's, let's move. We'll be back in a minute for the amps. In the meantime, *Melvin's* coming with us eh, Mel?"

"What?" Melvin uttered before Sid yanked his floppy hair in his fist and marched him downstairs.

We quickly gathered up our stuff and followed suit. Sid flung Nigel/Melvin in the passenger seat of Eleanor's car and guarded him whilst Bobby and I loaded our equipment in the back.

"Right, get back up there and get the amps. Tell them once we've got them safely loaded Melvin here will be released … what the fuck is he doing?" Sid wrenched the car door open and snatched Melvin's mobile phone from his ear then slapped him across the face.

"There'll be no' phoning the polis, Melvin. Try anything else and I'll break your fucking fingers, a'right?"

Shouts of encouragement for Melvin and curses of abuse at us were thrown from the windows up above. Bobby and I ignored them and returned to the flat to get the last of our equipment. The mood in the flat was understandably sour as we mumbled our goodbyes and apologies at the way events unfolded.

We returned safely with the amps and bundled them into the car.

"Right, man, let's get the fuck out of here before they call the polis," I hissed at Sid.

"I've been thinking … that lot up there just broke my pride and joy. Get your arses back up there and get all the champagne and whisky you can get from them. If you see anything of value, take that too," Sid said as he hawked then spat on the pavement, enjoying his new role as a self-appointed gangster.

"Whit?! Look we got what we came for let's just get the hell out of here, man," Bobby pleaded

"Aye come on, Sid, this is stupid. We're no' fucking robbing them, let's make tracks," I said, but Sid had that gleam in his eyes.

"Look, you pair of arseholes, get back up those stairs and get that booze afore I slap you both. Nobody breaks my guitar without paying."

"But what'll we say, 'eh we've got our stuff back, cheers an' aw that but now you've got to gie us your booze and jewellery?' They'll no' stand for that man. It's stealing. They'll call the polis if they haven't already done so."

"I dinnae care what you say to them just don't come down empty handed, go on, get," and Sid pointed back to the main door of the flat.

Bobby and I shrugged then turned around and headed for the entrance.

"This is bloody crazy, man. He's lost it," Bobby muttered as he tried to get in the door. "Shit I took it off the latch when we came down."

"Oh, this just keeps getting better," I sighed as I buzzed the intercom.

"Hello?" The line crackled.

"Eh … Tony? We need to come back upstairs likes."

"Oh no you don't. Where's Melvin?"

"Aye we do. Eh we've left some leads behind. Melvin will be up once we've got the leads."

We stood outside the door; heads bowed to the metal box that housed Tony's muffled replies waiting for an answer.

"What the fuck are you two up to? Get on with it," Sid loudly whispered from behind the car as Tony returned to the intercom.

"We've just checked and there are no leads here, return Melvin to us immediately."

"Look, Tony, we're no' pissing about here, the leads are up there somewhere and we need to come and get them. If you don't let us up, then we'll drive off with Melvin and take him to a lock up garage where we'll stick on some Steelers Wheel and have a jolly old time with him if you catch my drift?" I replied, cringing at my ridiculous attempt to play the hard man whilst Bobby shook his head with the heaviest look of disappointment in his eyes.

The buzzer sounded and we pushed the door open and trudged back upstairs.

"Let me do the talking," I said to Bobby.

Tony was standing at the open door with his arms folded.

"There are no leads in here, we've searched thoroughly."

"Aye, we ken. We've no come for the leads we've come for your booze and jewellery," I demanded, getting into the swing of things.

"You've what?" Tony wheezed, unfolding his arms to place them on his hips.

"Look, mate, we're no' arseholes. Really. It's just that Sid's raging you broke his guitar and he's wanting a wee drink to drown his sorrows so if you can just give us a couple of bottles of champagne or whatever you've got spare to shut him up, we can get out of your hair and forget this whole sordid affair ever took place," Bobby interrupted, trying to soothe the situation.

"That's exactly what you are, a complete bunch of arseholes."

Tony's phone rang, interrupting his insulting tirade.

"Hello, Melvin? Are you alright?" he asked. "Oh it's you, what the hell do you want? All right, all right, just don't hurt him okay? ... Yes I understand ..."

Tony sighed heavily then shoved his phone into his pocket and took off for the kitchen. I wasn't sure what we should be doing at this point and looked to Bobby for direction. Moping about in a stranger's hall, a stranger whose hall we'd just wrecked and whose friend we were holding hostage is not the most comfortable situation to find oneself in.

"That must've been Sid on the phone there," I whispered.

"You think?" Bobby replied sarcastically.

Tony came chinking back with a large plastic recycling box full of an assortment of bottled beverages. He handed it to me and then proceeded to take off his rather glamorous looking watch and threw it in amongst the bottles. Bobby reached into the box and fished it out then handed the watch back to Tony.

"Look, we're no' like that, keep your watch, we'll go and get Melvin back to you now," Bobby muttered, barely able to retain eye contact with Tony.

"Sorry again about the plant likes," I mumbled as we turned around and trudged back down the winding stairs, arms laden with an assortment of alcoholic beverages, and out onto the street.

"Right we've got the stuff, let him go and let's get the hell out of here," Bobby seethed as he threw the box of bevy into the back seat of the motor.

"Did you get a good haul?" Sid asked excitedly.

"Now is not the time, Sid," Bobby replied, pushing past Sid to open the passenger door. "Right come on, Melvin, out you get, it's over."

Melvin looked at Bobby then to Sid before launching himself out the seat.

He sprinted down the street in the opposite direction of the flat.

"Guess he's not going back to the party then?" Sid chuckled to himself.

"Prick," Bobby spat as he jumped into the seat newly vacated by Melvin.

"What did you say?" Sid shouted as he got into the driver's seat. I climbed in amongst the instruments in the back and closed the door as we screeched off into the night.

"What the hell was all that about, eh? We got all our gear out safely. Going back for booze? That was just crass, we're not fucking animals," Bobby argued.

"We didn't get any jewellery though," I chipped in.

"You shut your face, Dick Turpin," Bobby said as he turned to glower at me.

"A'right take it easy, man," I pleaded.

"They broke my guitar. They got off lightly if you ask me."

"Aye, aye, we've heard it a million times, your precious guitar. It's a lump of wood, it'll fix. It's no excuse to behave like a bunch of hooligans. Drop me off at the bus station. I'm going back to Fife, and I'll be taking my £150 with me."

"No can do, Bobby. That £500 is going to pay for the fixing of my precious lump of wood. If you're no' happy wi' that you can take it up wi' him. He started all that shite in there," Sid responded by thumbing in my direction.

"Whit?! You were shagging some boy's missus," I responded.

"I wasnae shagging her, I just got a blow job and I would've gotten away with it if you hadnae behaved like a fucking thug chucking shit aboot the hoose," Sid bellowed.

"Look Bobby, I'll see you right," I sighed, consigned to defeat.

We drove to the bus station in silence except for the random tutting and sighing that escaped from Bobby's mouth as he intermittently shook his head.

Other than the house party gig, the Edinburgh Festival was a rip-roaring success for Champions Of The Underdog. We had made plenty of money, not as much as we would have earned if we were all still in our respective jobs, but a hell of a lot more than we had earned at the start of the tour. We had worked hard to get it though. Some days we were playing up to five gigs. We also received a large amount of positive publicity.

The Evening News had given us a half page spread in their festival pull-out and The Scotsman had reviewed one of our gigs, giving us a complimentary four out of five stars, stating that 'This local three piece are taking live music back to its roots by embarking on a gruelling tour playing venues the length and breadth of the country … don't be a chump, be a champ(ion) and go see them if they are playing a venue near you.'

This type of publicity had led to Sid receiving a large number of calls from venues demanding to host us as part of the tour.

Things were looking up.

By the end of August, Sid had received the insurance money (much more than he'd originally paid for the van) and had splashed the cash on a ten-year-old Transit van.

It may not have had our band name splashed across the sides but at least it didn't stink of fish.

We thanked Eleanor for the hospitality, and she appeared over the moon when we presented her with a Champions Of The Underdog T-Shirt, well it was the least we could do seeing as she'd saved us a fortune.

CHAPTER 18

We drove up the A92 through Fife towards Dundee, stopping briefly at home so Bobby could spend a wee bit of time with Mel. Sid and I, having nothing much to do and nowhere else to go, felt obliged to spend the time with our parents.

It was raining heavily as we pulled into town which gave the place that all too familiar depressing feel.

They say you can't fully appreciate your hometown until you've spent some time away from it. I know we hadn't been away that long, but I got the feeling I could spend a lifetime away from this place and still never come to appreciate its bleak charms.

After listening to the usual moans and groans from my parents, it was onwards and upwards to Bonnie Dundee.

The Silvery Tay resembled dirty puddle water as we crossed its stretch towards the bright lights of the city and the shelter of another cheap Travelodge on the outskirts.

The gig diary was fully booked and we had a fortnight's stay in the City of Discovery to look forward to.

As well as the gigs in town we would also play in:

Broughty Ferry
Monifieth
Carnoustie
Arbroath
Brechin
Coupar Angus
Montrose
Forfar
Blair Atholl
Kirriemuir
Perth
Dunkeld

Pitlochry
Aberfeldy
Blairgowrie
Crieff
Killin

The fortnight turned into three weeks, but it was an enjoyable extended stay. The gigs were fast and furious and as expected the ones in the city itself gave us the most pleasure as the fans cheered their support.

At the more boisterous gigs Sid would produce a couple of bottles of the champagne we had procured earlier from our good friend Anthony and sprayed the captivated crowd with its contents. This little idea (which he nicked from a now defunct band we gigged with in the early days called The Newtown Grunts, who used to spray their fans with Buckfast) went down a storm and soon earned us a reputation of decadence within our storming sets.

Our exposure in Dundee enabled us to get a live performance slot plus an interview on the local radio station, Tay FM.

This was quite a nerve-racking experience.

Sid, however, took all in his stride.

"You're no' wearing shades, are you?" I asked Sid, appalled at his clichéd appearance as we exited the van.

"Aye, too right I am, how?"

"You look like a dick and it's dark. Do you no' think it's a bit, well, clichéd?"

"Fuck you, I'm the front man. I need to wear these, it's all about the vibe I give off, if I don't believe the hype how am I supposed to expect everyone else to, eh?"

With Sid looking like a wanker, we strolled into the studios of Tay FM for some serious airtime.

The DJ looked as big a wanker as Sid did. He was a man in his late forties and, like ourselves, was still trying to convince the world he was in his late teens and was still relevant. He had the trademark Converse trainers combined with faded ripped-at-the-knee jeans and he proudly wore an obscure band name t-shirt. His receding hairline had apparently been styled and he also sported a collection of piercings and tattoos. Everything about him screamed 'look at me, I'm still cool as fuck. No, I am, honest.'

He and Sid exchanged exuberant greetings of mutual heartfelt admiration like a preening peacock viewing its glorious appearance in a mirror for the first time.

We played a couple of tunes then Bobby and I sat in the corner as DJ rubbish directed all his shitey lazy arsed questions at Sid. Sid sat there answering the questions like Rodin's The Thinker, spouting out innuendos with a gusto. He looked completely at ease, relishing this opportunity as if he'd been preparing for it his whole life.

"I have," he answered when we climbed back into the van afterwards whilst hailing his media performance, "every time I'm on the toilet I conduct a sort of mock interview with myself, it's great practice. All those years sitting there visualising this moment has paid off. I was a natural in there," he grinned as he drove the van from the radio station car park.

"So every time you take a shit, you're pretending you're being interviewed? By who?" Bobby smirked, trying his best to stifle a belly laugh.

"Aye. So what? It's good practice," Sid replied with a look of embarrassment which quickly turned to anger. "I came across like the experienced campaigner back there, unlike you pair o' fannies sitting there staring at your feet."

Not wanting to pour petrol on the fire but unable to resist the opportunity, I offered my view on the subject.

"I can just imagine him sitting there on the pan with his troosers roond his ankles replying to John Peel's well-versed question; 'Well John, we've just released our … eeeeeeeeeehhh … second album and it's gone … aaaaaaaaaaaaahhhhh … down really … "plop" … well with our … "splash" … eeeeehhhh … "fart" …' ha ha ha what a fanny."

Bobby and I rolled around the van in hysterics as we conducted more mock interviews with sound effects.

Sid brought the van to a sudden halt.

"Fuck you, you pair o' pricks. Get out, go on, fuck off."

"You're no' kicking us out, man? We were only having a laugh," Bobby chuckled whilst wiping tears from his eyes.

"That's exactly what I'm doing, you ungrateful bastards, go on, out."

"Oh come on, don't be such a bairn, man. Can you no' take a joke?" I asked through aching jaws.

"No' coming from you pair of ungrateful cunts. I've just given us some brilliant exposure and all you can do is take the piss, well how funny is walking home, eh?"

"Oh for fuck's sake, Sid." We could see that he wouldn't budge so we had no other option than to get out the van. No sooner had we closed the van door when he rammed the gear into first and wheel spun away from us.

"What a moody bastard," Bobby moaned as we turned to look at each other by the side of the road approximately four miles from our digs.

"Eeeeeeeeehhhh … plop," and we both burst into hysterics again "… what a fanny."

The walk was long and uneventful, and we made it back to the Travelodge in one piece in little over an hour. Bobby and I met up with Sid in the morning, debating what sort of mood we'd find him in. We were both quite surprised to find him in high spirits.

It turns out the radio play was indeed good exposure as some events organiser in the highlands had heard it and got in touch with Sid through our website.

Dougie, the event's organiser, was putting on a mini festival in October to celebrate the end of summer/start of winter solstice type bullshit thing and wanted us as one of his acts.

"You see, dick heads, all my years of interview practice paid off. I've just landed us our first festival slot," Sid beamed. "Dougie said I came across as articulate and a visionary and we were just the sort of band he wanted for a headline slot."

"Nice one, Sid. What's the festival called?" Bobby cooed.

"It's something like Sun and Moon, I cannae really mind."

"It's no' gonnae be one of these hippy pagan type things where everyone's dancing about naked with their faces painted, is it?" I asked.

"Who gives a fuck what it is, we'll be top of the bill. Anyway, with all those naked hippy chicks floating around you might actually get a ride."

Sid's dig hurt.

I hadn't had sex since Debbie and me split up over five months ago and it was turning me into a right moody bastard. It wasn't for the lack of trying either but each knock back I received took a little bit of confidence from me.

Finding some quality alone time to relieve my frustrations wasn't easy either, especially when you're cooped up with these two day in, day out.

We had a rare Saturday afternoon off, our first since we started the tour, and I was all alone. Sid was away 'sorting out things for the band' which meant he was away shagging his latest conquest and Bobby was off meeting

Mel who had come up to Dundee for the weekend.

All alone and with nothing to do I decided to go up to Tannadice to check out my beloved Dundee United who were playing a league game against Motherwell. I asked Sid to come to the match with me for old times' sake, but he wasn't interested, said he couldn't give a fuck about football. This was typical behaviour from Sid. If anybody or anything dared spurn him, he instantly hated them. Forever. Because he didn't get signed up to play professional football as a kid, he never kicked a ball again; when Debbie turned down his advances, she was labelled a miserable frigid bitch and people who disliked his singing or song writing were ignorant fuckwits who shouldn't be at a gig.

There's a name for people like Sid.

Bampot.

I needn't have bothered going to the game. I watched a dreich, dour, nil-nil draw played out in front of a piss poor, callous crowd. I came away from the match feeling as I always do when my team have played shite.

Depressed.

I remembered why I didn't come to watch them anymore. The football was third rate at best with the ball being constantly blootered from one end of the park to the other. First touches to control the ball were ultimately met with two-footed lunges to reclaim the ball from the misplaced first touch. The cost to get in and savour those delights was also ridiculous. By the time I'd had a couple of pre match pints, a couple of pehs etcetera, etcetera, along with my ticket for the big game, I was nearly £50 out of pocket.

I was in a melancholic mood as I trudged back down the Hilltown, vowing never to go back yet knowing I would always return.

We had a gig that evening, so I had to remove myself from my depressive state. Thinking about the tour and spending the next couple of months roughing it with Sid and Bobby playing to unassuming crowds did little to bring a smile to my coupon though.

I really hope this is going to be worth it.

CHAPTER 19

It was nearing the end of September when we rolled into Aberdeen. The nights were fair drawing in, and it was noticeably a few degrees colder up there. The granite city stood proud against the fierce backdrop of the freezing North Sea as we checked into our usual cheap lodgings on the edge of the city. The three of us cramming into another little room.

Again.

I was now fed up with touring. I was becoming increasingly pissed off with the same boring routine of wandering around whichever town we were playing in all day waiting to play a couple of sets in the evening then heading back to spend the night in our shitty room sleeping either on the sofa or bed with Sid or Bobby depending on the rotation.

It was like Groundhog Day except the towns and cities changed and Bill Murray sadly wasn't around to offer us his crazy insight.

Occasionally we would try and rehearse new songs but finding the space to do so proved harder than you would think. Tensions within the camp were at an all time high and the mood was at an all time low.

To the impartial spectator we may even have appeared to be like a proper rock 'n' roll act, turning up to gigs separately, not muttering a word to each other before or during the gig and then pissing off separately at the end only to spend the entire night sniffing each other's farts and listening to Bobby snoring.

We were like Fleetwood Mac without the talent.

Or the songs.

I wish we had Stevie Nicks.

Having said all of that though, the Aberdeen gigs were by far the best we had done in terms of appreciation. The large student following welcomed us with open arms and for the week and a half we spent in Aberdeen there was only one gig that we didn't do an encore and that was only because someone set the fire alarm off towards the end of our set.

For the couple of hours we were on stage each night, I felt energised again and at peace with myself and the world and I knew that completing this tour was the right thing to do, that we had to keep going.

It was only the other 22 hours that were torture.

Days turned into weeks and gigs rolled into one as we ventured up into the highlands.

Sid had sold this tour to me with a promise of amazing scenery and a chance to see some of the places we'd never seen before.

Other than obscure stretches of road due to piss-poor map-reading, this turned out to be utter bollocks.

As we were now in quite possibly the most scenic part of the country, I thought I'd take the van for a wee jaunty to explore the mystical highlands. Sid, however, was having none of it. The van was his and he needed it for, well he never exactly said what he needed it for, he just drummed up some excuse that he might require it at a minute's notice to go see somebody about another gig.

Utter shite.

Not wanting to be perturbed I set off on my own adventure and found myself viewing sites such as the Culloden battlefield and Urquhart Castle on the banks of Loch Ness with a bunch of ageing North American tourists aboard a cramped and somewhat dilapidated coach.

At first I found them all to be a right royal pain in the arse with their snap happy ways. They would all push past me and shove oversized zoom lenses in my face as they clicked away at various landmarks through dirty sodden windows whilst spraying me with an assortment of Tunnock's treats and shortbread which were lazily distributed by the guide.

Nothing depicts a desperate cry for authenticity better than stereotypical Scottish fare.

I could just imagine the punters showing their neighbours the resulting pictures back home in Texas.

"Jeez, Bob, great shot. What is it I'm looking at here?"

"Why that's Urrkart Castle on the banks of Luck Ness, beautiful ain't it?"

"Uh hu. Although it's pretty hard to see clearly through all the grime on the bus window."

"Yeah, well we would've gotten out the coach to take a closer look, but it would not stop raining."

In the end I warmed to their innocent questions and childlike fascination with our country's history. I acted as unofficial tour guide for them making up ridiculous stories simply for my own amusement.

"You see that spot right there?" I asked an unsuspecting punter looking out the bus window as we sat parked in a lay-by.

"Sure, that rocky hilly thing?"

"Aye, that's the spot. Well back in 1692 we were under English rule, much like we are today, only back then it was a violent, hostile melting pot of a place. There was a young Scottish Laird who went by the name of Whispering Whisky McSporran due to his love of the local tipple and because his vocal chords were crushed as he was hung by English forces for not bowing to an English Officer."

"They hung you for that back then? Sweet Jesus."

"Oh aye and for much less. The English were just going about hanging folk and chopping them up willy nilly and for the slightest thing too. Speaking Scots, not bowing their heads. One guy was even decapitated for daring to ask an English officer to stop raping his wife. Anyway, Whispering Whisky McSporran was hanging, kicking, and struggling from this tree. I think it could've been ... hmm ... that one over there, whilst the English laughed and spat on him. Suddenly from out of nowhere his brother Mad Malky McSporran appeared and with his bow took aim with a flaming arrow and shot it straight throw the hanging rope, splitting it in two, plunging Whispering Whisky McSporran to the ground. Mad Malky, carrying two claymores, that's a big Scottish sword that I'll tell you about later, threw one to his brother who caught it and leapt to his feet. The two brothers quickly embraced before standing back to back to face the English Army. There were at least 55 English, but some official reports say it was closer to 100. The brothers hacked and chopped and stabbed their way to victory. In the end the ground was awash with bloody, butchered English corpses. The brothers themselves were unhurt except for a small cut to Mad Malky's cheek. These two guys armed with only a sword each defeated an English legion. Pretty amazing stuff, eh? And that's what that rocky mound is, it's the grave of all the English soldiers that the McSporrans defeated."

"Wow, that is amazing. That's one couple of tough dudes."

"Oh aye they were that. But that's not all they did. Before the McSporrans headed back to their castle they rifled the pockets and satchels of the defeated English army to take what treasure they could. They found golden goblets and caskets of silver and gold coinage. They filled up the satchels with the plunder, but they couldn't find anywhere to put all the gold coins as they didn't have any pockets in their kilts. Mad Malky came up with a solution. He set about castrating the dead English army. Malky and Whispering Whisky scooped out the testicles and made wee purses with the scrotums into which they placed all the looted coins. They tied the scrotum pouches together and hung them around the front of their kilts. When they returned home, they received a hero's welcome as they threw the gold coins to the awaiting villagers and there was much celebrating and feasting. The scrotum pouches they used were the talk of the town and soon everyone was wearing these new McSporrans with their kilts to pay homage to the brother's magnificent achievement. In fact, we still wear Sporrans with our kilts today. That event is also responsible for the famous saying 'The English have got no balls'."

"I have heard that saying. I had no idea that's why you guys wore Sporrans. They never tell you this stuff in the guide books."

"Well they wouldn't, would they? These tour guides are all printed in England and as they like to think that we're all part of the same country they don't want to put in any of the stuff where they come across as pompous arseholes and we look like the heroes. There's loads of stories you never hear of, in about half an hour we'll pass the place where a bunch of Scots peasants armed only with dry sticks defeated a large advancing English army and subsequently invented the game of football by booting the decapitated head of the English king into a giant spider's web ..."

CHAPTER 20

I returned back to base feeling rejuvenated from my whistle stop tour only to find the collective mood much the same as it was when I left. Bobby was still moody and pissed off, so he spent his free time with Mel, and Sid was still being a selfish prick as he continued with his usual routine of shagging the local dames and finalising upcoming tour dates.

I should have stayed on that coach.

Sid, in my absence (not that I would've had a say anyway), decided we would skip Inverness and return there for the Sun and Moon festival towards the end of October so we headed on up the country to play some smaller towns and smaller venues in the mean time.

We drove along the slightly hazardous stretch of road known as the A96 to perform in the towns of Nairn, Forres, and Elgin to paltry crowds who were either too stoned or smacked out of their weather-beaten faces to appreciate us or perhaps they just thought we were shite.

Therefore, we about turned after the frosty reception we'd received and high tailed it through the Black Isle stopping to play an uneventful night in Dingwall before heading onto the smaller town of Dornoch. Passing through the town to our little B&B I was struck by how quiet the place was. This is normally a good indication to the size of crowd we would attract, and I was starting to get the familiar nauseating feeling in the pit of my stomach as I imagined another gig being played to a handful of punters who talked to each other throughout our set and would only show encouragement if we trashed our equipment or set fire to ourselves.

I'm happy to report that in Dornoch I was about to be proved very wrong.

The venue was a hotel with a large bar area suitable for hosting live music. If you had fifty people in there it would be classed as rammed and on that fine evening that's exactly the number we had.

With everyone packed into the room the atmosphere was vibrant, hot, and sweaty and we took to the stage to loud cheering.

Nothing better than a warm welcome to massage the ego.

The three of us all played out of our respective skins and due to the rousing reception we received, banter quickly flew backwards and forwards between ourselves and the crowd.

Sid was loving it. Bobby was loving it and I was loving it too. If you could play a gig like that every night, life would be sweet.

I noticed a girl in the crowd after about two songs. She had started the gig right at the back but had slowly worked her way forward so that by the end of our fifth song she was standing right in front of me which was a little unnerving at first.

After a few winks and smiles from her I was like a horny teenager. I slapped and worked my bass with renewed energy as I showed off my skills to this new fan. The fretboard was like an extension of my manhood. My hand slipped up and down, I caressed it slowly then beat it hard, never taking my gaze from hers. At the end of each song, she clapped and whooped and never took her eyes from mine.

I might just be in here.

We finished our set half an hour later than planned due to the crowd's constant chanting of 'one more tune.' We could only oblige and launched into a few older songs from Sid's back catalogue.

Afterwards, as we packed up our gear, I was approached by the girl that had been staring at me throughout our repertoire.

"Hi how are you? I'm Maggie," she smiled and offered me her hand.

"Pleased to meet you, Maggie. I'm Jimmy … eh … did you enjoy the show?" I asked, trying my hardest to appear cool.

"Yeah it was great, I've been hearing lots about you. I think you guys will go far."

"We're going to Thurso soon, that's pretty far … a ha ha ha ha."

Laughing at your own jokes, Jimmy, what the fuck?

Come on, I said play it cool.

"Ha ha ha," she politely laughed back, "do you fancy a drink?"

"Eh yeah that would be great. Let me just finish packing up this stuff and I'll come and join you."

I excitedly told Sid and Bobby the good news as we shoved our equipment into the van

"Which one is she?" Sid asked.

"The one that was down the front and couldn't take her eyes off me all night " I replied triumphantly.

"Nice work, man. Go for it," Bobby enthused, offering me his clenched fist to be bumped.

"The one with the hair like a burst mattress?" Sid snorted.

"Fuck off, you're just jealous that I'm getting some attention."

"Listen, pal, I could have any piece of fanny in that place if I wanted it. Unlike you I'm not restricted to one crazy haired burd offering me her wares. I've normally got three or four burds to choose between. It's no' easy being me by the way."

"Aye, well I don't see you batting away a legion of adoring lassies in there tonight. So if you don't mind I'm going back inside to charm the pants off this wee cutie. I'll see you chaps later, I dinnae want you two cramping my style."

"Aye whatever, Romeo. I wouldn't ride her into battle," Sid sneered as he closed the van doors.

I didn't care what he thought though because I was bursting with anticipation, I felt like I was … Reid brothers sing a long chorus time … 'sitting on top of the world.'

It was time for me to get back in the game.

Maggie and I chatted until chucking out time. I felt completely at ease in her company as I sat and listened attentively whilst she talked about everything and anything.

I was bursting for a piss at one point but couldn't find a decent opening in her constant chatter to make my excuses and relieve myself. Through fear of soiling my well-worn jeans, I had to cut the story about her teenage years short and made the agonising walk to the urinals. Inside, as I took the longest piss in the world, I panicked about what she thought of my hasty exit.

Was that a bit rude?

I couldn't help it though, I was in agony.

I wonder if she finds me interesting?

Was I being a dick?

Will she still be there when I return?

Fuck, I bet she couldn't wait to leg it.

Oh come on piss, she'll be half way home at this rate.

I hadn't suffered this much anxiety about a girl since I was a teenager.

Wash the hands, that's the stuff.

Quick check in the mirror, aye that'll have to do.

Right here we go …

No need to panic pal, see there she is right where you left her.

I was relieved and delighted to see Maggie still sitting there sipping her vodka and coke.

I don't know what all the panic was for, she loved my banter and she found me hilarious. She kept stroking my leg as she chuckled loudly at my latest witty remark, making me hornier by the minute.

She wasn't the best-looking girl in the world but she had that something, that aura, that made her … well … sexy. Yeah, that was it. She was sexy as fuck. She had an inner confidence too as if to say this is me, if you don't like it, there's the door now get the fuck out of my face.

She told me she was a primary school teacher and worked at the local school and because she had to work in the morning she couldn't get up to 'anything wild tonight.'

"Well I guess it is a school night," I replied and she laughed some more and stroked my leg again before digging her nails into my tender thighs.

Fucking hell, I'm gonnae burst if she keeps that up.

"Tomorrow's Friday so we can meet up then and have a few drinks and then see what happens …" she said with a glint in her eye that made me want to grab her and kiss her face off.

"Shite. We're playing up in Wick tomorrow so … where can I meet you?"

"That's cool, I can come up and see you play and then we could head back to mine afterwards … if you want to?"

I'd love nothing more in the world.

Don't sound too keen though, play it cool my boy.

"Yeah could do … fuck it, that sounds like an excellent plan."

We swapped phone numbers and I got a goodnight snog for my troubles. After her tongue entered my mouth, I got a bit carried away in the passion of the kiss and quickly worked my hand from her back to her chest and started to massage her breasts.

"Uh uh uh. Not on a school night, remember?" And she tilted her head back and laughed that infectious laugh of hers.

Fuck.

I think I love her.

I was feeling drunk and happy as I climbed into the bed I was sharing with Bobby, who was already fast asleep and snoring loudly. I switched off the bed side light and rolled over to sleep.

My phone beeped then vibrated loudly against the cheap wooden bedside table. I turned to check the message. The pitch-black room was illuminated by the rays of

CAN'T W8 2 C U TOMOZ NITE LUVERBOY SWEET DREAMS. MAGGIE XX

Apart from the fact that she texted like a 12-year-old I loved everything about my new woman, and I rolled over with a smile on my face to enter a beautiful peaceful sleep.

I awoke the next morning in the best mood I'd been in a long time. It's amusing to think that the knowledge of a guaranteed shag can leave you feeling giddy with excitement and bursting with energy.

I was also a complete nightmare to be around that whole day.

"Can you no' shut up about Maggie for two bloody seconds. She must be mental, the fucking tide wouldn't take you out," Sid argued after listening to me prattle on and on about her over breakfast.

"Not only is she taking me out, Sidney, my dear boy. Tonight, she is also going to shag me out. Out of my fucking brains that is a ha ha ha ha ha."

"Aye, we'll see. Once she sees you standing in front of her in the buff she'll be reaching for her Rampant Rabbit quicker than you can say 'I'll just get ma clothes' ha ha."

"Yes yes very good, Sidney, you really are a very witty gentleman. But speaking of which have you still got some of those Viagra on you?"

Sid had bought a number of Viagra tablets from a dodgy looking bloke in Aberdeen. They were only purchased (so he said) to assist him after marathon shagging sessions so that he could carry on fucking the next chick in the long line who were waiting patiently outside the hotel room door. "Sometimes I'm totally knackered and just want to go to sleep but that would just be selfish to the burds concerned so I pop one of these little beauties and everyone's happy."

Aye right Sid.

"And what the fuck are you going to do with Viagra? Have an all-night wankathon?" Sid roared with laughter.

"What the hell do you think I'm gonnae do with it? Look, I've no' had sex for donkeys and I dinnae want to make a tit of myself on the first night so come on, dinnae be selfish. I only want one."

"Viagra'll no' stop you making a tit of yourself, you're fucked on that one ha ha." Sid continued with his piss poor repertoire.

175

"Are you sure that's the best idea you've ever had, Jimmy?" chipped in Bobby. "I mean if you shag her on Viagra the first night, she'll be thinking this is how you shag all the time. She'll be sorely disappointed a few weeks down the line when you're wiping your cock clean on her curtains after a steamy two-minute session ha ha ha." Bobby and Sid both fell into hysterics at my sad predicament.

"Aye very good, lap it up. You're probably right though I don't want to be setting myself up for a big fall, maybe I'd better no' take it."

"Knowing your luck it'd get stuck in your throat and all you'd be left with is a stiff neck aha ha ha."

Cue more hilarious laughter from Sid and Bobby.

Pricks.

"You cannae take the piss out of me today, boys. I'm invincible. I'm on top of the world. I've got a great girl meeting me tonight for some fun and frolics and nothing you pair o' fannies can say will take the shine off it. Things are looking up for me, this could be the start of something new. A great woman by my side to share life's thrills with. The only other thing I need is for us to get signed, make a few million quid, and life will be just peachy."

"Aye, well I'm working on that. I've got a couple of leads that I'm chasing up so watch this space," Sid grinned.

"Really? Fucking brilliant, man, what's the score?" I asked, palpitating at the thought of ending this tiresome tour and retreating to a country studio with a kilo of cocaine and a vat of whisky to record our first album as professional musicians.

"Just wait and see. Patience, my friends, is a virtue. Besides, I dinnae want to tell you anything till it's set in stone otherwise you'll just get complacent."

"Oh man that'd be amazing if it works out, Sid. Mind and keep us posted as soon as you hear anything," drooled Bobby.

CHAPTER 21

We arrived in Wick at about 2 p.m. on the Friday afternoon and as the gig wasn't until 8 p.m. that night I decided to continue with my usual routine of walking around the town trying to get a feel for the place. I normally walk about with my hands in my pockets, trying to look moody and interesting so the locals will know that I'm the bass player in the best band in the country who's about to play a superb rocking gig in their town that very evening and that they should be extremely grateful for having someone of my high standing gracing their streets.

But that afternoon I'd just received another text from my new girlfriend.

1 HOUR 2 GO THEN IL B HEDIN UP ROAD 2 C U. IM XCITED ALREDY. THINK IL WEAR MY FK ME BOOTS HOPE THEY DONT PUT U OFF UR PLAYIN!! MAGGIE XXXX

Despite being concerned about the spelling education the children were receiving at Maggie's school I walked around Wick like a simpleton on speed. I was shouting 'hello's' and 'lovely days' to the bemused locals who didn't share my enthusiasm for the biting gale accompanied by horizontal drizzle.

I paid swift visits to The Wick Heritage Museum and herring mart and then paid a longer visit to Mackays Hotel for a couple of cheeky pints and photograph opportunity as it is apparently housed on the world's shortest street. But don't take my word for it, the fine folk at The Guinness book of records have verified it too.

Brilliant.

Maggie arrived as we were sound checking and she looked gorgeous. She wore her fuck me boots as promised and my concentration was already waning as I winked and smiled at her in between my checks.

"Jimmy, you've got all night to gaze into her eyes, can you no' just concentrate on getting this sound check sorted. You're messing up my rhythm."

"Sorry, Bobby. I'm just excited at seeing her and nervous too. I mean, tonight's the night."

"Christ you'd think it was the first time you'd shagged a burd, get a grip, man. She's no' exactly stunning, is she? But in your case any port in a storm, eh?" Sid sneered.

"Piss off. I just dinnae want to fuck this up that's all."

"You're thinking about it too much, it's only sex. If you're that concerned about lasting the pace, away and have a wank in the toilets. That should add at least a couple of minutes onto your minute and half. Aye she's a lucky girl."

Sid was right though; I was thinking about it too much. In fact, it was all I was thinking about.

I felt like a striker going through a barren patch. I'd been at my last club for so long that I'd become stagnant, a little lazy even. When I first joined, I was scoring all the time and I was putting in loads of effort, the fans loved me, they shouted my name in ecstasy when I scored. But towards the end of my career with F.C. Debbie there wasn't a lot for the fans to sing about. I was by my own admission disinterested in training. On match day I'd got into a stale routine and was happy just to stroll into the box and tap in the odd rebound off the post. Gone were the long tantalising mazy dribbles that left the fans begging for more. I'd become too complacent and although shocked and deeply hurt when I was released by F.C. Debbie, I understood that the club was only looking after its best interests. They were after a striker who showed hunger, desire, and commitment as well as scoring lots of goals. I was no longer that player. Instead F.C. Debbie had opted to sign a different type of striker, a good old-fashioned centre forward. Not a lot of skill but hard as nails and as loyal and daft as a pet dog.

I wasn't for the scrap heap yet though. I'd been thrown a lifeline and given a trial by Maggie United. Although not quite in the same league as F.C. Debbie, Maggie United was a club on the rise who hadn't yet fulfilled their potential and by signing me I just might be the man to lead them to the Premier League. Yes, I was that man all right. I can do this. I used to score goals for fun. I'll soon find the back of the net again, it's all about getting my confidence back and when I do, oh boy, I'm going to score a shit load.

The gig was a poor one.

We all played well enough, but the sparsely populated crowd seemed more intent on discussing the trials and tribulations of their working week than listening to us. Except for one drunk guy who was more than happy to be moshing out of time in his own little world whilst spilling his pint all over himself as well as the annoyed, listless punters.

I couldn't have cared less though.

This gig was a mere irrelevance that I had to put up with before getting to the main event.

Maggie watched me from a bar stool at the side of the room whilst sipping her coke through a straw and playing with her hair.

God she looks cute.

"Right, boys. I'm off, don't wait up," I announced as I loaded the last of my equipment into the back of the van.

"Enjoy your night, man. Hope it all goes well. We'll hear about it tomorrow," Bobby grinned as he grabbed me by the neck and shook me with a little too much force. "go get her, tiger."

"Aye see you the morn. Meet us back here about three, we'll be hitting the road shortly after," Sid mumbled from inside the van as he continued arranging the instruments.

"Nae bother, chief," I replied, rubbing my bruised neck. "Right, here goes nothing. It's show time."

Maggie drove us back to her place in Dornoch. She drove an old burgundy Fiat Punto that rattled and thudded over every pothole as we made our way down the road.

What is it with teachers and shite cars?

We arrived back at her flat and immediately downed a bottle of red wine to calm our nerves because the sexual tension was rife in the car. We weren't as chatty and as comfortable in each other's company as we had been last night. For Maggie it was probably because she hadn't had a drink, for me it was because I was shitting myself about putting in a good performance.

I wanted to get the initial shagging out of the way quick smart so we could relax and then spend the rest of the night exploring each other.

I was starting to feel tense and wondered what must be going through her mind.

Is there anything she expects of me?

She's a teacher.

I've never fucked a teacher before.

I hope she's not into dominating and spanking. I cannae be doing with that shite.

We kissed on the couch.

Not mad, passionate snogging, but gentle kissing. It was soft and sensual and not really what I had expected or was used to, but I enjoyed it anyway.

We pulled apart and Maggie led me by the hand into the bedroom.

My heart rate immediately rose, and I could hear its dull rampant pulse echoing in my eardrum.

"You get undressed. I'm just going to slip into something a little more comfortable," she winked and left to go into the en-suite bathroom.

I pulled my clothes off as fast as I could and threw them in a heap on the floor, remembering my socks at the last minute before diving under the pristine white, ironed, cotton sheets.

Nice touch.

"Fuck that's cold!" I gasped in shock

I lay on my back, taking in my surroundings.

There were a couple of photographs on her dresser that could have been Maggie with her sisters or maybe her friends.

Could be both.

She described them all in great detail last night but none of their faces matched the pictures I had made of them in my mind. They looked like holiday snaps, you know the one where one joker's pulling a stupid face whilst the others stand there grimacing unaware of the wacky person's hilarious stunt.

These covers smell nice.

She must use fabric softener.

Very welcoming.

Was that just for me or does she always use it?

What's taking her so long?

Wonder what she keeps in that wardrobe?

I peered under the sheet at my naked body.

Nothing much happening down there.

I started to panic at the thought of not being able to get it up.

Shit, I wish I'd got that Viagra just in case.

There was a click of the bathroom door then the sound of a light chord being pulled.

My heart was now close to palpitating.

Please don't have a weird-looking fanny.

The door opened and in walked Maggie from the dark looking like an angel wearing a see-through nightie

Holy fucking shit that is probably the sexiest looking sight that I have ever seen.

Her nipples stood pert against the silken fabric, and I could just make out the trace of a neatly trimmed Brazilian.

What a body.

It took about a millisecond for the signal from my eyes to be processed by my brain and then relayed to my cock who responded in the only way he knew how.

Attention!

The initial get-it-out-of-the-way sex was fast and furious and fucking tremendous.

I managed to last about six minutes which I thought was bloody good going seeing as I'd not had sex for seven months. Plus, I'd not had time to have a wank earlier.

The second session was amazing and saw us drinking wine whilst we fucked. A first for me and very enjoyable if a bit uncomfortable. I'd drained two very large glasses of the stuff and was tucking into my third as I fucked her doggy style.

I could feel and hear the wine sloshing around my belly as I proudly watched my cock burrow its way into her snug wet pussy from behind.

I had to be careful and not overdo it lest I shower her back with warm burgundy bile.

Afterwards, as we lay there naked and sweaty and speechless in tangled satisfaction, Maggie suddenly threw back the covers and darted out of the bedroom. I was too knackered and content to delve deeper into the meaning of her drastic disappearance.

She appeared a couple of minutes later waving a little zip lock bag in the air which I noticed on further inspection contained a white powder.

"I'd forgotten about this. I love fucking on coke," she beamed with that crazy look of hers.

If she'd put the contract in front of me there and then I'd have signed for Maggie United for life.

Yep, this is a club that's going places.

We snorted and fucked and fucked and snorted till I had nothing left to give. My cock was in tatters. It hadn't been that badly beaten since I'd discovered the joys of masturbating as a kid. I was terrified that the next time I came there would only be a waft of dust shooting from my cock like a wheeze of talcum powder from its squeezed bottle.

I was drunk and high and satisfied and in love, not just with Maggie but with the whole fucking world. I can't remember the last time I felt that way.

That feeling of utter peace and contentment.

The Grim Reaper could've dragged my pasty white arse out the door to use me as a sharpening stone for his rusty scythe and I wouldn't have objected.

Such is the power of sex and drugs and rock 'n' roll.

We kissed and cuddled and looked into each other's eyes but never uttered a word.

We didn't have to.

We could feel the connection, we could communicate by touch, by sight, by smell.

Bliss.

Not ecstasy.

Bliss.

There is a difference.

I had thought of them all as the same.

Different words to try and explain the meaning of joy.

Just words.

That night I felt I knew the meaning.

Not a meaning, a feeling.

Perhaps it was the coke, maybe the drink. But combined with amazing sex with a woman I didn't really know they fused to form a holy trinity of utter delight that no word in the dictionary could convey.

Bliss.

It didn't even come close.

I could see light starting to creep in under the curtains as I cradled Maggie in my arms and reluctantly slipped off into a majestic sleep.

I don't ever want to stop feeling like I do now

Bliss …

Bliss …

Bliss …

CHAPTER 22

"Wahay! Here comes The Shagger," Bobby announced to the world as I finally entered the lounge bar the next day.

"There are only two reasons a man has a look on his puss like that after spending the night with a burd," Sid exclaimed whilst pointing at my puss.

"Oh aye? And what are they then?" I asked warily.

"One, you couldn't get it up and left her feeling pissed off and frustrated or two, you shot your load after 30 seconds and left her feeling frustrated and pissed off."

Sidney was about to find out that there is actually a third reason a man could have a look like mine on his puss after spending the night with a burd.

"So what happened, man? You a'right?" Bobby asked, pulling his chair in closer to the table to assume the 'fuck, this could be serious chat'. "You want a pint?"

"No thanks. Aye I'm a'right …" my head dropped.

How to do this?

"Fuck it, aye gie's a whisky. Better make it a double."

"Well come on spill it, which one was it? Impotence or premature ejaculation?" Sid asked whilst rubbing his hands together with glee.

"Fuck off. Neither, I've no got a problem downstairs, everything's working fine and dandy."

"It's okay if you do, Jimmy, it happens to all of us at some point," Bobby shouted back as he made his way up to the bar.

"Does it fuck, speak for yourself, gay boy. I've never had a problem with my cock," boasted Sid, raising his fist in a triumphant phallic salute.

A couple enjoying their pub lunch at the next table looked over at the commotion and then at each other.

"Keep your bloody voices down," I whispered. "I've no' got a problem a'right? My knob's red raw with all the shagging I've done. It's just …"

"What? What's the matter wi' you then?"

"I don't want to talk about it. It's too weird, too embarrassing, you'll only take the piss."

"Ho ho ya beauty," shouted Sid, clapping and rubbing his hands together even faster, making the couple eating their steak pies look up again. "This has to be good. Here Bobby 'mon and here this. He's scared we'll take the piss … come on, hurry up wi' that drink I've got to hear this."

"Shut up, Sid. Stop being a prick. The whole bar doesnae have to ken about it. Look, Jimmy, we'll no' take the piss there's no need for you to get embarrassed or anything. It's probably something that's happened to us," soothed Bobby, nodding at Sid as he gently placed my nip on the table.

"Aye, sorry, man. I'll no' take the piss. Was it her time of the month? Was she a heavy bleeder likes? I mind I shagged this burd on her period and man, fucking hell, it was like a scene from a horror film. My cock and balls were splattered with blood, it was even halfway up my chest. I looked like I'd just walked out of a slaughterhouse having used my dick as the weapon," roared Sid.

There was a clatter of cutlery onto plates and the screech of chairs over laminate flooring as the couple sitting next to us threw their napkins onto the table in disgust and promptly exited the room.

"So, what happened then, come on?" Sid panted with excitement.

"It's just …" I couldn't get the words out because I couldn't really get my head around what had just happened.

"Just spit it out," Sid demanded.

"Okay. Okay," I let out a huge sigh then inhaled a double whisky as I decided to tell my tale.

"We had a great night. We were up all night shagging and drinking then shagging some more. I lost count of the number of times I came; my nuts are like fucking raisins now. I'd only seen some of the moves she was pulling off in a porno flick, it was fantastic, the best sex I've ever had."

"Well, what are you greetin' for then? She sounds like a right dirty bitch, you lucky bastard. I still wouldnae shag her though, it's that hair o' hers, looks like a heid o' pubes," Sid declared.

"Will you shut up? I'm getting to it. So, we passed out and only slept for a couple of hours 'cause we'd had a wee bit coke. Anyway, Maggie wakes up and the first thing she does is chop up a huge line and snorts it all in one go. She comes up with a wild look in her eye and says, 'Have you ever tried anal sex?'"

"Dirty bitch!" Sid exclaimed excitedly.

"So I'm thinking here we go, happy days, 'cause I've never really tried it before. Except that one time with Debs but I only got it halfway up before she started moaning that it hurt. So, she's got this look in her eye and I'm like holy shit I'm gonnae fuck her up the arse, but not only that, she wants me to do it too …"

"Dirty bitch!"

"So I say to her that I've only kind of tried it but I'm well up for shagging her up the arse. But she says, 'Not me, you', and I'm like all confused. 'What do you mean?' I say to her and she goes on to explain about butt plugs and fingers up the arse and the male G-spot and how her ex-boyfriend used to love it and—"

"Woah, woah, woah. Fucking hell, that's a bit much. You didnae take it up the arse, did you?" asked a horrified Sid.

"No, no she's right. The G-spot for a guy is near his prostate, it does work, I'm telling you," Bobby replied whilst gently sipping at his pint.

"WHAT THE FUCK?! You've taken it up the arse? You're fucking sick, man," Sid asked Bobby with a look of horror on his face.

"Piss off. Aye I've tried it. Mel and me experiment and sometimes she slips her finger up my arse when we're having sex. Honestly you should try it, it makes your orgasm so much more … powerful," Bobby pondered, waving his hands about like he was discussing the merits of yoga over a basic exercise routine.

"I'm no' hearing this right. Mel shoves *HER* finger up *YOUR* arse? And *YOU* let her? Jesus fucking Christ, I'll no' be able to look her in the eye again," Sid wailed.

"Look, will you let me finish my story?" Gaining courage from Bobby's experiences, I decided to continue. "So anyway, she talks me round to it, saying, like Bobby said, 'that it's the best orgasm you'll ever have.' So I took a chunky line for Dutch courage and—"

"No, no, no, no," Sid shouted, waving both his hands in the air in submission, "this is just wrong, I cannae believe I'm listening to this, you're just as sick as he is," and he pointed accusingly at Bobby, "the pair of you are fucking sick. Bloody poofters, man."

"I was just experimenting … I'm no' gonnae tell you anymore," I tailed off, feeling deflated by accusations of homosexual tendencies.

"Oh no, you cannae leave it like this. You've already crossed that line. Spit it oot," demanded Sid.

"Apparently loads of guys do it with their burds … I'm kneeling on the bed and she's lying in front of me 'cause she's gonnae suck me off whilst doing the deed. According to her that's when it works best. She lubes up this wee dildo thing and pokes it up my arse. It's not very nice I'll tell you that for nothing but once she takes my cock in her mouth and starts giving me head it does start to feel a bit better …"

A middle-aged couple sat down at the recently vacated table and a member of the bar staff came over to remove the half-eaten steak pies and wipe the table clean.

"I'm rock hard, right, and she's sucking me like I've never been sucked before in my life …"

"Dirty bitch!" Sid grinned, moving in closer.

"And she starts moving this thing up and down my arse and it's feeling really good …"

"See I told you, Sid. You should try it," Bobby enthused.

"Fuck off!"

The recently arrived couple clinked their glasses together and took a sip of their pint of bitter and gin and tonic in unison whilst staring lovingly into each other's eyes.

"… and she's sucking me faster and harder and moving this dildo deeper and faster and I'm about to cum and I mean I'm about to fucking explode. This feeling rumbles from the pit of your stomach, fires into your prostate or G-spot, cannons off your balls and then it comes shooting along your cock like water from a fireman's hose. All the time she's still sucking the heid off my cock and I'm shooting my load further down her throat when suddenly she whips the dildo out of my arse …"

"Oh no!" cried Bobby with his head in his hands.

"I lost control; I don't know what happened. It must've been 'cause I was coming or 'cause I'd never done it before," I whined.

"What happened?!" Sid asked wide eyed and open mouthed.

"I collapsed in a heap and shat all over her bed."

The couple spat their respective pint and gin and tonic into each other's faces before fleeing for the sanctuary of another table.

"Oh my fucking god. You stupid bastard," Sid shouted.

"I've heard that happens, man. It's cause your muscles are relaxed," Bobby added.

"How? Has it happened to you?" I asked desperately, hoping that he had suffered a similar fate.

"No, but a guy I went to college with, it happened to him so it's no' that big a deal."

"No' that big a deal?! He's just taken a dump on the lassie's bed," Sid cried hysterically.

"It gets worse," I whimpered.

"How the fuck can it possibly get any worse?!" Sid roared, slapping the table.

"Well, I was all embarrassed and that, but Maggie was like 'don't worry it happens' and I'm like she's just trying to make me feel better, so I picked up my clothes and nipped off to the bathroom to get cleaned up, wipe my arse you know? I got dressed quickly, thinking about how I've managed to completely fuck up the best thing that's happened to me in ages. I was actually punching myself in the face through utter rage, man. I calmed down but I was mortified, so fucking embarrassed … I mean I had to go help her get things cleaned up in the bedroom you know, cannae have a lassie you've just met cleaning your shite up from her nice covers. Anyway, I opened the door and the smell of shit hit me straight away, making me gag, but that shock quickly faded as I saw Maggie. …" I swallowed hard and shook my head as the image pierced my brain again "… writhing about on the bed covered in my shit."

"I'm gonnae puke, this is fucked up," Sid boaked as he bounded in the direction of the toilets.

"It was in her hair and everything …"

"Jeezo, man. That's pretty heavy shit. No pun intended. Honestly? She was covered in your shit? What did you do?" Bobby asked whilst casually sipping his pint.

"What the fuck do you think I did? I legged it. Ran out the door. I ran for miles before I managed to hitch a lift. I cut through bushes and fields so she wouldn't follow me. What the fuck is wrong with people?"

"You probably shouldn't have told us that story," Bobby said, averting his eyes from mine.

"I didn't want to tell you but you two made me. Christ the last thing I wanted to do was announce it to the bloody world. I cannae get my head round it. I think I'll be scarred for life. She was just like my old dog Sooty, you ken the wee Jack Russell? When we'd take her for a walk up the woods as kids she'd run into the nearest field and find the biggest cow pat she could find to roll around in. She'd come back panting and covered in the stuff."

"I think the best thing you can do is put it down to experience and never speak about it again."

"Aye nae bother, I'll just file it under shite shenanigans and shove it to the back of my mind and hope it never rears its ugly head again, eh? The annoying thing is up until then Maggie was absolutely fantastic. She's pretty and funny, bright and interesting. I really thought we were going to have something there. Now all I can picture is Mrs Melville my old teacher lying naked smearing herself in shite. It's horrendous. I think I need a good drink to get this out of my system. I'll tell you something though …"

Sid returned to the table and finished the remains of his pint which the hovering bar maid promptly collected.

"… I'm never having anything shoved up my arse ever again."

The barmaid looked at me and then to Bobby and Sid.

"Good night last night then, boys?" She smirked before returning to the bar with the empty glasses as my face turned beetroot.

"Right, I think that's as good a cue as any to get the fuck out of here and never show our faces again. Jimmy, you're an idiot. An unlucky idiot, but an idiot all the same. I never want to hear you mention that incident ever again. Dirty, filthy bitch," Sid groaned, shaking his head as he imagined what I'd seen.

"I'm hardly gonnae tell anyone that story, am I? And I don't want you two taking the piss either, a'right?"

"I cannae make any promises on that one. It does give a new meaning to you being shite in bed though, eh?" Sid replied before roaring with laughter at his own joke.

CHAPTER 23

We piled into the van in silence and drove north, heading for Gills Bay, stopping off at John o' Groats for a photo opportunity. This was my first visit to the place often mentioned in celebrity charity walks and I was left disappointed by the nothingness of the little village. Other than the fact it was the furthest mainland point from Land's End there was little else you would want to boast about.

At Gills Bay we picked up the ferry headed for St. Margaret's Hope on Orkney. The journey itself lasted about an hour and was a smooth crossing. I'd heard epic tales of stormy seas and gut-wrenching sickness on the ferry crossings to Orkney and Shetland but this was a stroll in the park.

We alighted, or is it disembarked?

Either way we drove off the ferry and headed for Kirkwall where we had a couple of gigs planned. We passed the famous Churchill Barriers which were constructed during the Second World War after a German U-boat torpedoed HMS Royal Oak. 833 crewmen perished, prompting Winston Churchill to put permanent barriers in place to stop a similar thing happening again. The waters are littered with block ships deliberately sunk to defend the Sounds and gives an eerie reminder of the tragedy that occurred over half a century ago. (Note to self. Stop plagiarising from tour guides. It makes you sound like an arsehole.)

This was also my first trip to the Orkney Islands and as we had a week there and only four gigs scheduled, I planned to make the most of my free days and actually get the chance to see some of the historic sites. In my head I pictured myself marching around Orkney like Neil Oliver gasping in orgasmic wonder at the primeval dwellings and standing stones.

After checking into our hostel, and with a free night on the cards, the three of us walked into town to sample some Orcadian hospitality. It gave us the chance to check out the pubs we'd be playing in and hand out some flyers and generally do a bit of self-promotion with the local music fans.

Eight bottles of Orkney Dark Island later at The Auld Motor Hoose put to bed any plans of exploring Kirkwall or meeting the fans.

Tomorrow is another day though, as they say.

"Fucking hell my heid feels like it spent the night in a vice," Sid groaned and with those immortal words we set off back into town to get ready for our evening set.

A couple of hair of the dogs were required to take the edge off the hangover before we eventually took to the stage to a fairly decent reception. The gig was progressing as well as could be expected after a night on the Dark Island but thankfully the adrenaline eventually kicked in, without which we would have played a much shorter morose set.

Sid copped off with a pretty young Kiwi girl and left the building pretty much as soon as we'd said our 'Thank you and good nights', leaving Bobby and me to pack up the gear into the van.

But it wasn't all bad.

When we headed back into the bar, neither Bobby or myself had to put our hands in our pockets all night which was a great relief as Sid had also conveniently forgotten to pay us, leaving us with only a tenner to share. The other plus was that we managed to flog a handful of t-shirts and CDs from the back of the van, leaving us with enough pocket money to see us right for a couple of nights on the bevy and Sid would be none the wiser.

Thank you, Kirkwall.

We played a second night in Kirkwall to pretty much the same crowd we'd played the night previously, so they weren't as keen to hear our songs or dip their hands in their pockets this time around. Mind you, I can't say I blame them, Bobby and me nearly bled them dry the night before.

Early the next morning we were up and hangover free and ready to go to Stromness.

Stromness had a much better feel about it than Kirkwall and I much preferred the town simply because of the Olde worlde buildings and street layout. The gigs, however, were much better in Kirkwall due to the fact that the crowd seemed to appreciate what we were trying to do.

There was no keeping of hands in pocket in Stromness.

Neither was there any selling of t-shirts or CDs.

The locals are either tight or smart. Or possibly both.

On the Friday we had a day off, so I had proposed an action-packed day of site seeing. Sid reluctantly let me take the van so I could visit Skara Brae and the Ring of Brodgar. He also eventually agreed to accompany Bobby and myself on the wee trip only on the condition that he could be photographed standing by the road sign for the village of Twatt.

I did get to have my Neil Oliver moment as I stomped around the ancient stones, looking back into Bobby's camera.

If only I still had my long locks to flick.

I'd love to come back here during the summer solstice.

Or winter.

Nah, fuck that it'd be freezing.

Summer it is then.

I'd sit with my back placed firmly on one of the stones and drink whisky all night and watch the sun come up. Not for any religious reasons, I just think it would be a really cool thing to do. To see the sun break the horizon at exactly the moment our ancestors predicted would be pretty fucking mind blowing. Other worldly.

How the hell did they do it?

Bobby smoked a heavily laden joint as we discussed this fact which resulted in him being left completely freaked out by the enormity it. Our visit to the Ring made me wish for a return to a simpler time.

No boss, no phones, no laws, no rules.

Just the sun and the moon.

And fucking.

Man, I sound like a hippy.

This is some good grass, Bobby.

I declined the weed as we visited the prehistoric settlement of Skara Brae. However, I didn't get to enjoy this crazy stone village due to the fact that Sid was 'bored stupid with all this shite' and demanded we 'hurry up' so he could get his photograph taken. After a quick birl round the stanes we were off to do Sid's thing.

We pulled up next to the site and Sid bounded from the van. He stood next to the sign grinning like a dafty whilst thinking that he was the first person in the world to have come up with the idea. Bobby took a couple of photographs and tried his best not to look too embarrassed.

Sidney, Twatt indeed.

Our whistle stop tour of the Neolithic sites of Orkney was a worthwhile expedition though. Bobby and I agreed to return and do the whole summer solstice thing properly.

Sleeping bags, bottle of Macallan, and a pile of weed.

With the storm clouds closing in as we journeyed back, I remember feeling refreshed from my brief glimpse of paganism and felt ready to tackle the chaotic mainland again.

Sitting on the ferry as we crossed the Pentland Firth, I remembered something that was bugging me throughout this trip.

There ARE trees on Orkney.

CHAPTER 24

The A836 was our chosen route, or rather Sid's chosen route to get to Ullapool so he could add to his wacky road sign photo collection by visiting the village of Tongue.

Twatt and Tongue.

Hilarious.

Sid wasn't only content with being snapped by the village sign. After stopping for refreshments at a shop he came running back to the van with a huge grin slapped across his face and proceeded to hand us the present he'd bought us. A nice pin badge with 'I love Tongue' written across. Bobby and I threw ours in the glove compartment, never to be seen again, but Sid pinned his to his chest and wore it with pride.

Wrong on so many levels.

We were driving through some of the country's most spectacular scenery whilst negotiating some of the country's worst roads, singing along to the radio when my phone rung.

I looked at the call display. 'Debs' it read.

My heart skipped a beat.

Was she phoning to say that she'd made a huge mistake, and would I take her back?

I hope so.

"Hey, Debs. How's it going?"

"Fuck you, Jimmy! What the hell do you think you're up to?"

"Eh sorry, you've lost me there, Debs."

"Don't play the smart arse, you've completely humiliated me, why did you do it, Jimmy? Why?"

"Look, Debs, calm down. I have no idea what the hell you're talking about."

"Those stupid videos you made of us are on the internet, you bastard. Why the hell did you do it? Get them off of there right now and I swear to God you'd better delete the originals or Daniel is going to kill you."

"Eh? Internet? I've not put anything on the internet, I swear …"

Sid started sniggering away to himself at the wheel and it suddenly all became clear in my mind.

I still had some video clips stored in my phone of Debbie performing various sex acts on me. They were filmed when we were still a couple, and we'd have a laugh watching them afterwards. I should have deleted them when we broke up, but I just couldn't do it. I admit with a slight feeling of shame that on the long, lonely nights since we'd split, I'd found comfort in watching them again. I felt that if I deleted them, then that would be it. It would finally be over. I foolishly thought that by hanging onto those images there might be a slim chance for the two of us.

Fear.

That's all it was. The fear of losing her. I guess it's the same with those people you read about in the news who've hoarded so much junk over the years that their house is now completely filled. It's the fear. The fear that they might suddenly need something.

Sid's sniggering had turned to stifled laughter, but I couldn't let Debbie know it was him who'd posted the clips on the internet because that would just finish her. I had to come up with something.

"Debbie, I swear, I never posted those videos online. I'd never do that to you; my phone must've been hacked. I love you—"

"Piss off. Get them off the internet now, you sick little prick, everyone at work has seen them and oh God … "

Debbie trailed off as she imagined what everyone was thinking of her. She started sobbing and I could hear rustling in my ear.

"Dinnae cry it'll be okay," I whined.

But she'd gone and been replaced by her psychotic new boyfriend.

"Right, you dirty wee bastard, you'd better get that shite off that internet within the next five minutes. What the fuck did you do that for anyway, eh? Think you're funny? Think you're the big man trying to get back at me, eh? The lassie's beside herself wi' worry so I'm gonnae put you through the same, a'right?"

"Look, Danny, there's been a big misunderstanding here, I didnae put that stuff on the internet, but I'll get it removed right away, you dinnae have to worry about that."

"Oh I'm no' worried. It's you that's gonnae be worried cause I'm coming for you."

"Look, man, there's nae need for aw that shite, I'll get it sorted, it's cool,"

I grovelled.

"Naw. It's no' cool. You've made her life a fucking misery. So now I'm gonnae do the same to yours. And that's no' a threat by the way, that's a promise. Get that shite aff the internet now, you sad wee man, and delete the original. Understand?"

"Aye."

"Good. Watch your back, Jimmy. I'm coming for you."

"Come on Danny—"

The phone went dead.

Along with the microscopic chances that I might have had of getting back with Debs. Sid's controlled laughter had now erupted like water bursting from a dam. The noise thundered round the van.

"Ah ha ha ha that was brilliant, you should have heard you, 'Oh please Danny, I love you Debs' ah ha ha."

"You fucking idiot. What are you playing at, eh? You've humiliated Debbie, you stupid prick." My anger got the better of me and I lunged to punch Sid but Bobby, who was sat in the middle, managed to deflect the force of the blow so I only managed to land a glancing blow on Sid's shoulder. He broke hard and pulled the van into the side of the road.

"What are you doing? Take it easy, man. I was only messing. It was meant to be a laugh—"

"Well I don't see anyone laughing here. Except you. You've gone too far this time. Debbie sounds like she's ready to throw herself from a bridge and now Danny Foster wants to use my head as a fucking punch bag. Aye that's totally hilarious, man, brilliant, well done. Tell him, Bobby."

"Aye that's totally out of order, Sid. Debbie didn't deserve that; you'd better apologise to her."

"Dinnae do that. That'll just make this a whole lot worse if she knows it was you who did it. She fucking hates you. The thought of you looking at her in those videos would send her over the edge," I exclaimed, shaking with rage.

"What? I thought she looked good in them, didn't know she had it in her," Sid mocked.

"Shut the fuck up. Just get them off the internet, eh? Why did you do it? When?" I raged.

"It was meant to be a laugh; I didn't know she'd react like that, did I? Anyway, you shouldn't leave your phone lying about."

"How the fuck was she meant to react, eh? Invite her family round for the big screening?" I screamed.

We both went into our phones. Sid to take the footage off the internet and myself to delete the originals.

I didn't even ponder.

With Danny Foster's words ringing in my ear, I hit delete.

"You done it?" I growled.

"Yes," Sid squeaked, not daring to make eye contact.

"Let me see."

Sid passed me his phone and I checked all the documents to see if he'd completely wiped it. I opened the van door, stepped out, then smashed his phone to pieces on the tarmac.

"What the fuck are you doing?" wailed Sid as he watched his iPhone being dismantled in front of him.

"It was either your phone or your head," and I handed him back his phone in little black shards.

CHAPTER 25

We drove to Ullapool in silence then parked up and ate our fish and chips from the award-winning chip shop that Sid had generously bought us. You can tell when Sid's feeling guilty because he acts as though nothing has happened but does his best to be nice to you so you'll stop being mad with him.

But I couldn't.

I couldn't forgive him for his latest stunt.

Over the years he's played pranks and taken the piss and we'd fallen out and made up again. But it was always between me and him.

This was about Debs and was unforgivable.

I ate my fish supper overlooking Loch Broom, but I was too angry, too bitter, too regretful to enjoy the view.

I slowly fumed at Sid's stupidity and my own selfishness that caused me to keep those clips that led to Sid's ridiculous 'prank.'

I thought of Debbie and the pain and anguish she must be going through. I thought about the hurt I'd inadvertently caused her, and I hated myself for it.

No, I despised myself.

But I despised Sid more.

He'll pay for this; I'll make sure of that.

As I picked up a handful of chips saturated with brown sauce, I thought of Danny Foster.

'Watch your back. I'm coming for you.'

I choked as I tried to swallow the chips. I coughed and spluttered and regained my composure but through tear-filled eyes all I could see was Danny Foster bearing down on me.

"You all right, man?" Bobby asked.

"Aye, wonderful. He's just ruined any chance I had of getting back with Debbie but other than that life's just grand."

Sid looked at me but could only maintain eye contact for a few seconds before he shoved a piece of fish into his gob and stared at his feet.

Fuck you, Sid.

"Fuck it, let's go get a drink. I really need a pint," I demanded.

We stayed in Ullapool for a couple of nights, playing a gig in each of them, but I really wasn't in the mood. My mind was preoccupied with Debbie and the resulting kicking I'd receive from Danny. 'Watch your back.' It was the only phrase that went through my mind. It was like a terrifying mantra that couldn't stop.

As I played on stage, I kept scanning the crowd to see if he would appear. But he didn't.

In a way I wish he would've so we could just get this over with. He could beat me to a pulp then we could carry on with our lives and live happily ever after.

"Come on, man, you've been playing shite for days now, get it together," Sid moaned at me.

"Are you taking the piss? It's thanks to you, ya fuckwit, that my head's a wreck. All I can think about is poor Debs and her nut case of a boyfriend who's ready to boot several shades of brown out of me at any minute. Apologies for being a wee bitty distracted."

Gigs came and went over the next few days as we stopped and played to various towns and villages. We went over to Skye and played a couple there, but I honestly cannot remember one gig from the other. Bobby tried his best to console me, and Sid even took us on a sight-seeing adventure of the island, but I couldn't appreciate its beauty. I had received another phone call from Danny asking if I'd removed the offending article and deleted the original to which I replied yes.

He replied with "Good boy. You're still a dead man though." I had done what he asked but the threat of violence had increased.

How can that be fair?

After a week of moping about in a zombie-like state and with my fear and paranoia increasing, Sid decided, as he'd been the cause of the 'big misunderstanding', he'd rectify and pacify the situation.

"Danny? A'right it's Sid. Let's cut to the chase here, there's been a mix up, it shouldn't have happened but it did and Jimmy's really sorry so let's just stop all the school boy threats eh? … So what are you saying like? … Okay well if you want to play it like that then here's how it's gonnae be. You lay a finger on him and me and Bobby will be round your door quicker than a flash to sort you out … Oh really? I dinnae think so pal. Aye? NAW, YOU'RE A

DEAD MAN! … I think I may have made it worse," Sid said nervously as he handed me back my phone.

"How the hell can it be any worse?" I pleaded.

"He's one angry dude. He kept going on about how you should have thought of the consequences before you posted the images online."

"I didn't post the fucking images, YOU did."

"Aye, well he doesn't know that. He's after you, man. Even the threat of me and Bobby didn't work."

"It's cool, Jimmy. Dinnae worry, man. He's full o' wind and pish. He'd know better than to try anything. He's just pissed off and trying to act like the big man cause it's all he knows. He's no' got the brain capacity to sit down and have a deep discussion so he deals with it in the only way he knows how to. Violence."

"Cheers, Bobby. You've cheered me up no end, I feel so much better now," I sarcastically replied.

"Dinnae worry, he'll be more afraid of the thought of Sid and me sorting him out."

"Dunno about that, Bobby. He did sound very angry like," Sid interjected.

"How, what did he say?" asked Bobby.

"Eh I'll tell you later," Sid said, nodding at me, hoping I wouldn't notice.

I did.

"Oh this is just one big fucking mess. Nice one, Sid," I groaned as my head sunk into my hands.

"Sorry, man. Dinnae worry, we'll look after you," Bobby consoled.

That week felt like the longest week of my life. I wanted to call Debbie to try and explain to her that the only reason I'd kept the videos was because I still loved her and wanted to be with her. It was all I had left of our relationship. I hadn't kept them for seedy reasons or to show them to friends. Nobody, up until the minute Sid decided to post them online under the heading 'My bitch ex-girlfriend', had even seen them.

They were for our eyes only.

I wanted to tell her that it was Sid who had decided to upload them and that none of this was my fault but most of all I wanted to tell her that I wish I could turn back the clock so I could tell Sid to shove his stupid tour up his arse and that we could still be together.

I couldn't call though because I was scared.

I was scared it would upset her more and it would definitely upset me to hear her upset as I listened to her calling me all the useless names under the sun.

I would just have to deal with this clusterfuck the best I could and move on.

So I text her with the pathetic explanation that my phone had gone missing during one of our gigs and whoever took it must've been responsible for the terrible deed. I ended it with many sincere apologies and a couple of kisses for old times' sake.

She didn't reply though.

If I hadn't waited for a couple of weeks to pass by before texting her this miserable made-up excuse, she might have believed me.

CHAPTER 26

Fort William was our next destination and we arrived on a cold, grey, autumnal day. The mighty Ben Nevis was obscured by cloud cover. I've been to Fort William on several occasions and still had never seen the summit. It could be a myth that it's actually Britain's highest mountain. We could be hiding a tiny little hill or a giant mountain peak under all that cloud for all I know.

"Seriously, behind all that cloud is the world's third highest mountain. You've got Everest, K2, and then the mighty Ben Nevis." Nobody would be any wiser.

My world was still in turmoil and my brain continued to send messages of guilt, fear, and paranoia to my stomach, leaving me feeling apathetic and miserable but with a heightened state of alertness.

My relationship with Sid had soured and we were barely talking.

It was a shame for Bobby who as per usual was stuck in the middle, but he did sympathise with my predicament. Normally quick with a soothing word or a speech of uplifting endearment there was nothing he could say to drag me from my morose. I had gotten over my fear of being attacked by Danny Foster whilst on stage so for two hours a night I felt free again, free from my destructive thoughts.

The rest of the day was a different matter.

Whilst in Fort William Sid received a call on his new phone from the organiser of the Sun and Moon festival advising him that it had been cancelled due to poor sales and this put Sid in a foul mood. Not because the festival had been cancelled, I think he was upset as he saw the lack of ticket sales as a direct insult to us because we were one of the top acts.

But what can you expect when there appears to be a new festival announced every week? Punters aren't made of money and they aren't daft, they can catch the whiff of a bandwagon being leapt upon from 3000 paces.

So Sid and me sulked about the town looking grimmer than the weather.

Bobby, thankfully for him, had Mel to lean on. She'd newly arrived to spend a couple of days with us.

Whilst having a quiet drink with Bobby and Mel, I asked her if she could have a word with Debbie for me when she returned home. I didn't want her to do my dirty work for me. I just wanted her to let Debbie know how sorry I was and that it wasn't my fault and maybe she could help smooth things over between us.

Come to think of it I did want her to do my dirty work, dirty work that I shouldn't have had to do but thanks to my good friend Sid she would have to.

I even got an angry phone call from my mother who had somehow heard the news of the unfortunate online incident and subjected me to another torrent of abuse about my disgraceful behaviour, not growing up and acting my age etcetera, etcetera.

How the hell did she find out?

I shuddered to think.

I suddenly had the image of my mum and dad perusing the internet for porn to spice up their love life and coming across the clip of Debbie and me.

I shook my head to rid me of the thought and went and found solace in a large quantity of alcohol.

Our final gig in Fort William was one of the better ones we'd played of late. Partly because of the volume I'd consumed but also because of the underlying anger and resentment coursing through my own and Sid's veins.

It was a fast, furious, wild and angry set we played, and the drunken Friday night crowd lapped it up.

The next morning it was with a heavy head and heart that we said farewell to Fort William and headed for Kinlochleven.

Ben Nevis still refused to come out from beneath the clouds.

About a couple of miles outside Fort William we could hear banging and muffled shouting coming from the back of the van.

"What the hell is that?" Sid queried and hastily pulled the van over into a deserted but scenic lay-by.

We all jumped out and waited to see what was responsible for the din. Sid opened the van doors and out jumped a young lassie with her hand clasped to her mouth. She shot passed us and dived into the bushes at the side of the road to throw up over wildflowers and discarded rubbish. The three of us looked at each other in bemusement. Once she'd finished being sick, she approached us, wiping her mouth with the back of her hand whilst squinting from the morning glare.

"Got any water?" she asked.

"No, no no. First of all, who the hell are you and secondly how the hell did you get into my van?" asked a stunned Sid.

"I need water … my head's thumping. You got any paracetamol?"

"Bobby, get her some water, eh?" Sid demanded whilst staring inquisitively at our intruder.

Bobby handed her a bottle of lukewarm highland spring that had been rolling about the passenger footwell for several days and she guzzled it down.

"No paracetamol?" she asked, gasping from the exertion.

"NO," we replied in indignation.

"You gonnae tell us how you came to be in our van?"

"I wasn't doing anything … I wasn't trying to nick your stuff or anything. I was at your gig last night, it was amazing by the way, and well I was really drunk and I couldn't go home in that state, my mum and dad would've killed me, so I saw you putting your stuff into the van and then climbed in afterwards for a wee sleep. I was going to leave in the morning, but I must've slept in."

"Did you lock the van?" Sid asked me with a penetrating glare.

"Aye … aye I think so," I replied, now starting to doubt myself.

"Well, you didn't do a very good job if sleeping beauty managed to sneak in, did you?" shouted Sid, pointing at the girl who by now had had enough of standing and was sitting cross legged on the lay-by kerb next to the van.

"Dinnae get smart wi' me, I've got enough on my mind thanks to you," I argued.

"All our stuff could've been nicked, you arsehole, then where would be, eh? All this work for nothing? You better buck your ideas up."

"Or what?" I shouted back and made to lunge for Sid but Bobby the human bear stepped in between us.

"Boys, boys, behave. Sid, from now on you're in charge of locking the van at night. Like he says, he's got other things on his mind, a'right? Now young lady, what's your name?" said Bobby, taking control of the situation.

"Molly."

"Hello, Molly. I'm Bobby, this is Sid and that's Jimmy."

"I know. I've followed you for ages. I was at both your gigs in Fort William, they were savage, but last night's was the best. I've been following you online and reading your updates, me and my friends had been looking forward to these gigs for months. I think you guys are going to be big."

"You think so?" asked a clearly delighted Sid. "Well, that's the plan anyway," he added in a somewhat cooler fashion.

"Oh yeah, this tour you're doing is a great idea, my pals and me are all big fans," Molly smiled.

"Thanks, so do you live in Fort William?"

"Yeah, but I hate it. It's boring, there's nothing to do—"

"Right well we'd better get you back home then," Sid interrupted as Molly started a teenage rant.

"Aye jump in the back, Molly, and we'll drop you off," I added.

"Eh, can I not come with you to Kinlochleven? I was coming to your gig tonight anyway, so you'd save me getting a lift. I don't mind sitting in the back."

We all looked at each other and then back at Molly.

"How old are you, Molly?" Bobby asked.

"I'm 17," she replied before polishing off the last of the tepid water and rubbing in the dribbles on her Debbie Harry t-shirt.

"You don't look it, you look closer to 15," Sid stated.

"Fuck off!" At that she dug out her wallet which was hooked to a chain on her ripped black jeans and fumbled around inside. "See?" she protested and held up a green bit of plastic whilst tapping it with her free hand for added emphasis. "Here's my provisional licence, SE-VEN-TEEN, and I'll be 18 in a few weeks."

We all craned our necks for a closer inspection.

"Okay fair do's. I suppose we can give you a lift to Kinlochleven but you'll have to make your own way back from there we're no' offering a rock 'n' roll taxi service here," Sid chuckled. "Right, jump in and if you whitey on any of our gear I'll boot your arse all the way back to Fort William."

"Awesome!" Molly shouted and jumped into the back of the van, showing no ill effects from her puking episode five minutes earlier.

Oh to be young again.

We drove the short distance to Kinlochleven in contemplative silence as we enjoyed the surrounding scenery.

Driving along the edge of Loch Leven I watched the mist cling to the sides of the mountains like a damp blanket and wished I was at home with Debbie.

I was the damp blanket to her cold hard mountain.

Thoughts like that just left me irritable and unable to enjoy the moment so I closed my eyes for the last few miles in an attempt to shut out any other depressing images from my mind.

After arriving in Kinlochleven I went for a walk around the village partly because it's what I do but mainly to get away from the machine-gun-like drivel from a teenage lassie on the subject of music post 1999, in particular band names beginning with the letter A.

There wasn't much to the village itself as I shuffled through its deserted streets sucking on a Regal King Size which I had found earlier in the glove compartment next to our discarded tongue badges.

Free smoke-bonus.

The backdrop to the town, however, is spectacular. The rugged mountains covered in mist rolling down into the loch conjured up images in my mind of times gone by in this village. A village people born of hard work and toil, slaving away in the aluminium works.

The industry has all gone now to be replaced by, well, I'm not exactly sure what it's been replaced by. The village seems to be modelling itself on towns like Fort William and Aviemore in going for that whole extreme outdoorsy type place.

Come to Kinlochleven and climb our mountains and be sporty on our loch and be totally awesome whilst doing it.

I don't like this new way of selling the great outdoors to the younger generation. It's too shiny and false. There was a programme on the telly when I was a kid which I didn't care for too much at the time. Mainly because I was a kid and had better things to do but I recall it fondly now.

It was called Weir's Way. Tom Weir used to ramble about the countryside of Scotland telling stories and meeting the local folk in nothing but a woolly bunnet and plus fours.

Not a shiny cagoule in sight, oh no, he was a tweed man, hard as nails and probably weighed about a tonne by the time he came off the mountains having soaked up all that rain in his woolly gear.

Nowadays these wee towns like Kinlochleven are filled with shops selling you luminous clothing so you can be easily found by rescuers when trapped under an avalanche. Survival gear like ropes, folding shovels and axes in case you get lost up the mountains and have to bed in for the night until you can be rescued the next day. GPS devices so you can tell the mountain rescue team exactly where you can be found after breaking your leg having been distracted by the thick mist and accidentally plummeting from the side of the mountain.

It appears to me that the extreme sport outdoorsy type person of today is a city-dwelling fool who should never be allowed within 20 miles of a hill range or moor or loch to save themselves the embarrassment and the mountain rescue folk the time and hassle of rescuing them.

But having bought the Land Rover Discovery and sporting the hideous tweed jacket with pink corduroy trousers combo the satisfaction of poncing about the city without having tasted any rugged action starts to gnaw away at their Sauvignon-pickled minds. And so, having loaded up on shiny new luminous cagoules and a couple of tins of Red Bull, they head for the hills with a blatant disregard for their or the resulting rescuers' safety.

Pricks.

But I suppose you've got to move with the times and do whatever it is you have to do to survive the difficult financial climate. Adapt or die as somebody once said.

After all, it wouldn't make good business sense for the shop owners to appeal to the Tom Weir type people of this world who would perhaps only purchase a new pair of boots every 20 odd years and maybe a pair of laces every 10. Nope, better to jazz it up and sell it onto the unsuspecting morons who buy into the idea that climbing a hill or cycling a trail is AWESOME!

It's not.

It's enjoyable.

Let's just leave it at that, eh?

I returned to our hotel confused as to whether or not I agreed or disagreed to the promotion of climbing mountains and bombing up and down lochs on Jet Skis as awesome. Sure, it provides a living for the local folks, and it fleeces the people with too much money into thinking they need all this stuff to have an awesome time whilst doing their extreme activity of choice, both of which I am all for, but at what cost, eh?

If I'm ever asked the question of who would attend my ideal dinner party, you know like the one the broadsheets ask celebrities, then I'm inviting Tom Weir so we could have a lengthy discussion once the plates have been cleared over the state of modern outdoor activities and its impact upon the environment and society at large.

CHAPTER 27

The two gigs we had that weekend were played to an audience of mature hill walkers who were negotiating the West Highland Way. With most of the 96 miles behind them they only had half a day's walking ahead to reach their final destination of Fort William and felt they were due a wee celebration and so duly unzipped their luminous cagoules and let what was left of their hair down to sup pints of the local ale brewed in the micro brewery across the road and foot tap along to the sounds of the infamous Champions Of The Underdog.

Molly's thirst and knowledge for all things musical lead to her setting up and sound checking for our gigs.

She certainly knew her way around a fret board and the three of us were quietly impressed by her work. I could certainly get used to not lugging amps and leads from van to stage and back every evening.

On Monday morning we were packed up and ready to go to Oban when we said our goodbyes to Molly.

"Right, Molly, thanks for your help, it was much appreciated. How are you getting back to Fort William?" asked Sid whilst trying to sound like he actually gave a fuck about her wellbeing.

"Eh I dunno, I hadn't really thought about that. I thought I would join you for the rest of your tour …?" And her sentence petered out as she stared at her tattered converse shoes and fidgeted on the spot.

"I dinnae think so, hen. You'd better head home, I'm sure your mum and dad will be worried about you," Bobby butted in.

"But think about it, I could be your roadie. You said yourselves that I did a great job. No more carrying all your stuff from the van. I could tune the instruments and sound check for you. You'd look like a proper band. Don't you want to be a proper band or are you just going to carry on playing rock stars?" she accused whilst meeting all of our glares head on.

"Look, Molly, it's been really cool having you set up for us, I hate doing all that shite, but we hardly get any pay as it is plus there's no place for you to stay," I reasoned.

"And there's no room for you in the van. It's illegal to sit in the back without a—" Bobby added and he was just about to deliver a lengthy speech on the importance of health and safety when Molly thankfully cut in.

"I don't want paid, I could just crash on the floor in one of your rooms or I could sleep in the van, I could guard it. All you'd have to do is buy my food and I'd set up and dismantle and tune and sound check for every gig. You lads wouldn't have to do a thing, you'd be like a professional band just turning up backstage, having a few beers, walking on stage, and doing your stuff and then walking off again without having to lift a finger," Molly enthused as she painted a rather nice picture.

She really was quite infectious when she got started.

"So, just to make sure I'm hearing you right, you want to roadie for us for the rest of the tour and I wouldn't have to pay you?" asked businessman slash contract negotiator slash tight-fisted bastard, Sid.

"Yeah. Obviously, I'll need something to eat and somewhere to sleep."

"But no money will change hands and you're happy to crash in the van?"

"You cannae let a young lassie sleep in a bloody van, Sid."

Sid shooshed Bobby up with a dismissive wave of his arm.

"Yeah I don't want paid and yes I'll sleep in the van. Obviously if there's room, I'd prefer to be indoors but it's not a problem."

"And why would you want to do this?" said Sid, adopting what I took to be his interview face.

"Because I think you guys are going to be the next big thing and I want a piece of that action. When you get signed, I'll be your chief roadie and then you can start paying me. There's nothing for me back home and music is all I care about. Trust me, this is fate."

I looked at Sid and then Bobby and rolled my eyes.

"I'm no' so sure about this, Sid. What about you, Bobby?" I asked.

Bobby just shrugged and blew air through his cheeks in a non-committal way.

"Never mind what that pair think, Molly. You and me are going for a little chat."

With that Sid wrapped his arm around Molly's slender shoulders and took her back in the direction of the hotel.

I lit a cigarette and took a deep drag as I leaned on the bonnet of the van.

"What the hell do you make of that then?"

"No' sure," said Bobby, scratching his head. "A bit out of the blue, eh? It would be good no' having to carry all the gear but it's no' right no' paying the lassie, and making her sleep in a van's just asking for trouble."

"When has Sid ever cared for anyone's wellbeing? If he thinks he's benefiting from this then that's all that matters. I can just see him in there now making her sign a contract in blood on a napkin like he's Tony Wilson," I grinned.

"Ha ha aye or on the back of a fag packet. 'I Molly forsake all claim to any payment and must make do with sleeping in the van and eating leftovers from the plates of Jimmy or Bobby but never Sid. I do all of this with free will and … shit this fag packet's no' big enough' ha ha what a numpty," Bobby laughed, shaking his head in disbelief.

"So what do you think it'll be, napkin or fag packet?" I asked.

"Probably a napkin."

"Aye. I hope the sneaky bugger doesn't take advantage of her."

"What do you mean? Like …?" Bobby asked with raised eyebrows.

"No, no, he'll no' shag her. She's no' his type. Would you shag her like? I mean, you know, if you didn't have Mel?"

"NAW! She's only 17 for Christ's sake, I'm old enough to be her dad. How, would you?" Bobby asked with a disgusted expression on his face.

"Well she was just 17, you know what I mean," I belted out the Beatles hit to a grim stare from Bobby "No, no … I don't think so … I mean I'm no' too keen on all her facial piercings and she's a bit skinny for me. I like her enthusiasm though."

"But the age thing doesn't enter into the equation for you, no? Doesn't make you feel like you're a low-life dirty scum bastard?" Bobby scowled.

"Fuck's sake, Bobby. She's no' 12. I wouldn't leave a trail of Smarties up my leg to my unzipped crotch. She is above the consenting age so no, the age thing doesn't bother me, it's more that I dinnae find her that attractive. But who's to say that after a barren spell I might not change my opinion. Any port in a storm and that, eh? How am I a low-life dirty scum bastard likes?"

"Unbelievable. You were in your twenties when she was born, how's that port looking right now eh?"

"A'right, a'right. You dinnae have to go making me feel guilty for something I've no' even done … yet," I laughed and took flight but Bobby's giant fist gripped me by the collar.

"I dinnae find it funny, man. If Molly is coming with us for the rest of the way, then you boys better treat her with respect. She might be old enough in your eyes but she's still just a kid to me, a'right?"

"Easy man, fuck's sake. What's the matter with you? I'm sure she can take care of herself just fine."

I lit another cigarette and smoked it in the huff.

Having a puff in the huff.

What's got Bobby so upset?

I was only joking; bet he wouldn't have reacted like that if Sid had said it.

At that Sid came strolling through the car park with his arm still wrapped around Molly's shoulder.

"Right, girls. Say hello to the newest member of Champions Of The Underdog's back room staff. Miss Molly Bruce, three cheers, hip hip hooray," Sid shouted as he raised Molly's arm in salute.

"Congratulations, Molly. Good to have you on board," I shook her hand, but I was wary of maintaining eye contact for too long in case Bobby got the wrong idea and gave me a kicking.

"Sid, where's she going to sit? It's no' safe to have her in the back like a piece of equipment," asked Bobby who was too chivalric for his own good.

"Looks like she's gonnae sit in your seat, Bobby, seeing as you're so concerned for her safety. Jump in, Molly, you're in the middle," I replied, giving Bobby the thumbs up.

"Ha ha, you walked right into that, big man. Bang on the back if you need a pish," Sid added before jumping in the van and starting the ignition.

We drove back in the direction of Fort William so Molly could explain the good news to her parents about her change in career path.

Sid parked up outside her bungalow.

It looked like a nice house.

The garden was immaculate.

I could just imagine the type of people who resided here.

People like my parents. Parents that wouldn't take too kindly to a rag tag bunch of nearly 40-year-old men whisking their precious teenage daughter off to do their dirty work and God knows what else.

"Right, Molly, it's up to you now. I'm no' going in there. I can imagine their reaction. I'll keep the motor running in case we need to beat a hasty retreat," Sid said with a concerned expression on his face.

Perhaps he was having second thoughts.

"Shut up. They're not that bad. I won't be long." Molly got out the van and ran up the path to her front door like a child returning home from school with exciting news.

Bobby's right, she is too young for this.

This is a ridiculous idea.

Sid wound his window down.

"Shout if you need anything," he cried.

The front door opened, and Molly disappeared.

"The more I'm thinking about this the more I dinnae like it. She's only 17 for Christ's sake. It just sounds wrong, man," I whined.

"Shut up. It'll be fine and she's almost 18. If you're happy to be our chief roadie then I'll drive away right now … naw? Didnae think so."

I shook my head in disapproval and stared straight ahead.

After ten minutes, Molly came back out and approached Sid's window. By the redness of her eyes, we could tell she'd been crying.

Sid slowly lowered his window down.

"What's up?" he asked.

"They want to meet you," and she turned to go back up the path.

"On you go then. I'll be staying put," I stated.

"Get your arse in there," he demanded.

"No way, this is your call, you can go and meet them."

Bobby banged on the metal of his cage. We could just make out a muffled "What's going on?"

After a heated whispered debate, the three of us trudged up the path like naughty schoolboys about to receive a dressing down from the headmaster.

Fair play to George and Barbara though, despite being completely pissed off with their daughter and the three of us, they did their best not to let it show. Sid was on his most charming behaviour as he told them about our great plan. They reluctantly agreed with Molly that music was all she had wanted to do but countered her argument that perhaps going to college would be the best course of action. Molly wasn't budging so with heavy hearts George and Barbara reluctantly gave their blessing for Molly to join the band as chief roadie with the condition that she would return home to further her education if things didn't work out.

It was a weird situation to find ourselves in, especially as George and Barbara could only have been a few years older than ourselves.

But with Sid's charm and Bobby's parental instincts in full bloom they felt reassured that Molly was in safe hands.

I just got the sneaky feeling that it was me they weren't too sure about.

Molly grabbed a rucksack full of clothes and after finishing our cups of tea we were back in the van and on our way.

I was glad that pointless little chore was over with, but at least it had preoccupied my mind for a short while.

"Right, finally. Oban here we come," Sid shouted, and we all waved cheerily to George and Barbara as the van trundled off.

CHAPTER 28

O n route to Oban we took a wee detour so we could stop to pay our respects to the victims of the massacre of Glencoe. Sid parked the van at Kingshouse Hotel. I wasn't sure how you went about paying respects to a family that you knew little about or had anything to do with seeing as the aforementioned massacre happened over 300 years previously, but we all agreed that it was something we should do.

I stood in the car park and breathed in the sight of Glencoe. Maybe it was the weather or maybe it was the fact that I knew some terrible deed had been committed here centuries before by the treacherous Campbells or perhaps it was both but I swear a chill ran right down my spine as my gaze took me past Buachaille Etive Mor and up towards the Devil's Staircase.

There was definitely an air of melancholy that gripped the place. If you dwelt on it long enough, tears would definitely form.

"Let's get back in the van, this place is giving me the creeps," Bobby shivered.

You would think that being cooped up in the back of a van with your head resting on a guitar amp for the next hour or so would be reason enough to want to stay outdoors in the fresh air for as long as possible, but Bobby could sense the atmosphere more than the rest of us.

"You bunch of Jessies, you don't even know what this is all about, do you? You're Sassenachs, you'll never understand. But me," Molly said, thumbing her chest, "I'm a highlander, it's a different way of life up here. Always has been, always will be, so don't give me your shit about feeling the chilly atmosphere. It's not a part of you. If you want to feel atmosphere, take a walk through Ranoch Moor on a wet and windy day." And she pointed in the direction that I took to be Ranoch Moor but it could have been anywhere such was my ignorance.

With that the melancholic atmosphere evaporated quickly and Bobby, Sid and me looked at each other like a bunch of gullible tourists.

Embarrassed, I shuffled about and stared at another bunch of hills instead.

"Right, Oban it is then," Sid said, clapping and rubbing his hands together to end the farce.

We drove to Oban with the splendid Loch Linnhe on our right and the magnificent mountain ranges whose names escaped me to our left. My enjoyment of the views however was spoilt by self-indulgent tales from Sid as he told Molly about the history of Champions Of The Underdog and our flirtations with fame and fortune and subsequent phoenix-like rise from the ashes to obtain our rightful place in rock history as the greatest live band Scotland, if not the world, had ever seen.

The sad thing, I thought as I listened to his biased recollection, was that he actually believed it. He'd twisted the stories to suit himself so we would sound legendary.

We were anything but.

Hell, if I hadn't been there since the inception of the band, I'd swear he was describing AC/DC. Even sadder was the fact that Molly hung onto his every word like she was a disciple and he Jesus of Nazareth.

"You're our wild child, Molly. You know like The Doors song?" Sid announced to a starry-eyed Molly.

"Yeah I know it," And she closed her eyes and sang. "Wild Child full of grace, saviour of the human race, I love Jim Morrison."

Oh for fuck's sake!

"Not bad, not bad. You've got a decent voice there, Molly. Aye well that song was written about Danny Sugarman. He started working for The Doors when he was just a kid and he ended up managing them. Imagine that, eh? That could be you, Molly, the wild child of the Champions, fucking brilliant. So you like Jim Morrison, eh?"

And off he went again, somehow managing to confuse Jim Morrison's life with his own.

I don't recall you ever moving to Paris, Sid, and you're a wee bitty old to join the 27 club.

As if this torturous journey couldn't possibly get any worse, we were about three miles from Oban when my phone vibrated in my pocket. I retrieved it and opened the newly delivered text message.

It read: "See you're in Oban this week. Mite just see you there. There's something I need to give you ..."

"Fuck, fuck, fuck," I shouted, slamming my phone against the dashboard.

"What is it?" Molly asked, startled by the sudden interruption to her and

Sid's bonding session.

"It's another text from Danny," I ignored Molly and looked straight at Sid whose expression changed to one of concern. "He says he might see me in Oban," I continued. "Fucking great news eh, Sid?"

"He's full of shit. Dinnae worry about it he's only messing with you, he'll no' be there."

"Oh aye that's easy for you to say, you're no' the one with a contract on your head."

"Who's Danny?" Molly chipped in.

"Shut up, contract? I'm telling you there's no danger he'd come all the way out here. He's doing it to mess with your head and it's working. Why don't you get a new number or better still throw that old phone away?"

"What's this all about?" Molly continued as her confused gaze shifted between mine and Sid's.

"Ask Sid here. He'll tell you a wee story about how he fucked up any chances I had of getting back with my ex and how her new boyfriend wants to use my body as a stress ball."

"What are you talking about, getting back with Debbie? You're the one that dumped her, remember? Why the hell would you want to go back with her, eh?" he asked, goading me to tell him the truth that he already knew.

"It's complicated, I miss her. Just forget about it, eh?" I retreated.

"Do you want to talk about it, Jimmy? Sometimes it helps to talk to someone who's not involved," Molly kindly asked.

"No I don't want to fucking talk about it," I snapped and she recoiled like the scolded child she is. "I'm sorry, it's not your fault, I'm just a bit on edge the now. Loads of shit to deal with, my heid's no' right. Just forget about it, Molly, eh?"

"Sorry. I didn't mean to pry I was just trying to be—"

"Just leave it eh?" I sighed.

We trundled along the remaining mile in unbearable silence.

The constant chatter of self-praise and bands with two guitarists died along with my self-worth.

We parked up outside our hostel and clambered out the van.

Molly released Bobby from his martyred cell in the back and thanked him for his selfless actions.

"Ah that's better," he groaned as he stretched the last 20 odd miles of cramped isolation from his gigantic frame. "What's the matter with you lot?

I'm the one that's had a fret board jammed up my arse for the last half an hour."

"Dinnae ask, man. Dinnae ask," I replied.

CHAPTER 29

We took our bags into the hostel and I dumped mine on a rusty, squeaky bunk and left the others to their own devices.

"See youse later, I'm away for a pint," I grunted.

I was in need of some quiet time and there was no better way of doing that than by staring at my dishevelled reflection through a dozen optics from a comfortable stool.

Unfortunately, the bar keep had other ideas.

"Pint o' Guinness please," I grumbled.

"So are you here for the Islands or are you doing a spot of walking in the area?" he enquired far too cheerfully for my liking.

"Neither, I'm just passing through," I replied without looking at him.

"Oh aye? On a wee holiday, eh?"

"Aye something like that. Can I get a Macallan as well please."

"Will you be staying local?" he continued, ignoring my request for more alcohol to damage my brain cells so I wouldn't have to listen to his pre-recorded shite patter.

"Aye, just around the corner and a Macallan as well … please," I groaned, rubbing at my eyes, hoping that he would take the hint.

"Oh that's good. At the hostel, eh? Well if you're here tomorrow evening we've got a live band playing. Very good I hear. I spoke to their manager just yesterday, says we're very lucky to be hosting them," and he smiled proudly as he topped up my pint then wiped the sides clean of the creamy foam that had escaped.

"Is that right? Good for you."

"Oh aye that should bring the punters in and keep my till ringing. So what is it you do yourself?"

"This and that."

I grabbed the dark beer before its arse had even touched the bar and chugged it down my throat like I was the main attraction at the student union drinking challenge.

He looked at me anxiously as he handed over the Macallan. As if he'd watched other men down their pints in that manner then shook in terror from the corner as they subsequently trashed his bar.

I'm no' like that, man.

No need for fear.

"So … you like whisky, eh?"the barkeep queried.

What do you have to do to get a bit of fucking peace around here?

"Listen, thanks for the craic. Put the change in the tin, I'll see you around," I downed my nip and slammed it on the bar, omitting a satisfying 'aaaaahhh' as I did so.

I wandered up the town until I found a sign outside a hotel for a basement bar boasting the largest selection of malt whisky in Oban.

This'll do for me.

This indeed was more like it, a place with wee alcoves where I could sit and get slowly melted in silence. I ordered a double Macallan and produced my last twenty-pound note from my back pocket. I checked my wallet and was aghast to find it empty.

Fuck, I'll have to go back to Sid and get some money.

It was a humiliating ordeal, but I was fucking destitute and he hadn't paid us in weeks. I hadn't touched my cash line card in months as it was already overdrawn.

Every month the balance ran down as the bank charged me for the pleasure of borrowing their money. It was a never-ending spiral of debt. I would pay in the £200 cash that Sid paid me and every month the bank would take back £20 of any monies paid in to cover their non-existent costs because I'd had the cheek to borrow some of their precious funds.

Evil bastards.

I'd been deliberately trying to deposit a couple of hundred every month to bring the overdraft down and live solely on the remaining cash I got.

But as is life something or other would crop up to ruin my good intentions of saving money, such as my ex-girlfriend's psychotic boyfriend wanting to blooter the fuck out of me, and I would have to delve into my pot of money to buy alcohol to allow me to forget about my ex-girlfriend's psycho boyfriend wanting to kick the fuck out of me and so on and on the torturous circle would go.

Fuck it.

I spent the last of the twenty on whisky at the bar and then withdrew fifty at a cash line outside a Spar shop.

Feeling guilty at my lack of self-control on the money-managing matters, I served penance by purchasing the shitiest bottle of whisky they had in the shop and the harshest packet of rolling tobacco available in Oban.

The mind works in mysterious ways.

There is a lesson in there somewhere.

My carry out jiggled inside the bright blue carrier bag as it bounced off my thighs.

With my belly grumbling in anticipation at the fiery liquor it was about to be drowned in I marched to the nearest chippy and ordered a haggis supper.

Well, when in Rome.

I took my culinary delight and sat on the pier and ate my tea in silence.

Why is life so difficult?

I mean I'm the only one I know that seems to be struggling right now.

Why is life so difficult for me?

Take my sister for example; we've never been that close, but I've always respected her. Loved her even, although I'm not sure how much you can love someone you don't really know.

What do you want to be when you grow up, Clare?

A vet.

A vet, eh? Oh that's nice you'll be a really good vet.

I will be.

And off she pops, sails through school onto veterinary college.

First class degree please.

No problem, there you go, young lady.

Thank you very much.

Nice wee James Herriot style job in a borders village for a couple of years then it's off to New Zealand for a mega bucks job, huge ranch, cooshty lifestyle with her farmer husband.

Been good knowing you, Sis, sorry if I ripped your coat tails, was just trying to find out what it felt like to be you.

Shit, even Sid, a perpetual fuck up at school, is doing what he wants to do.

Okay he might not be a successful musician but at least he's heading in the right direction, he's doing something he loves, something he's passionate about. And Bobby? Well, he's always got his art, loves his art. And him and Mel are so perfect, perfect, perfect. It makes me want to greet.

What have I got? What have I got, eh?

Nothing.

Hee haw.

That's what.

I'm like my old man. Me and him are the same, see? Like two wee useless frightened rabbits caught in the headlights of life.

Most rabbits are daft and just rely on their primal instincts to flee. Flee from danger, go on daft wee rabbit, run away. But me and my dad are different, see. We're thinking rabbits. We're thinking what is that bright light? Where is it coming from? Why is it here? How did it get here?

Before you know it, we've been run over by the metaphorical car of life for having the audacity to stand up and question that which came before us.

And that, my friends, is my failing in life.

Questioning everything that comes before me, dissecting it until I no longer know what it is I have been chopping up into little pieces.

Where did it all go wrong eh, where did it all go wrong?

"You bought High Commissioner for a start."

"Yeah and you're hogging the spliff, come on, pass it on."

I slugged a fierce mouthful of whisky and passed on the joint.

Even this bunch of wasters think I'm a nobody.

I sat within McCaigs tower with a few random locals and foreign stoners for company, contemplating my existence.

Yet even they doubted me.

Several people from varying backgrounds laughed at me as I belched out my thoughts.

I sighed and looked out across the bay to the lights over Oban and the Islands.

The stars overhead shone bright with condescending twinkles.

It all made sense to me.

Will nobody understand what it feels like?

"Finish the bottle, I'm going to bed."

"Gee thanks, Jimmy. That's very generous of you. We'll be here same time tomorrow, mate, bring a decent bottle though, eh? Ha ha ha," somebody piped up, continuing the banter.

Their laughter echoed through my soul as I descended Battery Hill. I bounced from house walls to parked cars and back as I eventually made my way to the hostel.

I may have kicked a wing mirror or two clean from their holdings in anger.

For this I can only apologise.

CHAPTER 30

The only thing worse than waking up in a depressed state of mind is waking up in a depressed state of mind with a raging hangover.

Perhaps one and the same?

At least it gave me the excuse to wear sunglasses all day and play at being a rock star.

I spent my morning ambling about town on my own in a terrible mood.

It was Molly's first gig since officially joining the band as roadie and she was her usual excited, talkative, enthusiastic self.

I found her annoying in my current state of mind, but I was glad of her presence when it came time to set up our equipment in the Irish bar I visited yesterday. Her grafting enabled me to sit at the bar and order a hair of the dog to set me up for the gig. It was the same annoying, nosey tosser that was behind the bar.

Please don't talk to me.

"Two Bloody Marys please," I ordered.

"So are you with the band then?" he asked, clearly not recognising me from yesterday. "You must be if you're wearing sunglasses in here. Rock 'n' roll, eh?"

And he did a Chubby Checker style twist to emphasise his point just in case I wasn't sure what rock 'n' roll was.

Upon seeing his twisting actions, I suddenly remembered, ah rock 'n' roll.

"Aye I'm the manager," I dryly replied.

"Oh really? It was me you spoke to on the phone the other night, I'm Terry." He dropped the celery and shoved his grubby hand over the bar and into mine.

I reluctantly shook his sweaty palm.

"So, these boys are gonnae be big stars, eh?" he asked whilst returning to the discarded celery.

"Probably not."

I picked up my two Bloody Marys and headed for the solitude of a wobbly table.

I sat and watched Molly set up our equipment and slurped at my drink, discarding the celery on the table. I briefly thought about the health-giving properties in tomato juice and celery and picked up the sickly wilting piece and gave it a nibble

Fuck, that's rank.

I'd rather deal with the hangover than eat that shite.

Molly went about her work like a master technician, and I envied her enthusiasm, her blind faith.

She was starting out on her musical path and was full of hope. I was like her once and I longed to feel that way again.

Keen, eager, hopeful.

But after a number of setbacks and disappointments, life seems to kick the eagerness from you.

I'm a depressing bastard.

I need some company, spending too much time in your own head is a one-way ticket to being a sad, bitter, and lonely man.

The bar tender got right on my tits and the place was pretty empty so that only left Molly.

"Need a hand?" I offered.

"No thanks, I'm cool. Anyway, this is my job now, you go and relax and drink whatever it is you're drinking," she answered, staring warily at my glass.

"A Bloody Mary, you want to try it?"

"No way, it looks disgusting."

"It doesn't taste much better. Listen, sorry if I was short with you yesterday, it's just that I've got a few things on my mind and ..." I tailed off and looked into a mirror on the adjacent wall.

I've started but I can't finish.

Sensing my discomfort Molly stepped in.

"It's all right. Look, Bobby gave me a wee idea of what's going on. I'm sorry about you and Debbie, she sounds like a lovely girl."

"She was ... she is," I could feel the tears begin to well in my eyes. It was a good idea to wear the shades.

"If you want to talk about it sometime then ..." and then she tailed off, probably having sensed my discomfort.

"Thanks," I snorted the snotters back up my nose, "eh, do you want a drink?"

"No thanks, some of us have got work to do," she laughed and turned back to her tangled pile of guitar leads.

"Aye I'd better go and get ready," I turned to leave and dropped off my empty glasses at the bar.

"Is that you away then? Be back soon for the gig?" the cheery barman asked.

"Aye … no … eh … give me another two, eh? And have a drink yourself."

I sat back at the wobbly table and felt the vodka and tomato juice start to work its simple magic. Watching Molly graft away taking great pride in her work did start to make me feel a bit better.

What would I give to be a teenager again?

I actually enjoyed the two gigs we played in O'Donnell's. We went down well with the mixture of locals and passing travelling folk and we didn't have to buy a round again.

Irish bars are very hospitable places.

Even when they're not in Ireland.

We gathered in a wee café on the morning of our departure to have a good, cooked breakfast before we set off for our next destination.

Bobby or myself weren't actually sure of our next destination as I think Sid had now gotten to the stage of making things up as he went along or could get offers to host us. It was actually more enjoyable this way. It was a bit like Quantum Leap with The Magical Mystery Tour thrown in for good measure.

Where would we be going next?

Ooh it's so exciting.

Sid was in a cheery mood as we all tucked into our full Scottish breakfasts. Well Molly had the vegetarian equivalent which actually looked a lot more appetising than the pile of morsels that were swimming in the grease on my plate. The fried bread had been saturated with oil, so it floated alongside my bacon and rubbery-looking egg.

Do people still eat fried bread?

It has to be one of the most ridiculous tasting things we've ever decided to fry. I know we'll fry anything in Scotland, but bread? For Christ's sake it's bread, its main use is to sook things up on your plate. Not act like a sponge for a pan full of oil. That's all you can taste. The manky oil that it's been floating about in picking up wee bits of burnt bacon or sausage as it turns into a hard, useless piece of filthy toast. No wonder our arteries are all clogged up and we're dying at 50 if that's the sort of shit we're happy to ram down our thrapples.

Why not save yourself the time of dunking the bread in the fat and just pour the vile grease into a mug and drink it.

A nice greasy steaming brew on a winter's morn, aye that'd fair set you up for the day.

Ah braw.

"Are you listening, you divvy?" Sid shouted, sending a tiny wee piece of black pudding hurtling from his mouth to land on the back of Molly's vegetarian hand.

"Oh gross!" she wailed as she pinged it from her hand with a deft flick, launching it on a mission across the room where it landed amongst a wee old wifey's perfectly curled white hair. It nestled comfortably like a sleeping fly.

"Ha ha ha ha," we all burst into fits of laughter, prompting the other diners to turn and see what all the fuss was about. Even the wee wifey turned her head but wee blacksy wouldn't budge.

"Brilliant," Sid said, wiping a tear from his eye. "Right, as I was saying, I've got a wee treat in store for you all. We've worked bloody hard on this tour, and it's not been easy, but I think we're making good progress. So as a wee thank you and as a wee, well you ken ..." Sid was finding being nice harder than it looked. "We're gonnae take a week off and head to Mull for some camping and fishing and some getting back to nature."

"Oh superb, man. I really need a break, this tour's doing my nut in," I uttered as Bobby and Sid both looked at me with faces of hurt and disappointment.

"It's no' you guys it's just a bit, well you know intense at times and all the shit with Danny isn't helping. A wee break will sort my head out fine like," I continued with a bit more diplomacy so as not to hurt their tender wee feelings further.

"Aye tremendous, Sid. Have you got places in mind to stay?" asked Bobby.

"Nah we'll get the ferry over to Craignure and take it from there. We've got a whole island to discover. I want to do a bit of fishing so camping by the lochs would be best I think but we'll just play it by ear. We've got two gigs lined up in Tobermory but that's no' till next weekend so we've got just over a week to enjoy ourselves."

"Sounds cool, I've never been to Mull before. It'll be good to have a rod in my hand again and the wind through my hair," I offered whilst trying to sound all rugged.

"Whit?! Your rod's never oot your hand," cackled Sid, slapping his thigh.

"Aye very mature. We'll need to get some supplies, maybe pick up a couple of those disposable barbecues, eh?" I asked.

"Aye we'll stock up in town. I saw a wee fishing shop so I'm gonnae pop in there and pick up some stuff," enthused Sid.

"I saw a phone shop so I'll nip in there and pick up a new phone or SIM card and then I'll no' have to hear from that prick again. I'll meet you in the fishing shop, Sid."

"Okay then. Molly and I can go to the shop and pick up some water and toilet rolls and some food for the barbecue. Do you want me to get some pork chops or steaks for the barbecue?" Bobby asked.

"Whit?! We're camping, I plan on living from the land. There's fish in the lochs and there'll be rabbits and pigeons. I'm doing this aw natural, man. I'll no' need any food," proclaimed Sid, acting like the hardened backwoodsman.

"Aye you'd better pick up some food, Bobby. Just in case the fish dinnae bite or the rabbits are good at hiding," I said.

"Pussys," Sid replied.

"Get some bevy too. Mind the whiskers," I ordered.

After breakfast we each headed our separate ways to do our shopping. I picked up a cheapish refurbished phone and another SIM card so I'd have no more dealings with the knuckle dragger that is Danny Foster.

With my purchase complete I went to the Anglers' Corner to meet Sid. I opened the door and was met by an array of sophisticated weaponry from floor to ceiling. The gloomy shop had that musty smell. It was probably caused by the legion of Barbour jackets they had for sale.

I was suitably impressed by the shop though.

This is the type of shop that I detested as a kid because they smelt funny and were boring. But along with DIY shops I now find in my more mature years that I could quite happily spend an afternoon perusing their wares.

I spotted Sid in the corner being handed an air rifle from a jolly-looking staff member.

"Check this one out, Jimmy," he gushed as he handed me the rifle. "They've got loads of cool stuff in here, eh?"

"Aye they do," I agreed.

Sid was like a kid in a toy shop as he swapped one rifle for another then darted between fishing reels and walking boots, picking each one up and giving it a shake and a squeeze.

I walked over to the knife counter and looked at the shiny instruments of destruction.

"Cool, eh? I'm gonnae get me one for gutting the rabbits," Sid shouted as he darted over and pushed me out of the way, dumping his would-be purchases on the counter to stare menacingly at the weapons under the glass.

I stared at the knifes in wonder. There was every size and shape available.

A nutter would have a field day in here.

I asked to see a small hunting knife. I picked it up and the weight felt good in my hand.

This could come in handy.

If Danny Foster did happen to spring a surprise on me, he might think twice when I pulled this bad boy out.

Oh yes, this will do the trick.

"That thing's tiny, that's no use. Here, check this one out, I'm getting it," Sid flashed his massive hunting knife at me, cutting the air with a mixture of slashes and thrusts. "Smart, eh?"

"Aye very good, Crocodile Dundee. Do you plan on wrestling an alligator with that one?" I smirked.

"It's for the rabbits," he snipped.

"I'm sure they'll be delighted to see it."

Sid bought his knife and fishing reels and about a dozen other things that he'd probably never use, and I bought my little knife. It was only for protection; I didn't want to gut a man.

We walked back to the van laughing and joking about our trip.

"Man, those rabbits are gonnae get it," Sid said menacingly.

Bobby and Molly were already waiting for us, and we each inspected the others purchases.

I sat in the back of the van amongst our equipment for the short ride to the ferry port. In between regaining my balance, I saved all my stored phone numbers to the phone's memory and sent one last text message with my old number.

"Good afternoon you useless excuse for a human being. I have a new number now so this will be the last you hear from me. We're going off to Mull for a few days, so I'll hopefully see you there as you really disappointed us with your no show in Oban. Adiós motherfucker. Love and kisses, Jimmy."

I discarded the old SIM and fitted the new one and sent texts to Sid, Bobby, and Molly with my new number.

I felt as though a huge weight had been lifted from my shoulders and the foggy haze that permanently clung to my brain parted momentarily to let a little ray of happiness peek through.

I looked in the little carrier bag at my new knife and removed it from the hard plastic packaging. It came with a handy little carry case that you could attach to your belt.

Nice touch.

I removed it from its woven sheath and gripped it in my hand.

Aye I'd like to see you try anything now, Foster, you prick.

I copied Sid's slash and stab movements from earlier.

I laughed to myself at how ridiculous it looked but there was no mistaking the extra couple of feet I'd grown as I held the weapon in my hand.

It was like a child's blanky.

It felt comforting, reassuring.

It gave me strength.

I could now understand why the youths of today would want to carry one of these things. If I was living in a scheme, not knowing whether I'd be jumped or not, and I felt the cold steel against my skin as it rested beneath my waistband, I'd feel a lot more comfortable making that walk to the shops after dark.

I fumbled about with the sheath and eventually attached it to my belt and placed the knife inside. I pulled my jumper over the top and patted it gently.

This feels right.

CHAPTER 31

The ferry ride to Craignure only took 45 minutes but during that time the mist had gathered and then clung to the Isle of Mull so any chance of seeing some majestic scenery was sadly vanquished.

By the time we got back into the van and drove from the ferry the heavens had opened. The rain battered the windscreen as Sid navigated the road to our destination.

Salen Forest on the banks of Loch Frisa.

With window wipers going full pelt, the road classification quickly deteriorated from a major one to a minor one and then onto scary with passing places to finally a beaten track that was at best the width of a garden path.

Sid brought the van to a juddering halt at a clearing in the forest where the track suddenly ended.

"Looks like we'll have to carry the tents and stuff on foot the rest of the way," Sid pondered whilst peering out the small patch of windscreen that wasn't fogged up.

"It's pissing doon. I'm no' walking or carrying anything in that weather," I moaned.

"Yeah, let's wait a bit till it goes off," agreed Molly. "It's probably just a passing shower."

"Couple of pussys," Sid huffed, shaking his head in disgust. What he was really thinking was, 'I'm glad you two came to that decision. You are of course quite correct, it is pissing down and to get ourselves and our camping equipment soaking wet would be detrimental to this whole exercise. However I am going to keep up with the illusion that I am a tough and rugged individual who fears no man or beast and is certainly not afraid to get one's head a little wet so I am going to berate you both with childish insults until the rain stops and then I can get out and walk away with my tough and rugged reputation intact'.

"Are you two made of sugar? You'll no' melt it's only a wee bit rain," Sid continued with his tiresome banter.

Sid's chatter was brought to an end by Bobby banging on the driver's window. Sid slowly lowered the steamed-up glass a quarter of the way down. Just enough to see two dark brown eyes peering through the gap.

"Yes?" Sid asked, moving up the window an inch as tiny flecks of rain bounced off Bobby's head and into the van

"What's happening then?" Bobby questioned as he dragged his hand over his soaking brow, allowing more droplets of water to fall onto Sid's lap.

"Well I'm wanting to take all the gear up to our site but the two lassies here are frightened of a wee bit rain and are refusing to move till it stops so I guess we'll have to wait here till it stops."

"What? I'm no' sitting squashed in the back while you lot sit up here all cosy listening to tunes. It's bloody boring in there. Come on, man, you and me can take the tents and get our pitch all set up. Once we're in the trees it'll be sheltered."

"Eh … that's no' fair on us having to do all the work likes, we'll just wait till these two are ready so we can all do it," Sid's brain was working overtime attempting to come up with a plausible excuse.

"This rain's no' gonnae stop any time soon and I'm no' sitting in the back by myself all night. It'll be dark soon, come on, Sid. They can bring up the rest of the stuff."

"Aye, Sid, go on, you were just saying how it was only a wee bit of rain. Give Bobby a hand and Jimmy and me will bring up the stuff you can't manage," Molly smirked.

I like you kid.

Sid huffed and puffed then got out and slammed the van door. Molly and I could hear his mutterings as he opened the back doors and gathered up the tent with Bobby.

"Hey Sid …" I shouted through the inch gap in the open window as he walked by, arms laden with various forms of camping equipment.

He turned around with a look of contempt in his eyes, his lank hair strapped to his forehead by the weight of water it held.

"… dinnae worry, you'll no' melt."

Molly and I burst into laughter as Sid shouted an insult back at us but we couldn't hear what it was because I had already put the window up.

It was dusk by the time the two of us met the others at our campsite.

Bobby was right, the rain hadn't eased off but negotiating your way through a dark forest to find a tent in pitch blackness wasn't an option, so we braved the rain and brought the rest of the camping essentials with us.

The couple of hours we'd spent alone in the van passed by quickly. We talked mainly about music, but I opened up to Molly about Debbie and I didn't feel like a useless pleb whilst doing it.

I'd enjoyed her company and she made me laugh.

"You took your time, eh? Hope you weren't getting up to any monkey business in my van."

"Greetings to you too, Sid. Thank you for making us welcome in your campsite, we accept your generous offer to make camp with you and have brought with us gifts of beans and whisky in return," I mocked.

"Aye very funny. Put them in the store over there," Sid pointed to a piece of tarpaulin tied between two trees at a 45-degree angle with another sheet of tarpaulin on the ground. On top of which sat a large number of carrier bags which collectively comprised our 'store.'

"You've done a great job, guys. Nice pitch you got us here," Molly replied as she dumped our offerings in the store.

I couldn't actually see much as it was dark and cloudy but, with the silhouettes of the trees behind us, we were sheltered from the worst of the weather. I could hear the gentle lapping of the loch not too far in front of us. It did indeed feel like a good pitch. The boys had done a good job and were sitting proudly in front of a decent sized fire, each supping on a can of beer.

That evening we all sat huddled around the fire sitting on our Lidl folding fishing chairs with built-in beer holder in good spirits.

Telling jokes, sharing stories, and gentle piss taking was the order of the evening.

After drinking enough beers to put us to a gentle slumber we all retired to the massive six-man tent that Sid purchased with his nefound wealth before the tour commenced.

It wasn't the best sleep I had ever had but it wasn't the worst and as I listened to the trees blowing gently in the wind interspersed with the occasional splattering of rain dripping onto the canvas I fell into a dreamless sleep.

The next morning I wearily awoke and, after shuffling my way from the vice-like grip my sleeping bag held me in, I crept over the sleeping bodies and through the zipped tent door.

The first thing that hit me was the cold.

The second thing was the spectacular beauty of our secluded site.

I stretched the tired knots from my muscles like a goal scorer who'd scored the winner.

Arms aloft and pointing skyward.

The stretch felt as good as scoring a winner.

I wiped the sleep from my eyes, adjusted my crown jewels through the cotton prison of my boxer shorts and drank in the majestic view that stood before me.

The loch was only ten metres from our tent, and it shimmered like glass, reflecting the trees and hills on the banks at the other side. A couple of pockets of low-lying mist hovered on top of the water like magical candy floss. That was the only remnants of last night's rain. Otherwise, it was crisp, clear skies. The sun was starting to rise behind me, and little bursts of warmth streamed through the break in the trees.

Ahhh this is the life.

It would be great to have a wee cottage somewhere like this. Away from the hustle and bustle of everyday life …

"Morning, Jimmy," Molly cheerily uttered whilst poking her head through the flap and interrupting my poetic musing.

"Good morning, Molly. How'd you sleep?"

"All right. Wow this place is beautiful," she exclaimed.

"Aye it's no' bad, eh? Feast your eyes on that lot," I grinned as I introduced her to my theatrical backdrop. "Fancy a morning swim?"

"Eh, no thanks, looks a bit cold to me."

"Aye you're probably right."

After we were all up and dressed, Sid took charge of getting another fire going and Bobby had breakfast covered so I went in search of skimming stones to launch across the loch's unblemished surface.

Bobby announced that breakfast was ready, bringing the Loch Frisa skimming stone championship to an end. I had triumphantly beaten Molly hands down with my twelve to her measly niner. She had claimed hers was a twelver too and therefore the game was a tie, but she either can't see or can't count.

It was definitely a niner, tenner at best.

We sat and ate our scrambled eggs layered on top of campfire-toasted toast in silence.

I washed mine down with a sumptuous cup of steaming black coffee.

There's nothing like eating alfresco.

Out of doors.

Naw, ootside.

That sounds more appropriate.

Aye, you cannae beat eating ootside.

The first couple of days of our wee holiday passed by in absolute tranquillity.

Each of us were invigorated by our surroundings and we were happy to be in each other's company for the first time in ages, but we were just as happy to go off and enjoy our own.

However, things started to take a turn for the worse by the Thursday evening.

On Thursday morning Bobby was off painting the surrounding scenery and Molly was happy to sit by the fire playing her acoustic guitar so Sid and I decided to spend another day sat at the water's edge trying to catch at least one fish.

They had eluded us in the previous day's encounter but today was the day that would change. Yesterday Sid had gotten as far as hooking one but after a fiercely contested battle, lasting approximately five minutes, the fish was declared the winner as Sid's line snapped, allowing the underwater morsel to swim for a life of freedom.

Albeit a life of freedom spent with a shiny new piercing protruding from its gaping gob.

The morning started amicably enough with the two of us sitting on our folding chairs, rods held firmly in hands, eyes narrowed on the still water patiently waiting for the first sign of a bite so we could spring into action.

A lovely bottle of Balvenie 15-year-old single barrel Speyside malt, which was solely procured for this trip, was cracked open and generously shared between us.

"Ah that is absolutely beautiful," Sid remarked, smacking his lips as the whisky went down his throat. "Mind when we used to sit by the burn near ma hoose like this when we were kids?" he continued.

"Minus the whisky though. Aye that was rare. Just the sound of the water and a couple of stolen cigarettes for company," I replied as the memories appeared in my mind's eye.

"Sitting crunching on our Pot Noodles for lunch 'cause your flask was shite and couldn't keep the water hot," Sid reminded.

"Ha ha, aye you're right. They were good days, man," I nodded at the images in my mind.

"You always used to fall in the burn. I think you did it on purpose so you could wear my clothes," Sid laughed.

"Walking back to your hoose like I'd pished masell aw dripping wet and your mum going daft at me for falling in again. Ha ha. It was the only time I got to wear cool clothes," I chuckled.

"Aye but they were only meant to be worn till you got back to your own house. You'd give me my clothes back in dribs and drabs. I lost count of the number of t-shirts and jeans you nicked off me over the years all because of that bloody burn," Sid moaned.

"Guilty as charged, me lord. Why do you think I fell in so often? It wasn't because I liked the taste of the dirty water. It's the only way I could own some clothes with designer names on them. Anyway, you had loads of clothes, you didnae even wear half of them."

Our stroll through fishing trips gone by ended abruptly as I felt a sharp tug on my line. My ninja-like reflexes burst into life.

"Got you, you wee bastard!" I shouted as I pulled sharply on my rod to ensure maximum impact with the barbed hook. "Get the net, get the net," I shouted excitedly.

After a bit of reeling and rocking and toing and froing I brought the fish into the edge of the loch.

"Quick get it in the net. It looks like a beauty," I roared with pride and sheer delight.

Sid scooped up the trout in the giant net and brought it to shore.

"Would you look at that," I gasped as I gazed in wonder at my first catch in years.

A magnificent brown trout lay convulsing in the net. It slapped its tail hard against the pebbled ground and flicked itself over and back as it tried its best to escape the impending doom.

I reached down to pick it up.

It felt cold but heavy in my hand.

Probably a five pounder.

I tried to gently remove the hook from its mouth as the shiny hook had unfortunately pierced the side of the trout's mouth and re-entered its eye. This was easier said than done as the fish flopped about in my grasp, making me tug and pull at the hook as I battled to lead the little dance.

I ended up shoving the hook further into its eye and as another spasm of twisting and shaking racked its gilled body I pulled the hook out with so much force that I ripped the damaged eye clean out and nearly took half of its head with me.

"Take it easy man, Christ you're no exactly Paul Young, are you? You're supposed to remove it gently so it doesn't feel any pain. Give us it here," Sid grabbed the trout from my sodden and slimy grasp and placed it on the shingle. It looked at us through its one good, pleading eye whilst its mouth opened and closed with the frequency of a broken automatic door.

Smack!

Crack!

"It's a fish, Sid. It's no' a bloody Bond villain you're dispatching. Look, you've battered the other eye out now, fuck's sake," I complained.

"What? You're supposed to give it a couple of firm dunts to put it out of its misery. I had to after you tried to decapitate it with your bare hands," he countered.

"Aye there's firm and then there's mashing its head into the bloody ground. Would you look at it?" I picked up the once proud amphibious creature and pushed its eyeless crushed face into Sid's

"Eugh," he howled as he batted it away. "It doesn't look the bonniest. You're no' eating the head anyway so quit your moaning. Blind brown trout, ha ha it sounds like an old blues singer."

"So? It was my first catch in ages I wanted it to look good. I cannae take a picture of this and stick it on Instagram now, can I? Folk'll be like 'whit the fuck is that meant to be?' It looks like it's been chewed by a cat."

"Ha ha. I woke up this morning. Dee de de de de. With a hook in my eye. Dee de de de de. It was really painful. Dee de de de de. I started to cry. Dee de ..." Sid played an imaginary slide guitar to accompany his made up song.

"Shut up. At least I've caught a fish."

"De de de and now I'm getting smacked on the heid oh why oh why? Dee de de de de."

"Fanny." I shoved my way past Sid and placed my mutilated catch on a piece of driftwood. His witty song lyrics continued for several long verses, but his jovial mood found a watery grave soon after.

I re-hooked my line and cast it into the water. The maggot encrusted hook had just plopped through the shimmering surface when I clearly had another bite.

I was still watching the ripples on the water, caused by the maggots' headfirst plunge, disperse when it happened and so was caught ever so slightly unawares.

But the old fishing instincts soon kicked in and once again I was pulling back hard and engaging in the old game of cat and mouse.

Or rather human and fish.

This catch took me slightly longer to wind in and I felt a lot more resistance on the line. It was clearly a monstrous catch.

I was, however, slightly disappointed when I did land it in the net. Although it was slightly bigger than the previous one, I'd guess about a five and a half pounder, I'd already had visions of pulling out a beast of a catch and posing proudly with it. I'd already seen in my mind's eye the photo that would appear in the angling section of The Daily Record under the 'catch of the week' heading.

Still, you can't win them all.

"That's two-nil to me, Sid. Get it right up ye!"

"Fuck off. Jammy bastard."

"Woke up this morning. Dee de de de de. With a plan to hatch. Dee de de de de," I had my own blues riff going on now.

"Right, this is boring, I'm away to get my gun. I'm gonnae do some proper hunting."

And with the deflating sense of failure and shame in his eyes Sid stormed off in the huff.

"You're no' singing any more, you're no' singing any more," I shouted at him as he picked up the bottle of Balvennie and made a hasty retreat for our camp site, but he wasn't biting.

Just like the fish on his line.

I sat and smoked a cigarette in quiet contemplation, satisfied at my day's work so far.

I watched Sid from afar as he threw his rod into the store and rummaged around for his gun before stomping off through the trees and finally out of my view.

It's the small victories that count.

He could have left me some whisky though.

Without as much as another nibble I decided to call it a day a couple of hours later. My final tally remained two brown trout, but I was more than happy at that, and I walked back to the campsite with my catch thrown proudly over my right shoulder and my triumphant rod over my left.

The hunter gatherer returns, bringing food for his tribe. Praise me, love me, worship me for it is I and only I who have brought you morsels to eat.

The fire was blazing nicely and Bobby, Molly, and myself sat contentedly staring into its flickering orange mass when Sid returned.

"Looks like you're not the only one bearing gifts, Jimmy," Sid beamed as he tossed a rabbit by the hind legs to land in front of the three of us.

"Oh gross!" Molly shrieked as she leapt to her feet, kicking over her folding chair with built-in beer holder, sending her bottle of beer flying from said built in beer holder to spill its amber contents wastefully onto the mossy ground which greedily drank the brew, leaving nothing more than a frothy mound as evidence.

"Where the hell did you get that? It doesn't look right," queried Bobby as he stared at the lifeless beast through squinting eyes.

"Where do you think? In the woods. It was a great shot, man. You should have seen it, I was about 50 feet away when I caught a slight movement out of the corner of my eye. Just a wee flinch, nothing more. I turned slowly and could see the tips of a pair of ears sticking out above the grass."

"Oh here we go," I sighed.

Sid shot me a mean stare that said shut the fuck up and let me tell my amazing story.

I relented and allowed him to carry on.

"I crept over a few branches so I could get it in my sights. The wind was starting to pick up, so I had to judge that as well as the distance. I had a clear head shot in my sights but just as I was about to pull the trigger something spooked him, and he looked at me. He looked right into my eyes through the sights and he legged it. He was zig zagging left, then right then left again," Sid was aiming an imaginary gun left then right then left again to give us some idea of the immense task he faced.

"I still had him in my sights and just as he was about to feint right again, I aimed two inches to the right of his head to compensate for wind speed and distance and gently squeezed the trigger. BANG! Down he goes. Right in the back of the head. Clean kill. No mess. No mistakes. Just a brilliant bit of shooting. One shot, one kill."

Sid sat down and pulled out a cigarette, he lit it, inhaled deeply, then blew the blueish hue violently from his mouth. "You see, fishing's all about luck. There's no skill to it. Bait your hook, chuck it into the water and wait and see if any thing's daft enough to munch on it."

Molly had retrieved a fresh beer and picked up her chair to move it out of view of the dead bunny.

"Sit down quickly, Molly, you're gonnae love this story. The big game hunter here is gonnae share his secrets into the art of shooting," I dryly interrupted.

"I don't want to hear your stupid stories, it's cruel and disgusting," she countered.

"But shooting, that's a skill pure and simple. You've got to judge for conditions, light, wind, distance. Sometimes, like today, you've even got to look your target right in the eye and blank out all emotion. Silence the voice that says 'I can't do this'. You've got to hold your breath, feel your finger on the trigger and with clear conscience say it's you or me and then squeeze that trigger," Sid concluded whilst staring into the fire like Marlon Brando's character in Apocalypse Now.

"It's a rabbit, Sid, no' the Vietcong," Bobby muttered, shaking his head in disbelief at Sid's shamelessness, "and by the looks of it, it's no' a very well one either."

"Aye you're right, Bobby, it doesn't. What's up with its face? It looks like it's been heid butted by an angry badger," I added, trying to pop Sid's inflated ego.

"What are you talking about? It looks fine, it's a wild rabbit from the Isle of Mull, it's no' meant to look like the wee ones we see running about back home. It's got to be a bit tough to survive the harsh island life. It's probably been through a few scrapes with other rabbits."

"A few scrapes? It looks like General Woundwort," I riposted.

"Myxomatosis. That's what's it's called. Myxomatosis," Bobby stated scratching his chin like the wise old owl he is. "It's a virus that was introduced to control the rabbit population. This one looks like it was suffering from it."

"Pish. Mixaeymytoesis," Sid grumbled

"You aren't going to eat that thing, are you?" Molly enquired, making a repulsed face.

"Aye of course I am, I shot it, I'll gut it and I'll make a nice stew out of it. It's the way things were intended. The world's gone too soft nowadays eating all that processed shite. It's about time we went back to living off the land. Folk weren't as sick in the old days when they were out hunting and eating their catches."

"Amen brother," I clapped along with Sid's righteous speech.

"And you, Molly, you wouldn't survive for a start with all that vegetarian pish. If Armageddon came and we had to start again, how would you feed yourself, eh? Eh?" Sid continued with his rant whilst picking up his catch and shaking it by the hind legs at Molly.

"I'd eat fruit and vegetables like I do now."

"Oh aye and what about your proteins? The body needs proteins to build and repair muscle, you wouldn't get that from your fruit and vegetables, would you, eh?" Sid wasn't backing down.

"I'd get it from pulses and—"

"Look, this is all very topical and interesting, Sid, but all the same you should throw that thing away and I'll put some pork chops on the barbecue. You said it was running away when you shot it?" Bobby asked with a raised eyebrow.

"Eh aye, how?"

"Well if it did have Myxomatosis it wouldn't be able to run at all so unless you're telling porkies and it wasn't just lying at your feet I guess it should be all right to eat."

Check mate to Bobby.

"Whit?!" Sid shuffled in his seat and rubbed his left ear with his right hand. In poker that is what's known as a tell. We all now knew that Sid was bluffing. The trouble was Sid hated losing face so he would continue with this charade and carry on regardless, whatever the consequences may be.

"You calling me a liar like? It took off at full speed, Usain Bolt couldnae keep up with this thing. You're only jealous cause you've no' got the balls to kill an animal. You're just as bad as her," Sid argued, turning the attention back to Molly's vegetarianism.

"Sid's telling the truth, Bobby. I've seen him shoot, he's really good. Let the man eat his kill. I'm away to get my fish cleaned up so I can eat them. I'm bloody starving. Come on, Sid, let us hunter gatherers go prepare our food like real men," I schemed whilst wondering how far Sid was prepared to go with his lies.

The truth was I had never gutted a fish in my puff. I hate the smell and the thought of my fingers rummaging through some poor fish's insides to drag its guts out gave me the dry boak.

I like fishing, don't get me wrong, and I have no problem killing a fish, but I always gave my catches away to neighbours or relatives and let them deal with the real grisly stuff.

But it'd be worthwhile going through the whole rigmarole just to watch Sid eat that manky rabbit.

Dusk was coming in fast so Sid and I had to set up our chopping shop promptly.

"I'm away for a pish first," I advised Sid and then legged it into the woods. Once I'd found a quiet spot, I whipped out my new phone.

Thank fuck I can still get a signal.

I hit YouTube into the Google search engine and after a couple of minutes of nothing it finally registered. I typed in 'How to gut a fish' and I was rewarded with a four-minute crash course on how to gut a fish.

Fuck I'm no' sure I can do that.

Just breathe through your mouth, Jimmy, breathe through your mouth.

By the time I got back to the butcher/fishmonger area, Sid had already cracked on and removed the fur and head from old Bugs.

"Nice work, Sid. You're a dab hand at that," I offered as he held the skinned beast up by its hind legs, admiring his handy work.

I placed the nicer-looking fish out of the two on my makeshift chopping board log and took a deep breath. I knew Sid was watching me over my shoulder. He'd be ready to pounce on the first sign of any weakness, so I had to take the fight to him.

"Scalpel please, nurse," I joked, trying to lighten the moment.

Oh fuck I'm about to cut open a fish for the first time.

I placed my left hand firmly on the top side of the fish and with my right hand shaking ever so slightly I brought it up to rest under the chin of my fish just like the guy in the video had said to do.

He called it a chin.

Do fish have chins?

Come on stop stalling, he'll know you've never done this before.

"I'm making the first incision," and I guffawed again.

With a sharp prod from my virginal knife, I was through the skin.

Take it easy, breath through the mouth.

Now slide the knife back to the anal fin like the boy in the film said.

Not too deep mind, we don't want to puncture the guts.

That's it, see nae bother. Easy peasy.

I made a couple of incisions under each side of the neck and then removed the dorsal fins. Sid was suitably impressed and had gone back to his grim work, leaving me in peace to get the worst of this over with. I laid my knife down then turned the fish on to its back.

Deep breath. Be cool.

I opened its belly up just enough to stick two fingers in.

Rank.

It felt cool and slimy, but I grabbed a hold of some piece of mush and pulled it quickly.

I was surprised at the ease with which I removed its innards. With another quick tug they were completely free, and I stood in amazement as I held this dangling string of blood and guts at arm's length.

In shock and delight at completing this arduous task successfully, I let my guard down and took a long deep breath through my nose.

The stench filled my olfactory system, flew inwards towards my brain which in turn promptly relayed the stinky message to my stomach.

Oh fuck!

"Just gonna get rid of these gu ... bleurgh ... ts." My mouth filled with bile and a few chunks of stuff, probably scrambled eggs and afternoon Balvennie.

Sid looked up from his chopping block, but I think he was too preoccupied with his own bloody mess to notice the leakage spilling from my closed but not closed tightly enough mouth. I sprinted to the loch and flung the fish guts into the water which were closely followed by the contents of my own.

I shook my head then dunked the fish carcass in the water, removing the last of the innards and blood with a swooshing action.

Spitting the last chunks free from my mouth I headed back to my work bench.

Right, that's the worst of it over, let's make this last bit quick then I can watch Sid suffer.

I removed the head, tail, and remaining fins with a few deft slices of my knife and threw them in the loch to join the other sunken parts. I'd already made up my mind after the trauma of gutting my first fish that I would just discard blind brown trout.

No way was I going through that again.

Think I'll continue getting my fish slightly less fresh but ready to cook from the supermarket.

"Right that's me done here," I said as I made my way over to Sid. "One fish ready for the fire. How are you getting on here? Fuck me that stinks," I gasped.

The bloody mess on Sid's log resembled an abortion and he was up to his elbows in blood.

"Aye he doesn't smell too pretty but there's some good meat on this buck," Sid was busy slicing up some sort of muscle into bite size pieces as I approached.

"Looking good though, mate," I lied. "I'm gonnae wrap this wee bugger up in tin foil then sit it next to the fire. I'll see you when you get back." I left Sid to his bloody carcass and chuckled to myself at the thought of him actually going ahead and eating that diseased thing.

Too stubborn for his own good, that boy.

It'll be the death of him.

By the time my fish was cooked, and Sid had made his braised rabbit concoction, Bobby and Molly had already eaten their respective dinners of pork chops and baked beans on toast and were happily sitting back with their beers watching the circus unfold.

In my panic at being faced with gutting a fish for the first time I had completely overlooked the fact that fish are bony little shits. I should have made my mother nature calls excuses and left to go watch a video on de-boning a trout but I was too hungry and lazy to go through all that, so I had to make do with picking at the pieces of meat with my fingers whilst trying not to choke on any bones.

My evening meal was more of a poor starter than a main, but it was all I had and I was too proud after my macho display to admit defeat and ask for a pre-packed supermarket pork chop.

"Ah that was rare. There's nothing like catching, gutting, then cooking your own tea. There's something kind of spiritual about it, you know?" I stated, knowing full well that it was a load of bollocks.

"Aye you're spot on there, Jimmy, my boy," replied Sid, waving his wooden spoon at me. "Does anybody want some of this, there's plenty and it's really good."

We could all see Sid was struggling with his culinary classic of Myxomatosis-infused rabbit lovingly stewed in its own stinking juices before being boiled to an almost chewable state amidst a sauce of Bisto gravy granules.

Voilà.

His jaws were working ten to the dozen as he laboured with the toughness of the meat. Hats off to the boy though there's no way in hell a sane person would've eaten that stinking gruel. A hungry, homeless tramp would've told you to bugger off before dining on his own piss-soaked leather shoe rather than entertaining the thought of eating Sid's braised rabbit.

It just goes to show you what an amazing bullshitter he is, so good in fact that even *he* believes his own lies and is willing to put himself through absolute torture rather than have someone question his authenticity.

After about five mouthfuls even Sid's legendary bullshitting wasn't enough to convince his stomach that this food was edible, so he had to concede and put his bowl down.

"That was delicious," he beamed. "Could've done with some wild garlic and some wild mushrooms though, it was a bit too rich without them. Still, that was the best meal I've had in a long time."

We spent the rest of the evening in a primal trance staring into the fire, smoking joints, and sharing whisky and watching Sid grow restless by the minute.

"I'm away for a wee walk, nice evening for it ..." Sid stumbled over his chair and vanished into the blackness.

"You a'right, mate?" Bobby called out but he was already gone.

Molly picked up her guitar and entertained us with some indie clichéd shit, but it was good to sit back and listen to somebody else play. She was a really good guitarist and a decent singer too. Bobby and me just nodded along and tapped our feet. Halfway through her rendition of a Green Day song, and approximately 25 minutes since he disappeared, Sid stumbled his way back into the camp.

His face gleamed with sweat in the fire light.

"You okay, man?" I asked, a little concerned by his appearance.

"Aye I'm cool, I'm gonnae hit the sack though, I'm feeling pretty tired. Must be all this fresh air," he croaked.

With that he headed for the sanctuary of the hard ground and his sleeping bag.

"You think he'll be okay?" I whispered to Bobby as Sid clambered into the tent. "We shouldn't have let him go ahead and eat that shite; it was bloody stinking. I cannae imagine how it must've tasted. Yuck," I shivered at the thought.

"He should be fine. I searched Myxomatosis earlier and it's not contagious to humans, he'll just have an upset stomach and more than likely a dose of the shits in the morning. Bagsy no' sleeping next to him tonight. Serves him bloody right for his stubbornness," Bobby stated

"Poor Sid," Molly added.

"Poor Sid nothing, he's his own worst enemy," replied Bobby, emptying the last of the whisky down his throat.

CHAPTER 32

I was awoken early next morning by Sid who inadvertently kicked me in the ribs as he made a lunge for the tent door. I awoke with a fright and turned in time to see my perpetrator fighting with the zip on the door. He managed to open it just in time for as soon as he stuck his head through the opening, I could hear him vomit at the entrance.

He collapsed and his body went into some kind of spasm.

"Sid? Sid?" I slid out from my sleeping bag and went to shake him.

"Come on, Sid." I pulled him back inside the tent. His face was a greyish white.

On a Dulux scale it would be called whitey white. That sickly pale gloss colour normally associated with a nasty hangover.

I gently slapped his face.

"Come on, Sid. Wake up. Sid?"

Fuck.

"Bobby? Bobby?"

"Eh what. What is it?" Bobby moaned, half asleep with his eyes still closed to reality.

"It's Sid, he looks terrible, we've got to get him to a hospital. Think that rabbit's poisoned him."

Bobby leapt out of his sleeping bag and checked Sid's pulse.

"He's still breathing, right throw a jumper on him, come on, we'll go take him to the hospital. I hope to fuck they've got one on this island."

"What's going on?" Molly asked, worriedly pushing past Bobby and me.

"It's Sid, don't think he's doing too well, we're gonnae take him to a hospital," I said, shoving her back out of the way.

"You stay and look after the stuff, we'll be back as soon as we can," Bobby reassured.

"I heard him throwing up in the middle of the night, but I thought he'd feel better after that," she answered.

"Aye well he's no' feeling better," I snapped.

We each took an arm of Sid's and threw it over our shoulders and half dragged, half carried him on the ten-minute walk to the van. Halfway there, Bobby picked him up and slung him over his shoulders.

"Right, you get on that phone of yours and get details of the nearest hospital. With any luck there'll be one in Tobermory," he demanded whilst lugging the unconscious Sid.

I left Bobby to the task and frantically searched my phone for the nearest hospital.

"There's one in Salen," I announced triumphantly.

"Good that's no' too far from here, come on."

We carefully placed Sid in the van, he groaned as we did so, and his eyes rolled in his head.

"Do you think he'll be all right? I thought you said that thing wasn't harmful to humans?"

"I dunno and it's not," Bobby was in response mode and jumped in the driver's seat. I wanted to argue that when Sid wasn't driving I was next in line to be the driver, but it didn't seem like the right time for petty squabbles.

Bobby handled the road to the hospital with precision and speed and in 15 minutes we arrived. Bobby ran in ahead as I tried my best to resuscitate Sid from his slumber. I had only managed to unfasten his seatbelt when two men brushed me aside and with Bobby's help pulled Sid from the van and into the little hospital.

I watched them go through the automatic doors and couldn't move.

I hate hospitals.

What if he doesn't come back out?

I shut the van door and walked in to find Bobby sitting in the waiting room with his eyes closed and the back of his head pressed against the wall.

"Is he gonnae be okay? Bobby?"

Bobby slowly opened his eyes and turned to face me. His eyes were bloodshot, and he looked petrified.

"I honestly don't know, man. I don't know."

Fuck.

I put my head in my hands and rubbed my face because I didn't know what else to do.

This wasn't good.

Thoughts of doom and gloom had started to enter my mind and were multiplying at a frightening force.

"Hello?"

I jumped with a startle as the man before us began to speak.

Please God let him be okay.

"Are you the fellows that came in with Sid?"

"Aye, aye we are," we both replied, swallowing hard as we feared the worst.

I didn't want to hear his reply.

"What's happening?" Bobby asked nervously.

"He's fine. He's just got a nasty case of food poisoning. I hear you lads have been camping, which one of you cooked the sausages that made him sick?"

"Whit?!" I replied. "Sausages?" I asked, confused by the turn in events.

"Thanks doctor, we'll sort it out. Can we go in and see him now?" Bobby interrupted, obviously having advised the other doctor on the true chain of events that led to Sid's admission.

"Yes of course you can. You know you've got to be careful when you're cooking meat on a fire, although the meat may look cooked on the outside more often than not it's still uncooked on the inside. He'll be fine in a couple of days he just needs rest and the lost fluids replacing."

We thanked the doctor for his heroic performance in delivering Epsom Salts to our sickly friend.

"That shame-faced bastard told them we poisoned him?" I whispered through pursed lips to Bobby as we made our way into Sid's room.

"Sshhh, it's cool. They know what really happened, Sid just wants to save face. Don't let on."

"Sidney. Good to have you back, mate. You gave us a bit of fright there," Bobby beamed.

"Aye how you feeling?" You lying prick, I wanted to add.

"A'right, lads? Aye I'm alive. I feel like shit though, doctor's reckon I've picked up some sort of infection or something. It must've been off that dead sheep I passed when I was out shooting. It was lying in the middle of the path with its guts all hanging out and I've thought I was being helpful moving it out of the way, you ken? But I've no' washed my hands properly after touching it and that's where it's come from. We're gonnae have to cancel the gigs in Tobermory though I cannae play feeling like this."

"Is that right? A sheep, eh? One of those ones with the long ears, big teeth and fluffy white tail …" I tried to finish but Bobby stepped in front, obscuring me behind his large frame.

"Aye that's what it must've been. Anyway, good to see you're up and at 'em. Take your time getting ready, we'll head back to the camp site and get packed up and we'll collect you in an hour or so. You still want to head for Tobermory?" Bobby said quickly, turning the subject back in Sid's favour.

"Cool. Yeah, I'll need a couple of days in a warm comfy bed to get my strength back. These parasites are in my bloodstream, so I need rest and recuperation. I'll be fine by the Monday then we can head back to the mainland."

With our heads spinning as to whether Sid had food poisoning due to an undercooked sausage, a parasitic disease/infection caused by manhandling a dead sheep, or some sort of gastric disorder brought about by eating a rotten bunny, we set off back to the camp site to collect Molly and all our belongings. The walking wounded was dutifully picked up and handled with kid gloves and we set off in search of Tobermory.

Due to Sid's critical illness he had to be put up in the finest hotel with friendly accommodating staff, luxury Egyptian cotton bed sheets and 24-hour room service should he need some cheese on toast at 3 a.m.

The rest of us, however, were deemed fully fit and able bodied and had to make do with the local hostel which came equipped with its own linen which was synthetic at best.

Sid had phoned ahead to the Mishnish Hotel to cancel our two-night residency there which had angered the owner due to the additional revenue he had outlaid pending our arrival. We were booked for the Saturday and Sunday night which were the busiest times for the local publican, and I could fully understand his annoyance.

Which was why I paid him a visit.

I then announced the plans to Bobby and Molly in a local bar overlooking the picture-perfect painted houses made famous by that terrible children's TV series.

You know, the one with the theme tune?

The one that gets stuck in your head all day and haunts you like a demonic vision driving you to distraction?

I'll tell you what the fucking story is. Here, here's the story, whack, batter, kick, thump. How do you like the story now, Archie, eh? Not so fucking amusing when your face has been hammered to a mushy pulp, is it? Go on, fuck off back to your poncey pink castle and leave us in peace.

No? Maybe just me then.

"Sid will be raging, Jimmy," Bobby pondered as usual, blowing through his cheeks as he viewed the premonition in his mind.

"Fuck Sid. If he's daft enough to eat a shitey rabbit then have the audacity to make up some stupid sob story about it, leaving us bored out of our minds in a shitey hostel whilst he lords it up in some posh hotel getting wanked off by the cute wee chambermaid …"

"Breathe, Jimmy," Molly pleaded.

"Aye cool it," Bobby added.

"Why? It's always the same," I argued, slamming my pint down on the table for effect. "We're always the ones to suffer because of him. Well, no more. Are we supposed to just mope around here aw weekend whilst he gets over his wee tummy bug? There's nothing to do. At least going ahead with the gig without him would give us something to look forward to."

"We could take a boat trip out to Staffa, see Fingal's Cave?" Bobby suggested.

"I COULDNAE GIE A FLYING FUCK ABOOT FINGAL'S CAVE."

The four older chaps who I take it were the locals all turned round to stare at the three of us sat in the corner then tutted and muttered something indecipherable under their rasping breaths.

"I couldn't give a fuck about Fingal's cave, I care about number one and so should you two. Look, if we do these gigs it'll be good for us 'cause we'll get some much needed dough, it'll be good for the band cause we'll be getting more publicity and it'll be good for the folk of Mull and the owner of the bar cause they'll be getting a night of rocking entertainment and money in the till. Everyone's a winner," I argued.

"Except Sid. He'll take the huff big time for sure; you know what he's like. There is no Champions Of The Underdog without him," Bobby replied.

"Well, that's his tough titties. It's his own fault," I countered.

"So you're going to sing then?" Bobby questioned, a little bit too aghast for my liking.

"Yes. Is that such a big deal? My voice is just as good as Sid's, and you know it. Molly can take lead guitar eh, Molly?" I asked in the hope that I'd at least get her on my side.

"Yeah, no problem, I mean I know most of your songs off by heart anyway I'll just need to work out a few of the solos. I'll not be as good as Sid, but I can do it for sure," she added confidently.

"There you go then, it's all sorted. The boy at Mishnish is more than happy to go ahead with it without Sid. He's shelled out about a grand on extra booze and promotions so come on, Bobby, let's do this. It'll probably be a lot more fun without Sid anyway. It's no' as if he's Joey Ramone, he's no irreplaceable. Fuck, nobody on this island has even heard of us. Do you think the crowd will suddenly start chanting 'we want Sid, we want Sid' when I start singing? They couldn't give a toss. As far as they're concerned it's a chance to get pissed whilst listening to a new bunch of wankers rather the usual muck they've got to put up with."

Bobby took a long slug of his pint, put his empty glass on the table, then licked the foam from his top lip as he mulled over the finer points.

Mulled over on Mull?

That's a good title for a song.

Mull over on Mull?

Aye that's no' bad either, I'll sort it out later.

"Aye a'right. But let me tell Sid, you'll just wind him up and then there'll be a battle for me to wade into."

Those were the exact words I wanted to hear. I had no inclination of breaking the news face to face with Sid.

"You'll no' regret it, mate. This is gonnae be magic," I smiled. "Right, whose round is it?"

We finished another couple of beers then headed for the door. Molly and I returned to the hostel whilst Bobby went to tell Sid the good news.

Bobby returned two and a half hours later.

There were no visible signs of physical violence but that was only because Sid couldn't punch his way out of a paper bag seeing as he'd just shat and puked three stone of his body mass away in the last 24 hours.

"Well, how'd you get on?" I asked excitedly, perched on the edge of my bottom bunk.

"Yeah, what'd he say?" Molly added, popping her head over the top bunk.

"How'd you think? He hated the idea, said there was no way we were performing under our name without him. He is The Champion of the Underdog. I got all the usual bollocks how it's like The Doors performing without Jim Morrison or Jimi Hendrix being replaced by a member of The Feeling. He's ready to rip your head off by the way. I'm no' even going into the gory details, you're getting the cleaned up diplomatic Bobby version of events."

"Well, what can he do about it? Ring his wee bell and get the maid to run down here and boot me in the balls? He's as helpless as a shitting dog. We're doing it, end of story," I concluded.

"Aye he knows there's nothing he can do about it and that's why he's raging. He's cooped up in his cosy wee room shut away from the rest of us and he's not in control. I guess the root of his fears, and I'm surmising here, is that we might form a splinter group without him."

"Ha ha fucking brilliant," I rubbed my hands in delight. "I can just imagine him sitting up there stewing, all like …" and I put on an extra whiny voice for effect "… nobody loves me, everybody hates me, I'm so misunderstood'. What about Underdog Champions as our new name?" I gleefully grinned.

"Come on, man. Dinnae be crass," Bobby butted in. "If we all go round there in the morning basically telling him we're only doing it for the good name of the band and that there's no way we'd be anything without him it'll be so much easier in the long run, AND …" he held his finger up for silence as I omitted a large groan. "And, he'd be in our debt for showing that the Champions are nae blooses. Despite being a man down, we always carry on with the show. There's not one of us bigger than the band. We do it for the fans." He nodded his head as if to say his word was gospel.

"Oh come on, I'm no' going round there and licking his arse telling him how great he is, no way," I rebutted.

"No, Bobby's right, we've just got to let him know he's needed and that we're basically doing it for him and then we can show the people of Tobermory what's been missing from their lives," Molly said as she jumped off the top bunk. "This is gonnae be amazing, my friends are going to be sooooo jealous. Bobby, give me the van keys I'm going to get my guitar so I can practice."

CHAPTER 33

On Saturday morning, after we had broken our fast at the local bakery, we paid Sid a visit. It didn't go as bad as I'd expected for the simple reason we did exactly as Bobby told us and let him do most of the talking with Molly and myself merely chipping in with a few 'you're amazing, Sid' and 'as much as it pains us to play without you we're going to have to do this for the good of the band.' Etcetera etcetera etcetera. The bile almost stuck in my throat as I formed those words. But we got what we came for, his reluctant blessing.

Well, Bobby got what he came for.

Molly was a coiled spring of nerves and excitement all day and despite being excited myself I was also very nervous at the prospect of my début as a front man. My nerves soon turned to anxiety and then into fear.

Have I properly thought this one through?

I had been so caught up in my idea of winding Sid up that my brain had forgotten to remember that I'd never sang fully in public before. Yes, I've sang backing vocals and performed the various harmonies with Sid for years but that's easy because you're hiding behind the main man himself. I'm playing second fiddle to the legend that is Sid Hughes. Being a front man was a whole new ball game and it suddenly dawned on me that I didn't think I could do it.

I was irritable all day and couldn't sit still. In my panic I got the keys from Bobby and took the van for a spin just to clear my mind. In all honesty it was so I had a private place to practice singing. I turned the keys in the ignition, pushed The Original Bad Company Anthology into the CD player and then slammed my foot on the accelerator pedal.

Ba da dah doo do doo, do do do doo! I slapped the steering wheel hard to the cracking drum beats of 'Can't Get Enough.'

"Well I take whatever I want and, baby, I want you," I belted it out at the top of my voice, drawing strange looks from the townsfolk and tourists as I motored out of Tobermory.

Should maybe put the windows up.

It was great to be out on the open road with just my voice and the musical accompaniment of Kiss, Foreigner, Led Zeppelin, and Bad Company for, well, bloody brilliant company.

The weather was of the grey dull misty kind that we've become accustomed to in Scotland.

The cold and damp seeps through our clothes and onto our skin and soaks through into bones and marrow before finally drip drip dripping into the root of our souls, turning us into a bunch of angry, moaning, hard bastards who seek some sort of solace from the eternal colourless wet dirge by consuming steaming hot tea by the gallon and alcohol in an even higher volume.

Still, I think we put a brave face on it.

I drove all day through the winding road that is the B8035 which permits a top speed of 20 mph whilst you negotiate hair pin bends, playing chicken with passing motorists as to who is going to be first to pull into the passing place and avoiding the many sheep that feel it is their right to use this road as a bed, toilet, and or meeting place with their sheep pals to discuss the order of the day.

None of this fazed me, however, as I sang from the top of my lungs with a gusto blowing away the cobwebs of diluted backing vocals and harmonies to leave a powerful lead vocal voice in its place.

After three hours of driving and rocking out I found I had reached the end of the road.

Or Fionnphort as it is named.

A picturesque wee village overlooking the Holy Isle of Iona. This is where St Columba set up his base before taking off on a tour of Scotland (not unlike our own, minus the religious undertones) hoping (and probably praying) to convert the pagan Pictish people of this soggy land to his Christian ways. Quite what these Pictish people, a people who were just as happy to fuck each other as fight, thought of St Columba I am not sure, although there are probably a few books written on the subject I for one have no interest in reading them.

I parked the van as the rain started to pour down with enough frequency that it required the second setting on the windscreen wipers to keep my view of the Holy Island visible. By view I mean grey mist. I couldn't actually see the island, but it didn't stop me getting out of the van to take a closer look. I made my way to the tiny beach that snuggled into the side of Fionnphort. The Calmac ferry had just departed on its ten minute crossing to Iona and it bobbed up and down nauseatingly.

Huddled up against the wind and rain I looked out to where the Abbey could possibly be situated and thought of the old Scottish kings that were buried there. Men vying for power and control of a divided nation.

Power, that was the key.

It's what we all want in a way, whether it be over our thoughts, our family, friends, or our people. I lit and smoked a cigarette and let a wave of melancholy submerge me again.

There's something about the history of this nation that made me feel sad, confused, and proud all at once, sending a tingling shiver up my spine.

With that I jumped back into the van and looked out one of our own CDs so I could judge my newly invigorated singing voice alongside Sid's.

I took what I thought would be the quicker route to Tobermory, the A849, but this was slower than the other route. It was just as scenic though as the mist swirled around the various peaks with unpronounceable names giving the place that comforting eerie feel.

It was almost 6 p.m. by the time I got back, only to find Bobby and Molly in a panic as to my whereabouts.

"Where the hell have you been? We couldn't get through to your phone, we're on in just over an hour," Bobby barked, sounding more uptight than his usual laid back self.

"Relax, man. I just went for a wee spin, it's all good. Are you ready to rock?"

It was all good.

I felt a lot better than I did that morning and after a great sound check with our new guitarist and a couple of doubles in my belly, I was in a confident mood.

We started off quite slowly and nervously as you would expect with a hastily rearranged line up, but after a bit of banter with the attentive crowd we quickly got into our stride.

I felt amazing.

I was hitting every note and Molly was doing us proud on lead guitar. Bobby put in his usual solid, unassuming performance at the back. I was getting a great response from the crowd who were well up for it.

After our set Bobby, Molly, and I embraced in a sweaty euphoric cuddle.

"That was without doubt *THE* best moment of my life," Molly shouted in our ears as the audience's clapping and cheering died down.

"You did us proud, kid. You were brilliant," Bobby purred.

"Aye you were, and you get to do it all again tomorrow. Come on, we'll give you a hand taking down the gear then we'll come back in here and celebrate with the punters," I added breathlessly, my heart was still hammering in my chest from the exertion and adrenaline.

Dismantling and packing away our instruments and amps is my least favourite job, in part because it's boring but mainly because it brings you back down to earth quicker when all you want to do after a storming set is party with your newly formed fans.

But tonight was an exception.

The three of us all mucked in and within an hour of finishing our set we had packed everything away and were sitting at the bar drinking with our new best friends whilst receiving all the gracious praise and back slaps we could handle.

"I could get used to this," Molly shouted over all the drunken voices as she slurped on a bottle of beer.

"Aye, I'll bet you could. So could I," I surprised myself by saying that and I drunkenly analysed my statement as I stood taking a piss in the toilet cubicle.

I could get used to this?

There was nothing out of the ordinary about this gig.

We've played to bigger and more raucous crowds in bigger venues than this.

We've played better than this.

But I've never been the centre of attention before.

The focal point.

The one having the banter with the crowd.

The orchestrator of the band.

The leader.

The power.

Fuck, it's like a drug.

It's infectious.

Now I could see through Sid's eyes why he loved this job so much. Bobby and I had lost the initial thrill of playing live years ago. I suppose it was a case of familiarity breeding contempt. We were just bit part players and although it was still thrilling to hear the roar of appreciation from the crowd, it was nothing like feeling that roar when it's you that's standing centre stage. You that's announcing the next song and it's you that's holding the audience in your palm as they listen to you and only you.

I could definitely get used to this.

That night, carried by the wave of ecstasy and desire, we drank till closing time and then got invited back to a local's house to carry on the party.

Which we did.

It was light when Bobby made the executive decision that we should stumble back to the hostel.

For a wee lassie Molly had kept up with the frantic drinking pace tremendously well.

With wide smiley drunken faces, the three of us linked arms and trudged back to the comfort of our bunk beds.

On waking a few hours later, despite feeling like I'd spent the night boxing a kangaroo in a barbed wire cage whilst using an old sock as a gum shield, I still couldn't get rid of the feeling of exhilaration.

The memory was too fresh.

Bobby was already up and had gone to visit Sid to tell him how rubbish it was playing without him and how the crowd were good but not as good as they would have been if he had been there and so on and so on and so on.

We spent a collective, lazy Sunday eating Pot Noodles in our dorm and talking about that evening's gig. We'd managed to sell a few of our CDs and a couple of t-shirts so we planned on taking more for tonight's performance and I'd do my bit to promote them more in my new role as lead singer/front man.

I'd asked Bobby and Molly to meet at The Mishnish at 5 o'clock because I wanted us to have an extended sound check.

What I actually wanted to do was give Molly enough time to rehearse a couple of songs that I had written. I'd written loads of songs in the early days of the band which in my humble opinion were just as good.

No.

Some of them were better, a lot better than the ones Sid had written, so when I played them for him, I was expecting muchos praise with the promise of a Lennon/McCartney equal writing royalties partnership. What I actually received was a volley of abuse about how my songs were weak and slow and that the lyrics lacked feeling and that the whole musical content I'd just subjected his ears to made him want to quit the business altogether.

He was like Simon Cowell before Simon Cowell had invented himself and instead of a Lennon/McCartney song-writing partnership, I was left feeling like the Ringo Starr of song writing.

Jimmy, you really are a very naughty engine.

So I gave up on my song-writing quest, believing everything Sid had said and, I quote, 'I'm your friend and I wouldn't want to see you humiliated on stage by playing that shite.'

Well, I finally knew the truth.

He felt threatened by me because he knew I could be just as good a writer and front man as him.

Tonight that would all change.

We met at 5 p.m. and set up our equipment and after Molly had checked the microphones and tuned our guitars, I sat them both down and explained that we would be playing two new songs for tonight's show.

This did not go down well with Bobby, a man who would do anything for a quiet life and the thought of offending our dear old friend Sidney would give him anything but a quiet life.

"That's a bad idea, mate. Sid will not like this one little bit," he groaned and shook his head.

"Bobby, he's stuck up in his room shitting through the eye of a needle, he'll never know. Stop being a big Jessie, eh? Do it for me pal, I just want to see how they go down. I might even start writing again if it all goes well," I pleaded.

And so, after much time wasted debating the pros and cons with Bobby over my two songs, he eventually agreed (as he always would) and we set about rehearsing them.

Molly picked up the changes in no time at all and I had to admit my songs did sound impressive when accompanied by crashing drums and a ringing lead guitar.

The crowd wasn't as busy or energetic that night mainly because it was a Sunday evening, and most people were laying off the booze so they could begin their working week in the morning with fresh heads. None the less it was still a very enjoyable gig, and my two songs did receive a good reception, no better, but no worse than any of our other tunes, justifying my decision to include them in our set.

It did feel pretty amazing singing my own songs for the first time.

I was like a proud father introducing my two babies to the world.

My ego had been stimulated again and I liked it.

I love it.

I want more of it.

We packed up and shared a couple of drinks with the sparse crowd who had stayed behind to chat. A couple of people from the house party last night had made it back to see us again but were taking it easy and nursing lager shandies.

We didn't sell anything on the merchandising front, but we'd just been paid so we were more than happy with that. Plus, we certainly added a few more 'likes' to our Facebook page. All in all, a successful enjoyable evening was had by everyone and the three of us walked back to our hostel in quiet contemplation, lost in our own wee world, enjoying the moment that had passed, safe in the knowledge that it was indeed a unique moment in the history of Champions Of The Underdog and one that would never be seen again.

Well, perhaps not under that name.

But the seeds had been sown in my mind.

CHAPTER 34

We were awoken early next morning by Bobby's phone ringing for far longer than it had to, instantly ruining my wonderful dream and putting me in a crabbit mood.

"That was Sid," Bobby yawned, rubbing his eyes. "He's downstairs waiting on us, he's ready to go, we're heading for Lochgilphead. Apparently, we've got a gig there tonight."

"It's 7 o' clock," I moaned whilst staring at the inside of my eyelids.

"Aye but the ferry leaves at 9 o'clock. Come on, let's get our arses in gear, he didn't sound in the best of moods."

"For fuck's sake. Good to hear he's back to normal, eh?"

We got dressed, packed our bags, then ambled to the car park to find Sid on his phone leaning against the van. We threw our belongings in the van as Sid finished his call.

"You lot took your time, we've got a ferry to catch," he huffed.

"Good morning, Sid. Glad to see you back on your feet. We're all good, thanks for asking, how are you?" I asked through a clearly fake smile.

"Fine. Get in the van. You're in the back, Jimmy. Bobby's spent enough time in there."

"Eh? How am I in the back. What about Molly? She's no' been in there yet."

"She'll get her turn. Today it's your turn, now get in the back," Sid glared, daring me to challenge his authority.

"I dinnae mind going in the back again likes," Bobby chipped in, trying his best to turn down the simmering heat.

"No, Bobby, you've had your turn, fair's fair." Sid's eyes never left mine as he answered Bobby.

"Fuck's sake," I moaned and opened the back doors.

What's the matter with his greetin' puss this morning?

The journey from Tobermory to Craignure only took 25 minutes but it felt longer as I clung to the inside of the van, slowly seething at Sid's outburst.

We parked up in the ferry queue at Craignure and while Sid was busy buying the tickets for our crossing I spoke to Bobby whilst massaging some feeling back into my numb arse.

"What's the matter wi' him?"

"He turned up at the gig last night," Bobby whispered, looking over his shoulder to see if Sid was in the vicinity. "He came in for the last half an hour and sat at the back. I didn't even see him. He saw us play your songs and he's pissed off."

"Fuck. He was spying on us? He could've come and seen us last night if he was that pissed off?"

"He said he was too mad, that he would've ended up hitting one of us so he left it till the morning. He thinks you're wanting to break up the band and do your own thing."

"What? He's crazy, man. I think that poisoned rabbit has affected his brain," I checked the horizon and could see Sid making his approach with the tickets in his hand. "Shit, he's coming."

"Look you'll have to talk to him, Jimmy, otherwise these next few weeks will be unbearable …"

"Right, here's your tickets," Sid dished out our tickets like a parent handing out dinner money to his three disobedient children. "Don't lose them. I'm away to get some breakfast. The ferry leaves in 45 minutes. Be back here in 30." And he turned and walked off in the opposite direction.

"Go," Bobby nodded that I should follow him.

"Aye all right, but what am I meant to say to him other than that he's a deluded paranoid freak?" I asked.

"Just tell him it was a one off, a wee break from the norm. Just don't go losing your temper and making things worse. I cannae be arsed dealing with you two bairns aw day."

"I've no' even done anything, it's him that's got the problem," I defended.

Bobby just sighed and waved a dismissive hand at me and turned to go in the other direction with Molly, leaving me standing there alone and feeling flat, wishing I felt like I did when I was standing on stage in Tobermory.

Once inside the harbour cafe I ordered two bacon rolls and a coffee and placed them on the table where Sid had sat. I pulled the rickety wooden chair from under the Formica topped table to sit down.

He didn't even look up from his plate of fried meats.

This riled me.

To hell with diplomacy.

"What's the problem, Sid? Your puss has been tripping you all morning," I launched in.

"What's the problem?" he mumbled before swallowing his packed mouthful of food and wiping his lips with the back of his hand, leaving a shiny wee trail of bean juice glistening in the sunlight.

"You're the problem," and he jutted his pointing finger at me in case I wasn't sure who he was talking about. All I could look at was the slimy orange trail on the back of his hand as he shook it in my face. I fought hard not to piss myself laughing which would make everything worse. "I suppose Bobby told you I saw some of the gig last night?"

"Aye he mentioned it. What did you think? Pretty good, eh?" I couldn't help myself.

"What the fuck were you playing those songs for? They're not Champion's songs, they're not good enough. So you think you're a front man now, eh?" he seethed.

"Look, man, get aff your high horse. It was a one off," I slurped my coffee then looked him square in the eyes. I knew he felt threatened by me because he had seen for himself how good we were without him and how good I was as a front man and how good my songs were. And I now knew the tactics he'd employ that would supposedly beat me into submission so I'd lie down and accept his word as gospel.

Well sorry, Sid, my boy, I'm not falling for those tricks any more.

But go on, take your best shot, tell me how bad we were and how terrible I was and how pathetic my songs were.

"You'd never make it as a front man anyway. Your voice isn't good enough and you spend too much time talking with the crowd. They're here to listen to music no' listen to you talking shite ..."

Ouch, he's hurting more than I thought.

Sid likes to think of himself in the same guise as his musical heroes, Liam Gallagher and Jim Morrison. A brooding figure who prowls across the stage like a caged lion, demanding to be respected by the gathered crowd who have come to see his majestic presence. A legend in his own mind who should be worshipped by the masses who are beneath him in every sense of the word. He is a God and as such should be treated like one and if your eyes are lucky enough to meet his as he scans his flock with a vacant, distant gaze then you are truly blessed for you have been fortunate enough to have looked through the window of his soul into greatness. For he IS blessed, he IS greatness, and he IS the saviour of musical apathy.

I, on the other hand, adopted a more natural form during my two-night stint as front man for Champions Of The Underdog. I took the absurd notion to act like a human being as I shared jokes and stories with the audience whom I also treated as human beings before entertaining them with our collective group of songs.

End of story.

And then I would go and mingle and listen to their comments and praise and let them purchase me many beverages after they had had the pleasure of listening to our songs and I had had the pleasure of playing them our songs.

Simple.

"… so dinnae get carried away with yourself on some crazy notion that this is the start of something new for you, cause it's not. This is my band, and they are my songs, and you'll never tear this band apart," Sid continued with his rant.

"What are you talking about? I think your brain's been fucked up with that food poisoning—"

"It wasn't food poisoning; it was a parasite. I saw you, remember. You were loving it up there, being the centre of attention for once in your sad wee life. I saw the gleam in your eye, and I know how your mind works, Jimmy."

"Is that right, eh?"

"Aye so you can forget about breaking up the band, Bobby and Molly are with me—"

"Breaking up the band? Have you lost it? Do you think I'd break up the band after destroying the best relationship I've ever had just to drag my sorry arse around the country with you? Do you think I'd break it up after alienating myself from my parents to do this tour? I've got no girlfriend, no job, and nowhere to live, why the fuck would I break up the band? This is the only thing I've got in my life, get a grip," I tried to sound as pathetic as I could for Bobby's sake. But I was already formulating a plan in my mind.

When we were finished with this never-ending tour, I was going to form my own band.

My band.

And I'd take Bobby and Molly with me.

"I suppose. I dunno. I think I'm still suffering from the effects of that disease I had, and it's made me a bit paranoid."

"That's understandable, mate. You've been through a lot lately," I replied, putting on my best sad face for full effect.

Poor wee Sid.

"Ach I guess I'm just feeling a wee bitty depressed, I mean this tour has hardly been a success, has it? I thought we would've been signed up by now but instead we're off to Lochgilphead to play to a few dozen punters for a couple of hundred notes. It's getting to me, man. I'm better than this. We're better than this. We should be getting recognition for that." His head slumped into his hands as he let out a huge sigh.

"Look, we've been in this together since the beginning and yes it's been tough at times, but it's also been a great fucking laugh, so come on, keep the chin up. What have we got, four or so weeks left? There's still time, keep the faith," and I slapped him on his pathetic shoulder. He looked up at me through tired, almost defeated eyes.

You're fucked, pal.

"You're right. Sorry, man. I was feeling a bit left out there when you did the gigs without me, and my imagination went into overdrive. Being stuck in a bedroom all weekend on your own isn't healthy."

"I thought you would've had that lassie from reception up to keep you company?"

"Aye I did, but I was too weak to shag her, so she just wanked me off instead. You want to smell my fingers?" And he held them in front of my face as a huge grin spread across his.

"Get lost, you dirty bastard."

How the hell does he do it?

Even in his sick bed he pulled, lucky bastard.

"You were good though ..." but he couldn't finish the sentence because it would make him puke up his freshly eaten cooked breakfast therefore wasting his money.

"I know," I replied.

"Hey dinnae get cocky, you weren't *that* good."

Bobby and Molly entered the building and upon seeing Sid and me talking and laughing decided it was safe enough to approach and join us for a coffee.

"I've been thinking," Bobby said as he nibbled his carefully dunked shortbread. "Why don't we go over to the Outer Hebrides? I mean, it's been brilliant fun touring the islands and exploring the scenery and Harris and Lewis are supposed to be beautiful. White empty beaches, rugged landscapes, the folk there would love to hear us play. They cannae get that many bands going over to play, we'd be doing them a real service."

"Exactly, that's why were no' going," Sid answered, instantly bursting Bobby's little romantic vision. "Nothing good ever happens over there, it's just full of sheep. If we went over to Stornoway we'd ruin their little world with our amazing tunes. It'd be like stumbling upon a lost tribe in the Amazon and letting them taste Irn-Bru, they'd go mental for it, but they could never have it again. They'd be fucked, imagine them running about in their wee grass skirts licking anything and everything trying to recreate that sweet sugary taste. It'd drive them crazy. Nah best just to leave them alone. What they dinnae know cannae hurt them."

So a planned trip to the Outer Hebrides, one of the most rugged and scenic parts of our fantastic nation, was struck off the list because our leader didn't think the simple islanders could handle hearing us perform live.

I'd like to spend a day inside his head to see where he gets these notions from.

He really is a fucking idiot.

CHAPTER 35

Over the next few nights, we played a meaningless bunch of gigs to weekday crowds in Lochgilphead, Inveraray, and Helensburgh.

The one highlight was a gig we played at The Drovers Inn. A rustic pub at the top end of Loch Lomond that looked about as old as the hills behind it. With the low ceiling in the bar and the open fire blaring, the atmosphere was great and we had a brilliant night of drinking and banter after we'd finished.

Molly had been promoted too.

After seeing her in action at The Mishnish, Sid had decided to put her on rhythm guitar, leaving him with more time to prance about the stage like a proper front man should.

She still had to set up and dismantle our equipment but at least Sid gave her a few pounds for her efforts even if it did mean me and Bobby's cut of the cash was reduced.

We drove down the Bonnie Bonnie Banks of Loch Lomond although how bonnie they actually were on that particular autumnal morning I cannot say for I was stuck inside the back of the van, spending my time updating our blog whilst being shunted from one side to the next as Sid negotiated the A82.

Our destination was Glasgow. We'd use the city itself as a base and then ferry our happy little group to the outlying areas before coming back to the city centre to play to the best crowds in the country if not the world. Apparently.

Our base as per usual was a hostel in the city centre but I was pleasantly surprised by the standard of this one. Sid had done us proud and had managed to cut a deal with the manager by probably telling him he was lucky enough to be housing the hottest live band in the country in his humble establishment.

We managed to get a four-bed dorm so we wouldn't have to worry about getting our stuff nicked by other punters. Not that we had been particularly worried on our adventure so far because none of our stuff had been touched.

But we hadn't been staying in Glasgow.

After settling into our new base which consisted of throwing our bags down, checking the state of the sheets and deciding on who would sleep on which bed, we all jumped back into the van because we had a gig that evening in Greenock.

I'd never actually set foot in Greenock before, but I had prejudged the town as a bit of a shit hole. My impression of Greenock as a shit hole had been formed whilst watching Scotsport and Sportscene as a kid in the 1980s. Upon seeing images of Cappielow, home of Greenock Morton F.C., beamed into my living room. The ground appeared to be a bit of a dump and there was this massive crane behind the terracing to the left of the park which loomed over the stadium as a constant reminder of the great ship building days gone by but which were now pretty much extinct.

But as I strolled through its streets with the setting sun creating a pink haze over the town, I was amazed by the beauty and quality of the architecture in the main buildings. Had they been built in Edinburgh or Glasgow they would have been marvelled over, but as it was just Greenock …

Well, you know?

I also learned that Greenock was the birthplace of the famous Scottish inventor James Watt. To celebrate this fact, I popped into the James Watt pub for a cheeky pint to toast his roaring success with the steam engine.

I felt more relaxed about the gig now that I had seen the town for myself. It wasn't the dump I was expecting.

The gig that night at The Steamie was played to a drunken, pumped up, mostly teenage/underage crowd.

The drunken, pumped up kind that like to lob alcohol at you whilst you play.

This was much to Sid's annoyance as he felt it showed a lack of respect towards the band. I thought it a nice touch though as I cowered in the background and looked on as Sid was constantly splattered by plastic cups containing the dregs of Tennent's lager.

The crowd hadn't heeded Sid's earlier warnings about throwing cups and like a bunch of delinquent children they actually threw more at the band. The cups that were frequently launched at us appeared to contain a greater volume of liquid too.

The inevitable eventually happened and I saw it all at close quarters.

A wee fanny about two rows from the front of the sparse stage took a couple of sups from his newly purchased pint, did the universal 'ahhh' of enjoyment and then pulled his right arm back over his shoulder and hurled the plastic tumbler containing the best part of three quarters of a pint with as much strength as his puny wee arm could muster.

I watched in awe as the stream of lager that shot from the projected cup spilled tiny amber droplets onto the sweaty heads of the bouncing row in front.

The plastic pint didn't falter in its trajectory, and it must've been travelling at approximately 75 mph when it connected with Sid's confounded coupon.

As it had only been thrown from ten feet away it hit Sid's face like a big wet punch which sent his head snapping back in shock. That shock instantly turned to anger as Sid stopped singing mid verse, shook the drips from his face, and launched himself headfirst into the crowd in true Axl Rose fashion.

He swung a fist in the general direction of the perpetrator but unfortunately for the young lad in question whose hapless jaw connected with Sid's angry fist it wasn't the correct direction. The innocent guy dropped to the floor in a broken heap as Sid grabbed the next guy who was closest to him and held him by the throat whilst screaming obscenities in his face. The offender who had caused this unsavoury scene slunk away through the crowd whilst presumably thanking his lucky stars that it hadn't been his chops that had just been busted.

Bobby threw down his sticks and waded through the crowd to try and diffuse the situation. His massive bulk was enough to make anyone stop what they were doing and pay him attention. He pulled Sid from his latest victim as dozens of plastic pint glasses rained down on the stricken twosome thrown by teenage thugs on the periphery of the brawl. Sid had shaken himself free of Bobby's grip and returned to his square go with anyone who was within swedging distance. He used his guitar as a shield come axe, sending chopping blows upon anyone who strayed into his path.

I stood on stage watching the scene unfold as my mind drifted back to a similar incident several months earlier at The Crown. By the time I'd finished reminiscing the mini riot had been broken up as the sturdy bouncers grabbed anyone who looked like causing trouble and threw them out the door, including a very irate Sid.

"No need for an encore then, eh?" I said to Molly who looked on in disbelief.

"What the hell was that all about?" she spluttered. "That was mental."

"Sid's like a Gremlin, you dinnae want to get him wet," I laughed, trying to make light of the situation. "Come on, let's get this stuff packed away and into the van."

"Are they nutters gonnae be waiting for us outside?" Molly asked with genuine fear in her eyes.

"Eh, I dunno?" I hadn't thought that far ahead but now that she mentioned it there was more than a good possibility that the wee neds would be hanging around awaiting our exit so they could unleash more fury.

The main door to the pub slammed open as Bobby and Sid pushed their way through the bar and marched on up to the stage.

"Fucking wee bastards, eh?" shouted Sid. "Fucking chucking beer at me, eh?"

"Aye that was out of order, come on, let's get out of here before any more shit happens," I replied in haste.

"They're not going to be waiting outside for us, are they?" asked Molly, voicing her earlier concerns to the whole group.

"They'd better no' even think about it, the mood I'm in," Sid seethed, throwing his guitar leads into his case with venom. "Where were you when it was kicking off, eh?" His furious eyes met mine.

"Eh … I … by the time I knew what was going on it was all over with …" I stammered.

"Standing up here like a big pussy while me and Bobby sorted the wee cunts out. You should've been in the mix wi' us two."

"You boys seemed to be doing all right for yourselves; anyway, laying into a bunch of kids isn't really my thing, man," I smiled and held my hands up in an attempt to deflect the heat from me.

"If they're old enough to stand there and drink and then throw it at me then they're old enough to suffer the consequences. It's nice to know who your friends are though eh, Bobby?"

There he goes again always looking for someone to take his side.

Strength in numbers, eh Sid?

"Look, let's just get out of here, this has been a disaster. I don't even want to talk about it," Bobby moaned as he wiped the dregs of spilt beer from his cymbals.

"Big Bobby was quick enough to get steamed in, unlike you, you wee pussy," Sid jabbed his finger in the air, thrusting it at me.

Suddenly it's all about me again.

I never threw anything at you or caused the rammy but I'm the one who's taking the brunt of your anger, how's that?

Aye for that simple reason.

You've just stood and watched, eh?

Molly didn't do anything either and she's no' getting this hostile reception.

"Molly didn't do anything either," I complained.

"Whit?! What the hell do you expect Molly to do? She's five foot and weighs six stone soaking wet. What the fuck do you want her to do?"

"Yeah, Jimmy, what was I supposed to do?" Molly argued.

Now I had managed to piss off Sid and Molly all thanks to some wee bastard who threw a pint.

Where's the justice?

"Will you all just shut up and let's get out of here," Bobby roared as he continued dismantling his drum kit.

We did as we were told and hastily bid a retreat from our one and only trip to Greenock. I had half expected a bit of trouble on the way out as we bundled our gear into the van, but none was forthcoming. I was relegated to the back of the van for my earlier stance of pacifism.

I pondered as I sat in the black silence.

What would Gandhi have done?

CHAPTER 36

Sid had decided that the weekend gigs would be played solely in Glasgow for obvious reasons and the midweek gigs would be played in the general Strathclyde and outlying area.

As a band we'd never played in Glasgow before.

Even in the early days.

I tried to think why this might have been and I had a faint recollection that the three whipper snappers held Glasgow with disdain, and we had refused to play there. Not that we were ever offered the chance.

Glasgow has a reputation of being the funniest, friendliest, prettiest, hardest city in Scotland if not the world.

A reputation only held intact by its inhabitants.

It was because of this arrogance that Glasgow is the centre of the universe that we decided to shun it altogether.

We were tired of playing what we thought at the time were 'amazing gigs' only to be told by some weegie punter afterwards that it would've been miles better if it was played in Glasgow. Rather than being held in some sort of mythical awe by us, a musical Oz if you will, it was held in complete contempt.

With hindsight, had we played to a Glasgow crowd earlier in our careers we probably would have made it by now.

Nice 'n' Sleazys was the venue for the upcoming Saturday night. We were keen to put on a bit of a show after the debacle that was the previous night's gig. I wasn't holding out for much when I walked through the doors carrying my bass and amp as menacingly as I could. The place was a bit of a dive but that didn't bother me, I felt more comfortable in places like this.

The punters, however, were dressed like there had been an accident at the Belle and Sebastian cloning plant.

"Oh for fuck's sake," Sid groaned as his eyes made contact with what I had just seen.

"The times they are a changing, my man," I replied, rolling my eyes.

"Aye but do the times have to be so pretentious? Does anyone need to wear a pair of spectacles that big?" he asked.

We dumped our stuff on stage and headed for the bar, leaving Molly to carry on with her initial role of setting up.

Molly fitted in a treat with the paying public though. Young, cool, and although I wouldn't class her as pretty, she had a certain look to her that I'd describe as interestingly attractive.

A few of the art school dropouts walked to the stage to chat with her.

I supped a beer in the corner, ignoring everyone, pretending to be on my phone so nobody would talk to me.

They were less than a generation in age from us, but I felt as though we were centuries apart.

I blame technology.

It's developing too quickly, leaving this latest generation frustrated and impatient.

As a youngster I had a Spectrum 48K computer. The games were shit and they took a day and a half to load. But at the time it was the most amazing thing on the planet. I had to wait years for my next computer, a Commodore Amiga, only purchased so I could play Sensible Soccer. Then it was a number of years later that I bought my first console. Three pieces of technology over a span of some 15 years. Each one better than the previous but all three equally enjoyed and overused.

Patience, that's the key. These days there seems to be a new phone, a new console, or a new bit of technology that I've never even heard of making an appearance at the end of every week.

These folk have no perseverance. They rant and they rave about saving the planet and bang on about how much we waste yet look at the technology they own. It's all the latest, up-to-the-minute shit that's available. They don't hang on to a phone or laptop or tablet that's two months out of fashion oh no, that gets chucked in the bin as the latest edition hits the shelves.

The point I'm trying to make is that us, we, Champions Of The Underdog are *THAT* out-of-date technology.

The people who buy the music, who influence the wider public, are young and flighty. They'll love us initially as we grab their attention for five minutes. But their brains and imaginations will soon grow bored and listless and then they'll discard us like the out-of-date software that we are.

Use By.

Best Before.

Out of date.

They've never experienced the delight in going back to that old Spectrum 48K a decade after it was first used. They rubber keys all worn. Teeth marks on the edge of the plastic board where I'd thrown a wobbly at my failings in Daley Thompson's Decathlon.

And starting it up.

The memories, the shudder of pleasure, the agony and the ecstasy of the whole loading process. I played with that machine for years, long after it had been preceded by faster and smarter technology, because I loved it.

Because it was mine.

Just like the music we as a band still listen to hasn't changed.

Because it's ours.

We've invested so much time. Many hours of sitting, drinking, smoking, and laughing. Listening at times in pure silence and with great intent trying to fathom out a chord or new piece of melody that we'd never noticed before.

We own a piece of it.

It's ours.

"So what are you into then?" A pretty looking girl with what can only be described as a Hitler haircut asked me, pricking the bubble of my insightful ramblings.

Pop.

"Not the same as you, hen," I sighed and with a shake of my head I returned my attentions to the bar.

What am I into?

I shook my head again.

The state of youth today.

You're just getting old.

Fair play to the crowd though. They shook me from my slumber with some energetic dancing and whooping. Our tunes went down a storm and the four of us left the stage after an hour of non-stop noise to thunderous applause.

We were all beaming grins and wide smiles.

When you get nights like these it makes me wonder why I ever did anything else with my life. The band, the music, the crowd as one. A triptych of energy absorbing and reverberating within and without.

It was almost spiritual.

I can now say, having experienced my first Glasgow gig, and without any sarcasm, that Glasgow crowds are by far the best in Scotland. I won't say the world because that would be unfair. But without prejudice I can definitely say the best in Scotland.

Well so far.

There are still a few places we haven't been to yet.

The night ended on a high as we were invited back to one of the happy punter's flats for refreshments. Bobby declined as Mel was through for the weekend but Sid, Molly, and me thought it'd be good for a laugh.

I retract my earlier statement about the youth of today/technology because that was a terrible generalisation to make.

'Never judge a book by its cover' is a phrase I often use when preaching to others but seldom do I put it into practice.

The party was housed in what I would call a typical art student's flat.

Posters, paintings, and various hangings adorned the walls. Lazy, socialist regalia was splattered everywhere as if to imply that this lot were the first generation to have a conscience.

I have a deep-rooted mistrust of people who wear or display images of Che Guevara.

Do they fail to see the irony?

Despite all of this I found myself warming to them as we relaxed to some obscure jazzy beats. The kind of jazzy beats that I would normally find irritating and pretentious but in this context strangely worked.

We sat and chatted on many subjects, ranging from art and music to politics and the evolution of technology. Well, if we were going to be all grown up about it, I thought I'd at least pose some sensible questions.

Sid and Molly were perched on the other side of the living room engaged in some deep and meaningful conversation with a couple who nodded and gestured with frantic arm movements that I took to imply agreement.

I was sat next to a girl who introduced herself as Abbie who was twenty and in her third year at Glasgow School of Art.

Ordinarily I would have shunned her for no other reason than she was an art student. This is because the people I'd met over the years who were art students or who had previously attended art college tended to be arrogant, self-indulgent wankers.

Bobby was the only exception to the rule.

But then again, he had an actual talent.

He is a naturally gifted painter who doesn't feel the need to tell the whole world and anybody else who will listen how talented and creative he is.

For this and many other reasons he is one of my best friends.

Abbie quickly fell into the same category as Bobby. She was shy and self-effacing, and I instantly warmed to her. Not only that, she was pretty cute and had an enormous pair of tits that I could see my hands all over. I played it coy and told her how creative and amazing she was as she reluctantly pointed out a mass of clay that could've been an accident but was in fact one of her 'sculptures' and she in turn played it coy with me telling me I was a gifted musician who wrote great 'music.'

It wasn't long before I had my tongue down her throat and I made my move to get her to a place of tranquillity where we could take things further so I could see those amazing tits in all their glory.

"There's no rush, Jimmy," she panted, pushing her hand into my chest to abort our tryst. "We've got all night, let's build up the tension. Besides, I don't want to be one of those annoying couples who just snog all night."

I fell in love with her right there.

We sank, entwined in our beanbag, and carried on with the party.

After hours of interesting chit chat, beer drinking and joint sharing, somebody introduced a cocktail to the room.

It was described as mushroom tea.

Sid and me immediately looked at each other in fear.

Mutual hallucinogenic flashbacks flashed back into our minds.

"Eh, would that be the magic kind?" Sid asked.

"Of course. Is there any other kind?" Much chortling throughout the room commenced at the bearer's witty riposte.

"No' for me, pal. I'm passed all that shit. Hallucinogens are a young man's game," Sid replied with glowering eyes. He motioned for me with the universal 'come on, it's time for us to go' head nod but I palmed him off.

"It's okay, it's a pretty mild hit, just something to wind the party down with. I've infused it with honey and whisky to take the bad flavour away. You should try it," advised the mixologist.

"A mushroom flavoured hot toddy? That sounds simply spiffing, old bean," I replied, trying to deflect the attention from Sid and me.

Sid was insistent that he was partaking in none of that jiggery pokery and said we should leave. But I didn't want to, I was having a rare old time.

He mouthed something along the lines of 'stupid prick' to me.

Actually, I wasn't interested in taking any of the mushroom brew either.

That was until Abbie intervened.

"You should try it, Jimmy. It is very mild; it just exaggerates things like touch and smell and taste."

I tried to fob her off and impress her by exaggerating that Sid and I had taken LSD and mushrooms millions of times and nearly died the last time we took acid and that we were only now just getting over our Sid Barrett/Peter Green psychosis.

"Why do you think he's called Sid? That's not his real name," I told her with a stern look on my face.

"Oh you don't have to, I don't want to force you, I just wanted you to share what I'll be experiencing … later. It'll be amazing feeling your skin on mine."

If ever there was a case of my dick overruling my brain, this was it.

I knew I shouldn't have drunk it but all I could think about was her naked body, glorious tits, and all the fucking we'd be doing. Hell at that stage I would've drank bleach had she asked me to.

With an erection that was trying its best to burst through my jeans like the Alien from the unfortunate man's chest in the film, I grabbed the large Thermos flask that housed the warm mushroom brew and slugged a dose.

It tasted as bad as it sounded.

There wasn't enough whisky in Scotland to disguise the earthy fungal taste.

It made me gag.

I wiped my eyes and passed the flask onto Abbie as Sid stared at me from the other side of the room, shaking his head with a disgusted look slapped across his face. I simply smiled at him and shrugged my shoulders. Molly, despite Sid's warnings, took a slug, in fact everyone except for Sid took a slug so it was at this point he decided to exit the party because he didn't want to spend his night 'listening to a bunch of tripping arseholes slavering shite.'

Abbie was right, it was a nice mellow hit. I felt what I can only describe as snugly.

Yep that's it, snugly.

That sounds about right.

Like a cat in front of the fire.

Maybe it was because I was cuddled up in a bean bag or maybe it was because I actually felt like a mushroom.

Underground.

All safe and warm ready to push myself through the earth's crust to a higher level of consciousness, a new beginning so to speak.

No, a new birth.

Is that just hippy bullshit or is this stuff really fucking good?

I spent what seemed like an eternity touching and stroking and kissing Abbie. I stared at her in wonder and couldn't stop smiling.

She was like an angel.

My desire to fuck her brains out had been replaced with a strong desire for connection. Of body and soul. But not in the ball aching way like an hour previously. It felt strange but at the same time so right.

Her white skin radiated light and love.

Love.

What is love?

Baby don't hurt me.

Don't hurt me, no more.

Man, I hate that song.

But I felt myself nodding along gently to its infectious beat. I laughed to myself at the ridiculousness of it all.

Haddaway. Getaway. Stayaway. Findaway. Lookaway.

More laughter, this time everyone.

"Can anyone else hear Haddaway?"

More laughter.

I felt connected with Abbie in a way that I'd never felt with any other human being before.

Was she 'the one?'

Is there such a thing as the one?

What is the one?

This is the one.

The only one I know,

one love,

one way or another,

you're still the one.

What the fuck?

How'd Shania Twain get in here?

Oh no there she goes again but she sounds like me.

Man, I feel like a woman.

"Quick I need another song."

More laughter drifted by that babbled off the walls and rippled past my ears.

Ripple?

Ripple, ah that's better.

Ripple in still water, when there is no pebble tossed, nor wind to blow.

Abbie's skin felt fucking amazing.

Like cotton sheets.

No.

Silk sheets.

I was connected with everyone. The room. The world. Life.

Life. Oh life, oh life.

Something to do with toast?

I took a few tokes of a spliff that floated by me and the serene and gentle world of love and truth that I was gently cocooned in violently collapsed.

My trip up until that point had been more to do with my mind and conscience. The visual side to it had simply consisted of the colourful auras that I could see emitting from and through everyone in the room.

It reminded me of the hazy glare from streetlights when the haar rolls through.

After inhaling the mighty weed something else was triggered in my brain which brought about a cacophony of sliding colours. At first this was hilarious, but my peace was somehow shattered.

The melodic jazzy beats that filled the air moments ago suddenly sounded like snake-charming music infused with the whining din that's played in Indian restaurants.

I could feel the fear slowly creeping through as the adrenaline kicked in to let my brain know that something wasn't quite right.

I quickly did a bit of mental chatter to myself.

Everything's cool, Jimmy boy, you've taken some mushrooms and they were fantastic but the weed has messed it up a wee bit and now we're tripping pretty seriously. Nothing to panic about though. Just ride it out and then we can get back to feeling nice and mellow and then we can shag the night away with Abbie.

Abbie.

I turned to face her and obviously recoiled in shock as I saw Debbie's face replace hers.

"Debs?"

"Are you okay, Jimmy? You've gone pretty white. Do you want a drink of water?"

I could hear Abbie's voice and I knew she was sitting there but all I could see was Debbie and it was her lips that uttered those words.

Oh man this is totally fucked up.

"Eh yeah, eh … I'm a'right, Abbie. Ma trip's just taken a wee turn for the worse. I'll be cool," I lied.

Inside, my head was a fucking train wreck. Abbie tried to touch my face, but it felt as though sandpaper was being slowly dragged across my cheeks and it was Debbie who was doing it.

I flinched and threw my hands up in defence.

"I'm just gonnae go to the toilet," I mumbled but the words wouldn't come out properly for my tongue was stuck to the roof of my mouth. I rolled and lolled about like an upturned turtle as I tried to evade the clingy grasp of the beanbag. I finally wrestled my way clear as I attempted to convince myself more than anyone else in the room that I was 'all right, I'm all right.' I imagined everyone talking about me as I left the room, and this simply added fuel to my paranoid fire.

I fumbled my way through the hallway in the dark and finally found the bathroom and, once inside, shut and locked the door. I filled the sink with cold water and splashed my face with it. I looked in the mirror at my dripping features.

I looked normal, albino white but normal.

Fuck. Fuck.

This is some powerful shit.

I attempted to calm my racing heart by retracing peaceful images from my mind. All I could see was Debbie. All I could feel was Debbie. I sunk to the floor with my head in my hands as the terrible feeling of guilt and excruciating pain of remorse gouged and tore its way through my mind and then my heart.

I saw for the first time how I had treated her. Truly treated her and not just the way I'd imagined I'd treated her. Because for some obscure, crazy, fucked-up reason …

I was her.

I was inside her.

I saw myself mistreating her because I was Debbie.

I saw how I'd justify myself by telling her that I was a great partner because I'd never cheated on her. And I hadn't.

But by thinking I had done this great heroic deed of not corrupting our relationship I excused myself for not complementing her. For constantly putting her down. Ignoring her needs. Putting myself and my friends first. By not taking our relationship seriously. For not loving her properly. The way she deserved. That was all she wanted. To be unconditionally loved.

Isn't that what we all want?

I'm sorry Debs.

I'm so so sorry.

I sobbed and cried until I couldn't catch my breath.

I'm sorry Debs.

Why did she put up with all my shit? My neglecting her, the false promises?

I've been a complete and utter selfish bastard, yet she'd stuck by me for over seven years.

Because she loved you.

I can see it all as clear as day now.

She believed in you.

Most of all she hoped for a future with you.

As and with a family.

The newly scabbed wounds of her departure from my life were ripped open and vinegar was poured over the top of them which burned through my emaciated flesh.

I wailed uncontrollably as I writhed about the bathroom floor, trying desperately to console myself and my loss.

The only thing I could hear though was Joni Mitchell warbling 'You don't know what you've got till it's gone,' like a record that was stuck.

Over and over, she sang.

'You don't know what you've got till it's gone.'

'Till it's gone …'

'It's gone …'

'It's gone …'

'Don't know what you've got …'

I rocked myself to her words. Hating myself a little more each time she repeated them.

Love hurts but the truth hurts more.

I'm a cunt and I didn't deserve her.

I'll never get to have her again.

Aye you're right so sook it up.

"Are you okay, Jimmy? Jimmy? We heard screaming, open the door."

I jumped like a sleep kick as the banging at the door penetrated my subconscious.

I slowly lifted myself up and staggered towards the door.

"Jimmy? Jimmy?"

I turned the lock, and the door flew past me.

"Thank God." Abbie and Molly flung themselves at me and held me tightly.

I sobbed into their collective embrace.

"What's wrong? We thought you'd tried to harm yourself, man," Molly soothed.

My head was all the over the place although I did feel slightly better for my primal screaming.

"I'll be cool," I sniffed, wiping my tears with the back of my sleeve. "Just some stuff that needed to come out …"

"Debbie?" Molly asked and I vacantly nodded.

I made my excuses and promptly left.

I needed to be on my own.

I apologised to Abbie as best as my fragile state would let me and told her to get my number from Molly and to call me soon. Molly wanted to come with me, but I told her I would be fine and assured her that I wasn't going to top myself.

I pleaded with her that under no circumstances was she to tell Sid about this. After both agreeing she let me leave and I walked the darkened streets of Glasgow town alone and still tripping.

I wandered until I found a park.

I needed to be with Mother Nature.

I just wanted to be listened to and not judged.

I found a large oak tree and hugged it tightly. The bark felt rough against my face, but I could feel the energy from within. I gripped the base of the aged trunk and I heard her say 'it's all right, son.' More tears rolled down my cheeks and converged with the course casing of the trunk to seep like salty sap until they were absorbed into the earth.

From whence we came.

I just sat there holding the tree and mumbling my failings to it.

It didn't judge me.

CHAPTER 37

I awoke a couple of hours later with a pain in my left arm.
Pins and needles.

I was still slumped against my wooden counsellor. My head hurt to buggery, but my brain felt normal. Well as normal as it was likely to have felt after being mind fucked by crazy mushrooms.

I passed a church clock which told me it was 8.30 a.m. Not literally told me, I wasn't still tripping. I saw with my slightly blurry vision that the big hand was pointing towards the six and that the wee hand was in between eight and nine.

Easy when you know how.

I sneaked back into our lodgings and climbed into bed without undressing. My dozy head connected with the soft embrace of the pillow, and I had just closed my eyes when,

"Well, well, well. If it isn't the 24-hour party people."

Ah fuck.

My eyes flashed open, and I could see Sid propped up on one elbow on his bunk.

Staring at me.

"How was it then? Did you shag that lassie?"

"It was a'right, feel a bit rough now likes but I've felt a lot worse after a hard night's drinking. Didn't get to shag Abbie, we were both a wee bitty too fucked to fuck. Just got a snog and a wee grope but I've got her number for next time."

"You fanny. What did I tell you about taking that shit? You could have been shagging her all ways if you hadn't touched that stuff. Did you see the tits on her? Fuck me, some size for a wee lassie. I was thinking about firing in there masell but didn't want to spoil it for you."

"Oh aye? That was good of you," I satisfied myself with the knowledge that there would be no way in hell Abbie would have entertained the idea of going anywhere near the self-indulgent cretin. I would've told him so, but I just wanted to get some rest.

"Where's Molly?" Sid demanded.

Obviously he was well rested, therefore everybody else should feel the same as him.

"I dunno, back at the party?" I was getting pissed off now.

"A'right. Did you no' wait for her?"

"For fuck's sake I'm no' her auld man. She wasn't ready to leave and I was, so I left. Is that a'right?"

"Aye a'right calm doon wee man, dinnae get aw aggro wi' me cause you fucked it up with that burd."

"Piss off."

He was right. I had fucked it up.

Again.

Maybe not though.

Some lassies love that sensitive shit, and you don't get more sensitive than greetin like a bairn on some stranger's bathroom floor over a lost love.

"Right, well, you cannae stay in bed aw day. I told Bobby we'd meet him and Mel in town for breakfast. So come on, shift your arse."

"Oh for fuck's sake," I shouted and threw back the covers.

"I'll gie Molly a phone and let her know," Sid announced whilst smirking at my predicament.

Sid and I tramped through the streets of Glasgow to meet Bobby and Mel.

The cold wind cut through me like a knife, and I bowed to its superiority.

We eventually found the place, a wee café supposedly off Argyle Street but in my condition it was like walking from Aberdeen to Inverness.

After fake kissing and hugging our greetings with Bobby and Mel we sat down at the table to chew the fat.

Or in my case stare blankly at the menu as I tried to decide what type of food substance had the best chance of staying put in my belly for the foreseeable future.

"So how was the party?" Bobby asked cheerfully whilst sipping on his cup of coffee.

"It was a'right. Too many arty farty types for my liking though. No offence to you two," Sid nodded at Bobby and Mel. "I left when they brought out the magic mushies. Fuck listening to them discussing Van Gogh whilst off their tits. Dafty here got wired in though. Messed it up with some hot wee chick as well, eh?" Sid sat shaking his head at my supposed faux pas.

"How the hell did I mess it up? We spent the night chatting and it was really nice. She's got my number. We'd just overdone it on the magic tea front. Just 'cause everything revolves around shagging for you it doesn't mean I'm a failure if I haven't jumped into bed with her on the first night. Is there no romance left in the world?" I moaned whilst staring at an omelette that had arrived at the adjacent table.

"Piss off," Sid squealed. "Stop trying to act like the gentleman just cause Mel's here. You would've shagged her, and you know it, but you got all fucked up on the magic mushies and didn't have it in you. Therefore, you messed it up."

I just shook my head and rolled my eyes at Mel in disbelief that he would suggest such a thing.

Bastard was right though.

We discussed the varying successes of the tour so far for Mel's sake with Sid making the venture sound a whole lot more exciting and rewarding than Bobby or I could have.

I pushed the Spanish omelette that I'd ordered around my plate whilst listening to his terrible anecdotes.

Molly arrived just in the nick of time to spare us the sordid details.

"Oh aye and where have you been all night, you dirty wee stop out?" Bobby laughed as Molly sheepishly pulled out a chair and sat her weary bones down. She looked tired, guess the party carried on for a while.

She looked at me through hazy eyes and I returned her gaze with a wink and a wee shake of my head. The kind of nod and head shake that says 'remember our agreement'.

Keep shtoom.

"Sorry, Molly. We started eating without you, we weren't sure if you were joining us or not," I said, feeling the need to give her another knowing wink.

"That's cool, I'm not really hungry. I could do with a coffee though."

Bobby, ever the gentleman, went off to order her a coffee whilst Sid made a shite joke about Molly taking it like she does her men.

I leaned in close and whispered, "How's Abbie?"

"She's good, she's asking for you. Said she'd give you a call later."

Ya wee beauty.

I hadn't fucked it up.

I'd hit the bar with an open goal, but the rebound had fallen right at my feet.

I should have tried that sentimental stuff years ago.

A young lad brought over Molly's coffee.

"How's it going? I was at your gig last night, brilliant. I'm feeling it today though," he cheerfully remarked.

"Fair play to you, man. I'm no' feeling that great myself," I replied.

"You enjoy it then?" Sid asked, his ears perking up the minute a compliment was dished out his way.

"Yeah it was great craic. Sure you've a great sound going there, so you have," the enthusiastic waiter declared.

"Why don't you pull up a pew and join us for a coffee then, my man. Sorry I didnae catch your name?" Sid carried on, his eyes growing brighter by the minute.

"Sean. I'm getting my break in five minutes so I'll join you, thanks."

And so it was that Sean sat with us and added further fuel to Sid's glorifying storytelling of our tour thus far.

"Have you ever thought about doing a tour of Ireland, you know, like you're doing now? Jeez you'd be mad not to. You'd be huge over there. We love this kind of stuff back home; you'd be treated like legends. Nobody ever bothers to tour the small places back home and they're the best places to play. You should think about it, it might not make you rich but you'd earn enough all right and you'd be treated well, we love our musicians. Look at David Gray, nobody over here gave a feck about him. It was us that made him."

Bobby, Mel, Molly, and me all looked at each other and then back at Sean as if to say 'Aye that'll be fecking right pal,' but Sid got in there first.

"You think so?" Sid was now sitting forward, giving Sean his undivided attention.

"For sure, we love live music. But hardly anybody does gigs the way they used to—"

"Exactly, Seanyboy. That's what we're all about," Sid butted in, wagging his finger violently to the table for emphasis. "We're all about getting back to basics, making music the way it was meant to be heard. Live. These days it's all about your five minutes of fame on some shitey television show or some pasty fuckers recording a homemade album in their bedroom and pumping it out through the internet. We *ARE* different. Tell me more, I'm listening."

"Well like, you know how American acts that couldn't get a break in the U.S. came to Britain and then had success back home, Jimi Hendrix for example. British bands that are struggling over here should go to Ireland—"

"Haud on the noo, pal. We're no' struggling. You saw for yourself last night, we can draw a decent crowd …" Sid argued with a face that dared anyone to say otherwise.

"No, no I didn't mean it in that way. I mean bands that *should* be successful, that *should* get the recognition they deserve in their homeland but don't for whatever stupid reason. Go to Ireland, you'll get the rewards."

"I'm liking your thinking, Sean. We should talk more, my man."

Sid and Sean sat engrossed in their caffeine-filled debate whilst the rest of us sat looking at each other in fear, disbelief, disgust, and excitement depending on which chair you sat in.

Sean had to get back to work but Sid followed him over to the counter with his arm clamped firmly around his shoulder like they were long-lost pals.

"I'm not liking the sound of this, Bobby," Mel whispered with pleading eyes at Bobby. "I need you back home."

"Dinnae worry, baby. We'll be finished this soon enough. I'm not going on another tour like this," he replied.

"Aye fuck that," I chipped in. "This has been bad enough and we've got our home comforts just a few miles down the road. There's no danger I'm doing this in Ireland."

"What? Oh come on it'd be brilliant fun, imagine doing this but playing to crowds who actually get it?" Molly piped up.

Her enthusiasm was not catching this time.

"I'll forgive you this once, but only because you're young and you haven't had your enthusiasm crushed by that numpty over there yet," I moaned, feeling worse by the minute.

Who except the Spanish would think that a full dinner encased in an eggy glue is an acceptable option for breakfast?

"If you want to do a tour of Ireland it'll just be the pair of you. You can be like the white stripes," I mumbled in between swallowing mouthfuls of egg.

"Or the shite stripes," Bobby laughed and our hands met across the table in a triumphant high five. Mel just shook her head and put her hand over her eyes and sighed.

I sensed her anger and frustration and thought it best to change the subject.

"Anyway, enough about that, how's things back in the Kingdom, Mel?"

Mel gazed up from her melancholia poo with a startled look on her face.

Her eyes shifted to Bobby's and then back to mine.

"Fine, fine. Everything's … still the same." She returned her gaze back to Bobby who did a nodding motion of his own as if to prompt her.

She sighed.

"I need to tell you something, Jimmy. I suppose it's better hearing it from me than somebody else."

This immediately sent my respiratory system into meltdown and my anxiety reflex into overdrive.

Fuck, what's happened?

Somebody's got cancer?

"What is it?" I softly asked.

"It's Debs …" Mel whispered whilst trying to retain eye contact with me.

All I can hear is my heart thumping in my ear, I think I'm going to be sick.

She can't be, God please no, why did you let this happen?

I picture her lying in a grave having been killed in a car accident driven by that wanker and I feel like I'm going to explode.

She can't be dead. Come on please no, no, no. Not Debs.

But it's worse.

CHAPTER 38

"Debs is pregnant."

I've never had the wind knocked out of me by a statement before. But that one delivers a lethal fucking blow.

I splutter, choke.

Can't breathe.

I reach for my coffee cup but knock it from the saucer, releasing the dark flowing liquid from its clay dam to be soaked up by the thick white tablecloth.

"What? How?" is all I manage to squeeze out before asphyxiation occurred.

"Debbie and Danny are having a baby. I met her last week for coffee … she's really happy, Jimmy. I know it's not what you wanted to hear but it's better that than reading it from somebody on Facebook. Bobby said I should tell you." Her eyes were shimmering with tears. Funny that I should remember a thing like that as I tried to comprehend her devastating news.

"Eh right. Okay. Good for Deb," I kicked back my chair and slumped forward, resting my hands on the table for support. "I need to get some air."

I lurched for the exit as Bobby shouted something in my ear. He grabbed my arm as I fought my way outside, but I shrugged him off.

How did that happen?

I was just trying to struggle my way through breakfast without puking and now this?

I staggered like a drunkard through the busy shopping streets of Glasgow.

I tried my best to stifle the agonising scream that was surging through my mangled body.

It manifested itself in a curdling mumble as I gulped back my grief.

I bumped into some shoppers as they made their way up the street.

Seeing my pain, they tried to restrain me and asked if everything was all right.

Will it ever be all right?

Not now.

I somehow made it back to the dorm room where I promptly collapsed into bed and buried myself beneath the covers.

My heart feels like it is ready to break.

That's my baby.

That is my baby.

That should be my baby.

No Debs. Why? Why?

That was supposed to be us.

Me.

Us.

Not like this.

I love you … Fuck.

She's only known the guy for a number of months and now they're having a kid together?

Fucking hell, she doesn't hang about.

When she wants something, she goes for it.

Big style.

I can't seem to grasp the idea, the concept of Debbie having somebody else's baby.

Not just someone.

HIS baby.

Round and round it goes, the thoughts, the images, the sick, gut-wrenching anxiety and grief of it all.

My brain simply can't take any more endorphins or adrenalin or grief, so it does what it always does in times of stress.

It shuts down.

I awoke after a couple of hours of dreamless sleep feeling a bit better. The news from Mel was still fresh in my mind but what could I do about it?

Nothing.

Sure, it hurt like hell every second I thought about Debs and the happy wee family that she was going to have but it quickly turned to hatred when I thought of who she was playing happy families with.

I didn't want to do the whole self-indulgent, woe-is-me thing. I had to keep my mind occupied for my sanity's sake.

Besides, haven't I just met a lovely new girl?

She's not Debs.

We had a gig to prepare for so that would keep me busy for a while.

I just had to ignore the cruel images that kept appearing in my mind. They showed an old-fashioned hallway with an elegant oak staircase. Adorned on the walls as I made my way up the stairway were pictures of Debs, Danny, and baby in various poses.

All happy, all smiling.

At the top of the stairs on the landing was my head. Mounted onto a piece of wood like a hunting trophy.

My gormless head.

Defeated.

"Right fuck this I'm going for a drink," I shouted to myself.

I phoned Sid to get the details of tonight's gig and told him I'd meet them all there. He was surprisingly kindhearted, said he'd heard the news and felt for me.

Probably still feeling guilty about the phone incident.

Who am I kidding?

He doesn't have any feelings other than those that affect him.

I took a taxi to Great Western Road, home of a few decent-looking bars, one of which we'd be playing at tonight. I ducked into the first one I came to and ordered a pint and whisky chaser. I had just sat down and was away to enjoy the first slug of my pint when my phone rang. I didn't recognise the number, so I was pleasantly surprised to hear it was Abbie on the other end and she arranged to meet me for a few drinks before the gig.

You see, Jimmy boy, think positive and positive things will happen.

Fuck Debs and her happy wee life, who needs her?

CHAPTER 39

A bbie showed up looking absolutely gorgeous, banishing all thoughts of Debbie from my mind. We were only on our first couple of drinks when everybody else showed up.

"Dinnae you be getting him pissed now, he needs to be on top form tonight," Sid jokingly pointed to Abbie.

"I'm sure he's more than capable of doing that all by himself," she replied.

We all sat and chatted over a few drinks whilst Sid kept trying to bring up the subject of going to Ireland at every possible occasion. Bobby thankfully kept shooting him down and changing the subject. I could tell Mel was not amused by this new development. By now we only had a few more weeks left and our mammoth six-month tour would be over and she could return to a normal life with Bobby.

The gig itself was as uneventful as I'd expected a Sunday evening show to be, even if it was in Glasgow. The place was pretty busy, and the crowd were appreciative enough, but it just lacked the energy of last night's gig.

The best was yet to come.

As was I.

Whilst Molly was packing up, Abbie asked if I wanted to come back to hers.

Too fucking right I do.

We all said our goodbyes with Sid giving me strict orders to meet up at midday tomorrow for a band meeting.

Aye aye Captain.

I won't bore you with the details of my night with Abbie.

It was good.

No, that's not the right word for it.

She has an amazing body, and I devoured every inch of it, it's just that the sex wasn't amazing like I thought or hoped it would be. Perhaps I'd built it up too much in my head. There was just no real passion. Sure, we got hot and sweaty and both climaxed. It just lacked that wee bit of fire, that wee bit of primal lust. It was lovemaking rather than fucking.

Maybe she just wasn't that into me.

Perhaps the age gap was too large and now that she'd ticked that box I'd be kicked to the curb?

Still, it was nice.

That's what it was.

Nice.

We drank wine and talked and kissed and then had sex. It was a bit too structured. But maybe that's how these arty types roll.

At least there was no weird up the arse stuff!

I was still trying to figure out the previous evening and how I felt about Abbie when we met to have the so-called band meeting.

"Spare me the gory details, Jimmy, but did you shag her last night?" Sid blurted out as he took his seat at the table.

"Not that it's any of your business but yes, we had sex and it was fantastic," I replied, feeling uneasy discussing my sexual misdemeanours whilst there was a teenage girl sitting next to me. I gave Sid the eyes and a nod to make him aware of that fact.

"It's a'right, Molly's no' wet behind the ears. So, who shat on who this time?" Sid burst into a fit of childish laughter as Bobby snorted out a stifled chortle whilst Molly just looked scared and confused.

"Aye very funny, eh? Let's just get on with this poxy meeting. I've got better things to do than listen to you take the piss. What are we here for anyway?" I fumed, feeling my face turn a slight shade of burgundy as I looked at Molly out of the corner of my eye.

"Sorry, man. Couldnae resist," Sid chortled for longer than was necessary.

What is it they say about folk who laugh at their own jokes?

"Right, I've been doing some serious thinking. I'm not going to lie to you, this tour hasn't gone as well as I'd hoped it would. By now I thought we would've been snapped up by a big label, or at least some sort of label, but we've not. God knows why, we've put on some really amazing gigs, our songs are first class and as a live band I've not seen any others who are as tight as we are. But it's their loss. So I've been thinking, we've only got a few gigs left before this tour ends, I say we go home, get a bit of rest and homemade grub, and then come back in the new year and take this show on the road to Ireland." Sid clapped his hands together then spread them wide as he awaited the response of his darling audience.

"That's a brilliant idea, how ever did you come up with something as radical as that?" I smiled sarcastically.

"Aye I know it was Sean that planted the seed, but I've been doing the forward planning. Sometimes you've got to take a step backwards to move forwards."

"Nut. I'm no' happy with this," Bobby stated matter of factly. "We've been away from home for nearly six months. I cannae do this any more. We gave it our best shot, it didn't work, let's leave it at that."

"What do you mean, you're no' happy? Or is it Mel that's no' happy? She cannae bide the thought of you trying to better yourself …" I could see the exasperation in Sid's face rising that somebody had dared to challenge his authority.

Especially Bobby.

Good old laid-back Bobby.

As dependable as a farmer's dug and just as loyal.

"Shut the fuck up," Bobby shouted as he stood up and slammed his palm onto the table. Our drinks jumped and so did I. Bobby was obviously aware of this and sat back down again but he didn't take his eyes off Sid's as he seethed through gritted teeth. "Now you listen to me, I've jumped through hoops for you. But I'm not doing it anymore. When does it end, Sid? So we go to Ireland and dinnae get spotted there, then we go somewhere else and somewhere else and on and on it goes, us dancing to your merry tune. I cannae live that way anymore, this is affecting my relationship, it's affecting my life. My life, not yours, mine. I'm not doing it."

I'd never seen Bobby respond like that. I didn't know whether to applaud him or shit myself. He can be one mean motherfucker when he needs to be.

"So Mel stamps her feet and you've got to come running home? Fine, fuck off then, drummers are ten a penny, we'll just go to Ireland and make it without you. But dinnae come running back to me begging to return to the band when the money's rolling in." Sid wasn't for backing down either.

"That's fine by me, I might as well just go now then. You shouldn't have a problem finding a drummer for the rest of the gigs seeing as we're ten a penny," Bobby threw back his chair and turned for the door.

"So that's it then, eh?" Sid stood up and shouted back to Bobby. "You're just gonnae walk away in the huff cause Mel's no' letting you out to play?"

Bobby didn't even look back. The big man kept his dignity and simply walked out the door.

"Nice one," I said, shaking my head at Sid.

"What? He's the one that walked out. Fuck him, we don't need him."

"Is that right? So are we just gonnae cancel the rest of the gigs or have you got a spare drummer in your pocket that just so happens to know our tunes?"

Sid's anger had gotten the better of him, but I saw the realisation slowly dawn on him as he considered the consequences.

"Well, I think it's a brilliant idea, Sid. We should totally go for it," Molly's enthusiasm still knew no bounds.

"Look I'll go and talk to Bobby. You calm down and ... ach whatever," I waved my hand at Sid and his pathetic childish nature. I had no positive words to say to him.

CHAPTER 40

I fully understood Bobby's point of view as I headed back to our digs to try and pacify him. This was a new situation, however. It was always Bobby who would pay Sid or me a visit with some calming words of wisdom to iron out the ridge-like crinkles that had formed during another of our ongoing feuds.

Bobby didn't want to go to Ireland because he didn't have to. He had everything he needed at home. He only agreed to do this tour because he knew he'd be helping Sid and me out with our quest to become rich and famous.

I was envious of Bobby.

Not in a bad, jealous way. I just wished my life was more like his. He was content with what he already had. He had the girl of his dreams by his side, he had a talent with his art, and I just knew that that would take him places in life, but he put all that, his relationship, and personal ambitions on hold to help out his two best pals with theirs.

Or in my case floundering ambitions.

As I walked down the cold streets with my jacket wrapped tightly against my body to keep out the worst of the winter wind, but failing miserably, I thought about how best to approach this.

The easy, kind-hearted way or the tough love, sook it up, Bobby, stop being a big bloose way?

The more I thought about it the more I thought that I couldn't do another tour without Bobby. He's been the glue that's held this band together for so long. Without him, Sid and I would tear each other to pieces. Once Sid has an idea in his head, it's going to happen. He's like a dog with a bone. He's not for letting go.

Could I survive doing this all over again for God knows how long?

In another country?

Molly is naturally delighted with the idea and why shouldn't she be? She's young, full of energy and shining bright with enthusiasm that hasn't yet been tarnished by years of disappointment and failure.

Sid? Well, this is his baby, he can't desert it now when he's been given another crack of the whip. He's not about to turn down an opportunity like this.

After all what's the alternative?

Going back home with his tail between his legs, resorting to the good old ways of playing the local boozers and doing the occasional wedding reception?

No way José.

He's daft but he's not stupid.

And what about me?

Well I've got nothing else to go back home to. No job, no house, no girlfriend, and no idea of what I'm going to do with what's left of my life.

So that's that decided then, off to Ireland I go.

I arrived at our dorm to find Bobby packing all his clothes into his rucksack.

"Hey, man. What's happening?" I asked gingerly.

"Just packing up my gear. Head to the station when I'm done." He didn't even look up at me, just carried on stuffing pants and socks into his duffel bag.

"Eh? So that's it? You're just going to end it like this?" I can't quite believe that Bobby's quitting the band.

Not like this.

"Do you want me to go out and get some party hats?" he replied, shoving more garments into the bag.

"That's not what I meant. Look, let's go for a wee drink, eh? You and me. Talk about things, you know?"

This is harder than I thought it was going to be.

Cannae get the words out.

"I'm not changing my mind, Jimmy. There's no way in hell that I'm going to Ireland."

"That's fine, I'm no' here to change your mind it's just … dinnae quit like this, man. It's not right. You're the reason we're still in the band. The glue. You know, holding us all together. Glue. That's you. Glue," I stammered as I flapped my arms aimlessly trying to beef up my statement.

Stop saying fucking GLUE!

They had failed miserably and naturally slumped to my side.

Bobby, on either seeing my huge discomfort in doing this kind of thing sober or the fact that he actually wanted a drink himself, agreed to my suggestion.

"Aye a'right," he sighed "'mon let's go."

Thank fuck for that.

After walking for a few minutes in the icy cold blast we chose the first bar we came to. Ordinarily we would have avoided this sort of establishment like we would've avoided a ned being taken for a walk by his pit bull but because it felt like our eyeballs might freeze over at any minute, we chose warmth over substance.

It was more of a brasserie than a boozer, the type that sells alcohol as an afterthought. I ordered a couple of drinks and returned to the table to find Bobby blowing on his hands to try and establish some warmth into his chilled digits.

"Cheers, mate."

I took a large slurp from my pint.

Ah braw, I needed that.

"Aye, cheers."

We sat and took in our surroundings. Stared out of the large window at the dreich day and the huddled masses that trooped by with grim faces.

Avoiding the topic of conversation.

"Same again?" I asked as I drained the last of my drink but noticing that Bobby still had over a half pint left.

"Eh aye, I'll get these though."

"No it's cool, you finish your drink."

I returned with another couple of pints. Whilst at the bar I'd been working up the courage to tell Bobby not to quit the band.

"Dinnae quit the band, man. Not like this."

That was it, that was all I had. Shot straight from the hip.

"I have to, I'm not doing this anymore. Sure, I'd love to, but when it's starting to affect my relationship with Mel then I've got to call it quits."

Bobby then opened up to me about their plans to start a family and subsequent failings.

Mel had recently suffered a miscarriage.

I was devastated for them both. It had only happened in the last week, so it was all still very raw for them. I think Debbie's news made it all the harder for them. Despite Bobby's best efforts to put a brave face on things, I could see he was struggling.

"She's beside herself with guilt. Keeps asking if it was her fault, something she had done. We only found out a month ago that she was pregnant, and she keeps blaming herself that she had had a few nights out with us before she knew. She thinks that's why it happened. The partying, you know? Especially at our age."

I just nodded my head and kept my mouth shut.

I didn't know.

How can I possibly know what that feels like?

I didn't know what to say to make things better and it made me feel useless.

Is there anything I can say?

"She's changed, man. I'm really worried about her. She's become distant, keeps telling me she's fine but she's not. I need to be with her, to look after her, to be there for her. I'm not putting the band first like you did. I'm not fucking this up."

Cheers mate. Is that what everyone thinks?

I fucked it up?

I know now that I did but does everyone feel like that?

Fuck.

It makes you look like a right useless prick, eh?

"You all right, mate?" Bobby asked, snapping me out of my selfish pondering.

"Eh? Aye, aye. I'm just trying to get my head around it, that's all. I'm gutted for you both. I don't know … what else to say … I'm here for you."

I felt awkward, extremely uncomfortable. This was a hellish topic to be discussing and one that was made all the more extreme because it was somebody that I loved at the other side of the table. I tried my best at putting a positive spin on things.

"Look, everything happens for a reason. Sometimes we don't understand the reason at that particular time but you've just got to trust in it …" I didn't believe that bullshit any more than he did but it was all I had. My pathetic attempt to show some support and offer some soothing words to my best friend came out as some clichéd, new age, horse shit. "There's nothing Mel could've done, maybe you should get her some counselling. For both of you, just to, you know talk about it and stuff. It might help?" I offered.

"Yeah … maybe." Bobby just stared into the bottom of his glass.

"Or you could just get plastered and have a good greet about it and see how that feels?" I laughed, trying to worm my way out of this horrible situation.

I wish Sid was here, he'd know what to say.

"That's what I feel like doing." He drained the last of his pint and started on the next one.

Thata boy.

After four or five pints we decided to head to pastures new.

Somewhere a bit darker and dingier that felt more suited to somebody spilling their grief and guilt.

I was conscious of the time.

We had a gig tonight, well we were supposed to, but our drummer had just walked out. I was sat here listening to him pour his heart out. The details of which got more personal and angrier as the volume of drink increased.

You're almost there, mate.

Whisky should do the trick.

I ordered a couple of nips for each of us then lifted one in a toast.

"Did the bairn have a name?" I asked.

Bobby shook his head as the tears started to flow from his crumpled face.

"Didn't even have a fucking name …" he sobbed as the tears gave way to the inevitable flood of grief that had been dammed for some time.

It's a strange thing seeing a friend cry.

The natural instinct is to try and console. Put an arm around his shoulder and tell him that everything's going to be all right.

I didn't, I couldn't.

Instead, I just sat opposite, watching him huddled over in pain as his body lurched and heaved with convulsing muffled sobs.

It was very uncomfortable.

But I told myself as I stared at him that it was what he needed.

A good greet.

Let it all out, pal.

I finished my drink in silence.

The good thing about this type of boozer is that nobody bats an eyelid when confronted with the sight of a man crying into his drink. The regulars and bar staff have seen it all before.

They've been there themselves.

The situation might not have been the same, but they've been there.

We all have.

I could feel the collective sigh of despair at the sight of another good man down. So they all carried on with their drinking as if nothing happened, relieved that it wasn't them spilling tears into a glass.

"Drink it, Bobby," I offered, shoving the whisky into his shaky hand. "Get it doon ye. What doesnae kill you makes you stronger, eh?"

He looked at me through red eyes and laughed before clinking my glass and chucking the cheap whisky down his throat. He gasped then reached for the extra nip and downed it too.

"I ken this is hard but speak to Mel, maybe get her to stay through here for the rest of the week. Get her away from everything and everyone back home. Christ that toon can be a depressing and unforgiving place at the best of times so it must be a million times harder for her now. She'll be closer to you, and you can keep an eye on her, make sure she's a'right, ken? Listen, why don't you stick it out with the band, man? Just do these last few gigs, have a proper farewell and then that's it over and done with. You pair can go on and live your lives in peace whilst Molly and me get our ears chewed by Sid." I smiled at him, hoping he would return the gesture.

"I dunno. I'm no' sure. I dinnae ken what to do. Mel's always the strong one, keeps me on an even keel."

His tears started again.

"Hey, you keep each other on an even keel. Dinnae go playing the big useless lump on me now. She needs you just as much as you need her. So come on, get it together or you're only gonnae make things worse. Sure, you might feel like shit, feel like chucking in the towel but you cannae or else you'll lose her. Who's the one that's always there for me and Sid? You. You're the sensible one, the smart one. So be that guy. Dinnae go feeling all sorry for yourself now. You've got to be the strong one, help Mel. You can do it, mate."

Where's this coming from?

Keep it up though, it sounds fucking authentic.

"Can I?" he snorted, looking up at the bar.

I got another round in and we drank and he spoke and I listened.

In his drunken state he told me more than he probably should have.

The idyllic lifestyle that I thought they both had didn't seem so rosy the way he told it. But every couple has their problems. Especially when you've been with that person since you were just a kid.

How are you to know any better?

You've nothing to gauge it with.

That's life, eh?

My phone rang, interrupting the discussion.

Sid.

Fuck.

"Where the fuck have you been? Why are you no' answering your phone? We're on in an hour."

My mind tried its best to evaluate the volley of questions but due to the volume of alcohol that was rendering it useless I didn't even bother. I stood up and made to move away from our table so Bobby wasn't in earshot.

Fuck I'm drunker than I thought.

I staggered towards the other side of the bar where two rough-looking bald guys were playing darts.

"I'm talking to Bobby," I hissed, trying to keep my voice down but judging by the look I received from Bobby I was doing a terrible job of it.

"Fuck Bobby, I've managed to get a boy to sit in for tonight, we've had a wee practice and he'll do," snapped Sid

"Whit are you talking aboot? Bobby'll be playing tonight cause he's our drummer … always has been … always will be. He's had a bit of bad news, but he'll be a'right. Dinnae you go replacing him with anybody … a'right?"

"For God's sake, Jimmy. Can you no' lay off the booze for two fucking minutes?" Sid shouted in despair.

We ended the conversation with a bit of verbal sparring, but I promised him we'd both be there within the next 20 minutes to play the gig or neither of us would be there.

To which Sid reluctantly agreed.

"'Mon, Bobby. Uncle Sid needs us to play tonight," I slurred as I shouted at him from halfway across the bar.

"He's sorry he lost the rag with you, and he welcomes you back with open arms." I emphasised this with a wild sweep of my arms, sending two pints flying from a thirsty punter's newly purchased grasp.

"For fuck's sake," the punter roared as the spilled lager soaked into his faded denim jacket.

Bobby was up and on his feet within seconds.

"It's a'right pal, calm down. Here's a twenty, get yourself another couple on me, we're just leaving," he offered.

The sight of a massive black Scotsman bearing down on him offering not fists but notes, notes in which to buy more drink than originally purchased, reduced the inconvenienced gentleman to a grateful wreck.

"Gaun yersell big yin," the angry wee man shouted as he greedily snatched the note from Bobby's grasp. The realisation at how his mild misfortune had suddenly opened up a door of drinking opportunity manifested itself in a wide, rotten-toothed grin.

"You're a'right, big man." He pointed then slapped Bobby's back.

He's back.

There's the Bobby we all know and love.

Ready to protect and defend the ones he loves at any cost. If anyone can help Mel get through their pain, it's the big man.

"Come on, big fella. Let's do this," I grinned.

CHAPTER 41

The gig was pretty awful, mainly due to the drunken state Bobby and I found ourselves in. I can normally handle a tune after a good few libations, but Bobby was bloody hopeless.

It would've been better if he'd left the band.

I explained Bobby's predicament to Sid, and he apologised to Bobby and welcomed him back into the band. His apologies were short lived however when Bobby reiterated the next day that he wouldn't be joining us for our tour of Ireland. So, Sid did what he always does when he doesn't get his way, retreated in a big huff.

Tensions were awful, you could feel it as soon as you stepped into the room. I was just glad it wasn't me on the receiving end of Sid's notorious silent treatment for once.

Molly assumed Bobby's normal role of peacekeeper but she mainly sided with Sid for obvious reasons. She was playing the game well and didn't want to upset Sid for fear of being kicked out of the band. I couldn't blame her; she was ambitious and, like Sid, would stop at nothing in her search for fame.

Mel did indeed join us. She and Bobby checked into a hotel for the week to spend some quality time together and try as best they could to get over their loss.

I felt terrible for Bobby, he was being forced out of the band that he had helped create over something that wasn't his fault. I can't even begin to explain how I felt about Mel. I didn't know what I could say to her to try and make her feel better.

Feeling useless, guilty, and helpless, I avoided the topic altogether.

I was glad the tour was coming to an end, especially as the mood in the camp at present was depressingly low.

Sid was ruthless in his quest to make something of his band, even to the point of excluding his best friend who along with his partner had just suffered a miscarriage.

Does this man have any morals?

After all we'd done for him over the years this is how he treats you. I'm not even going to get started on the Debbie incident because that just made me furious.

Yeah, I was pissed off too at how the tour had gone. I along with Sid and probably Bobby assumed that by doing this tour we'd have at least drawn enough attention to merit a record deal. Maybe not with one of the big players but at least some sort of record deal. I didn't for a minute expect it to end like this with one of our founder members quitting in tragic circumstances and then being frozen out by the driving force.

But hey, I signed up for the rock 'n' roll job a long time ago, so I guess it goes with the territory.

It was with a horrible feeling of shame that I made up my mind.

This band wasn't going to go anywhere with somebody like Sid in charge.

Bobby was right, so we tour Ireland then nothing happens than we go to London and try there, and nothing happens and on and on it goes.

Us dancing to Sid's merry tune as he chases rainbow after rainbow.

There isn't a pot of gold, is there?

I had toyed with the idea ever since our gig at Tobermory.

I could be the main man.

It had been my most enjoyable gig since the early years, and it gave me back the energy and drive that had been missing in my life. Hell, it even made me forget about all my troubles.

Maybe it was time to quit the band too?

Maybe Bobby and me could form a new band when we got back home?

Get some young blood in with new ideas and go in a new direction.

Do it all by ourselves?

The way everybody except Sid is doing it.

Through the internet.

The more I thought about it the more I knew it was the right thing to do.

We don't need Sid.

I don't need Sid.

Let Molly and him chase their tails in search of something that isn't there.

Do you know why?

Because the songs aren't good enough.

It's no fluke that some bands make it on the strength of one song. It's because that song resonates with the masses. It invokes a feeling in them.

I remember the first time I heard songs in my youth such as Smells Like Teen Spirit and Live Forever and the way they made me feel. And as I delved deeper into the musical past and heard songs by Dylan and Carole King for the first time I was blown away by their simplicity. The alluring lyrics entwined with addictive chord hooks.

The list is endless.

All the great bands and artists throughout the years all had one thing in common. Their songs had simple childlike melodies but with a back beat that amplified it. They all had something to say too, but they didn't just say it, they made me the listener feel it.

Like it was me they were singing to.

I understood them.

They understand me.

The shit we're currently peddling is the account of one man's mission to be heard at any cost. We're stuck in a dictatorship and the General is too blinkered to see that he's lost sight of his destination.

I've lost count of the number of times I'd approach Sid with a new song I'd written only for him to shoot it down and I stupidly believed him when he told me it was terrible because I trusted him and I valued his opinion.

Not anymore.

I'm out.

It's time for a new order, it's time for a revolution.

This revolution will not be televised, brother.

CHAPTER 42

It was a cold, snowy morning when I took the call. I couldn't bear to be in the same room as Sid and Molly after the way they had been treating Bobby, so I left early to go for a walk.

Walking helps me clear my head, right any wrongs that need fixing. It enables me to find solutions whilst answering the usual self-doubting questions that drift through my mind.

The best place for doing this I find is out in the countryside where you can hear the birds' gentle chatter and listen to the rustle of the hedge rows and trees as they blow in the wind. Being with nature soothes me. That and the fact that there's never a bunch of annoying half wits nearby shouting at the top of their lungs shattering my peace.

In Glasgow, as with any other city or large town, areas of natural beauty are rather infrequent due to the expanding lumps of concrete that decimated them.

The botanic gardens were situated at the opposite end of town, and I couldn't be arsed walking that far for a moment's tranquillity so I opted for the Glasgow Necropolis. Not quite your secluded woodland but just as good because the dead for the most part tend to give you peace.

Peace to find peace.

I wandered past the large monuments and gravestones, checking to see if any of the deceased souls shared the same birthday as myself.

Nope.

Although somebody named Samuel Brown died on my birthday.

Well, my birth date.

It would be another 94 years before I graced the earth.

Rest in Peace, Sammy, ma boy.

The wind had picked up and swirled the snow in a multitude of directions, giving the cemetery a spooky Dickensian look. I wouldn't have been surprised if a few gravestones were shifted and some of the corpses clambered out to do a rendition of Thriller just for me.

It was just that kind of atmosphere.

I dug the vibrating phone out of my pocket.

It was Sid.

"Hullo?"

"Jimmy, where are you? Get your arse back here I've got some amazing news, you're no' going to believe this, meet us at the Wetherspoons on Sauchiehall Street. Hurry up."

And he hung up.

Well, I'm wandering about a snowy cemetery.

Okay I'll return to meet you presently.

You're probably right I won't believe it.

Sauchiehall Street you say?

I'll be there, post haste.

Sid sounded like the picker on Blind Date who found out that the two hotties he had turned down were in fact complete munters compared to the beauty that stood before him.

Utter relief.

Amazement.

Excitement.

Uncontrollable lust.

Unashamed ecstasy.

Thoughts of what could possibly be making him so happy entered my mind as I retraced my steps back through the near-deserted cemetery.

I made my way over the bridge and turned for one last time to survey my surroundings with the knowledge that the solitude I felt at that particular moment in time would be forever banished in a short while.

"What time do you call this?" Sid moaned as I made my way towards the table where he sat with Bobby, Mel, and Molly.

"Early afternoon?" I replied flatly at having my peaceful walk disturbed by his demanding phone call. "What's this all about?" I asked the congregation warily as I spied a couple of bottles of champagne on the table.

"Dunno man, he wouldn't tell us till you got here. Think we've got an idea though," Bobby responded excitedly as he winked at Sid.

All the problems and arguments of the past week seemed to have been forgotten as Sid's face cracked and a huge smile beamed from his face as he winked back at Bobby.

Aw that's nice.

"Right, grab a glass," Sid demanded as he popped open the first bottle of champagne to whoops and cheers from everybody, except me.

For some reason I couldn't quite get into the swing of things.

"What's going on, Sid?" I asked as he filled my glass. The bubbles fizzed up the sides before spilling over my glass and onto my hand.

I sooked the sour liquid from my hand and noticed that it was Dom Perignon.

Very nice, Sid, this must be for a good cause.

Without meaning to sound ungrateful but going to anyway, I actually detest the stuff. The fizz, the sour taste, and the fact that its reputation is up its own arse. It is my humble opinion that the folk who drink champagne despise it too, but as it's viewed as a drink of the upper classes, the rich and successful so to speak, ordinary people clamber over each other to buy the stuff and quaff it back like a teenager who has just had their first taste of alcohol and think to themself 'my god, this tastes horrendous, but my peers seem to be enjoying it so I'd better just go along with the majority so I can keep up with appearances.'

We're Scottish for Christ sake, we've got a perfectly good drink of our own to use in such times of celebration. I'd much rather have a nice Macallan or Balvenie to toast with than this pompous French shite. We've even got the under classes buying Cava and the likes now.

Something that they'd never purchase but owing to the power of suggestion and advertising feel obliged to do so.

Champagne, much like Sid, is overrated, thinks it is better than it actually is and after an evening spent in its company leaves a foul taste in your mouth.

"If you'll shut up and raise your glasses, please," Sid announced, trying his best to keep his excitement intact. "I'll tell you what's going on. It seems that after lots of hard graft our efforts have finally paid off. Champions Of The Underdog have just received an offer to sign with a record label in London," he closed his eyes and looked to the heavens and mouthed 'thank you.'

We all looked at each other in disbelief.

Not quite grasping what he'd just said.

I heard it myself, the word 'signed' but it wasn't sinking in.

"We've been signed?" Bobby whispered, reluctant to announce it louder in case he'd misheard Sid and would subsequently ruin the whole event by raising his voice.

"We've been SIGNED!" Sid shouted as he threw his glass in the air, sending bubbly liquid flying upwards like a feeble volcanic eruption.

"What?" Bobby squealed. "No way. We've done it?"

"We've actually been signed?" Molly squeaked.

I couldn't quite believe what I was hearing.

It was something that we'd all been wanting, no, expecting to hear since we started this crazy ride but just like discovering that a sick elderly relative had finally passed away there was still that sense of shock and disbelief when it finally came.

We were all stood around a massive faux oak table.

Glasses were in a cacophony of raised positions.

Faces were contorted with different stages of bemusement.

"I dinnae want to sound all repetitive, but are you saying we've been signed?" I asked. I was conscious of the words in my head.

This is surreal.

"That's exactly what I'm saying boys. WOOHOO! Christmas has come early for the Champions," Sid announced, sending the last few drops of his pishy drink skywards.

"How? Who? YES!" Bobby shouted. And we all started jumping about and hugging and kissing and ruffling each other's hair.

It was just the three of us.

We embraced and kissed and cuddled some more and banged heads in a tribal euphoric moment of madness and self-congratulation. All our years of toil, playing to mediocre and apathetic crowds would be over. The years spent trudging our gear from town to town only to be rewarded for our efforts with a crescendo of awkward applause would be over. The years trying to convince Debbie and my parents that we'd make it would be over.

I forced the image of Debbie from my mind as quickly as I could.

I'd dreamed of the day that I'd come home to tell her that we'd finally made it, take her out shopping and buy her all the things that she wanted, see that smile on her face as she realised that I was a 'somebody.'

As I came round to our current predicament, I realised in our excitement that we'd left Mel and Molly standing on the periphery sharing a somewhat less salubrious celebration than the one the three of us were currently indulged in.

Bobby grabbed Mel and affectionately kissed then hugged her. Sid ran around the table and grabbed Molly and threw her about like she was an old tracksuit. I, having no one to celebrate with, suddenly became aware of my surroundings and noticed that the entire bar population was staring.

Heads turned and eyes fixated on us as if we were some rowdy but poorly attended Stag do.

Heads shook in disappointment at our bawdy rabble.

But I didn't care.

We'd made it.

I turned to re-join the celebrations.

"So who signed us, man?" Bobby laughed, wiping the last of the tears of joy from his eyes.

"We'll I've not actually signed anything yet," Sid uttered as he refilled his glass.

You could hear the groan resonate throughout the building as we sensed that all too familiar, hopes-raised-only-to-be-brutally-crushed moment again.

"What do you mean, you've no' signed anything yet? So, it can still go tits up?" I fumed as the memory of our last brush with fame or lack of it entered my mind's eye.

"Dinnae worry, I've got it all under control," Sid grinned as he pulled a pile of papers from his inside pocket. "This is legally binding." And he flapped the papers in front of our faces.

"They're called Nearly Man records. They're based in London. I took a phone call a couple of days ago from some guy telling me they'd like to offer us a deal."

We were all still standing as Sid began to tell us his tale but, sensing it was going to be a long one, I grabbed the bubbly, refilled my glass, and sat down, prompting the others to do the same.

"Now at first I was all suspicious, pull the other one, pal, I told him, but after a discussion he seemed genuine and insisted that we would be his latest signing. Now, I didn't tell any of you this at the time because, well I didn't want to tempt fate, you know? We all remember what happened last time, you know, pre-empting and that. So I asked him to call me back in an hour or two whilst I did my research. I phoned a few of the boys I knew in bands down in London, but they hadn't heard of them, so I went online and checked them out. They're a fairly new independent label who, like ourselves, want to give the music back to the people in the way it used to be, you know by having bands doing large tours and giving great live performances."

"Would we have to be based in London?" Bobby asked reluctantly. The anxious look on his face amplified his fears.

"Bobby, I know what you're getting at and if it means keeping the band together, no we don't have to be based in London. You can return to our dead-beat town safe in the knowledge that you'd only have to be available for future tours and recording contracts. I, however, will be leaving as soon as possible to relocate to the big smoke." Sid raised his glass to himself and then drained the contents.

"Haud on, you're saying you've no' signed anything yet but it's still official? How does that work? I dinnae want to be the voice of reason here but I do want to know everything's sorted before we get too carried away," I asked in confusion, still trying to get my head around this latest development.

"Good question, Jimmy. Now your Uncle Sid here is a smart man, and I wasn't about to let an opportunity like this slip through my fingers so after researching the label online, who by the way turns out to be run by some ex-Oxford educated rich kid with a huge inheritance burning through his pockets. You should see their offices, fucking hell, totally swanky and the recording studio looks minted. Anyway, he asked me to come down to London to sign the contract. But I had a better idea," Sid had that familiar gleam in his eye as he prepared us for the rest of his tale.

"I'm definitely moving to London," Molly chipped in. "I can't wait to tell everybody back home."

"All in good time, Molly. All in good time," Sid continued. "So after some heated discussions I managed to secure our services to the Nearly Man label. On one condition though I might add," and he held his finger up for effect.

"That we conclude the deal after a special gig at King Tut's."

We simply stared at each other in amazement.

Sid had actually got us a deal and we'd be completing said deal after a gig at King Tut's. *THE* King Tut's. Where Alan McGee signed Oasis.

"So we've signed but we've no' signed until we play a gig at King Tut's?" I asked, even more confused by the developments.

"Exactamoondo, my boy. I played hard ball with Dennis, told him that we had a few other options and said that if he wanted us to sign with his label he'd have to conclude the deal after we've played King Tut's. Deal or no Deal. Well after that it was like stealing sweeties from a bairn," Sid congratulated himself with a dusting of the hands and a beaming grin.

"Aye, but this can still go tits up, right?" I sighed. "I mean, when you told us it was legally binding, it's not though, is it? He can still pull out of this?" Once again, I hated to be the messenger of doom, but this all seemed to be a bit convenient and with our track record there was still time for us to spectacularly mess up our one shot of glory.

"Au Contraire, my good fellow. You see, I got Dennis to sign his side of the bargain to show that he meant business," and he again held up some more papers for effect, drawing our attention to the inky mass that was Dennis Smith's signature. "So there's no backing out on his part. All *we* need to do to conclude the deal is put our squiggles on the relevant parts and Champions Of The Underdog can celebrate their first record deal. Then we hand over the paperwork to Dennis after we've played the gig at King Tut's, job's a good one."

"So the King Tut's gig's more of a ceremony then, you know, handing over the baton type thing?" Mel asked with a bewildered look on her face.

"Exactly, Melanie," and Sid did a 'Give Us A Clue' nose touch and finger point for emphasis. "Tonight's the real party, we sign our names and the deal's done but where's the story in that, eh? We'll keep it quiet so when the fans turn up at King Tut's and see us getting signed on stage they'll be blown away. It's all about entertainment these days, why do you think the X Factor's so successful? That Simon Cowell may be a massive cunt, but he's got brains, I'll give him that. Entertainment sells so that's what we're gonnae give them."

He's some boy.

There was much more celebrating, this time it was more euphoric as it dawned on everyone that there was indeed no way of fucking this up. All we had to do was sign the papers and we as a band would have a record deal.

I couldn't believe it.

I should never have doubted Sid and his vision.

It might have taken us a bit longer than we'd initially thought it would, but we were finally at the big boys' table.

"Mel get your camera out, I want this moment consigned to history," Sid exclaimed, pulling out a fancy pen from his pocket.

"So what's the deal, man?" I asked as we all bunched up to pose for the photo.

"Well, here's the juicy part. By signing this piece of paper, we are duly obliged to complete three albums worth of material with Nearly Man records. If by the second album the sales are significant enough, we can enter into a further deal worth a lot more money."

"So do we get some sort of signing on fee, or how does this work?" I asked, having little clue on the proceedings.

"There's the small matter of an advance payable to us on completion of the paperwork and the gig at King Tut's." Sid smiled, ignoring the most important part.

"How much?" Bobby asked expectantly. "What are we getting?"

"Well, after a lot of haggling I've managed to get us a nice figure. It was much higher than what was initially put on offer," Sid grinned, remaining coy and enjoying the power he held over us.

"How much?" we all screamed.

Sid was playing us like Hitchcock.

"Well there's the small matter of £100K advance—"

We erupted once more in a writhing mass of jumping and screaming and shouting and backslapping and drink spilling.

"£100K?" Mel gasped, looking at Bobby.

"Yep, plus they're giving me two grand to provide drinks for the big gig. We're actually eating into that now with this stuff so make the most of it," Sid laughed whilst raising his drink in salute. "Champions, Champions, CHAMPIONS!"

We all joined in the with the chanting.

We embraced each other like long-lost friends. The earlier remonstrations between Bobby and Sid and the lifelong love-hate relationship Sid and I maintained were all forgotten memories.

Despite saggier, harsher features and with less hair, we still resembled those three young lads who had started this journey a long time ago.

Keen, energetic, excited by a lust for life.

We could do and achieve anything if we put our minds to it.

"What about the gig tonight?" Molly asked before refilling everyone's glass.

"Gig? What gig? Fuck that, playing to fifty punters in a smelly wee hole? We've hit the big time now, there's no need for us to slum it anymore," Sid replied. "I've cancelled our last few gigs, the only one that matters is King Tut's in a week."

A giant hurrah engulfed our table, prompting more looks of derision from the nearby tables.

Mel snapped away with her camera as each of us posed whilst signing our names on the relevant space provided to conclude our first record deal.

I was like a young footballer signing his first professional contract. I stood hunched over the table, pen poised to make its mark, a cheesy grin spread across my inebriated face.

I didn't feel like I thought I would though.

I mean, this was all we'd ever dreamed of when we formed the band so it was strange that I felt a little sad.

Perhaps it was because the hard work had all been done, sometimes the striving is more enjoyable than the actual acquisition.

It was the end of an era.

That and the fact our hard partying days were well behind us so we wouldn't be able to take full advantage of our newfound rock 'n' roll status.

Sid gave Molly a handful of notes to buy some more champagne.

I'd never seen him this generous but then again it wasn't his money.

"They didn't happen to give you some of that £100K in cash, did they?" I asked Sid on the sly. My pockets were decidedly light, and I could've done with a sub.

"Dinnae be daft, man. They didn't even give me the two grand for drinks. I've to keep the receipts and I'll get it back on Saturday when I meet Dennis."

"So what do you make of this Dennis then?" I asked anxiously. "He's no' going to rip us off or anything?"

"What? No. At first, he seemed like a bit of a weirdo, but after all our conversations … he's just a bit of a twat really. He's loaded so he doesn't need to work. I suppose he thinks by doing this, it classes as work. I've grown to like him, he's a'right."

"So how much are we getting, Sid?" Bobby interrupted, not beating about the bush.

"I telt you, £100K."

"No, each. I mean are we splitting it equally? I dinnae think it's fair that Molly should get the same as us when she's only been in the door five minutes. No offence to Molly likes," Bobby offered.

I knew exactly what he meant.

It would be interesting to see how Sid wormed his way around this one. It wouldn't have surprised me if he'd actually been offered £200K to sign and he'd pocketed the other £100K. He's a sneaky, tight-fisted bastard. He never lets us see any of the finances or the money that we get for the gigs. We just accept the notes he dishes out to us with mild gratitude and crumple them into our back pockets without question.

That's the way it's always been.

Guess it always will.

"Well, I've thought long and hard about this," Sid looked upwards in a pensive sort of way to add weight to this little problem of his. "And you're right, Molly cannae get the same share as us. That's only fair. But at the same time, I've paid out a helluva lot of money to support this tour, so I think it's only fair that I'm reimbursed for the great lengths I've gone to to drag this band to the top. Wouldn't you agree?"

Bobby and me just looked at each other then back to Sid and shrugged our shoulders.

"Aye I suppose so," Bobby replied when it appeared Sid was not going to carry on with his great speech until he'd received some vocal reassurances from us.

"You suppose so?" Sid uttered in bemusement; he looked a trifle pissed off at our blasé reply. "If it wasnae for me bank rolling this little adventure, where do you think we'd be, eh?"

"How much?" I asked, cutting his rant short. I didn't need to hear the bullshit behind his logic for ripping us off.

"Eh?" Sid replied in befuddlement. He was obviously expecting to be allowed to finish his little speech, so my interrupting threw him somewhat off course.

"Spare us the speech, Sid. How much do you want?" I countered. The look on his face was one part flabbergast and two parts constipation.

"It's not about how much I want, Jimmy. Who's the one who bought the van? Got the new gear? Paid for all the hotels and petrol? Got us all the work in the first place? Christ if it wasnae for me you'd still be working in that shitey job of yours."

This celebratory party was in danger of turning sour, so I thought it best to wrap it up. Besides I could see Molly paying for the champagne at the bar and wanted to conclude this before she returned.

"Look, we're very grateful for all the hard work you've done and if it wasn't for you, we'd all be languishing down some stinking hole. Let's not make this bigger than it has to be though, eh? Just tell us what you're taking so I know how much I'm getting," I sighed.

"Taking? I'm no' taking anything. I'm simply being reimbursed," Sid seethed as he leaned over the table to give me the eyeballs.

"A'right, a'right. This is supposed to be a celebration, remember?" Bobby stepped in, waving his hand at me. "We do appreciate everything you've done, mate. Without all your hard work we'd be nowhere. Jimmy's just no' got a way with words." Bobby gave me the eyes telling me to shut the fuck up then returned his attention to Sid. "So, take however much you need, a'right? Remember, this is just the beginning. Let's no' start fighting before we've even begun, eh? Come on raise your glasses, CHAMPIONS, CHAMPIONS, CHAMPIONS!"

Molly returned to the table, assisted by Mel with two more buckets of champagne. I decided to leave the discussion of money alone for the time being and went off to the bar in search of a decent drink. I returned with a pint and a nip to continue with our celebration.

"I take it you won't be going to Ireland then?" Mel asked Sid reluctantly.

"Fuck no," Sid instantly replied. "I mean, not at the minute. We've got an album to produce first, eh, boys? We'll probably go there at some point to tour, but it'll only be for a few days so dinnae panic, Mel, Bobby'll no' be gone for long."

Bobby squeezed Mel by the arm as she returned a look that said 'I'll be by your side forever'.

Lucky bastard.

I'm so fucking lonely.

The rest of the day went by in a haze of alcohol and memories as we bored Molly with tales from the band's past. Mel, despite not being her usual self, was selfless enough to forget about her tragic circumstance and shared her own tales of woe and despair about following our great band over the many years.

Much laughter and piss taking ensued.

It was great to be in everyone's company and see us all happy.

Really happy.

It was just like the old days.

I was disappointed that Debbie wasn't here to share in this moment but, after listening to Mel's tales of sleepless nights and lonely weekends due to Bobby's absence, I understood why Debbie had had enough.

I can only guess as to why she put up with it for so long.

So, feeling detached and in need of some companionship, I gave Abbie a call so that she could come join us and share in our revelry.

CHAPTER 43

I awoke the next morning in Abbie's bed with a niggling hangover. It had been a great night, the best I'd had in a long time. Only because we were a team again. All the indiscretions and fuck ups of the past were forgotten about as we sat and drank to the future and drowned the sorrows of our yesterdays.

We had three days to waste before the biggest gig of our lives, so Sid, Bobby, Mel, and Molly all returned to their respective homes in order to boast, celebrate, organise support and surmise before returning to Glasgow on the Saturday to play King Tut's.

It would be the 23rd of December so there would be a double reason to celebrate.

Typical, Christians stealing somebody else's party and making it their own.

I for a couple of reasons decided to stay put in Glasgow. I had no need to return to my parent's house and our town. I could do without hearing their false praise and the thought of seeing Debbie and Foster playing happy families turned my stomach to water.

That place was dead to me.

Plus, I had managed to scrounge a couple of grand of my advance from Sid after he had finally divulged the amount that we were all to receive.

He, as leader and financier and general bloody good bloke, would be rewarded with 50 grand. 'Small reward' as he put it for all his financial backing and the personal fortune he stood to lose if we hadn't secured a record deal. There was no point in moaning about it despite my thoughts that the figure he was rewarding himself with was a bit steep, especially as all the stuff he had purchased was for his own benefit (van, guitars, amps, computer, air rifle etc.) and that the small amounts of money he'd had to outlay (petrol, hotel and food bills, pocket money for Bobby, myself, and latterly Molly) were more than recuperated by the payments we had received from our gigs.

We had sacrificed our financial well-being and future for his visionary gains. But I couldn't be bothered going into the details and arguing over the small points so I quietly fumed over his decision to reward Bobby and myself with £23,000 each leaving Molly to invest the £4,000 she would get for only a couple of months work.

Instead, I spent a peaceful couple of days exploring Glasgow and the surrounding areas during the day before meeting up with Abbie to expand our blossoming relationship as the moon shone.

The weather wasn't ideal, but I spent a nice morning walking through the botanic gardens gathering my thoughts and planning my future.

The deciduous trees reciprocated my mood.

Empty and barren in appearance but bursting with energy below the surface which would manifest in an explosion of activity during the coming seasons.

I also visited The Kelvingrove Art Gallery.

I'm not the biggest fan of art galleries simply because I don't understand the work involved. I can appreciate the effort and the skill that it takes to accurately replicate the subject matter, but the little descriptive notices displayed next to the work offering insight confuse me greatly.

Perhaps it's just me.

I struggle to feel the emotion these pieces supposedly convey.

On the plus side it would give me a few brownie points with Abbie as I slipped in 'The Glasgow Boys' to a conversation.

Most of the stuff was boring, I preferred Bobby's paintings and sketches to the muck that was on show.

Maybe we'll see his stuff adorning the walls sometime in the future. Although judging by the descriptions the wee notices mentioned he'd be better off killing himself and enjoy watching the fruits of his labour being dissected by drooling critics from beyond the grave.

The rest of the band phoned me at regular intervals to say they had a massive support coming down for the big show (Molly). They had discussed with each other the pros and cons of being in a professional band and had both agreed it would be in their best interests to go ahead with the current regime (Bobby and Mel). And had spoken to radio shows and music magazines to secure their attendance at what would be the greatest night in Scottish musical history ever (Sid).

I failed to share in their enthusiasm but by the Saturday morning, when they all returned in a triumphant mood, I forgot about my troubles and was swept along on the crest of their giddy ecstatic wave.

"You all set for this then, man?" Sid asked as he wrapped his arm around my shoulder and pulled me in close as we stood in the hotel foyer where he'd be spending tonight.

"Aye," I reluctantly replied.

"Told you we'd make it, didn't I? All those years ago, eh? Just you, me, and then Bobby McGee. Who would've thought it, eh?"

"Dunno?" I shrugged, trying my best to dodge his self-indulgent discussion.

"Me," Sid responded forcefully as he thumbed himself in the chest with his free hand. "I never doubted us. Not my ability as a songwriter or singer or guitarist." He thumbed himself with each word adding emphasis to his reputation. "Thousands might have but I never, and that's why we're here today. Dinnae forget that, Jimmy."

"I won't, Christ whit's the matter wi' you?"

"Dinnae go fucking this up. Stay out of the bar. This night's for the fans as much as us, we need to be at our best," he whispered menacingly before squeezing my neck like a python strangling its pathetic prey.

He strolled off into the clutches of some pretty young thing whose skirt was shorter than his attention span. He looked back at me as he strolled up the carpeted stairs to his room and did that thing with his fingers. The thing that started in films but now everyone appears to be doing. He pointed two fingers at me then returned them to his eyes as if to say 'I'm watching you'.

Calm down, you're no' in the SAS

Dick.

He laughed at me then returned to his latest squeeze and kissed her cheek, slapped her arse, then continued up the stairs on his triumphant march.

What the fuck was that all about?

If he's like this now he's going to be a complete nightmare once the real fame begins.

Some people were born to be famous.

He wasn't.

He just thinks he was.

I had already updated the masses on our website and social media sites informing them of our great news and inviting them to the show of a lifetime under the words of 'You probably won't remember where you were when Glen Michael halted his cartoon cavalcade. Or what you were doing when John Menzies closed their shops. But you will remember where you were and what you were doing when the mighty Champions Of The Underdog signed their first record deal. BE THERE!'

Cheesy I know but I went with it anyway.

There wasn't really much else for me to do. Normally I would take a walk around town and venture into a few boozers to partake in the local hospitality but with Sid's words ringing in my ears I thought it more responsible to be on my best behaviour.

Don't want to fuck this up after all.

Instead, I did what I hadn't done in ages and returned to my cheap hotel room and picked up my trusted bass guitar. It had been with me from the beginning, through thick and thin.

I plucked its well-worn strings and closed my eyes, picturing the scene that would unfold this evening. This was going to be an evening we would never forget.

I sat there and slapped at the strings, playing the songs that I had played a million times before.

It was almost like blinking or breathing.

It was second nature.

These songs were embedded in my psyche. They were as much a part of me as anything else that went before. They were my creations, adding emphasis to Sid's chord structure and giving meaning to Bobby's drum kicks.

I sat back and smiled and slapped.

This is going to be brilliant.

CHAPTER 44

My strumming had been too rhythmic and soothing for I had obviously fallen asleep.

I was awoken by the ringing from my phone, or rather the vibrations in my pocket that gave an extra dimension to my mid-afternoon dreaming.

"Hullo?" I answered.

"Hey what's happening, man? Have you been drinking?"

"Whit? Naw," I replied in confusion to Bobby's questions. I wiped the sleep from my eyes and rubbed my head to stir some feelings back into the old grey matter.

"You sound a bit drunk, get it together, mate. We want to be on top of our game tonight."

"Piss off, you sound like Sid. I've just woken up; I must've dozed off. I had nothing better to do seeing as you boring bastards dinnae want to embrace the rock 'n' roll lifestyle. I mean, what's the point of being in a band if you cannae go for a wee drink in the afternoon, eh?"

"Take it easy, pal. I was just checking to make sure you were a'right. You seem pretty quiet of late, didnae want you missing the big night, that's all. We're all meeting up at a wee restaurant in town before the show, Sid's treat, well Dennis' treat really. A journalist from the Fife News is going to be joining us too. Wants a scoop on the local lads turned good. Brilliant, eh? Be there for 4 o'clock."

I assured him that I was fine and sober and that I'd see them on time, ready and equipped to face the questions and probes from the journalist in question.

We'd conducted an interview with the Fife News before we started the tour, so I guess it was only fitting that we concluded one with them too. I couldn't see the pensioners of the region reading the piece, but it would allow our former schoolteachers to argue over who thought we'd go furthest.

I got dressed, taking some time to decide which clothes to wear. This was going to be a big night after all, I wanted to look the part. I put on and discarded more outfits than a lassie on a first date before finally going with the old favourite of faded jeans and creased shirt.

Back in the beginning I used to worry about my appearance, about whether I was rock 'n' roll enough.

We never really had a style of our own.

I wondered if that would all change now?

Probably not.

But I thought I'd better make an effort anyway. Usually I just threw on what clothes I had to hand that weren't laced with the previous night's dinner stains.

After a quick spray of cologne, I was good to go.

I met the rest of the team in a little Italian joint.

They all seemed nervous.

Another throwback to the old days.

We'd been doing the same old shit for so long that nervousness had been replaced with boredom and mild contempt.

This was different.

My stomach was churning wildly as I tried my best to eat the lasagne I had ordered. Thankfully Sid had requested a couple of bottles of red wine to wash it down with and I fought with Antoinette, Sid's latest conquest, to get as much of the vino down me as possible.

She was catwalk pretty.

She had that waif-like look, all cheekbones and pouting lips.

Like myself she also had a penchant for the booze.

Maybe she was just nervous too.

Her eyes constantly surveyed the table and in particular mine as Sid kissed her neck and fed her garlic bread.

Is she coming onto me?

I hadn't invited Abbie to dinner as she was working on some project, although she assured me she would join me later.

I refilled Antoinette's glass and she held it up to thank me.

God her eyes are amazing.

They had that feline quality with more than a glint of mischief thrown in for good measure. She reminded my crotch of Vanessa Paradis as she sang 'Joe le Taxi.'

Where the fuck does Sid find these lassies?

We ate and drank and toasted ourselves until we ran dry of parodies. Sid paid the bill then we took a slow walk to the nearby King Tut's. Mel arranged us in a fashion that only a seasoned photographer knew how to.

There was a significance there as we posed outside the venue for our final shots before we entered the music industry as a professional band.

I'm not the biggest fan of having my photograph taken, especially in this sort of forced manner, but after a few glasses of the red stuff I was more than happy to look moody and menacing as Mel clicked away whilst directing the shoot.

We went inside to mingle with the early punters and the other bands that would be supporting us whilst poor Molly continued with her role as roadie and gathered up our equipment. I felt a little guilty as I watched her struggle with the weight and size of the amps but didn't feel guilty enough to offer some assistance with her burden. After all, she wouldn't be doing it for much longer.

Happy with this conclusion and relieved at my clear conscience, I slithered my way to the bar for a sneaky drink, casting shifty side glances in case I was spotted by Sid or Bobby.

We had two local bands supporting us tonight and despite the fact that neither of them would be on for at least another hour there was still a large turnout.

I could feel the butterflies straining to hatch from their cocoons in my stomach.

A couple of whiskies should do the trick.

With nothing else to do I retired to the green room where I was congratulated by a few members of the warm-up bands. We swapped stories about gigging and touring, and I couldn't help being impressed by their vision. These people had done a hell of a lot more gigging than we had at their age and the venues they'd played in were on a par with what we were only doing now.

I was joined by the rest of the band and then finally Abbie. We all got stuck into a couple of the beers that had been left out for our consumption and as I drank a bottle of slightly warm lager, I got to thinking of the demands we'd make for our own riders.

Sid, due to his lack of imagination, and Molly, because of her youth, would probably go for the clichéd bottle of Jack Daniels. Bobby probably wouldn't ask for much. He's more of a take what you're given kind of guy. As long as he had some weed, he'd be happy.

Me?

Well, I'd be asking for the finest malt whisky money could buy as well as having half a dozen cases of Belhaven Best chilling in the fridge.

I smiled to myself as I imagined our indulgences growing as the years went by, becoming slaves to our own hype. Fighting with each other for an equal share of the limelight. Turning up to gigs and recording studios in separate vehicles due to our insecurities and addictions.

This is certainly going to be interesting.

Abbie brought me back to the present with a peck on the cheek and a "How you feeling?"

I was as nervous and unsure of myself than any time I could remember. I had that horrible feeling of anxiety that affects you like amphetamines.

I couldn't sit still.

Take a drink, put it down.

Pace to the other side of the room.

Go outside and have a smoke.

Pace up and down the street.

Smile inadvertently at chatty punter whilst comprehending nothing they've said.

Walk inside.

Pace about room again.

Drink some more beer.

On and on and on.

Unlike the high of amphetamines, I wasn't in the mood for chatting to anyone. I needed to be alone, to drown my thoughts and fears in a vat of whisky away from the judging prying eyes of the world.

Trouble was I couldn't.

Tonight, all eyes were on us.

On me.

To relieve some of my angst Abbie and I decided to watch the bands that were on first. Mel and Bobby joined us, leaving Sid to plump his ego with the 'fans' and music journos who were happy to listen to his egotistical speeches. Molly was her usual excitable self but spent the time amongst 'well jealous' friends and her family.

The support bands were very good, competent musicians who appeared at ease with their surroundings and the growing crowd.

Sid interrupted our little gathering halfway through the set of the second band.

"Just got a text from Dennis, his flight's been delayed so he'll miss the start of the show. Fuck's sake," he fumed.

"Aye but he will get here?" Bobby asked.

"Aye. He said he would. In the worst-case scenario, he'd get a taxi up and be here in time for us finishing. Fucking typical though, eh?" Sid shrugged, waving his hand about the crowd. "All these people have turned up to see us and this happens."

"It'll be cool man, he'll be here. So he's a wee bitty late, big deal. Relax, man. We're the Champions remember," I added, trying to calm him as he fidgeted from foot to foot.

"Suppose so. Right are we gonnae head backstage and get ready? Mel, you all set with the camera?"

"Sure am. I'll be down the front when you come on, but I was thinking of taking the rest of the shots from back here to feature the crowd," Mel replied waving her camera in the air.

"You're the boss. Right c'mon, lads, let's do this," Sid motioned for us to join him and we eased our way past the near-capacity crowd, receiving shouts and slaps on the back of congratulations as we did so. The crowd by now had swelled to the capacity 300.

Faces smiled and shouted and stared and closed in all around me.

I'm not sure if I can go through with this.

We got back to the sanctuary and relative quiet of the green room and sat down with our instruments. The first band were busy tucking into beers and sandwiches and were congratulating themselves on a job well done.

We left them to continue with their celebrations as Sid prowled around us.

"Right, Dennis'll no' be here till we're on but dinnae let that distract you from the job at hand. This is our night. It's what we've all been expecting, where we've been trying to get to. Well we're finally here, so remember, it's just like any other night except tonight we end it as a professional band." Sid's rousing pep talk resembled how I imagined Sir Alex Ferguson to behave in the Manchester United dressing room. He was stirring his troops before the cup final with words of reassurance and hope.

The only difference being we already had our name on the cup.

"Think of your wildest dreams and you'll no' come close to the journey that we're about to embark on."

The three of us sat there staring up at him behind guitars and drumsticks as he continued. I half expected the old eat thunder, crap lightning spiel but it never came.

A girl came into the room to announce that we were on in a couple of minutes, turning my guts to liquid again.

It's now or never.

Elvis serenaded me from on high.

"Come here," Sid motioned us to join him in a football-style huddle. It seemed so ridiculous that I thought I might burst into a fit of laughter. We'd never done this before a gig and to do it now seemed absurd, embarrassing, but strangely fitting.

We joined him; arms linked over each other's shoulders with heads bowed in the middle like a self-righteous rugby scrum.

"We are Champions Of The Underdog and we are the best band in the country. We're who they've all come to see, come to celebrate. Embrace it … love it … live it."

Sid was in his element.

I looked at him through raised brows and felt that if there was anybody I wanted to be delivering this speech, it was him. I couldn't do it and Bobby, despite his calm approach, certainly couldn't do it. I guess at a time of change or crisis you need a leader, somebody that's ready to grab the bull by the horns and address the situation.

Sid did not disappoint.

I felt proud of my mate.

He hadn't wavered in his belief of us reaching the big time despite the setbacks and knocks and being constantly struck with the shit-covered stick of life. I admired his diversity and no holds barred, blinkered vision.

Tenacity.

That's the word.

He's the kind of guy you would rather have on your side than against.

"Champions, champions, champions!" Sid chanted and the rest of us joined in quickly. Soon the room was a wall of noise, forcing the others to stop what they were doing and stare in wonder at the scene that developed before their amazed eyes.

Three oldish men and a young woman linked in a huddle, bellowing the name of their band over and over like a freakish mantra.

"Come on!" Sid screamed as he raced out of the room towards the stage. The band who had just finished walked past us offering high fives of support and congratulations, but we just left them hanging as we rushed past in search of that stage. We were like troops going over the top, focused, scared, excited, and ready to face our destiny, whatever that may be.

The wall of noise that hit us as we leapt to our positions was deafening.

It brought a lump to my throat as they cheered and screamed and clapped. *Will it always be like this?*

Rather than let the enormous welcome fade before announcing our gratitude to everyone for their attendance and support, Sid went straight for the jugular.

"1,2,3,4" and crashed into the opening riff of our first song 'Tragic Magic', catching the three of us a little off guard.

We thought, well I certainly did, that we would go on stage and soak up the atmosphere before getting into the swing of things. Sid, never being shy to deliver a speech, would surely love this opportunity. But his decision to rip right into our set was an inspired choice. The place went fucking mental and the mosh pit turned into a frantic mass of fist punching arms, entangled hair, and po-going legs.

Our years of experience showed as we fell perfectly in line with Sid's manic pace. Even Molly, who had only been playing with us for a number of weeks, showed her skill with a guitar and kept immaculate rhythm. Sid bellowed and screamed into his microphone. During a song my eyes are usually focused on my bass or on a particular spot in the crowd but that night I couldn't take my eyes off Sid. He was possessed with a rage, a fervour of the like I'd never seen before. It was as if he was angry, no, seething at the rejections we had received in the past. It really pained him and also bemused him that we hadn't been signed before now. I guess all his frustrations were finally coming out. It was his way of showing the world that after all the rejection we were finally arriving at the top table, so you'd better pull up some extra chairs.

We ended the song to more thunderous applause, but Sid didn't take his foot off the gas. We launched straight into the next song, leading to more mayhem on the packed dance floor. We were halfway through our set before Sid addressed the crowd. He wasn't much of a talker whilst we performed, he preferred to do that before and after the gig, but you were normally guaranteed a few 'thank you's' or 'this song's about' from him.

The cheering died down as it became clear we weren't going straight into another song.

Sid had a swig of his beer and approached the microphone.

"Well. It's been a long time coming, eh?"

Cue much cheering, clapping, and foot stomping.

"But you know what they say? Better late than never."

Cue more cheering and shouting.

"Tonight, we conclude our first record deal …"

More clapping etc. etc. etc.

"Now Dennis Smith from Nearly Man records is on his way up from London as we speak so once this show's over we're going to put on the mother of all fucking parties …"

Mayhem, beer's being launched, more hooting.

"… 'cause this is long overdue, eh? This should've happened fucking years ago, so we've got a lot of catching up to do. But we've got the experience, so we'll be at the top in no time, mark my words."

I was still staring at Sid as he gesticulated with venom towards the crowd. I couldn't help but think of Nuremberg as Sid spat out his disgust at the state of the music industry and at the lengths it would go to to forsake real talent for profit. He portrayed us as the victims of a society in decline. A society happy to embrace mediocrity. The gathered mass lapped up his dictatorial bombast in silence except for a couple of random shouts of encouragement and agreement. I stood and gazed in amazement at what Sid had become and I knew that I was doing the right thing.

For all the pain I'd caused and had suffered, this was going to be worth it.

"1,2,3,4!" With that Sid drew his speech to a resounding close as the near silent crowd found their voice again and bellowed along at the resumption of the show.

We played for about two hours and came off stage to find out there was still no sign of Dennis Smith.

CHAPTER 45

"He's no' fucking answering, his phone's switched off," Sid roared whilst banging his phone against the painted stone wall of the green room in a rage.

"Well that's a good thing, man. He's probably in the air. Calm doon, it'll be cool." Bobby's attempt at appeasing Sid was fruitless.

"Aye, it'll be fine. The contract's signed anyway so dinnae panic, everything's cool," I added.

"Everything is not fucking cool," Sid seethed. "He's meant to be here so we can hand over the contract on stage. Everyone's here for that moment, it's symbolic, it's what we planned. It's nae use him turning up once they've all gone home and we just hand it to him in the dead of night. Where's the romance in that, eh? Where's the glory? It's how I planned it. The lights, the crowd, the media. Them all seeing us make it. I told you we'd make it. DIDN'T I?"

Sid was in danger of losing it. The fact that we had now been signed didn't matter to him anymore. He wanted the pomp that went with it. The rest of us were just happy to finally get some recognition for all our hard work and effort but that wasn't enough for Sid. He wanted all the trimmings.

What would it matter if Dennis didn't turn up until later on?

The end result would still be the same.

So nobody was there to witness this humongous event in history, big deal?

"Big deal?" Sid screamed as he marched backwards and forwards kicking various objects that were in his path. "Of course it's a big fucking deal."

The other band members that were still hanging out in the room quickly dispersed, except for one young lad who missed his opportunity and now cowered in the corner behind a bottle of beer doing his best to avoid eye contact with anyone as Sid continued his tantrum.

"This isn't how it's meant to happen," Sid rubbed his forehead frantically.

"Eh guys …? This crowd aren't going to be happy until you've done an encore," said a head that had peered around the door.

"Whit?!" Sid shouted.

"Encore? They're getting a bit restless now, you should get back out there."

"Nae bother, hen," Bobby replied whilst gently pushing her head back and closing the door behind her.

"She's right, man. Let's get out there, I can hear them banging," Bobby said.

"Aye come on dinnae let this ruin the big night," I offered. I put my arm around Sid's shoulder, but he flinched it off and walked out of the room.

We joined him on stage, and we played another three songs, but the energy of our set was flat due to Sid's preoccupation with Dennis' arrival.

Or lack of.

We mouthed our thanks to the respondent crowd at the end of our encore and ambled off stage again.

Sid was back on his phone straight way.

"He's still no' answering, useless cunt." And he threw his phone onto the battered couch.

Closing time was drawing nearer so I made my way out front to the bar for a drink.

Nae point in wallowing in Sid's gloom.

I drank a pint as various people asked me when and where the signing party was taking place. I fobbed them off that it was supposed to be here but that the man in question, Dennis Smith, had failed to show due to problems with his flight from London. With only 20 minutes to closing time most of the crowd had dispersed in disappointment and confusion. Only the hardcore fans, friends, and family remained.

"What's going on?" Abbie puzzled with a frowned expression.

"I've no idea. It's turned into a bit of a damp squib," I replied disheartened. "We'll probably end up handing over the contract in the morning in Sid's hotel room. Bit of a let down really but these things happen I suppose."

"You all right?" she quizzed, being more supportive than I wanted her to be.

"Aye I'm fine, just got a few things on my mind. Things didn't turn out like I thought they would but hey, life goes on, eh?"

"Yeah, at least you've still got the future to look forward to."

"Aye," I supped at my pint. "Look why don't you head home; I don't think anything's gonnae happen tonight. I'd better stay and make sure the rest of the guys are a'right. I'll call you tomorrow, eh?"

Abbie looked hurt but she kissed me then turned for the door. She looked back and blew me a kiss.

I didn't return the compliment.

When I went back to the green room Sid was busy chucking out the reporter from The Fife News and some other journalist for having the audacity to question the night's proceedings.

"Fucking vultures, man," he bawled. "Let's get this shit into the van."

He threw his guitar into its case and chucked leads into bags. He picked up his stuff and lurched past me.

He looks tired.

His eyes are glazed.

This isn't going to be easy.

Bobby and I helped Molly with the amps and the rest of the equipment. Neither of us even spoke. Sid's incensed mood had soured the party atmosphere.

Outside in the fresh air we loaded our equipment into the van as the last of the stragglers queried the next plan of attack. They were all drunk and were keen to continue with the party despite the circumstances.

"There is no fucking party," Sid shouted. "Go home."

Nobody moved. The crowd just shifted and swayed, somebody whispered something that led to sniggering before erupting into full blooded drunken laughter.

"Go!" Sid shouted as he slapped the side of the van. The resultant din was enough to shock their system and gain their drunken attention. "Go on, fuck off. Get tae fuck!"

The crowd slowly lurched away as Molly said goodbye to her parents and friends, assuring them that she'd see them in the morning.

Sid slumped to the pavement with his head in his hands and sighed.

"Best night of our lives, eh? Fucking disaster. Wait till I see that English cunt …"

Bobby slid down beside him.

"Look mate, it's all right. Everything's still on. So we didn't get to do it in front of the fans? No harm done. We've still got the contract and the three albums to do."

"Eh … actually … we don't," I mumbled.

CHAPTER 46

Sid and Bobby looked up at me as Molly and Mel drew closer.

"What?" Bobby asked in confusion.

"There is no contract. No Dennis Smith. No Nearly Man records," I continued.

"What are you talking about, Jimmy?" Sid asked dismissively.

"It was me. It was all me. I'm Dennis Smith, I made up a website for the company, made a fake contract. It was a joke. To get you back for what you did to Debs and me—"

"Whit?! Shut up, you're no' funny, man." Sid glared into my eyes, daring me to defy him.

"I'm not trying to be funny, it's the truth," I uttered whilst trying my hardest to remain composed.

"NO. No, no you're lying. This isnae funny, this is bullshit, eh?" Sid replied. He pushed himself up from the pavement and came towards me, shaking his head in disbelief.

"It's not, I did it to teach you a lesson, make you see how it feels to be the butt of the joke for once … I was supposed to announce it on stage after our last song but I chickened out …" I stammered whilst slowly taking backwards steps.

"Tell me *THIS* is a joke, Jimmy?" Bobby queried as he joined Sid in standing to attention.

"What's this all about?" asked Molly whose look said she was as confused as everyone else.

"I'm Dennis Smith," and I launched into my London accent to prove it to Sid. "Alright fella? It's me, Dennis. Look sorry about the misunderstanding, mate, but there is no contract. It was a joke. A laugh innit?" I dialled Sid's number with the spare phone I had bought in Oban and held it up to him as his own phone rang.

The realisation slowly dawned on Sid's ashen face as he looked at the name displayed by the incoming call.

I don't know why he answered it.

Everybody could see I had just dialled the number.

But he did.

Praying that this was all just a sick joke and Dennis Smith really would be on the other end of the phone.

"Hello," he answered hesitantly whilst maintaining his vacant stare at me.

"Hello?"

I slowly brought the phone to rest on my cheek and sighed.

"It's over, Sid," I gently spoke into the receiver.

His face contorted with confusion and pain.

"Why? How?" he mumbled whilst looking like Caesar must have felt as Marcus Brutus revealed himself. I felt a surge of remorse as I saw his reaction. I silently watched as he blinked a single tear from his eye. I stood motionless in the cool night air as it meandered down his cheek. I was so mesmerised with my own thoughts and feelings that I didn't notice him lunge at me. The wind rushed from my lungs as we crashed to the cold, hard pavement. The aching blow snapped me from my hypnosis, and I quickly attempted to get back on my feet, but he was on top of me before I had the chance. Sid's pounding fists rained down on my body as I pulled my arms up to protect my face from the attack. Blinded by his pain and his rage he swung wildly in my general direction. Thankfully none of his punches actually managed to connect with my head. My arms took a battering though as they defended my face.

"You fucking bastard!" he screamed as he continued with the assault.

Bobby grabbed Sid and pulled him from me. As I struggled to get to my feet, I could see he was kicking out and struggling to return to his onslaught, but Bobby held him in a firm grasp. Mel and Molly just stood and stared in horror and disbelief.

"This cannae be happening. YOU'VE FUCKING RUINED ME!" he howled like a lunatic.

"Why, Jimmy? What's this all about, man?" Bobby asked, still puzzled by the dramatic turn in events.

"To get back at him. Let's see how funny he thinks it is to be humiliated. I did it for us, I did it for you," I groaned as I patted my ribs for signs of serious damage.

Sid was still kicking out and writhing as he frantically tried to free himself from Bobby's firm grasp. Bobby flung him to the ground in a heap and walked towards me. I started to move backwards.

Quickly.

It was one thing being hit by Sid, but Bobby?

"What do you mean for me? You've ruined everything. I'd made plans." Bobby threw his hands in the air in disgust.

"If we end it now, we can start our own band," I pleaded and I raised my battered arms in defence. "This'll never end, Bobby, he'll keep marching us around the country, Ireland, London … God knows where else after that and we'll never get signed. We're no' good enough. We're SHITE!" I roared.

I didn't see him approach.

I was more concerned with Bobby's looming advance, but Sid cracked his fist off my jaw and sent me sprawling to the pavement once more.

I could taste the blood in my mouth as it poured freely from my lip.

It tasted bitter.

Just like my friendships.

I heard Mel scream and looked up to see Bobby dragging Sid away as he swung a kick in my direction.

"Get tae fuck!" Bobby shouted and chucked Sid away like he was a rag doll.

I wiped blood from my mouth and cackled hysterically to myself as I admired the maroon streaks that smeared my hand.

"It'll never change, man. It'll just go on and on like it always has. Me and you dragging our sorry arses all over the place as we jump through his hoops. Well, no more. Now is our chance for freedom. Go home with Mel. Live your life in peace. Dinnae make the same mistake I made," I spat blood onto the concrete and wrestled with the remaining salty tasting strings that clung to my chin.

"You ungrateful wee bastard," Sid raved as he violently thrust his finger at me from within Bobby's firm grasp. "I did everything for you, we could've been something … you've ruined everything you, you … FUCK!" Sid pointed his head to the heavens and omitted a blood-curdling scream that would've made the most valiant knight defile his gleaming armour, haul his whinnying steed into a U-turn, and denounce his chivalric ways forever.

"You did it all for yourself, Sid. You always have. You don't give a fuck about the rest of us. It's over. Go home," I pathetically batted the cold night air with my less painful arm in a dismissive gesture to Sid.

When Bobby eventually released Sid from the tranquillising grip he held him in, Sid stalked the silent street like a caged animal, he didn't know where to turn. He tugged at his hair, threw punches into the night air, kicked parked cars, and wailed profanities as he did so.

His tantrum reminded me of Basil Fawlty, and I smirked through the pain of my split lip at the thought.

The wrathful glares I received from the other three transformed my grin into a sombre pout though.

Driven to distraction through manic rage, Sid stormed to the back of the tour van, yanked open the door, grabbed my guitar case, and hurled it down the street. A car approached and had to swerve as the case skittered towards its wheels. The cab driver honked his horn and gesticulated at us.

Next, Sid produced my amp which promptly cracked as he launched it onto the concrete. Just for good measure he then booted it hard, ripping the canvas covering.

"Take your shit and get the fuck out of my sight, you evil little cunt," Sid pointed and marched round to the driver's seat. His key had barely entered the door lock when he suddenly whipped it out, turned around and came marching over to my defenceless position. Bobby, presumably expecting this, charged over and held his hands out to block Sid from attacking me again.

"You've got two grand of my money. Fucking gies it," Sid sneered and he held his hand out in expectation of a prompt payment.

"Dinnae worry, you'll get your money back," I replied lamely.

"Gies it … fucking now," he demanded.

"I've no' got it," I lied. I had most of it, but I wasn't telling him that. Two grand was scant consolation for having no job and no home to go back to.

We stood there staring at each other as a couple of taxis drove slowly by hoping to witness some carnage. The drunken inhabitants in the back seats would be none the wiser to the events that were currently taking place between lifelong friends.

"You'll get your money," I repeated and puffed up my chest to add some pride to my lie.

At this uncomfortable stalemate Sid shook his head and threw a few shadow punches at me.

"You're a fucking dead man, Jimmy. It's no' Danny Foster you've got to worry aboot noo, it's me." And he did that eye pointing thing again as he hauled open the driver's door and jumped into the seat. "Youse coming?" he shouted through the half-opened window to the visibly shocked others.

I walked over to Bobby and Mel.

"Sorry, folks," I pleaded. "It wasn't meant to end like this, but it did have to end."

"You've gone too far this time," Bobby fumed, barely able to maintain eye contact with me.

Mel just stared at me in resentment and shook her head in disgust.

"Why, Jimmy? Why?" was all she kept saying.

I shrugged my shoulders. I'd told them why, but they wouldn't or couldn't accept my reasons.

"You've made us look like a right bunch of arseholes," Molly broke in on our uncomfortable discussion and punched me in the face. The blow didn't hurt but seeing the abhorrent looks on their faces sure as hell did.

Molly got into the passenger side and slammed the door shut. The engine revved hard and the exhaust pipe belched noxious fumes into the already polluted atmosphere. The tyres screeched into life, mimicking the driver's earlier cries of grief as Sid put his foot to the floor and raced down the street.

I was left standing there with Bobby and Mel who, lost in hurt, grief, anger, and despair, simply shook their heads at me once more and walked off down the street.

"I'm sorry folks," I shouted after them. "I'll give you a call later … when it's all calmed down."

I stood on the pavement and watched them fade into the distance.

They didn't look back.

It was then that I felt the throbbing pain of my wounds and realised how cold it was.

A shiver ran down my spine as I fumbled in my pocket for my cigarettes. In the mad rammy the box had been crushed and so had the contents inside. I didn't care. I lit a smoke and inhaled deeply, gazing all the while at the blue reek snaking from the tip to disappear into the cold night air. The cigarette resembled my own appearance. Dishevelled, broken, and limp. I smoked it down to the filter.

I hobbled over to the remains of my amp and nudged it with my foot to determine how much life was left in the old dog. It split in two as my foot made contact. Dragging it to the side of the road I went in search of my guitar which I found nestled snugly under the wheels of a parked car. I picked it up and brought it under a streetlight to inspect the damage. The case was scuffed and dented but when I examined the contents the bass guitar was still in one piece. It was a lump of shit. I had to constantly retune it whilst playing.

Some things just don't know when to give up.

I eased my aching body down and sat on the cold pavement and smoked another cigarette.

Things hadn't gone the way that I had planned them. Yes, the end result would've been the same, but playing it out on an empty street where nobody could see or could feel Sid's humiliation felt like it hadn't been worthwhile.

You've naebody else tae blame, ye couldnae even garner the courage tae dae it properly, could ye? Fucking bloose!

It was harder than I thought it would be, all those folk staring at me. I just couldn't find the right time.

Yer arse, ye'r a fucking pussy that's aw. If ye'r gonnae dae a job dae it fucking right or dinnae dae it at aw!

I'd planned it for some time.

Once the seed was planted there was no going back. Sometimes it was all that got me out of bed in the morning. Sid hadn't just embarrassed me with his stupid online prank, he'd humiliated and traumatised Debbie and for that there could be no forgiveness. She had done nothing to deserve that sort of treatment and the way in which he laughed it off as if it was just a joke … well let's just say it triggered a little spark in my brain.

I'd spent serious time developing the website for Nearly Man records to make it look authentic, cutting and pasting relevant photos from obscure websites for that bona fide feel. I was rather chuffed with my efforts. If all else fails, and by the look of it, it already has, I can always try my hand at web design.

I'd purchased a cheap, spare phone whilst in Oban, not for any other reason than it came with a new SIM so I wouldn't have to be pestered by Danny Foster's threatening texts. It came in handy as I used this to operate under the guise of Dennis Smith.

At first, I wasn't convinced Sid would fall for it, I mean Nearly Man Records? King Tut's? The clues were all there. But sometimes people are too blinded by their own desires that they only see what they want to see.

A record deal.

That was all he'd wanted since we started this farce all those years ago.

I thought it fitting that he should have one before it all came crashing down before his eyes.

All be it a fake one and only for a few days.

Why did I do it?

Revenge mainly.

I had been entombed in a silent bitter rage from the moment Sid decided to show the world the contents of my phone.

That was just nasty.

Evil.

There was no justification for his actions.

It was a moment of lust between two people who were in love and meant for the viewing pleasure of specifically my eyes only.

I wanted to, no, I needed to avenge Debbie.

By perhaps doing so it was my intention that she would see that I was finally ready to cut all ties with Sid. That I needed her a lot more than I needed him. My original plans weren't as drastic but when I received the news that Debbie was pregnant, therefore dashing all hope of a loving reconciliation, my anger, hurt, and hatred were consumed by one thought.

Destruction.

Sid had destroyed the one thing that I held dear. Now I would destroy the one thing that meant more to him than anybody or anything.

His band.

It would've been easy for me to simply quit the band and return home, but where is the fun in that, eh?

Besides, I would be the only one to lose in that scenario.

So instead my mind set about formulating an idea, a plan that would not only dissolve the band but destroy its reputation. What could be better than the hype surrounding a recording deal that would not only be the talk of the town but of Scotland?

Especially when you had an egotistical maniac at the helm who was only more than happy to tell the world of our newfound fame.

Sid was delightfully obliging in sticking his head over the parapet.

All I had to do was take aim and then fire.

If you're going to go down, you might as well go down in a blaze of glory.

I had repeated the pros and cons in my head until I'd convinced myself that the couple of cons didn't really matter. Sure, the reputation of the band would lie in tatters, but I wasn't the one shouting from the rooftops that we were the greatest band that ever existed.

I had been saying the opposite.

It was unfortunate that Bobby and Mel were going to get caught up in the crossfire. But I'd felt justified when Sid and Dobby fell out and Bobby announced his intentions of quitting the band at the end of the tour.

Molly?

Well Molly was young; she'd get over it. This could even be the making of her.

Fuck you, Sid, you had this coming to you.

I'm only sorry that it has taken me so long to see that it's not me that has needed you throughout the years.

It was you who needed me.

Well, no more.

I didn't ruin your life.

You fucking destroyed mine.

I picked up my guitar and headed for the luxury hotel which I had had the foresight to book knowing that my actions would lead to my exclusion from any further band activities.

It was after midnight.

I realised it was now Christmas Eve.

Bah bloody humbug.

Once in my room I took out my newly purchased laptop (courtesy of Sid's kind advance) and set about concluding my plans.

The grape vine would be slow.

Almost non-existent if Sid had anything to do with it.

I could picture him now, concocting some dramatic lie to tell the disappointed fans. It would probably be something pathetic like the terms turned out to be terrible or the money wasn't good enough. He'd probably be telling everybody that I was kicked out of the band for some pathetic reason. Well, I wasn't going to give him that opportunity. Not when I had the World Wide Web at my fingertips.

I poured a drink from the mini bar and toasted Sid before draining the contents.

I had changed all the passwords to the band's various sites, not that Sid had ever contributed anything to them before but when he saw what I was about to write he'd erase the damaging content as soon as he could.

Now there would be no chance of that.

Check mate.

CHAPTER 47

Fans, friends, and family, it is with some regret that I announce the shocking news that Champions Of The Underdog are no more.

After more than 20 years together it is, and some of you may agree, a decision that is long overdue. After (nearly) completing a gruelling six-month tour of our beloved nation and with a record deal in the bag this decision may seem preposterous.

So why now?

Well, if you'll make yourself comfortable, I will tell you.

For many years we have struggled to make an impact on the music scene. Not just in our magnificent country but on the world at large. Not satisfied with this outcome our glorious leader Sid Hughes decided that it would be a good idea to prolong our agony by making us agree to do a tour that would take us all over Scotland, forcing the good people of towns and cities who hadn't had the misfortune of hearing our mundane tunes to surrender to his will.

For this I sincerely apologise.

There is a good reason for us not setting the heather ablaze and subsequently gaining the trust, admiration, and respect of the music fraternity.

We're pish.

No' guid enough.

It's as simple as that.

We peddled songs that were one dimensional and self-serving and we had the audacity to complain when nobody took us seriously or gave us some much-needed attention.

For this we also apologise.

When we started this crazy journey as a bunch of teenagers, I can truly say that it was the best time of my life. There is no better feeling in the world than hearing the roar of approval from a jubilant audience. Sadly, as the years have gone by, the adulation has also gone, leaving one of us with a sour taste in his mouth.

'You should be worshipping the ground we walk on. Why don't you love us? We're fucking amazing,' he would rant.

If that truly were the case, then you *WOULD* be worshipping the ground we walk on. But you are no fools. You know a good thing when you see it. Don't blame yourselves. HOW CAN YOU IDOLIZE SOMETHING THAT DOESN'T EXIST??!!

Rather than watching us stumble on blindly like a lame, old dog becoming frailer and more disorientated by the day, I took the harsh, although some may say entirely justified decision to put that lame, old dog out of its misery.

BANG!

Your suffering is now over.

Rest In Peace.

Terminating a band that has been awash with mediocrity should have been a quiet and easy job that nobody really had to hear about.

But where's the fun in that, eh?

So it was that I decided to end the final chapter in our long and painfully boring story by adding some fireworks.

Call it something to remember us by.

Sid Hughes, a lifelong friend of mine, did something to me which I can only describe as inexcusable.

For this I can never forgive him.

With hindsight, I should have called it quits with the band when the incident happened and set about explaining his actions to the concerned party.

But I didn't.

In an act of cowardice, I chose to forget that the incident occurred and continued on with our quest to gain fame and notoriety.

It was this 'incident' that finally opened my eyes and set this ball rolling.

To be laughed at, made fun of is one thing. But to humiliate somebody to the detriment of their health is a bridge too far.

So, I made up a fake record company.

I won't bore you with the details. If you are reading this then you will, I have no doubt, read the other articles delivering the good news of us signing our first record deal, we've finally done it, hit the jackpot etc. etc. etc.

Well, we haven't, or should I say we hadn't.

In Machiavellian style I have ended the story of Champions Of The Underdog.

I did it neither for praise nor pity.

I did it because it had to be done.

Some of you may weep. Some of you may laugh. Most of you will not give a flying fuck and carry on with the rest of your lives in peace.

Bobby, I am sorry that it ended this way. You of all people deserved better and I failed you. You are now free of the burden of playing a part in this parody and can carry on with the life that you and Mel always planned. Hopefully through time you will be able to see that I had to do this and that you can forgive me.

Molly, it was fun whilst it lasted. But you'll get it over this. You're young and talented. More talented than Sid would have you believe. Go and follow your dreams. Learn from this.

I have hurt a few people in my life but none more so than the one I love most. My actions and non-actions have led to our relationship being beyond repair and this will haunt me for the rest of my days. Alas, it is my burden to bear.

I know it is of no consolation to you that I am truly sorry for the pain and suffering I have caused you. But I offer my apologies honestly and sincerely anyway in the hope that we can meet again someday as friends, although I will always want more.

And you, dear reader?

Carry on as normal.

Nothing more to see here.

Peace, love, empathy.

Jimmy Steel.

I shut down the laptop and finished the last of the drinks in the mini bar. I felt relaxed and slightly merry.

It's good to talk, to get things off your chest, and although my talking was performed behind the sanctuary of an electronic mail statement, it still had the effect of soothing my conscience.

I'd said my piece.

I chuckled to myself as I thought of Sid's response on reading it. It wasn't literary genius, but I said what I needed to say.

He would be uncontrollable with rage.

Brilliant.

The thought of me snuffing out all his years of toil and effort would almost give him a stroke. I was like McCartney announcing to the world that the Beatles had split. Sid would assume the John Lennon role with ease.

I only wish we were one tenth as good as them.

I'll sleep soundly tonight, Sid, but thanks for asking. You cunt.

CHAPTER 48

I awoke in the morning with a renewed sense of vigour.

Unlike Scrooge there was no sound of bells tolling or any sign of snow on the sleepy streets beneath but like the miser himself I had experienced a jarring epiphany the night before.

I showered, packed my bags, and checked out of my lodgings with a smile on my face and a spring in my step.

I felt fresh, the shackles of constriction had been broken and I was like a new man.

I exchanged 'Merry Christmas' with everyone I met as I walked down the busy thoroughfares of Glasgow. The streets were packed with angst-ridden shoppers rushing about like bees on cocaine. They buzzed from shop to shop, never quite appeasing their appetite for nectar. Last-minute gifts were purchased and thrown hastily into bags as they flew past me in search of the next item on their list. At this time of year, I would steer clear of this madness like one would a disgruntled Jihad screaming extremist with a smouldering rucksack strapped to his back.

But feeling joyous I took great delight in revelling in the bustle.

I had made no plans for the immediate future. I was well aware of the fact that I'd be returning to live with my parents in my dreich old town.

But that would change.

I would put a plan of action in place.

In the meantime, I was just going to enjoy the feeling of merriment that encapsulated me. If a little crippled boy had crossed my path that morning, I would've sent him packing with the largest turkey he could've carried.

Or the 21st century equivalent.

Probably a PlayStation or Vape.

I even took time to purchase some gifts for my folks to celebrate this Christian farce.

I bought my mum a nice lambswool scarf and my dad a DVD about gardening.

I couldn't wait to see their smiley wee faces.

On the train home I read a paper and pulled faces at a little kid who kept looking over the seat that backed onto mine.

God bless you, son.

God bless each and every one of us.

I didn't bother signing into our websites to see the commotion that had followed my outburst.

I had lit the match.

I didn't need to watch the inferno.

I'd switched my phone off because I knew there would be a few calls coming my way.

Mainly from Sid.

I had nothing to say to him.

Yet.

I jumped off the train at the station and made my way along the short distance to my parents' house, whistling as I did so.

I was met by a few people who offered me congratulations on the band's newfound success. I told them briefly that the band had split and let them go on their merry way, bamboozled by my announcement.

I should have known what to expect but I was too engrossed in my own little festive snow globe to think about my parents' response when I explained to them what had happened to the band.

They were a lot angrier than I had anticipated.

Their anger was centred around the fact that I had quit a good job (in their eyes only), ruined a perfectly good relationship with and the reputation of Debbie (in all our eyes), had embarrassed myself and them by my actions and on top of that it was all for apparently nothing as I had spent the last six months in a self-centred muddle of God only knows what sort of debauchery only to end it by ridiculing my friends and ruining everything they had worked for.

Well, when they put it like that …

My snow globe crashed to the tiled floor in a million tiny fragments. The liquid spilled across the solid surface and ran down the grout lines. The little glittery flecks of snow looked pathetic as they clung to the wetness.

I was like a fish out of water, slapping and flopping against the cold tiles.

I was also cold.

Disappointed.

Hurt.

Angry.

"I thought you'd at least be pleased to see me, eh?" I rummaged around my bag for the presents I had bought them. "Here," I offered as I threw them onto the kitchen table. "I was going to wrap them but what's the point? You'd probably tell me I'd wasted too much paper. Merry fucking Christmas," I roared and slammed the back door shut as I made my exit.

Fuck it's cold.

I'd left my scarf and hat in the house, but I'd be damned if I was going back in there again.

I'd rather freeze.

Now that I was out in the cold grey streets, I realised that I had nowhere else to go. My old flat was gone. I couldn't go and see Debs. It was still too soon to call on Bobby and Mel. I was in my hometown on Christmas Eve and I had nowhere to go. Nobody to be with.

I'd never felt so alone.

I pulled my jacket tighter to keep the worst of the wind out, but it only succeeded in keeping the self-loathing in.

I stopped at a shop and picked up a packet of smokes before heading for the nearest pub.

The bar was packed as I nudged and squeezed my way up to it. People had finished work early for the day or were off completely and the tables were full of middle-aged people wearing those cheap paper hats that slump out of crackers whilst screeching those annoying horn things that stretch out when you blow them.

What the fuck are they called?

I eventually got served, downed my pint, and promptly left as I was sick of the cheery pricks attempting to put a paper hat on my head whilst blowing those stupid screeching things in my face.

The next pub I came to, The Cross Keys, had a reputation for being the hard man's pub.

And for a reason.

I'd only frequented it once in all the time I've lived here and whilst enjoying my short stay I was lucky enough to see a punter get a pint glass shoved into his face. I'd never really felt the need to return.

That was over 15 years ago.

Perhaps it's mellowed?

It hadn't.

It was full of the same hard-looking ruddy-faced men that had always drunk there. This was a proper old-fashioned boozer where the largely male only clientele came to drink.

Not to chat or discuss how their day had gone, but to sit in silence and stare at the decrepit walls and drink.

Lots.

You'd be lucky to buy a packet of crisps in this place never mind the gastronomical delights that riddle the bar menus of today's contemporary watering hole.

The rigid punters stared at me with scorn as I made my silent and slightly uncomfortable approach to the bar. They were inspecting my appearance and overall right to enter an establishment such as theirs but upon hearing my order of 'a pint and a nip' they were satisfied that this newcomer was a serious drinker not to be fucked with.

At least that was what I was hoping for.

I downed my Famous Grouse and took a large slug of my pint.

"Same again," I grunted as I stared at my reflection in the dusty, mirrored pane imprisoned by cheap branded fonts.

I looked as miserable and as mean as any one of the desperate fuckers in this shit hole.

I felt a sense of belonging at last.

Maybe this is my place in life now?

Washed up with nowhere else to go, spending my days staring into the bottom of a pint glass as my anger and hatred grew contagious.

"Same again."

Nah, I'm better than this.

These people are nothing like me.

I'm not going to get trapped in a cycle of self-loathing and despair, pissing my life away as I contemplate past regrets.

This is a chance for me to start all over.

The slate's been wiped clean.

I don't have Sid's chain around my neck anymore, I can do or be anything I want to be.

I knew one thing though. I needed to get out of this town once and for all. There was nothing for me here.

So where should I go?

Do I want to be in another band?

I liked the idea of fronting my own band, but I couldn't be arsed with the hassle of starting from scratch again, having to find new band mates.

I could go to Edinburgh or Glasgow and try my luck through there?

Nah, that's still too close to home.

Donald Smart?

My old School pal.

He lives down in London

I could get in touch with him, see if he'd put me up for a while till I sorted myself out, could get a job or maybe go back to college.

Aye, I could retrain in something completely different.

"Another round, pal," I snorted.

With the drink pumping through my bloodstream and the new ideas rattling around my mind, I started to lighten up. My dark mood had been replaced with one of drunken hope.

Life's what you make it, eh?

I heard the opening piano bars and drum beat to Talk Talk's 'Life's what you make it' enter my mind.

Wise words indeed.

Top tune too.

How the hell could we never write anything as good as that?

One great song, one great tune.

That's all you need.

A catchy number so the world sits up and takes notice and then you've got it made.

We couldn't even do that.

No, Sid couldn't even do that.

I could though.

Aye, of course I could, look at all the shite bands that have made it on the strength of one good tune.

There are fucking thousands of them, the rest of their songs are utter bollocks, but they carved a career out of one solid song.

One song.

Surely I could do that?

Aye life's what you make it indeed.

Never to suffer would never to have been blessed and aw that, eh Poe? You kent the story Edgar Allan.

This is my chance to show the world, to show my parents, to show Sid that I can be somebody.

"Last orders," the bar man grunted, shaking me from my sozzled thoughts.

I looked up at the dusty clock through bleary eyes.

"It's only half nine, man," I slurred.

"Aye, and it's only Christmas Eve so drink up," his threatening glare immediately quashed my rebellious comeback.

"Fair do's, my good man, I'll have the same again and get one for yourself, eh? Merry fucking Christmas."

The bar man stared at me like he stared at all his punters. With a slight tinge of annoyance mixed with utter revulsion. It didn't stop himself from pouring a large dram from the only single malt on display though.

Didn't even say thank you either.

Ungrateful cunt.

I sat and finished the last of my drinks whilst contemplating my next move.

All the other bars will be closing at a similar time.

What about the nightclub, it'll be open till one?

Nah, it'll be packed with the latest generation of wee fannies and without any pills I don't think I can handle the musical assault that the DJ will be dishing out.

I could stop at the shop and get a few cans and try and sneak in the back door of the house.

Christ I'll be like a 15-year-old again trying to sneak in without being spotted.

At least ye can tell them tae fuck off noo when they get on tae ye aboot the drinking.

Thankfully my parents were the early-to-bed type so if I took the scenic route back to theirs they'd be tucked up safe and sound and I wouldn't have to go through the heartache and tedium of another argument.

There was a light snow fall as I ambled from the corner shop with my carry out in hand. It didn't make me feel very Christmassy though. Quite the opposite in fact. The lighthearted drunken mood I'd felt just moments before had been evicted by the feeling that usually accompanies me at this time of year.

Melancholy.

Melancholic.

Alcoholic Melancholic?

Ha ha ha. Melancholic Alcoholic, that's better, must remember that one, great title for a song.

Probably been done though.

I was bursting for a piss, so I turned and walked down Lover's Lane.

Nobody comes this way so I could pee without fear of getting stage fright.

Aaaaaahhhh, that's better.

I shook my cock free of yellow dribbles and popped him back into the warmth of my pants.

The snow was falling harder, and I was cold.

I just wanted to be indoors.

To be warm.

I stopped walking momentarily to remove one of the cans from the carrier bag and was taking the first refreshing slug when I heard his icy voice.

CHAPTER 49

"Oi Steel? Ah want a word wi' you."

Oh fuck.

Danny Foster.

On Christmas Eve? What's the chances of that?

Maybe he just wants to shake my hand and offer me seasonal greetings?

I turned around to see him marching up the lane to where I swayed.

Judging by the fierce look on his face it didn't look like he was coming to exchange pleasantries.

"Look Danny I dinnae want any trouble, I've just got back and I—" I tried to appease him, raising both my hands in surrender.

He ignored my pleas.

As he marched closer, he switched the carrier bag he was holding in his right hand to his left.

I didn't even see it coming.

My drunken gaze was lost on his carrier bag amidst thoughts of what it might be housing.

Last minute sprouts?

But I sure as fuck felt it.

CRACK!

It was a surreal moment that probably only lasted about ten seconds, but it felt like an hour as I flayed and kicked in the struggle to get back on my feet. Through too much alcohol and probably mild concussion from the right hook he had just delivered to my jaw, I resembled Bambi on ice. Strangely I noticed that my carry out had sprung from the bag and was lying scattered on the pavement.

I didn't know what I was doing.

I was still scrambling about the ground trying my hardest to make some sense of it all when his next blow landed.

CRACK!

A swift boot to the ribs hurled me sideways and onto my back.

The air surged from my lungs, and I gulped for breath.

I cannae fucking breathe, I cannae breathe.

In my panic for survival my brain had failed to register the fact that Danny Foster was now leaning over me with my throat in his left hand whilst he gesticulated in my face with his right.

I could tell by his cruel mouth that he was bawling at me, but I never heard a word he uttered.

I still couldn't breathe.

My brain was still struggling to comprehend what was happening, so it chose (perhaps as a wee treat to take my mind off the excruciating beating I was receiving) to replay images from my childhood of me playing the Nintendo Game Boy I had just received for Christmas in 1991.

What would I be? 12? 13?

A Game Boy?

A Game Boy. Oh thanks Mum, thanks Dad, you're the best. I love you two.

I've only got masell a Game Boy, wait till I tell Ian, we can share the games …

CRACK!

FUCKING HELL!

The shooting pain from my nose gave my brain the jolt required to waken it from its confused hiatus and start formulating a plan quick fucking smart to save me from the hellish torture.

The blood from my burst nose was streaming into my mouth and I spluttered as it entered.

Obviously, due to the close proximity of Danny's snarling face to mine, it was inevitable that some of my coughing and spluttering would result in his twisted features being pebble dashed a scarlet red with my blood.

He didn't seem to appreciate the inevitable though.

CRACK!

SMACK!

CRUNCH!

He delivered three more blows in such rapid succession that the pain merged into one giant ball of agony rather than three separate hurts. He'd also managed to punch my front teeth out because I could feel them rattling around my mouth.

I did my best to fumble them out with my bloody tongue so as not to choke on them.

This fucker is trying to kill me.

I tried to move, to react, to do something to stop the madness but he's a big fellow and he had his knee pressed into my chest.

I was going nowhere.

This was only going to end one way.

I was mumbling "please, please," but through a lack of teeth and a burst lip I was simply spitting more blood into his contorted face which made him even angrier.

I tried to block his blows with my hands, but he batted them away like one would an annoying fly.

I'm going to die.

I am really going to die.

In this shitty town.

Beaten to death.

By this cunt.

Left in a bloody puddle.

To die.

Die?

Die.

FUCK THIS!

CHAPTER 50

An image from some time ago flashed into my mind. It was my eureka moment. I fumbled for an eternity, pushing past the snotty hankies in my pocket until I found it.

The blows didn't seem to hurt any more.

I flicked off the covering and released it from its slumber.

Danny Foster didn't see the strike coming due to his preoccupation with mashing my skull into the Tarmac.

But *he* sure as hell felt it.

With as much strength as I could muster, I rammed the blade into any bit of flesh I could find. I didn't pick a target, anywhere would do.

His shriek pierced the night air.

I recall being amazed by the pitch of it.

It sounded like it came from the ruby red lips of a woman in a 1920s horror film, that spine-tingling, blood-curdling scream.

I pulled the knife from his neck and his hands immediately ceased their assault on my face to inspect the damage inflicted upon his own carcass. Through a half-shut eye I could make out the sticky liquid seeping through his clenched grasp.

"You fuck …" he mumbled as he gawked at the volume of blood that drenched his hands.

He stumbled off me and keeled onto his side. He didn't move. He silently lay there prone on the road.

I was so happy.

So relieved.

I wasn't going to die.

I pulled myself to my knees in agony.

With the adrenaline fading, my body was left to its own defences which were limited at best. With as much effort as I could muster, I attempted to stand. My legs buckled and I threw up my evening's intake of alcohol. The watery contents mixed with the spilled blood to create a childlike painting of messy colour on the ground.

Foster was still lying on the narrow road clutching his wounded neck.

Fuck you, Foster, think you could beat me, eh?

His body was shaking.

No, it was convulsing.

Fuck, this isn't good.

I crawled over to where he lay and pulled him over. There was a lot of blood pouring from his wound. It squirted through his tightly held grasp.

Oh fuck, oh fuck, oh shit this is bad.

"Danny? Danny?" I mumbled through broken bones and skin.

His eyes flickered as rapidly as his body shook. He looked pale and his breathing was ragged.

He tried to say something.

I fumbled in my pocket and took out my phone. I attempted to hit 999 but my fingers were covered in blood and the phone squirmed from my grasp and crashed to the ground. I swiped and swiped but there was no response from the dead screen.

OH FOR FUCK'S SAKE!

My hands shook uncontrollably as I tried my best to hit the power button to startle some life into the useless machine and make the important call.

Vital minutes had been lost.

Finally, thank fuck.

I blubbered and rambled down the phone to the operator as I described Danny's wounds.

"You're going to be okay, man. It's going to be fine. The ambulance is on the way," I mumbled to him.

I tried to console him, stroke his head, comfort him.

What have I done?

I pulled his limp head onto my legs and cradled him.

My tears joined my blood and fell onto his face to add to the horrific masterpiece.

He was shivering.

I was shaking.

Foster's flickering lids eventually focused upon my own. Without a word of a lie, upon seeing my terrified expression I swear his pupils dilated and his mouth conjured that evil grin of satisfaction he so often wore.

The ambulance took forever to arrive. I tried my best to stem the flow of blood by firstly applying pressure with my own hands and then tearing a strip from my jumper to use as a tourniquet.

My relief was beyond words as I heard the wailing siren in the distance then saw the flashes of blue bouncing off the trees and buildings in the adjacent street.

The paramedics quickly went to work on Danny by applying some dressings and then carefully placing him in the back of the van. Upon inspecting my own wounds and judging them not to be life threatening they bundled me into the van alongside the prone Foster.

I swayed and swerved in the back of the van as we bade a hasty retreat for the Accident and Emergency ward.

I couldn't see what they were doing to Danny. I just sat there in a state of frightened panic at my own predicament.

"He's going to be okay though, eh?" was all I asked every few minutes.

They didn't bother to answer me.

They were too preoccupied with their own mission.

Attempting to save a man's life.

On arrival at the hospital the two paramedics were met by another two who promptly wheeled the bed out of the van and into the cold dark night.

Somebody else, it could've been the driver, ushered me inside to have my own wounds tended to.

I didn't care about my injuries, I just wished, no, I prayed that Danny Foster would be all right.

The doctor who cleaned up my face and administered stitches to the larger cuts on my skull asked what had happened.

I didn't have the courage to tell her the truth, so I lied and told her we were jumped on the way home from the pub. The doctor had to keep pausing her healing efforts to allow me to throw up.

My stomach had nothing left to expel so I retched bile into a cardboard bowl.

The doctor was applying the last of the dressings to my face when the curtains were swooshed open and a man in a lab coat filled the space.

My armoured love that once protected me is now rife with holes like the ozone layer, allowing penetrating blasts of wickedness to sear through and scorch my once peaceful soul.

The sucking sound of anxiety feeding on my negative discharge echoes around the hollows of my mind, mimicking the ghosts of a disused mine shaft and wailing with stagnant ventilation.

Powerful visions of horrific crimes flicker like flames, casting images of murder within me, threatening my conscience for every ounce of its sentimental worth.

My body shakes and vibrates uncontrollably as I wrestle, entangled with these bogus thoughts.

Humans stare out the corner of one eye as they watch my wretched face act out a tribal dance.

If the thoughts overcome me then self-inflicted pain is the only suitable remedy, torturing myself with acute jabs to my face or violent thrusts of my head repeatedly towards a hard blunt object bang, bang, banging until the thoughts rattle out into the open breeze.

Relieving me of heartache.

Leaving me with headache.

The shame I feel clings to me like the gagging stench of rotting flesh.

It lingers with every step I take.

Emotions never get high; emotions only get low.

So low.

Dragged deep towards the furnace of Hell.

This is when common sense departs on its own frantic journey through parallels, hopelessly searching between what is right and what is wrong.

What is good?

What is evil?

At night I toss and turn in a furious frenzy, bashing myself sore, shuddering until the thoughts cease.

Morning appears with a sudden crack and the first three seconds of the dawn are tranquil until my memory registers the new arrivals.

These intrusive thoughts, a manifestation of my predicament, ruin my day from the very start.

The nausea rumbles in my belly, interrupting my appetite.

But not my thoughts.

Never the thoughts.

Guilty reflections spew from my adrenal glands, spurt throughout my body and penetrate my brain in a futile cycle.

As I lie in bed at night, attempting to extinguish the pain, I can only pray for salvation.

CHAPTER 51

I was shaken from my internal paralysis by the doctor nudging my shoulder and repeatedly asking "Are you okay?"

"Eh ... aye, aye," I answered.

I was anything but.

Danny Foster died on the operating table.

The surgeon didn't attempt to sugar coat it. He just came straight out with it. No 'we did all we could,' like you see on the telly.

Danny's dead.

Because of me.

I killed him.

"If you'd like to go out into the waiting room the police will be arriving shortly and would like to speak to you," she added.

"The police? Speak to me?"

"Yes, so if you'd like to gather up your belongings and just wait for them there that would be great."

The doctor who had skilfully patched me up with such care and empathy was now promptly ushering me from the treatment room so that she could carry on with her busy night.

"Turn right at the end of the corridor and then next left for the waiting area, okay?"

I just nodded like a dumb school kid who clearly hadn't understood the instructions but didn't want to upset the teacher by asking them to repeat themself.

As I trundled off down wrong turns my mind was a blur of guilt and confusion.

I cannae speak to the polis, they'll know it was me.

Aye but self-defence, it was self-defence.

He's deid though!

I killed him.

Oh fucking hell.

356

Before I knew what was happening, I had already wandered past the waiting room and out into the open air.

The cold air hit me in the face like an icy slap, momentarily bringing me to my senses.

Go back inside and wait for the polis.

Only momentarily though.

I drifted in the direction of my parent's house with the surgeon's words swirling inside my head.

I couldn't speak, I could barely force myself to put one foot in front of the other.

Only through years of incessant motion did my brain enable my legs to function on auto pilot.

The snow fall was getting heavier, and it swirled with the wind, but I couldn't feel the cold anymore.

I put one foot in front of the other for as long as I could.

The trick is to keep moving.

I killed him.

I've killed a man.

The rational part of my mind kept trying to calm me down by repeating self-defence. It was self-defence.

I know it was self-defence but I killed him.

I found it hard to breathe, my heart felt like it was trying its hardest to escape from its internal captivity.

What's Debs going to say?

What are my parents going to say?

What the hell is going on?

How could this have happened?

Images of the hellish incident were replayed in my head.

Blood.

All I can see is the blood.

My blood. But mostly his blood.

I can still smell it.

I stopped next to a tree to smoke a cigarette. I needed to give my mind something else to concentrate on. My hands were shaking like a victim of Parkinson's Disease and I couldn't get the bloody thing to light.

My hands wouldn't stop shaking so I threw the unlit tube to the ground.

Got to keep moving.

Where?

Anywhere.

Nobody knows what's happened yet.

The townsfolk will be tucked up in their beds, gloriously ignorant of the terrible news that will soon rupture their hearts and appal their minds.

I killed him. Me. I'm a killer.

I stopped again and retched but there was nothing left in my stomach except agony.

Why me?

Why didn't I just stay at home?

Oh fuck, Debbie's going to kill me.

I'm so sorry, Debs.

It was his own fault, he came at you.

He wouldn't stop hitting me.

I've got no fucking teeth.

Aye but you didn't need to kill him.

I didn't mean to, I just wanted to get him off me.

Right in the main artery though?

It wasn't my fault, he was going to kill me. I just hit him once to make him stop.

This is fucking mental, man, you killed him. You're going down for this.

I didn't mean to … oh Christ.

I suddenly realised that nobody knew I was responsible for the crime.

Stop calling it a fucking crime, it was self-defence.

I thought about the consequences.

Would anybody know?

Was I seen?

Of course they'll find out. Have you still got the knife?

I dunno …

I checked my pockets.

… no it must still be lying there.

Well the first thing they'll do is find it and then match your DNA and the game's up. You've got tae go back and find it. Hide the evidence, eh?

I couldn't do it though.

Get your arse back there and get hunting for it. What's the alternative? Owning up and spending the next twenty years in the

slammer getting your arse pumped? Aye very good. Turn aroond and go find the fucking knife.

My legs obeyed and I trudged off in the opposite direction.

In a daze.

In a muddle.

Lost.

All the while my mind fought with the enormity of the situation.

I kept walking.

Snow swirling.

Blinded.

I can't do this. I'm too weak, too scared. I don't understand.

I changed course again as I struggled to piece together images and outcomes.

I had to do the right thing. For once in my life, I had to make the correct decision.

I walked up the steps to the entrance and with my hand still shaking I pressed the intercom.

After a brief moment I heard the buzz and click of the front door and made my entrance.

CHAPTER 52

I entered the police station around 3 a.m. on Christmas morning.

"IIT'S CHRIIIIIIIISTMAAAAAAS!" Noddy Holder bellowed in my head.

Aye, Merry Christmas.

I couldn't think of anything else to do. Well, anything better to do. I floated up to the desk and told the officer on duty that I had information regarding Danny Foster's death.

The officer looked at my battered face with as much confusion as I felt before replying tartly, "Oh yeah? And what kind of information would that be?"

"The kind that will require me to have legal representation," I smartly answered before flashing a toothless fake smile.

The officer's expression changed as his brain slowly worked out who I potentially was.

"You were meant to wait for us at the hospital," he huffed then pointed to a row of seats behind me. "Right, sit there." And he turned in haste towards a door leading to the back of the station before swiftly turning back to face me and pointing again he added, "And *DON'T* move."

The officer disappeared from view as I sat on the plastic chair.

A heavy sigh blew from my lips, making a slight whistling noise as the air escaped through the newly attained gap where my front teeth used to live.

At least that's the hard part out of the way.

Oh you think so, eh? It's no' even begun yet. You dinnae ken whit trouble awaits!

My stomach heaved violently again as the various intrusive outcomes were displayed in my mind's eye, leaving me gagging and clawing for air.

A side door was flung open and the officer from the desk who had brought a colleague for back up stood before me.

"Right, follow me," he barked before turning to lead the way.

I swayed on standing as the blood rushed from my head and the other officer caught my arm and ushered me forward.

I was put in what I presumed was an interview room and was told a solicitor was on the way.

Then I was left alone. Except from my thoughts.

This is another fine mess you've gotten yourself into.

My head sunk onto the table, and I shut my eyes, but the images of Danny's broken and bloody form kept coming to mind so I simply paced the room until I was brought a cup of tea.

Have you ever tried drinking a cup of tea with three missing teeth whilst images of death haunt your brain?

It's not recommendable.

The next time the door opened a tired-looking but smartly dressed woman offered me her hand in welcome.

She introduced herself as Grace Anderson, my appointed solicitor.

We both sat down, and she asked me to explain what had happened.

She listened intensely as I recounted the night's events when all I wanted to do was shriek with rage, cry, or scream. Release some of the pressure that fizzed inside me, but I didn't. I couldn't.

She would make an excellent counsellor. Or psychiatrist. Grace nodded and asked questions in a non-judgmental softly spoken way which left me thinking that perhaps she wasn't the person I needed to defend my honour in this time of crisis.

She also explained that I would be charged as a formality and would have to spend a couple of days locked up here until the courts opened after the festive period but that I was not to worry and that she would take care of everything.

Nae bother hen!

My main concern of "Will I go to prison for this?" didn't go unanswered but her reply was like that of a politician who doesn't like to give a straight forward yes or no answer and skirted around the guts of my question by referencing different pleas and judges and juries which confused me.

A feeling of terror followed closely behind the confusion, and it heightened when a couple of moody-looking suits knocked and entered the room and began setting up video recording equipment for my impending grilling.

Wonder which one's the good one?

They both stared at me for an uncomfortably long time before speaking.

Neither.

My previous concern with Grace being too nice and softly spoken to defend me was quickly quashed as she took complete control of the situation and rebutted many of the moody detectives' questions with curt replies of "Don't answer that."

It's good to see a professional at work, her performance allayed my fears of the worse until the detectives informed me that I was to be formally charged with murder and held at the station until brought before the sheriff.

Did he just say murder?

Murder?

It wasn't murder, he tried to kill me. I was protecting myself.

Only then did the turmoil inside manifest itself as my mind came to frightening conclusions.

"MURDER? I didnae murder him, he was trying tae kill *ME*."

I shouted and banged my fists against the table like a petulant child.

I stood up, looking for something to throw, but everything in the room was bolted down.

Probably due to situations like this, eh?

The anger felt good.

At least I felt something.

Grace tried to calm me and explain that it was just a formality, that the charge would be reduced at a separate hearing and that there were procedures to go through, but I wasn't listening properly. The rage inside me had been released and I continued to lash out and vent my fury, my hurt, and my shame by booting the table and slapping the walls.

The detectives pinned me to the ground when I tried to grapple and resist their harsh attempts to appease me.

Even as I was handcuffed and led to a cell I kicked and fought with all the energy I had left in me. My screams echoed down the dimly lit corridor as they shoved and fought me. I landed in a twisted heap, smacking my already damaged face against the cold hard floor.

A door was slammed shut behind me.

I lay prone listening to the guttural groans fleeing my throat.

They hurt but nothing like the pain of reality.

I sat alone in the cell, trying to make sense of the last few hours. The whats? The wheres? The whys?

My brain could muster no answers.

I kept thinking about Debs and how the news would be broken to her. Her new partner was dead, and her unborn child would be fatherless all due to my actions.

No, fuck that. It was because of HIS actions. If he'd just left me alone then everything would be okay but no, he had to have the last word. He had to attack me and now he's lying there on some slab, his body ice cold.

His eyes closed forever.

Fuck him.

I did what I had to do. If I hadn't it would be my cold, lifeless body lying there with my faced caved in.

I won't be going down for this.

The thoughts didn't reassure me though.

I lay on the bed and stared at the ceiling, noting how grubby the place looked.

How the hell am I going to get out of this one?

I heard keys at the door and when it was opened by an officer, Grace stood before me with a look on her face that I had seen my mother and Debs wear on several occasions.

Anger and shame.

After a brief lecture on my performance and future behaviour she asked if there was anyone I'd like her to contact.

I looked at her dumbly in disgust.

Who the fuck could I contact?

Merry Christmas, folks, I'm in jail but you enjoy your turkey, eh?

What for, son?

Oh for nothing really folks, just a wee bit o' MURDER.

How the hell was I going to explain this one?

Just tell it like it happened.

Do you think they're going to believe me? Come on, it's Mum and Dad. I can just imagine the scene. They'll probably sell up and move to New Zealand upon hearing this.

Oh the shame, the shame I've brought to the family.

It's Christmas Day, my friends hate me, my parents couldn't care less about my whereabouts, and the one person I love just so happens to be the girlfriend of the guy I killed last night.

In SELF-DEFENCE.

"I suppose you better break it to my parents at some point. Give it to them gently though and tell them it was self-defence."

She nodded and made for the door.

The officer from the desk replaced her in the cell and removed the handcuffs.

He then put his lips horribly close to my ear and muttered, "If there's any more shite from you these will be going straight back on, a'right?" He shook the cuffs in my face and smiled.

I nodded obediently and rubbed my chafed wrists.

The door slammed shut and locked, leaving me alone with my thoughts.

Needless to say, I didn't get a wink of sleep. How could I with the thoughts that flew through my head.

The images.

Always the pictures.

Thoughts and recollection coming to wrack my body with anxious tics.

After hours of pacing, sitting, kneeling, standing, and trying anything I could think of to find some sort of solace, the door opened and a tray of tea and toast was brought in for me to stare at like some abstract artwork that I did not understand.

I couldn't eat.

I couldn't drink.

I couldn't shit.

I couldn't piss.

I couldn't sleep.

I couldn't function.

I really needed a drink. Or anything with mind-numbing properties from which to relieve myself from the surreal affliction.

With the courts being closed for the festive period I would have to sit it out until I could be presented before the Sheriff in two days' time.

Might as well get used to my surroundings. A ten-foot by eight-foot room with luxury en-suite in the corner.

At least there's nobody to tell me off for leaving the toilet seat up.

Oh Christ.

I thought of poor Debs and images of her breaking down upon hearing the news entered my mind.

What have I done?

Visions of Danny's mum wailing with grief also flooded my head as my conscience fought with my sanity.

The wee woman had had a miserable life, but she loved her two boys despite all the pain and embarrassment they inflicted on her with their actions. She didn't deserve this horror.

Oh no …

The guilt gave me the dry boak.

Shut up, you cannae think that. It was you or him, right? He started it.

By now the sordid incident would be the talk of the town. I could just imagine the curtain twitchers discussing the events and my guilt as they rammed turkey sandwiches down their insatiable throats whilst watching the usual Christmas drivel on telly.

Surely they'd come to sensible conclusions when they heard Danny Foster's name being mentioned? He was a menace. They all knew that.

They'll probably thank me for it when I get out of here.

The thought of meeting my parents filled me with dread. Would the power they still hold over me ever fade? They loved nothing more than lecturing me on non-entities like quitting my job and still playing in a band at my age. Imagine their fury when they were told about this little episode? It would make every other past argument seem a trifle trivial.

Fuck them, we dinnae need them anyway.

When I do get to see them, they'll have had a couple of days to stew and get used to the idea of producing a killer son.

Maybe they'll be cool?

CHAPTER 53

After spending two of the most horrendous days of my life holed up in a cell with only my intrusive thoughts for company, I was brought before the Sheriff for a committal hearing or judicial examination or whatever the hell it was called. The amount of legal terminology that's been mentioned in the past few days has been ridiculous. I've understood about a tenth of it and drew my own conclusions and nodded dumbly at the rest of it. At Kirkcaldy Sheriff court I spoke to Grace again who told me she had been busy preparing my case. I had been so caught up in my own inner turmoil the first time we met that I'd forgotten to thank her for her efforts thus far.

On Christmas Day too.

"With all that you've told me about Danny and his previous threats and with witness accounts from Bobby and Sid testifying as such, and with all your various injuries, I think we stand a great chance of winning this case."

This statement pumped a few gusts of air into my completely deflated spirit.

No plea was made as I stood before the crown to confirm my name and address.

Minutes rolled into hours. The hours slowly rolled into days and days limped into weeks.

The only thing of note was my transfer to the remand wing of HMP Edinburgh.

Which is colloquially known as Saughton prison.

WHAT THE ACTUAL FUCK??!!!

Being completely ignorant of the legal system in Scotland I ridiculously thought that I would be granted bail and packed off to enjoy the comforts of my parent's hospitality whilst I awaited my trial date but due to my previous charge of assault on Frank Harrison and the political/religious leanings of the Sheriff I couldn't have been more wrong as I sat in the back of a G4S van complete with blacked-out windows to await my fate in the more modest surroundings of Saughton Prison.

I was aghast with apprehension and blind panic as yet again violent images corrupted me. Thoughts of horrific beatings and rape flooded my mind.

This can't be happening to me.

Prison?

I'm an innocent man.

My only crime was to get the better of my perpetrator.

During the arduous ride from Kirkcaldy to my abode for at least the next week, my stomach heaved and lurched with every bump in the road and every sharp corner the driver negotiated. I attempted a couple of glances out the window as we followed the route.

The colour of the sky reflected my mood, dark and forlorn.

I couldn't take it all in. My brain was a lump of useless mush.

Housed inside the van with myself were a couple of young lads who constantly boasted about their crimes without a care in the world. They laughed and made jokes as if we were on our way to attend a jamboree.

This angered me but it also scared me. I can't show fear.

I mustn't show fear.

Any sign of weakness would be preyed upon inside. I answered their stupid questions bluntly and with a scowl. Not to look hard, it was not physically possible for me to act in any other way.

When I replied 'murder' to their question they suddenly eyed me up and down with a bit more caution. They stopped asking me questions. It was the first time I had been glad to use that term about myself since this whole farce started.

I thought I was going to vomit as the gates opened and we entered Saughton Prison.

I'd viewed the grim exterior from afar on a couple of occasions but now I would be going up close and personal.

I shouldn't be here among these types of men.

It was absurd, beyond my comprehension.

My worry was for nothing.

I was to be housed in Glenesk, the oldest part of the prison where the remand prisoners are kept.

Once I got to grips with the bleak surroundings and my head around the fact that this was to be my home until the next hearing and potentially until my trial date, I thought I adapted pretty well all things considered.

This was due to the processing I had to endure. It felt like spending a day at the job centre.

There was form after form to fill in all of which were to be completed in front of the ever-so-helpful empathetic guards. Or should that be screws?

I was asked questions ranging from whether I had been in prison before? NO.

Do you have any drug problems?

Only when I can't get any.

I mean NO.

SIR.

Joking at this point in the process was futile and my attempts to lighten the mood were met with looks of derision. I was just another piece of shit as far as these guys were concerned.

It was a day of bureaucracy.

And waiting.

One and the same?

I was given my prison-issue clothing of jeans, sweatshirt, a couple of t-shirts, and some jogging bottoms and put into another room where I was stripped of my own clothing and searched.

THOROUGHLY.

Wearing my smart new gear, I was checked over by a nurse who recorded my height and weight before ushering me into another office to sit and wait on my next round of questioning.

The next guy was actually quite friendly, and I found myself chatting away freely to him.

I told him my story and he looked at me with that sort of 'Aye right pal, they're all innocent in here' look. He's probably heard a million little sob stories before. The only trouble is my story is actually true.

He spoke in detail about visiting rights and phone cards and mealtimes and a whole load of other stuff that my muddled brain just couldn't cope with.

It was like my first day at high school all over again. New rules, procedures, and routines to follow in a foul-smelling building, all the while trying to avoid a kicking.

Hours after I came into this hell hole and armed with my bed linen, spare prison-issue clothing, and a bag containing a plastic plate and cutlery, I was led to my cell.

Even getting there is a slow and laborious process. The guard unlocks one door and I follow him through and wait for him to lock it behind me and watch him check it to see if it is indeed locked properly just in case I get any crazy ideas about running away. Then it's onto the next door and the next door and the next. I don't know what I'm moaning about, time is the only thing that I've got an abundance of at the moment.

My cell door was unlocked and opened. The guard stood with his arm outstretched as if he was the bell boy whilst I inspected my room at The Ritz.

There was a scrawny-looking guy sprawled on the bottom bunk watching something on the wee portable telly. I slowly walked in like the new boy at boarding school and stood there transfixed, trying my best to make sense of my new surroundings.

The door shut and then locked, always locking, behind me.

I could hear the jangling of the guard's keys fade as he wandered off to complete another task.

"A'right, man?" the croaky voice asked from beneath my eye line, breaking the spell from which I was currently under.

"Eh aye?" I answered as I placed my belongings onto the vacant top bunk.

"I'm Billy by the way," and he thrust his hand into my knee. I bent down to shake it whilst inspecting the creature that it belonged to.

Golum.

That's what he reminded me of. That skinny wee guy from The Lord of the Rings film. Straggly hair and sunken eyes with the dental plan of a medieval peasant.

Well if I cannae kick the fuck out of this guy I'm humped.

Terrible to admit it but I'd imagined myself being holed up with some hulking brute who would use me as and when it pleased him. I breathed a huge sigh of relief.

"A'right, Billy? I'm Jimmy. So, where's the phone to order room service?"

"Room service?" Billy slapped his leg and roared with laughter.

With nothing else to do I joined in with the guffawing.

Got to keep my spirits up. It's good to laugh.

Billy cackled and wheezed and coughed until I thought he was going to choke to death.

It wasn't that funny.

He stood up and continued to hack away. After wiping away the tears he regained his composure and I came face to face with my cell mate for the first time. The top of his head was level with my chest.

"That was a good one, mate, room service?"

Billy showed me where to put my belongings, which was pretty much obvious seeing as there was only a little dresser, a bunk bed, and a toilet and sink in the room.

He chatted away, asking me what I was in for and if I'd been in before. You know, just the usual prison banter, whilst I made up my bed.

I explained my bruised and broken appearance whilst telling him my story.

"Aye well if the fucker came at you first, he got what he deserved, eh?" With that I warmed to little Billy. He hadn't judged me or asked me any probing insinuating questions like the police or guards had.

A man whom I'd only met minutes earlier was happy to listen to my story and then find favour with my actions.

Billy then told me his own story. He was here because he'd robbed somebody to fund his heroin habit. Poor Billy was a victim of circumstance. Raised on one of the tough Edinburgh schemes by an alcoholic mother and junkie father he didn't stand a chance. Kicked out of school at an early age he'd been involved in crime in one way or another since childhood. I couldn't help but feel sorry for the wee guy. He was only 42 but he looked more like 62. Uneducated and ignorant through no fault of his own. His tale depressed me. Sadly, he didn't seem to mind, this was the only world he'd known. Do a crime, go to prison, get released, do another crime, and go back to prison. On and on it went, a terrible cycle that he could not or would not break.

I lay on my bed thinking about what his life must've been like and I felt grateful for the chances I'd been given. My parents, my friends, my schooling. Things that I had taken for granted, bemoaned and didn't really care about. They all seemed so important to me now and oh how I missed them. Even my old town. How I longed to walk its desolate streets.

There was nothing on TV that I wanted to watch, I had no books to read and neither did Billy. I thought for a stupid second about listening to some music. That was when it dawned on me.

I have nothing.

I couldn't nip to the cupboards and get a packet of crisps, pull open the fridge door and clutch a cold can of beer. I couldn't wear my favourite jeans or stick the heating on when I was chilly.

I was now bound by rules. Even the time wasn't mine.

As there was nothing to do, I attempted to get some sleep, but it didn't come. Instead, I tossed and turned whilst trying to console myself that I would only be here at worst until my trial. I was back up in court next week for a full committal hearing and there was a slim chance that I could be granted bail but Grace had advised me not to get my hopes up and said that I could be in here for a wee while, so I was under no illusion that this was going to be pain free.

I've got to be strong, adapt, conform. Take it a day at a time.

CHAPTER 54

I must've eventually dozed off because when I awoke, I was met by a stench that no man should bear witness to.

I could also hear Billy defecating loudly from within the thin partition walls of our cell toilet.

Billy must've heard my disgusted groans because he shouted in reply to my stirring.

"This is me, same time every morn. Regular as clockwork like."

"Good for you, mate," I replied as I buried my face into the pillow to shield my senses from the squelching sounds and acrid smell.

I had never seriously thought about using a toilet in a cell before. I'd just assumed there would be a separate room for taking care of business, not some flimsy walls thrown around a stained pan as a result of European slopping out rules. It suddenly dawned on me that I hadn't taken a shit myself.

How long has it been?

Must be nearly five days now.

The thought of emptying my bowels in such close proximity to another human being would surely add to that toll. That would suit me fine. Hell, I get stage fright whilst trying to take a piss in the urinals of a boozer if some guy's standing next to me. Imagine trying to take a dump whilst a wee gadge is sitting on his bed three feet away?

I could actually hear him wiping his arse. The rustling of the toilet roll, the muffled swoosh of cheap paper being stuffed up his dirty crack. I could even make out a soft plop as he discarded the manky tissue into the festering pit. The pipes and cistern made groans of displeasure, much like my own as they flushed another evil package from the vicinity.

"Aye, gotta get it oot afore breakfast," Billy grinned as he bounded out of the door.

As if he was waiting for Billy to finish his morning jobby, the cell door was promptly unlocked and the guard announced that it was breakfast time.

Following Billy's lead, I grabbed my plastic plate and cutlery and filed into line with all the other cons on my floor and headed downstairs.

I was scanning the other inmates to see which ones could pose potential threats to my well-being but I appeared to be like a giant in here. Now I'm barely six foot, but this lot resembled a bunch of Oompa Loompas at a Sunday school picnic.

This should be a stroll in the park. Looks like this is the junkie wing.

Hundreds of emaciated bodies all cooped up like chickens at a tragic RSPCA call out.

Thankfully, due to my situation, I wasn't particularly hungry, but had I been starving I still don't think I could have eaten the shit that was on offer here. I carried the greasy-looking abortion on my plate back up to my cell and stared at it in horrified wonder. There is a dining area but one guard whom I spoke with on my arrival stated that the best way to survive this place is to keep your head down and keep yourself to yourself.

Who am I to argue with that advice?

Once safely locked back in our cell, Billy sat on his bunk and tucked into the beans and scrambled eggs.

I stood for a while before noticing a chair was hiding under the locker.

How can a chair hide in a room this size?

I pulled it out and sat poking and shovelling the monstrosity that adorned my plate. It tasted a bit like egg but that could've been down to conditioning, otherwise it was just a yellow lump. I cut a bit of sausage off and slowly put it into my mouth. I watched the arc of its journey from plate to mouth with disdain, inspecting the bits of gristle as it neared touchdown. I chewed and then chewed some more but again it tasted of nothing.

Is it a crime to have salt in here?

Billy noticed that I wasn't going to eat the remains of my delicious breakfast so promptly scraped my leftovers onto his plate then devoured the lot in one, scooping up and shoving the synthetic mass into his gob as if it was his first meal in weeks.

"Gotta keep your strength up in here, man," he beamed as he mopped up the last of the grub. His crooked mouth resembled a blown fuse box.

Seeing as he'd spared me the ordeal of eating that monstrosity, I thought it only fair that I should wash up. The plastic crockery had to be looked after and treated with as much love and care as if it was the finest bone china. It had to last.

Billy went back to his usual routine of lying on his bed and watching whatever muck was on telly whilst he waited for the call to go and get his methadone fix. Listening to his story I actually think he enjoyed his life in here. He could still get high although not as high and as regular as he would've liked, and he got fed too. I suppose this was like a wee holiday for him.

I've only been here a day and already I am going mad.
Are these my own thoughts?

I sat and stared at the stained ceiling from my top bunk and thought about my trial date. I grew more and more anxious the more I thought. Despite trying my hardest, I kept thinking about the worst possible outcome. It terrified me. No, it was more than that. The anxiety filled my body until I was visibly shaking and had to jump down from my bunk and pace the few metres that I was permitted to in the enclosed space. The walls were closing in on me, I could touch the ceiling, the reek from the toilet constantly lingered and the incessant shrill from the portable TV persecuted my senses …

"Jimmy? Jimmy? Come on, man," Billy gasped.

I was struggling to breathe. I grasped and pulled at the iron bars that stood like ancient sentries mocking my futile attempts to breathe the fresh air of freedom.

I was that close.

Billy lightly slapped my face as I lay heaving on the ground.

"Fuck off!" I screamed and I shoved him hard, sending his seven-stone body hurtling towards the steel door. The sight of his fragile frame crashing against the cold metal shook me from my panic attack.

"Billy? Sorry, man. I'm so sorry. I didn't mean to …"

He gazed up at me with confused frightened eyes and cowered when I offered him my hand.

"I'm so sorry, I dinnae ken what's happening. I'm no' used to this, I cannae take it, I think I'm going crazy in here."

He reluctantly took my hand so that I could pull him to his feet. We just stood and stared at each other. I couldn't think of anything else to do so I hugged him. He flinched like a beaten child as I attempted to embrace him.

I held him tightly more for my benefit than his as I sobbed my apologies.

He squirmed free and stared at me with derision.

"How do you did it? How do you cope being cooped up in here all day? The thoughts, the claustrophobia?" I asked.

"You just have to, otherwise you'll no' survive. I dinnae want you going crazy on me so you'd better get your heid sorted or else I'll be telling the guards and you'll be getting shifted somewhere else."

I sat in the chair and rubbed my head, trying to stimulate some peace into my mind.

"I didn't mean to hurt you, I kind of lost it there. Didn't know where I was. I couldn't breathe, I just want to do something. This, just sitting here all day is doing my head in. Fuck I could do with a drink."

Billy laughed.

"Well you'll no' be getting one any time soon so get used to it."

I couldn't bring myself to make eye contact with him, so I stared at the floor as he slouched back into his favourite position and continued watching the telly as if nothing had happened.

I was ashamed at my pathetic outburst and, like I always do in these situations, I felt the need to over compensate by being extra nice.

"Look man, I'll do your dishes for you … or whatever you need help with … I'm not a bad guy … I'll give you some smokes when I get them."

I didn't look up from the spot on the floor that had gripped my attention as I attempted to right my wrongs.

"Dinnae worry aboot it. It'll take time for you to adjust, your kind is the worst though. Too many thoughts and too much time to think them. Just try and forget everything, dinnae think at all."

He was right, I had to adopt an almost meditative approach to my contemporary lifestyle. To co-exist in harmony with my surroundings. It sounded like a load of old Hare Krishna bollocks, but it was perhaps what I needed to do in order to survive until my trial date arrived. After all, I didn't want to turn up to court as a bumbling wreck. No, I needed to be strong, I needed to get through this and come out the other side a free and better man.

CHAPTER 55

On my third day inside I got to meet with my parents for the first time since this whole bloody mess started.

I'd spoken to them briefly on the phone when I arrived just to let them know that I was doing okay but I was dreading having to face them.

When they eventually appeared, I was expecting a volley of abuse from the pair of them, but they just sat there shaking their heads asking "How?" and "Why?" over and over again as I sat holding back my tears.

They were more concerned with what the neighbours were thinking.

"Because he tried to kill me, Mum," I explained but she couldn't retain eye contact with me.

"But a knife? Why the hell did you have a bloody knife with you?" she asked again, her eyes shifting between mine and her vending machine cup of tea.

"I've told you this already, for my own protection. If I didn't have the knife with me, you'd have been down the morgue identifying *MY* body. Would you rather that happened? Eh?"

Their lack of an answer told me what I already suspected.

"Look at me, come on, LOOK AT ME!" I screamed, forcing their eyes to look at my battered face.

"I've got a broken nose, broken cheekbone, fractured eye socket, burst lip and three missing teeth. I'm in agony here and all you two can think about is poor Danny. Fuck Danny. He did this to me; he was trying to kill me."

"But … but, you could get a life sentence for this … murder?" my dad sighed as he raised his hand to his face and rubbed it slowly.

"It's not murder if someone's trying to kill you, Dad. It's Culpable Homicide. I was protecting myself; I did what I had to do for my own safety. Why can you not see that?"

There was no "Good to see you, son. We're glad you're safe." "Is there anything we can get for you?" or "Don't worry we'll do everything we can to help get you out of here."

I just wanted to hear some words of encouragement, Some words of love.

I needed to hear them. To know I wasn't alone and that they would help me.

But they never came.

That hurt me more than I thought it would. Especially as I never expected to hear those words anyway.

With more huffing and puffing and sighing from us all they got up and left.

The guard escorted them from the room. They didn't even look back. Weighed down with the shame of producing a 'murderous' child they shuffled off to the sanctuary of their home to hide from the inevitable intrusion a murder inquiry in a town like ours would bring.

Parents, eh? Who needs them?

An unexpected but pleasant surprise arrived in the form of Bobby who appeared an hour later.

"A'right, mate?" he asked in a this-is-a-very-uncomfortable-and-terrible-situation-to-be-in way.

"Aye just peachy, room service is pretty shocking but other than that I cannae complain." I attempted a laugh, as did Bobby, but we only succeeded in producing a modest shrug between us.

Where's Billy when you need him?

"So what happened? Your face is a mess."

"He got me. Like he said he would," I told Bobby the story of walking back from the pub and then being attacked.

"Phew," Bobby blew the air from his pursed lips as he tried to make sense of it all like I had done in the long hours since.

A few weeks previous I had left him, left them all in Glasgow scratching their heads as to why we suddenly didn't have a record deal and now the big man was here. Listening to my fucking mess. It was too much for me.

"I'm sorry, mate," I started. "For what happened with the band. ..." But through lack of sleep, shock, and the enormity of my situation, I just wailed my limp apologies instead.

"It's cool," Bobby soothed as he got up to comfort me. He was quickly ushered back to his own side of the desk by one of the guards in the room.

Cannae have any real emotion in a room like this, eh no, pal?

It's 'cause he thinks your passing drugs.

I regained my composure as Bobby sat down again.

"Look, forget about that, man. We've got something more serious to worry about now. I'll get on the case and start looking into lawyers for you and—" Bobby pitched.

"Thanks, but you dinnae have to. I've got that all sorted, the solicitor has been brilliant so far. I just need you to be there for me, mate. That's all I need. Believe in me."

"Aye, aye … nae bother."

I asked him about Sid and he told me he'd spoken to him. Sid had heard the news but didn't want to come and see me. He was still too mad about the band. Good to know who your real friends are though.

Bobby gave me a squeeze on the arm on the way out and raised a clenched fist in salute.

"If you see Debs, tell her it wasn't my fault," I asked but he just nodded in a non-committal way and shook his closed fist again.

I went back to my cell and curled into a ball and got a decent kip for the first time since I arrived here.

CHAPTER 56

Minutes again merged into long hours that teetered on the edge of turning into days as I grew accustomed to my environment. Accustomed is not the right word.

Neither is tolerated.

Endured?

No.

Survived.

Even that word cannot begin to suitably describe the terrible range of emotions and narcissistic thoughts that besieged me from the second I opened my eyes in the morning until they merged with my dreams during the twilight stage.

The distraction of being registered in various forms of activity ranging from seeking employment to gaining access to the library and obtaining a phone card took up only a small percentage of my day. I would even harass the officer in charge with many unrelated questions in the chance that I could engage in a decent, meaningful conversation.

The only other thing of note was being refused bail again at the full committal hearing. It seemed a complete waste of a journey, but it got me out of HMP Edinburgh for a while even though I was only in the courtroom for ten minutes at most.

Apparently, the next step is an Intermediate Trial Diet or some nonsense like that and then the actual trial can proceed once all the paperwork has been sorted. It could be at least another month or two before that happens, so it was back to my cell to scratch another line into the wall and wish my life away.

My days seeped slowly into weeks of wake up, ignore Billy's grunts and smells as he excretes his vile waste, get breakfast, return to cell, ingest breakfast, do dishes, lie on bed, talk to Billy, take a shit (only if Billy's away getting his fix), get dinner, return to cell, stare in disgust at dinner, do dishes, sit on bunk staring out of window, one hour recreation time to shower, play pool, make a phone call, walk about in the exercise area and fantasise of Steve McQueen/Shawshank Redemption style liberation, back to cell, pick up tea, back to cell, swallow tea, do dishes, lie in bunk listening to Billy laugh at shite on telly, close eyes, try to sleep.

Don't dream.

Never dream.

My parents paid me another brief visit. I had expected the normal routine of me sitting there shifting uncomfortably in my seat whilst my mother lectured me on the topic of how useless and embarrassing I was to the family, during which time my father would nod or frown or shake his head accordingly. None of which happened. For the first time in my life, I was in charge of our little family get together. Who would have thought that a simple incarceration was all it would take for them to finally shut the fuck up and actually listen to my opinion? My mum, God rest her wee soul, even brought me a packet of cigarettes. Only one packet mind and not the kind that I would ever buy myself but fearful of her son's well-being whilst doing porridge she had thoughtfully purchased a packet of 'cancer sticks' so I could use them as a bartering tool to maintain my anal virginity. Well, anal virginity from an actual penis.

Rubber butt plugs did not count.

It was probably the most uncomfortable hour that I have ever spent in their company. I almost longed for the routine sparring we went through. But they just sat there dumbfounded.

"Good to see you, folks. How you doing?" I had to show them that I wasn't a total wimp, so I put a cheery spin on things to mumbles of "Fine" and "We're coping with the unwanted attention."

"Dad, you're looking well, how are you keeping?" I asked. He didn't. He'd lost a lot of weight and his skin had that sickly translucent appearance that highlighted his veins in a neon turquoise fashion.

Through habit he looked to my mum for approval before nodding that he was "Fine" and "would be returning to work soon."

"No he'll not. He'll be taking his retirement and liking it," Mum declared as Dad fidgeted in his plastic chair.

I know how you feel, old man.

I told them about my meetings with the solicitor and that I'd be appointed a really good lawyer for the trial and that Grace thinks we'll win the case etcetera etcetera.

I put their concerns for my safety at ease by reporting that the reputation of this place was worse than the reality. For some strange reason I felt like a child again as I explained how well I was doing and that everything would be okay. My instinctive need for approval from these two people who showed me anything but, slightly confused me and further weakened my already limp spirits.

There were minutes of excruciating silence as we each looked at the other before drawing our gazes onto the bare walls.

Sighing.

Too much sighing.

Has the exhalation of breath ever sounded so disdainful?

A kid who was presumably visiting her dad was acting up and started screaming and shouting which interrupted our little shindig.

"Kids, eh?" I tutted, trying my hardest to start another conversation.

Who in their right mind would bring their kid to this sort of environment? Bloody hell, no matter how badly the doting daddy wanted to see her, the poor wee bugger should not be subjected to this nightmare.

Getting nothing more in the way of chit chat I asked about my sister Clare. This would normally kick start them into a pantomime routine of animated drooling whilst waxing lyrical about her heroic exploits.

Nothing.

Zilcho.

Nada.

Hee Haw.

They didn't even tell me what Clare thought about my situation. They simply muttered that she was doing fine and that they hoped to go over and visit her under that long white cloud in the near future.

Give big Sis my regards, eh?

The whole episode felt like being in a lift with a bunch of strangers.

You know, that moment where you're all stood shoulder to shoulder invading each other's private space, trying desperately to think of something topical or witty to say to break the agonizing silence and divert your focus from the urgent need to fart. Nobody daring to make eye contact with anybody whilst somebody in the corner huffs and puffs and gazes at their watch or plays with their phone not because they need to know the time or to check their messages but because it gives them something soothing to cling to rather than strike up a mundane conversation with the reprobates that they've had the misfortune to be entombed with for thirty seconds.

The gasps of relief are almost audible as the doors ping open and you can continue with the rest of your day.

The ping was more of a shriek as the annoying kid attempted to break free from her mother's firm hold, prompting my parents to turn their heads to view the commotion for themselves then tut their annoyance as they swivelled back to view then look away from their own delinquent child.

"Look, you don't have to stay till the end, I know this cannae be easy for you. I won't mind." I hoped they would take me up on my get-out-of-jail-free offer. With much adjusting of clothing, they thankfully accepted my offer. It was as strange a goodbye as I've ever received from my folks. They just got up and left and quickly made for the sanctuary of the door and the outside world that awaited them.

That was it, a simple nod and goodbye.

That wouldn't do.

"Mum … Dad," I shouted as they made for the exit.

They stopped in their tracks like a couple of thieves who'd been sprung just yards from the shop door.

I walked over and embraced them both individually. I took my time hugging them, feeling the closeness of their bodies against mine, allowing my senses to soak up the bereft contact. I could smell my mum's perfume and my dad's hair lotion (the ones they had both used since I can remember) and let their respective scents nestle comfortably in my brain.

"I love you," I said as they both regained their composure.

My mum looked at me and nodded as my dad patted me on the arm.

They don't do public displays of affection.

They don't do any kind of affection.

A prison is not the best place to try and correct this lifelong affirmation.

I watched them walk to the door and wait for the guard to escort them out. They walked through into blissful normality and then the door closed behind them.

I was left with a terrible feeling of nostalgia when they departed.

Later in the evening, as I sat on my bunk, my memory bank permitted me snap shots of years gone by. Family holidays, birthdays, Christmases. All the times when I enjoyed being in their company.

I loved them.

They loved me.

We did have some good times.

Fun times.

Lots of them.

Over the years I'd exaggerated their old-fashioned ways.

They *were* good parents.

They were just born in the wrong century.

That was the first time I had hugged them or told them I loved them since … I thought hard about it … I don't know when.

Probably primary school.

Mind you, they weren't a pair for engaging in such an act.

Proper conservatives.

Hugging is for liberals.

The memories, although making me smile, naturally brought tears to my eyes as I longed for the things that I didn't have.

Be strong though, man.

Got to be strong.

Show no weakness.

Be tough. Hard. Like a rock.

CHAPTER 57

Day *thirtysomethingorother* began much the same as any other day in the clink, with me burrowing my face in the pillow trying my best to escape Billy's noxious fumes.

The window's got bars on it for fuck's sake, you'd think that they'd be able to open just a smidgen to release the toxic vapours?

My day got better though. I'd finally received clearance to enter employment. After much toing and froing and dotting of I's and crossing of T's the powers that be had deemed me responsible enough to work in the kitchen. I would start on the bottom rung of the ladder but that didn't bother me one iota. By donning an apron and wielding a mop, it enabled me to be free from my cell for a few extra hours each day.

Ah the space. The freedom.

After being suitably instructed on my responsibilities (cleaning the floors, washing down the work surfaces, and emptying bins.), I was free to skip about the kitchen and surrounding area with as much gay abandon as that guy from Singing in the Rain. I held my mop like a Spanish dance partner as I tangoed my way across the tiled surface. Being a jolly fellow, however, gets you strange looks in a place like this, so I quickly curtailed my enjoyment and set about scrubbing the tiles with a moody-looking puss. I briefly thought about maintaining my act as the happy-go-lucky nut job because I'd noticed that being mentally unstable in here gives you a certain amount of leeway from both the screws and the cons. Unfortunately, rational thinking got the better of me and I came to the conclusion that it would be damn near impossible for me to keep up this ecstatic charade whilst mopping the floor and scrubbing down grease-ridden chopping blocks.

However, being in the kitchen did allow me to come into contact with like-minded individuals, or as like-minded as I was ever going to get whilst residing at The Hotel De La Shitehole.

It's not what you know.

It's who you know.

Prison food, much like prison life, is atrocious.

There is a reason why the scran tastes so bad.

The government allocates each prisoner approximately £2 per day for food supplies.

Next time you're out doing your weekly shopping, see how far you get trying to feed yourself with a budget of £14, eh?

Exactly.

You'll be eating porridge for breakfast, eggs for dinner, and pasta for tea. And no' the good kind either. Oh no, you'll be treated to a brand that's far worse than the supermarket's own value range.

Now, I'm not here to bemoan this fact. To paraphrase roughly from our cousins across the pond, "It's not exactly a vacation I'm on here." "If you didn't want to eat that shit you should've thought of that before you did the crime, punk, yada yada yada."

Number one, I didn't commit a crime, it was self-defence, and number two, the last thing that crossed my mind as I did what I had to do to stop that violent Neanderthal from beating my face to a pulp was 'I do hope that one doesn't inflict injuries upon this fellow human being that are severe enough to require one's detention at Her Majesty's Pleasure for a non-specific period of time whilst the judicial system fumbles around with some colour of tape. Red? Yes red. That's it, red and regularly postpones one's hearing before finally arriving at the conclusion that it has wasted just the correct amount of taxpayer's money and everybody else's time before deeming it suitable that the hearing should indeed go ahead on the date that was aforementioned several months previously so that everybody can get on with their day and everything will be bloody marvellous. Oh one more thing, did one mention one is lactose intolerant?'"

Hanging around the kitchens for the best part of the day allowed me to come into contact with some serious contraband, contraband which unfortunately wouldn't allow me to get high and forget my pains, but it would make my mealtimes more palatable.

Black pepper.

This powdered condiment was as sought after and harder to come by than crack cocaine. Primarily as it is banned in most prisons because at some time, someone, somewhere, thought it'd be a good idea to crush up pepper and spices and blow them into a guard's eye, disabling him momentarily so that they could do whatever it was they wanted to do without the guard being able to see. Nice trick, but your selfish act ruined dinnertime for every prisoner ever since.

Prick!

But like I said, it's not what you know it's who you know.

I'd befriended Big Fred, the main kitchen hand, by giving him my phone card to use. Well, I didn't really have anybody to call. It's not like I was on holiday and could phone up for a chat to discuss the weather back home. Hearing about how well everybody was doing and how great their lives were just made me depressed so Fred might as well get the use out of it.

In return, he gave me a small bag of pepper and some chilli flakes. With all the thought and precision of an international drug smuggler I stuffed the wee bags into my pants as my shift ended and I headed back to my cell. I couldn't help but have a wry smile to myself as I thought how absurd this situation was. A grown man being reduced to hiding meal time accompaniments next to his tadger. However, I did enjoy the feeling of self-satisfaction of getting one over on the screws.

Another day another dollar.

I'd kept my head down and my nose clean as I counted the dull days until my trial. The worst part was not knowing when this would occur. If I had a date to aim for then it would make this whole farce a little bit easier to stomach, literally. But as of yet I still hadn't received a trial date. I suppose it would be a bit like running a marathon without having mile markers. You're hurting but thanks to the markers you know that there's only five miles to go before the pain stops. Well, I was hurting, but I had no idea how long I had to go on hurting.

Grace visited again to keep me updated on the progress of my trial. Apparently, her team had been working hard compiling evidence but there was still no trial date yet.

This hit me really hard as I was desperate for some sign of an end to this torture.

Feeling as low as I've felt in this place, I retreated to my bunk and chain smoked the remains of my last packet of cigarettes. I fought with my emotions to stay in control of the situation.

But it was hard, really fucking hard.

I wanted to tear the walls apart, rip the bars from the window and smash this cell to pieces but I couldn't put Billy through another episode of my inner turmoil.

This was a terrible joke. I was stuck in this hell hole whilst some civil servant hummed and hawed.

Can I stand this pain much longer?

You'll just have tae.

CHAPTER 58

After more red tape and crossing of I's and dotting of T's, and due to the fact that there was also a waiting list, I was finally allowed access to the prison library. I had big plans of checking out all the legal literature I would require to transform myself from legal novice to outstanding QC. I left with a handful of books on subjects ranging from The Law Of Human Rights to Criminal Law Essentials. The only thing missing was a copy of How To Win Your Trial For Dummies.

The initial glimmer of hope that warmly cuddled my body as I fantasised about my triumphant showing at the High Court was extinguished by the time I reached page two of Crime Law Essentials.

I sat on my bunk reading then re-reading the same paragraphs. I'm not sure if it was due to my anxiety, pent up aggression, or the cacophony of legal terminology on display, but nothing would sink into my brain. I'd never considered the debilitating effects or the workings of dyslexia before, but I think I may understand it a little better now. Nothing I read made sense. I knew most of the words, lots of them I didn't, and the letters didn't jump around the page, but I could not make head nor tail of it.

This was hopeless.

In my haste to have something meaningful to do to take my mind off the disabling thoughts and substance-withdrawal-like pains that racked my body, I returned the useless books before the free time was over and consoled myself with a book about Buddhism and an Ian Rankin novel.

Well whilst doing time I might as well read about crime.

Nothing, nothing, nothingness. That is all there is.
I have a terrible amount of time.
Time in which to do nothing.
Nothing, nothing, nothingness.
A terrible time is what I am having.
Yet there is nothing, nothing, nothing I can do about this.
Nothing, nothing, nothing.

Except write shite poetry and try and keep myself sane by not thinking about time.

Nothing, nothing, nothingness.

Bobby paid me another visit. It made me feel depressed. Not because of all this nonsense but because I couldn't feel happy for him. Or Mel.

He announced that Mel was pregnant again. Understandably they were both a bit anxious after what happened last time, but he was chuffed to bits. Mel was too so he said. I felt nothing though. Just empty. I told him it was great news and how happy I was for them both and that I hoped it all went well this time. But they were false words. I said them because that's what you're supposed to say to a friend in a situation like that.

Society expects that sort of behaviour.

It demands it.

So I adhered, went along with it.

Who am I to upset the apple cart?

What I wanted to tell him was 'I don't care about your happy wee life. I'm locked in this shit hole, barely even breathing fresh air. I'm in control of nothing. I eat when I'm told, I shower when I'm told, I walk about outside when I'm told. The little things that you'd think I'd be in control of I'm not. When I want to sleep I can't because my head's full of horrible thoughts. When I try to take my mind off the relentless thoughts by reading, I can't concentrate. I can't smoke when I want because I have to ration them. I can't take a shit when I want to because it's just not right taking a shit in such close proximity to another human being, paper thin walls or not. I can't even breathe when I want. I'm so tense that I suffer palpitations and hopelessly gulp for air like a landed fish. I want to be happy for you, Bobby, I really do but I just can't. I say I am but I don't really mean it cause I can't feel it.'

Can you mean it if you don't feel it?

Maybe you can. I don't know.

I love Bobby and Mel, my parents.

I still love Debs.

Don't think about her.

But I can't feel it, I can't feel the love.

Does that mean I don't love them?

Am I just full of hate?

How do I feel?

I am so lonely,
I'm so depressed.
My mind is in turmoil,
my life is a mess.
Feelings of terror,
feelings of despair.
This is just crazy,
this is unfair.
I wish this was over,
I yearn to be free,
from this confinement
from the monstrosity
that is the anguish
that assaults my brain.
Sending me heartache,
sending me pain.

CHAPTER 59

I've been here for the worst part of three months now and my mental health continues to tip toe along the thread-like wire that straddles the gaping gorge of insanity.

I was brought some amazing news by my knight in shining armour, however.

Or to be more precise, my legal counsel in cotton slacks.

Grace came forth through the engulfing mists of time with news of my Indictment. I was still no clearer on what this was or meant but it turned out that I had a date for my trial.

A date.

A fucking date.

There it was staring back at me from the paper like a divine apparition.

I scanned the pages up and down but all I could focus on was that date.

I sighed a long-repressed sigh.

That felt good.

I exhaled all the negative fibres that had clung to my lungs, rendering me breathless for such a long time.

At long last I had something to aim for.

My mile marker.

I could take this pain for a little longer.

I looked up from the page with gleaming eyes and smiled at Grace.

"I could kiss you," I beamed.

"Let's not get carried away, Jimmy. We've still got a long way to go," she professionally replied.

I swallowed hard and returned my focus to the papers.

Also contained within the Indictment was a list of all the character witnesses who would attend the trial. I scanned the pages again but this time I allowed my eyes to interact with my brain, enabling me to interpret the list.

I saw names I recognised – Bobby.

There were many that I didn't which puzzled me. I was just about to enquire when I saw it.

Deborah Smith.

I froze.

My heart began to thump harder, and I could feel tiny beads of sweat forcing their way to the surface of my brow.

I swallowed hard again but this time there was no moisture present.

Recognising her name in its birth certificate format brought the reality of this gig home to me.

She'd be on the prosecution team?

Against me.

She'd be after my blood, my life.

Blinded by her determination for revenge.

To avenge her deceased lover and unborn child.

She always hated being called Deborah, that would add to her fury.

I knew that it would come to this but now that it was a reality, I wasn't sure if I could bear to be in the same room as her.

My feelings were … fuck I don't know what I feel any more.

Put it this way, there was still emotional attachment.

The thought of her testifying against me, making me out to be a killer, made me feel sick.

Surely she of all people would know that I didn't mean to do it?

I may be many things, but a murderer is not one of them.

I warned her about him, what he was like, told her the stories.

She doesn't believe me.

She thinks you did it.

Why else would she be there?

She could've stopped all this.

But she hasn't.

She must really hate me.

Somebody once sang that there is a thin line between love and hate. I had no idea how thin that line really was. Just under a year ago we were still together, a couple. Lovers, friends, partners. Shit, this time last year we were on a week's holiday in Greece. Laughing and joking like teenagers, free from the worries and constraints of everyday life back home.

We were in love.

Now she wants to sentence me to a term in prison for having the audacity to protect myself.

I couldn't comprehend anything else that Grace said. I mean, I heard what she said, even watched as her lips moved to form the vowels as she spoke, but hearing is just the act of perceiving sound.

Listening requires attention.

CHAPTER 60

Knowing that my date with destiny was looming actually brought more anxiety and delusional nightmares as my subconscious and conscious mind fought for control. As the date approached, my dreams tangled with paralysis and when I awoke the recall left me confused as to what was really real.

Good evening and welcome to a snooze fest which tonight features withered opinions on topics as diverse as beleaguered right-wing fundamentalism by crusty unionists all the way through to Stalinist views on the minimum pricing of alcohol. Our roving reporter will also be out and about telling 'the man' on the street who's too stupid to form an opinion for himself what he thinks about the latest opinion we've seen fit to give him. But first we focus our attention on a new publication which hits the shelves tomorrow. It's titled 'The Daily Sun shines on Record Mail Star Jimmy The Independent Guardian of the Times Steel' and I'm delighted to announce that the editor, Jimmy Steel, joins me in the studio to discuss the paper's first edition with me. Welcome Jimmy.

Thank you. Can I just say how grateful I am for the opportunity to discuss today's news with you?

You can and you just have. So, Jimmy, talk us through the concept of this fascinating rag.

Well, I had this rather ingenious idea several years ago whilst breakfasting with a number of acquaintances during our residence at a quaint little self-catering lodge on the outskirts of Truro. Six of us sat down to breakfast that morning and under our arms we each carried a copy of our favourite newspaper. By the time we had opened the array of pages onto the little table there was no room to place our boiled eggs and soldiers, so that got me thinking. Rather than having lots of different newspapers cluttering up the kitchen table, wouldn't it be much tidier and economical to simply have one newspaper which covered all angles on the latest stories whilst at the same time appealing to each individual's differing tast?

Such as?

Well, it commences with lots of colourful pictures, and we deliberately run with badly researched gossip as the lead story but with each turn of the page you'll be surprised to find that the news becomes more relevant than the pictures. By the time you reach the centre pages where the encyclopaedic topics, which may I add are written in an authoritarian tiny font, discuss the latest companies to invest your spare billions in, you will feel as if you've had your mind blown apart.

Wonderful idea, so what do we have on page one, Jimmy?

Well seeing as it's a momentous occasion, what with it being our first edition, I thought we'd go with the revelation that Danny Foster used to pee the bed.

Eh, that's it?

Yes. Well, no. Further on in the story we mention the unfortunate incident at primary school when he apparently farted and followed through. It's an exclusive story. The other kids were so terrified of him due to his violent nature that the whole incident was forgotten, erased from memory. Until now. You're looking at some good research right there. I think the sepia photograph of a random child's unmade bed with realistic damp patches really sets the whole piece off.

Okay. So turning the page we have … WHAT IN THE NAME OF THE LORD IS THAT?!

Like I said, we cater for every reader's taste, even if that taste is misogynistic. So, sticking with tradition, what you're looking at on page three is an old photograph of Danny Foster's mum wearing a see-through bra with suspenders. The image is a bit grainy because it's a copy of a photograph taken from about 1980 when the Foster family were so poor that Danny Foster's mother took to posing in saucy underwear and offered services for cash.

You mean she was a prostitute?

That's how the story goes but again it's not widely known due to the Foster brother's ability to keep a lid on the family's affairs. Until now.

That's awful. I think we can quickly move on to the next story as page three is giving me the shivers.

Now here is a story about Danny's first brush with the law. I attained an exclusive interview with Mr and Mrs Robertson who owned the only shop in Danny's village. They've retired from the retail industry now, but their memories are still haunted by Danny and his brother's teenage reign of terror. The old couple go into detail describing how they banned the pair from the shop for stealing pornographic magazines only to find their shop windows had been panned in the next day. Nobody was ever charged with the offence, but it was well known in the village who the offenders were. Anyway, the lovely couple tell me about the morning they arrived to open up and were distraught to discover that their beloved shop had been broken into overnight. As they delicately crunched their way over the glass that used to be held in the front door, their eyes were met with a scene of carnage. Ambient goods lay strewn all over the floor, bottles were smashed, and tins were dented. Shelving had been torn from the walls catapulting its proud wares to all four corners of the outlet. Mrs Robertson nearly went over on her ankle as she skidded on some spilt fabric softener and the electric till was in pieces on the floor. Thankfully they had deposited their daily takings in the safe, but a sizeable amount of drink and tobacco was missing. The police didn't need to bother with door-to-door enquiries. There was only one door they needed to knock on. However, the Fosters, due to their age, only received cautions for their drunken rampage. When questioned they replied that they did it "'Cause they needed mair drink."

Interesting story. I like the photograph of the elderly couple sat gripping their seat.

Yes, I think it really highlights the impact that the gruesome twosome's antics had on the sweet old couple. Look at them, staring fearfully into the lens and clutching each other's veiny hands as if the Fosters could kick down their door at any minute to continue their unscrupulous rampage.

On the opposite page you've gone for a, and correct me if I'm wrong, an AR HERMANN font for the headline?

You are indeed spot on; I must say you possess an excellent knowledge of fonts.

Thank you very much, you could say I'm a font-ain of knowledge a ha ha ha. I trained as a compositor many years ago. So, tell me, why the sudden change of font?

Well this article goes into detail about Danny's second run-in with the local constabulary for dealing marijuana at school. Now I'm not condemning his actions, after all I've partaken in the odd doobie myself over the years, but his selling methods were, how shall I put it? Let's just say he didn't value customer satisfaction. Or loyalty. Or rights. You would have thought with all the money he was making and resin he was smoking that he would have relaxed a smidgen. Perhaps it was the amphetamines he ingested on a daily basis that fuelled his Mexican cartel style behaviour? Or perhaps it was simply because he was a head case? Anyway, I delve into great detail about how he was caught by The CID with substantial quantities of illegal substances on his person only for him to escape time at The Young Offenders Home because his big brother took the wrap for him. Literally. Ah brotherly love.

Okay so far you've unearthed a few minor stories about Danny Foster's chequered past, does the rest of the publication carry on in the same vein?

Funny you should mention that, if we just skip these next pages, they're mainly accounts about his expulsions from school and from people who've suffered some form of distress by Danny's hand. Ah, here we have the double spread pull out supplement.

Who's this serious-looking man we're faced with?

This is Lee Hooper, who has every right to look serious. Lee had an altercation with Danny Foster in 1998. At the time Lee was an 18-year-old kid from Leeds enjoying his first lads' holiday with his closest chums in Magaluf on the Spanish-owned island of Mallorca. Unfortunately for Lee, this also happened to be the same spot that Danny Foster had chosen to enjoy some much-needed leave from his stressful day job. A job that was so stressful it caused a slightly intoxicated Danny Foster to beat one of Lee Hooper's friends to a pulp and put the ill-fated Lee into a coma for two weeks. Lee's parents recall being faced with the horrendous decision of switching off his life support machine or leaving it on and praying that their boy pulled through. Their prayers were answered. Well, almost. Lee did wake up from his coma, but he suffered permanent brain damage and now requires 24-hour care. All because somebody looked at Danny Foster in a funny way. Remarkably the British Army swept in and took control of the situation, hushing up the incident whilst promising military justice would be imposed. I have no idea how they managed it, but the Army worked their powerful magic and saved Danny from a prison sentence (I think you'll find a mock cockney sergeant major accent works best for this next bit). *No need to punish him lads, he's one of us, what are we like eh? Bit of a drink, bit of a scrap, you can't beat it. The little bugger probably deserved it, I mean what kind of a poof let's themselves be put into a coma? Bloody civilians, they have no idea what it's like for us. We need to let off steam, it's all right for them sitting there judging us, thinking they're better than us because they had the common sense not to sign up for this shit.*

That is a powerful piece of investigative journalism. Did Danny really avoid a prison term?

Sadly yes. He ruined a man's life, yet he was allowed to continue with his. It was the talk of his village and the surrounding area. Although nobody was surprised when his name was mentioned in connection with the attack. Tragic.

Quite an astonishing tale, well unfortunately we'll have to leave it on that bomb shell as we've run out of time for this segment ...

What? There's still lots of powerful investigative journalism to show you.

Unfortunately, Jimmy, we're going to have to leave it there.

But we've not covered the best bit—

I'm really sorry, Jimmy, I've got my producer in my ear insisting we move on.

It's my tell-all story, my peaceful law abiding existence, my—

That's great but we really must press on—

I spill my heart out, it really is a wonderful peace of journalism.

Okay, thank you again and good luck with your publication.

You cannae leave it now, I've not told the world how sorry I am for destroying my life, my continued love for Debs …

Jimmy, if you'll just stop—

No … I came here to share my news and that's exactly what I'm going to do, now this page here has the romantic font and—

Jimmy, please.

You'll rip it …

Let go, Jimmy …

Oh no you've torn it, you stupid …

Can I get some help here… ?

CHAPTER 61

I couldn't have looked more befitting if I had tried as my Trial Diet loomed. My appearance resembled that of Christian Bale's character in The Machinist.

Skin and bones.

Sunken dead eyes, the lost and broken eyes of a condemned man.

A guilty man?

I felt horrendous as I attempted to put a Half-Windsor knot in my tie. My hands trembled as I pushed the woollen fabric through its final loop and slid the knot into place. It nestled gently against my throat, making me swallow involuntarily.

It was a harsh dry swallow.

Due to my drastic weight loss, I looked as though I had borrowed my father's suit for the big day.

A wee boy in a man's suit.

A terrified wee boy.

The jacket hung loosely from my bony shoulders and the multiple folds in the trousers created by the last hole in the tightened belt made it look like I had been fitted by a drunken tailor.

What shall we do with him early in the morning?

It was whilst being ushered into the courtroom by two heavily tattooed security guards that I clocked my bedraggled reflection. Tragically the only thing that I could think of as my date with destiny commenced was 'you cannae polish a shite.'

I can't do this. It's too hard, too painful, I'm still too raw.

I don't want to recall all the memories, all the emotions of the worst period in my life ever again.

I've tried so hard to forget them so that I can try and get on with my life.

How can bringing it up help?

I can feel the anger and bitterness bubbling to the surface once more as I try to do this.

It always returns.

Will it ever leave me?

My psychiatrist said that it would help me overcome the mental torment that I have suffered ever since I was subjected to that humiliating, stressful ordeal.

It was her idea to write all this stuff down.

Because I was such a 'closed book' and wouldn't 'open up and vent my feelings and frustration' to her due to a mixture of fear, embarrassment, and being judged, she thought it would be best if I expressed my feelings on paper instead.

My subsequent depression, anxiety, and anger are a manifestation of storing negative memories and emotions linked to my experiences whilst in prison and immediately beforehand.

Apparently.

No shit, Sherlock.

Five years of university and at least six years of speciality training to tell me that I'm feeling a wee bitty under the weather because I've been through a pretty tough time lately?!

Just hand over the Prozac and we can both get on with our lives, eh?

It's not that simple nowadays though. Handing out prescription medication like sweeties to alleviate symptoms is a bit like using an Elastoplast to reattach a dismembered limb.

You have to treat the cause instead of placating the symptoms.

And my symptoms need placated badly.

It's one of the reasons I'm writing this story. I didn't want to go over this again, digging up memories that are painful and upsetting isn't my idea of therapy. But my shrink thinks that by freeing your pent-up anger and negative emotions it will eventually lessen the heartache thereby easing the symptoms.

Cannae see how likes.

I was always taught that if something caused you pain then it is in your best interest to stay well away from it, it's a primal survival instinct. Don't keep going back in the vain hope that your body will adapt until the pain ceases to exist. That sort of behaviour is for the contortionist. Or guru.

I'm just a simple man with simple needs. In pain, need medicine. Take medicine, pain goes away.

That's too simple though.

The pain always returns.

Intrudes.

Destroys.

I replay the scenarios in my mind every day and every night. The what ifs, the buts and the maybes.

The different outcomes.

I don't want to think about it, and I try my hardest to distract myself but even when I lose myself in a great book or by writing a new song, I'm still aware of that irritating sensation in the back of my mind. No matter how deep I bury it in my subconscious mind I can still feel it beginning to itch. It's like the snowdrop flower breaking through the hard, frozen winter ground. Nothing will prevent it from its aim of being recognised.

You will never be able to fully understand what it feels like to have your character, your reputation, your essence ripped apart and violated by people who don't even know you, who don't want to know you and who don't care about you. You'll never begin to understand the abhorrent feeling of degradation as you're subjected to shameless lies for days on end.

Sympathy?

Maybe.

Empathy?

Never.

The courtroom was packed as I entered.

My eardrums were pierced by the deafening silence.

It reminded me of the time I got through to the final of the Rabbie Burn's recital during my second year at high school. My heart pounded just as hard and just as loud back then as I walked up to the lonely microphone on stage.

2000 or so eyes glaring into mine.

The majority of them begging for me to fail to satisfy their lust for humiliation.

Their eyes never left mine.

Not even when I tugged helplessly on my shirt and looked to the heavens for a prompt as I fluffed my lines.

"Is there for honest poverty

That hings his head, an' a' that;

The coward slave-we pass him by,

We dare be poor for a' that.

For a' that, an' a' that.

Our toils obscure an' a' that …"

Fuck.

I cannae remember the next bit.

What is it?

I've practised this so many times. It's in there somewhere.

Come on brain.

Oh fucking hell this is torture, they're all gawking at me.

"Um … for a' that … eh … "

My memory buckled under the pressure of a thousand pair of penetrating stares. Unable to continue I staggered from the stage to a cacophony of petulant giggles and sinister hissing.

At least I could go home afterwards.

Home?

Homeward bound.

I wish I was.

Homeward bound.

Home, where my thought's escaping.

Home, where my music's playing.

Home, where my love lies waiting.

Silently for me …

Aye, you can remember that nae bother though, eh?

Useless cunt!

I tried to maintain my focus on the security guard in front of me as he guided me to my position during the proceedings, but my eyes had ideas of their own. They betrayed my strict instructions and wandered in a carefree manner amongst the many faces that were gathered in the public seating area. Just like the recital audience the majority of them were here to see me fail. My neck muscles reluctantly gave way to the straining of my disobedient eyes, and I turned to catch sight of my parents. My mother maintained eye contact for all of a second before staring straight ahead. She must have thought that by looking directly into my eyes she too would be inflicted by the evils of this corrupted human being.

Her terrible son.

My father's appearance looked remarkably similar to my own, causing me to falter. Thankfully his eyes retained contact as he pursed his lips and nodded his support. That simple gesture meant more to me than I could have imagined, and it brought a fist-sized lump to my throat which departed as swiftly as it sprung when my fleeting glance came to rest on its next target. His malicious glower cast below deep-set brows was instantly familiar. The facial structure had changed due to the effects of ageing which resulted in my curious eyes seeking confirmation. They weren't to be disappointed because sitting next to the brutish figure was the slender frame of Danny Foster's mother whose desolate expression beheld a lifetime of despair.

That's Stevie Foster.

I risked another glance for affirmation, but I already knew it was him. He met my inquisitive peek head on for his wish of a slow and painful death upon me hadn't subsided from the moment he had heard the awful news.

Danny Foster was a bastard. A bully, a menace, a tormentor. A guy too ignorant to recognise or care that the carnage he inflicted upon people's lives on a daily basis would affect them forever. Perhaps it wasn't all his fault though. Bereft of a father figure he turned to the most suitable candidate to fill that void.

His big brother.

By all accounts Danny was merely the apprentice. Stevie, however, was the master. The original psychopath.

With a role model like that was it any wonder he turned out the way he did?

Fortunately, due to the council's housing allocation, Stevie and Danny had grown up in a small farming village ten miles from town. Unfortunately, his brutality wasn't confined to the walls of his quaint little village. As my town housed the only high school for a large catchment area, he was able to distribute his torture and mayhem to a wider unsuspecting public during his teenage years.

It's good to share.

Despite an age gap of six years and the fact that our paths seldom crossed, I still felt like I knew Stevie owing to the tales that were passed on from pupils in the years above us in a style reminiscent to Norse Mythology. Accounts of his loutish behaviour intertwined with various acts of barbarism and vandalism were recalled with childish glee by former classmates who had supposedly witnessed these actions in an attempt to frighten the latest batch of newcomers at school. Imagine my fear when I learned that his wee brother was in the same year as myself. After witnessing Danny's violent actions at close hand, I guess I have to be thankful of my parents' low sex drive otherwise I could have been in the same year as Stevie.

With a tutor like Stevie, I can clearly see where the apprentice gained his sorcery.

The lesser of two evils is always preferable.

Similar to myself, but owing to different circumstances, Stevie Foster had also spent some time at the expense of Her Majesty's Pleasure.

Like a whipped dog my eyeballs quickly obeyed their owners' initial instructions and they returned to settle on the back of the tattooed guard's creased shirt. To quell my roving mind, I set it the task of decoding the meaning behind the various inked swirls that were visible through the thin material of his cheap off-white shirt as he brought me to my designated position within the court.

Biker gang member?

Maori tribute?

Drunken weekend in Amsterdam?

Art school drop out?

Try as I might, I couldn't ignore the Superman-like laser eye blasts from the masses behind as I sat and faced the judge. Their collective revengeful energy produced enough scornful rays to keep me scratching the back of my head as the names of the jury were nonchalantly plucked from a glass bowl in front of me.

This was my lottery.

Does that civil servant even recognise that he is playing a major part in my fate?

To him it's just a part of the job.

"Ah'm the Clerk o' the Coort likes ken? Ah git up in the moarning, hae ma tea an' toast, kiss the wife an' kids cheerio then don ma robes an' wig. Maks me feel pretty important, ken likes? Like ah'm daein' something worthwhile, eh? Ah gets tae the Coort an' then ah stick aw they numbers in a bowl or whitever clear receptacle is at haun on the day. Ah once used a flooer vase, fancy that, eh? Onyway, ah gie them a swirl aboot an' then ah pick oot the numbers o' the jury wan by wan. Ah like tae pretend ah'm drawin' the Scoatish Cup fixtures, mak's it mair entertaining that way, ken? Ah love tae see the look oan their poor wee faces when ah pull their number oot the bowl. They've ay got the same look oan their faces. It's like ah've drawn them against wan o' the Auld Firm in the Semi-Final o' the Scoatish Cup."

Would I be lucky enough to be granted 15 individuals who had the intellect and foresight to see an innocent man in me?

It was hard to tell as I watched the collective that would be responsible for my fate make their way to their seats in the box.

What I wouldn't give for another of those spawny bastard chips right now.

From what I could gather in between deflecting the radiating beams spouting from my aft, the lion's share of the jury seemed to be treating this parade with utter contempt.

The gross inconvenience of it all.

"I'm giving up at least a week's work/profit maximization/ shopping/holiday/sitting on ma arse getting stoned for this nonsense/ barbarism/hindrance/disruption/piece o' shit?"

I was unsure whether to go for the 'I'm clearly innocent therefore pay me the respect I'm due, stare straight ahead at the wall because making eye contact would only be insulting to us both' look or the 'I'm pleading with you please, I'm the victim of a horrific miscarriage of justice, search deep within your souls and you will clearly see that I am a decent honourable human being who must be found innocent please, please, please' look.

Only they would be able to describe the expression on my face as I observed them constantly shifting their attention between the judge and me like spectators on Wimbledon's centre court.

CHAPTER 62

My memories are deceptive.

It's impossible to gain a clear insight when your mood is awash with the muddy waters of dread.

The flotsam and jetsam.

What can I possibly salvage from this wreck?

Where is my lagan?

I am having serious problems with this part.

I keep telling The Doc that it's making me feel worse, the symptoms are increasing.

Possible side effects of recalling trauma may include;

Insomnia.

Nervousness.

Loss of appetite.

Irritability.

Anxiety.

Headache.

Tinnitus (ringing in the ears)

Stomach problems including pain, indigestion, or heartburn.

Severe skin conditions, causing peeling and blistering of the skin, mouth, and eyes.

Palpitations.

Increased need to pass water.

Diarrhoea.

Flatulence.

Constipation.

Vomiting.

Kidney or liver problems.

Symptoms of aseptic meningitis.

High blood pressure.

Abnormal fluid accumulation in tissues of the body (oedema).

Heart failure.

Death.

FUCKING DEATH?

If you experience any of these symptoms, or have any other unusual symptoms or concerns whilst recalling trauma, please consult your psychiatrist immediately.

"Sometimes you have to take a step back to move forward."

Spare me your textbook tutorial and just *HELP* me.

Please?

How can I take advice from somebody who knows nothing about how I am feeling other than from what they have read?

It's almost as absurd as the celibate priest dishing out advice to couples having problems with their marriage.

YOU'LL NEVER FUCKING KNOW!

The Government's not so stupid when it comes to dealing with affairs they know nothing about. They'll happily convert thieves, smugglers, dealers, and hackers to gain the inside knowledge they crave. There's nobody better to learn from than someone who's been through it all before.

Yet I'm supposed to take advice from somebody with less life experience than myself, whose only experience with psychological woes include rejection whilst harbouring a slight Electra complex.

"Just carry on writing. It doesn't matter what you write as long as you release those feelings. Your angst, the bitterness, the hatred. Let it tumble out onto the pages, Jimmy."

FUCK, FUCK, CUNT, FUCK, PISSFLAPS, BASTARD, BOLLOCKS.

It doesn't mean anything. They're just words, expressions of aggression. Grunts would do but they don't have the gravity.

With her insight it probably means I have a fixation with my mother's breasts.

This is the end.

My trial lasted for all of four days. If I thought that being remanded in prison was arduous, I was about to be introduced to a whole new world of pain.

Mainly through shame.

Time flies when you're having fun.

Time doesn't even exist when you're subjected to torture.

There's only a swirling mass of confusion and terror interspersed with tea breaks and lunch breaks until the farce is adjourned by the bored-looking man in a wig.

Same time tomorrow, big man?

I wouldn't miss it for the world.

What the hell is the hair all about?

It's the 21st century.

No need.

To distract my mind from the verbal kicking it's receiving from the prosecution, I imagine myself attempting to explain to an eight-year-old Jimmy Steel the inner workings of a courtroom.

"But why do they have silly hair?"

"It's not their real hair, it's called a wig. It sits on top of your real hair, kind of like a hat."

"Why don't they wear a hat?"

"On top of the wig?"

"No silly. Instead of a wig?"

"I'm not sure, I think they wear wigs because back in the olden days everybody used to wear them and—"

"Where's your wig?"

"I don't get to wear a wig."

"How not?"

"Because it's only the important people that get to wear a wig. They think I've been a bad boy so I've got to sit here—"

"Like on the naughty step?"

"I suppose so."

"What did you do?"

"It doesn't matter ... I didn't do anything. Look, will you just listen? I sit here while that man and that women with the wigs on tell different stories about me and then those people sitting over there decide if I have been bad or not—"

"Where's their wigs?"

"They don't have to wear wigs."

"Are they not important?"

"No they are important, very important. They decide whose story they like best and then they tell that other man in the wig sitting over there—"

"Why is he sleeping?"

"He's not sleeping, he's listening ... so that bunch of people there listen to the two stories and tell the listening man if I have been bad or not and—"

"How do they know if they haven't got wigs on?"

"How do they know what?"

"Duh, if you've been good or bad?"

"Well if you'd shut up for two seconds and let me explain you'll understand."

Heavy sigh and shake of my head.

"Those two people there, see?"

"Uh hu."

"Well, this woman here is on my team and she tells that lot over there a story about how good I am and then that man on the other side, he tells them all a story about how bad I am and—"

"How does he know you're bad?"

"I'm not bad. He doesn't know I'm bad. But somebody told him I was bad so he's telling the people over there, they're called the jury by the way, that I was bad—"

"Who told him you were bad? He's bad."

"Nobody. It doesn't matter. Will you let me finish? I'm trying to explain this ... what was I talking about?"

"The droory?"

"Oh aye, so this woman here, well she's on my side, she thinks I'm good—"

"You are good."

"I know ... but ... thank you. She tells the jury a story about how good I am and that I'm not bad so she'll ask the jury to believe her story and not that other man's story ..."

"The baddie?"

"… and could they please take me off the naughty step and then the other man—"

"The baddie?"

"Aye, the baddie, he'll say no, no, no, no, believe *my* story he *is* bad, keep him on the naughty step."

"Cause you're stinky?"

"What?"

"Ha ha a ha ha ha."

"Aye very good … stop digging around up there … don't you dare eat that. Christ almighty … the jury go away and choose whose story is best and come back and tell that man there—"

"The sleepy one?"

"Aye him, they tell him to either keep me on the naughty step or let me go play outside and then he—"

"The goodie always wins."

"Not always."

"How?"

"Well sometimes the baddie will trick the jury and make them think that I am bad."

"He tells lies?"

"Well not as such … actually … pretty much, yeah. The baddie makes his story sound much, much better than the goodie's story so the jury will fall for his trick and tell the judge, that's the proper name for the sleepy man, to keep me on the naughty step."

"So the droory are baddies too?"

"No, they're just an assortment of human beings from a variety of backgrounds ranging from the educated, corrupt, racist, nepotist, to the ignorant, lazy, bigoted, sociopath who, rather than being picked on successful completion of a rigorous training programme that is designed to assess their mental and physical well-being and suitability to the serious task at hand, are summoned by post. After being chosen by the drawing of lots, successful candidates are then swiftly bundled off into a tiny room where they are forced to converse with each other in a style not too dissimilar to that of a doctor's waiting room. Deducing that they have absolutely nothing in common with a single one of their fellow jurors and that they'd rather spend a week entombed with smelly dread-locked protesters/fox hunters/snobby cunts, they shift and sigh and snort nervously whilst subconsciously deciding that the reprobate/moron/prick whose case they have had the misfortune of presiding over is guilty."

"What?"

"Nothing, I was just thinking out loud."

"Oh. So why do they need to have a wig again? Does it give them special powers?"

"No they just wear it as a sort of tradition. It's what the judge and counsel used to wear in the olden days."

"So … does that mean they're from the olden days?"

"No silly, they're just dressing up, so they look like they're in the olden days. You see their black cloaks?

"Yeah."

"Well that's the same things they would've worn in the olden days too."

"So why do they dress like they're from the olden days?"

"Fucked if I know."

CHAPTER 63

*W*id ye just get on wi' it?! Stop pissing aboot an' let's get this bit over and done wi' then ye can go back tae being a morbid, self-loathing wee prick, a'right?!

It's too hard, I'm hurting …

It's too hard, I'm hurting. Wid ye fucking listen tae yersell?! Stop greeting an' get on wi' it! Ye'r like a fucking wee bairn! It's too painful, oh boo fucking hoo! Ye think ye're the first person in the world tae be up against it?!

No, it's just …

It's just whit?!

I can't bring myself to …

Bring yersell tae whit?! It's no' fucking hard! Just tell it like it happened, easy peasy lemon fucking squeezy! Look, the sooner ye get this shite written doon, the sooner ye can show it tae that wee hippy bint so she can piss aff and fiddle wi' hersell over yer tragic misfortune. She's filling yer heid wi' shite! I'm telling ye, she's no' helping wan little bit! She's makin' ye saft.

Will you shut up and let me concentrate? I cannae write this with you constantly ranting like a lunatic. It's hard enough as it is.

Ye want hard?! I'll tell ye whit's fucking hard, listening tae you whilst ye wallow in a cesspit of self-pity day in day oot. It's like ye get some sort o' sick joy oot o' it, clinging oan tae the 'oh I'm so hard done by' act! Ye'r fucking pathetic, ye should be ashamed. Well it stops noo. I'm no' pitting up wi' this filth ony mair. Get it fucking doon oan that paper an' get it doon quick.

I've got to be in the right frame of mind to write it, this has been the toughest part so far …

Yer arse! Frame o' mind? Whit the fuck has that got tae dae wi' it? Ye ken how tae haud a pen an' ye ken how tae spell, that's the only ingredients ye fucking need. Ye'r no' aboot tae diffuse a bomb, are ye? There's no 'right frame o' mind' required. Stop using excuses.

Look I didn't ask for this …

Ask for this? Are you actually listening tae the putrid nonsense that's coming oot o' yer mooth or is it aw just word play tae convince yersell that ye're some sort o' martyr tae a cause that doesnae exist? Ask for this? Mind thon pictures oan the telly o' they starving wee bairns in Ethiopia? Aye? Those images that made ye feel sick tae the pit o' yer contented wee belly? Enough tae mak ye sell yer Millennium Falcon at some poxy 'bring and buy sale' so ye could rid yersell o' that queasy feeling, eh? Dae ye think they wee bairns asked fir that, eh? Wi' their bloated bellies and sunken pusses hoatchin' wi a thoosan' flees? Trying tae sook at their maw's droopy teat fir a wee bit nourishment? Sooking and sooking till the teat's rid raw but her teat's as empty as her belly? Mind o' that, eh? Dae ye think they asked for that, eh?! Eh?!

Piss off, that's not fair. That's completely different, a different time, a different place.

You want fair, eh? Well let me tell ye this pal, LIFE ISNAE FUCKING FAIR! Will you no' tak' yer heid oot o' yer arse fir wan day an' see that it's no' aw aboot you? Ye've got toy soldiers oot in Africa waging a war they ken fuck aw aboot. In the Middle East ye've got lassie's being pelted tae death wi' rocks for haein' the cheek tae look at anither man and there's lads being cut up fir fucking ither lads. Genocide, homicide, infanticide, democide, ecocide … there's mair cides oot there than a dodecahedron. Different time, different place? Whit aboot thae lassies locked up in that basement? Raped an' tortured by their own kin? Think aboot aw those pair bastards being shipped ower here fae aw o'er the fucking place sold on the promise o' guid times wi' plenty money in their poacket only tae fund oot they're being held as slaves or forced intae prostitution? Rape, slavery, torture, kidnapping …

Aye very good you've made your point, ever thought of going into inspirational speaking?

Shut yer puss ye hopeless cunt. An' dinnae get smert wi' me a'right? I'm telling ye this fir yer ain guid. The sooner ye get aw this through that thick heid o' yours the better it'll be for a'body. Life's tough. Really tough. The easier it gets tae live, what wi' yer modern technology an' aw that shite, the harder it becomes tae live. This freedom we've aw got noo gies us too much time. Time which we dae nothing constructive wi' an' ye ken whit they say aboot idleness?

Something about the Devil?

Aye ye'r right, something aboot the Devil, clever boy. Noo, I'm no' aboot tae get aw preachy oan ye wi' dogmatic matters regarding the Deil himsell cause there's ayways twa sides tae a story an' as yet I've no' heard his version o' events but for aw attempts an' purposes he's a handy cunt tae use in an argument so listen up bugger lugs for ye'r aboot tae hear something that maist folk arenae used tae hearing. People are bastards. An' I dinnae mean the 'Oh see him there he's a bad bastard' kind o' way. I mean human beings by default, by their basic nature, embedded deep within their Deoxyribonucleic acid is an evil so despicable it wid curl yer fucking toes.

Oh for fuck's sake, okay I'm starting to write now save your breath ...

I telt ye tae shut the fuck up an' listen. This is wisdom that ye cannae buy. 'Oh but there's good in everybody' they hopelessly whine whilst attempting to convince their languid brains that the shocking scene their eyes have bared witness tae wis a tragedy, a fluke, a wan aff. Let me tell ye something. It wisnae. People are angry, greedy, selfish, evil cunts. The only tragedy is in human beings trying tae convince themsells that they're inherently guid. Guid? Ah mean whit the fuck is that, eh? It's just a word. Guid, evil, right, wrang? Whit the fuck? Their interpretation o' 'good' is based loosely oan something written in a book aboot a boy who supposedly did amazing things an' loved his enemies. Come oan tae fuck? Fir the love o' Christ. Am ah the only wan getting this? He wisnae a King, he wis a fucking freak, stood oot like a sair thumb an' he paid the price for it. If onything use him as an example, learn fae his mistakes but dinnae go worshipping the cunt. That shrink lassie's a prime example o' the lunacy that comes by 'teaching good.' Does she honestly think that by spouting some technical words she's read in a book you're gonnae be magically cured?

At least she's trying to make me feel better, I mean, you're no' exactly doing a world of good are you? Fuck's sake, negative pish that's all you're good for.

Fir the last fucking time, close that whimpering trap o' yours, eh? Negative, negative? Positive? Negative, positive? They're only fucking words, like aw the ither wans they use that mean fuck all but are somehow held in high regard. Ye want tae ken aboot good? A'right I'll tell ye aboot good. Good is a myth. A Chinese whisper if it pleases ye? A theory drummed up centuries ago by the weak-minded who were tired o' aw the fighting an' stealing an' killing. By some strange occurrence they grew weary or simply couldnae handle aw the fighting an' stealing an' killing etcetera blah de blah. So the cunning wans, or fucking blooses if ye ask me, pit their heids thegither an' came up wi' this notion that getting alang an' helping wan anither wis far mair preferable than the previous stooshie and rabble. It wis a decision. A concentrated effort made by somebody who thought highly o' themsell. It didnae come naturally though, being good. If you listen tae Darwin, it's aw aboot evolution. We're just beasties like the ither wans oan the planet but the only difference is we've learned to think. Hurting, torturing, killing is natural tae us but somewhere alang the line it's been decided that that's no' right.

Like you said, it's called evolution. We've moved on, there's no need for all the fighting and hatred. You're contradicting yourself, we don't live in caves anymore, we've sent folk to the moon, people are good because it IS in their nature so dinnae give me your pish.

Oh aye, in their nature, is that right? Mind the time Sid brought his air rifle roond an' you an' him pit oot a loaf o breid in the back gairden so the nice wee birdies wid come doon tae dine? Dae ye mind? Aye? Well ye'll mind the carnage ye inflicted on those pair wee sparries as they landed wan after wan for a wee peck o' the breid tae stave aff their hunger pangs eh? BANG! BANG! BANG! Oh look a dozen wee sparries aw lying deid oan the groond. Mind how that felt eh? It felt GOOD! Dinnae lie, ah wis there mind? Ye wir aw pleased wi' yersell cause you were the big man, look at me, ah killed aw those stupid wee sparries, eh?

I was just a kid. I didn't know any better, that's a useless argument.

Is it? Is it really? That wis you in yer natural innocent form. A kid. Ignorant o' the rules an' regulations o' the world an' there ye were killing innocent wee creatures simply fir yer own pleasure. Killing, no' because ye wanted tae eat them or tae pit them oot o' their misery. Killing fir yer own simple pleasure. PLEASURE! Dae ye need me tae define it fir ye, wid that help? The only reason ye think it wis wrong is cause yer Maw came hame an' seen the destruction an' leathered yer stupid erse for the 'cruelty' an' then Clare had the cheek tae lecture ye aboot the 'feeling's of animals.' Tell me, who was in the wrang there, Jimmy boy? Eh? The innocent wee boy who didnae ken onything aboot onything who wis merely satisfying his primal desire for death and destruction or the institutionalised crabbit wifie who skelpt yer erse?

Me. I was, it was me who was wrong. I shouldn't have done it, but I learned my lesson.

There it is, pal. Ye've done ma work fir me. Excellent work, detective, why thank you Sir. Ye LEARNED yer lesson. Are ye too stupid an' blund tae see? Ye had tae be 'taught' that whit ye'd done wis wrang! Fall in line, Steel. Forward face. Quick march. Left, right, left, right, left, right, left …

What the is the point in all of this? You're just digging up shit from the past that doesn't even matter, how is this helping me? I'm trying my hardest, I really am.

Aw ma pair wee lamb come here an' get a cuddle fae somebody who doesnae gie a flying fuck. Look, ma point is, and this may come as a great big fucking shock tae yer glaiket puss, that human beings are born evil but they learn how tae be good. No' the ither way roond like they'd hae ye believe. It's natural tae be a hard bastard, a callous killer. The only thing that separates us fae the ither animals is oor giant brain an' it's capacity fir cold calculating killing. Pose it a question an' the auld grey matter will come up wi hunners o' possiblities, each wan mair gruesome than the last.

I'm not a killer, I've told you a thousand times I didn't do it.

I'm no' saying ye are, man, calm doon. All I'm saying is ye've got tae be tough. Harder than fucking granite. If ye carry on in this miserable state ye'll no' fucking survive. The doom an' gloom will engulf ye until ye dinnae ken if ye'r coming or going an' I can tell ye fir a fact that ye'll no' be coming. Be like yer name, Steel. Cold an' tough an' fucking solid, able to withstand ony pressure an' if ye'r really fucking lucky ye'll be worth millions someday. Jimmy Fucking Steel. There's nae shame in being called a prick or a cunt or ony ither genitalia-based insult. Fuck them, fuck them aw. We dinnae need them. If they cannae handle us well, that's their fucking problem, eh? Be ruthless an' be decisive, fuck tomorrow. As long as ye keep the heid, Jimmy boy, ye'll be fine an' dandy.

Second doubts. Questioning everything, every time.

Such a fear, now a fear of myself.

Hypochondriac? Killer? Psychopath?

One? Or maybe I'm all three.

Now I'm in charge here I tell myself, but the bully returns and interrogates me until I no longer know who's running the show.

Every thought that's positive, every memory that's fond, every ounce of love that I once oozed.

Stop.

Where have they gone?

Who dares to take over this station and undermine my authority, making decisions and coming to conclusions that shouldn't be made?

I do!

Who are you? Why have you come? To destroy me? Is this my fate?

Shiver.

Is this my destiny?

I shirk to think.

Or do I?

The deeper this goes the further I fall; something up here has always been wrong.

Is it the constant doubting of myself that has led to my demise?

Why don't you just do it? Go on, go on. Stab, kick, punch, bite, batter.

On and on it goes, who the fuck are you? Leave me alone.

I'm tired of fighting myself. No matter what *He* always wins.

Anything I do, see, hear, remember.

Why?

He always turns it around to suit *himself.*

I'm sinking, slipping, sliding further down this wretched stinking hill. As I near the bottom I see fire.

Hell!

Maybe not. But my feet are almost burning.

I'm not sick. *Yes, you are!*

I'm not mental. *You know you are!*

I no longer know who I am.

Always tired, a fear of being alone, can't share my feelings.

Bring me the good times.

This one-on-one battle is killing me.

I want to stop but I'm so scared as each day brings me more misery.

I wish I wasn't fighting.

I wish it wasn't me versus **me.**

These little episodes are a continuing thorn in my pasty flesh. I try to ignore them, no, I do ignore them, the content certainly but the frequency with which they are occurring alarms me. No that's not true, it's the content that alarms me. They're becoming darker, a lot darker than my usual thoughts. And they are *my* thoughts, it's *my* voice I hear in my head whilst **he's** making these speeches, these suggestions. I'm not schizophrenic, it's not somebody else I'm hearing.

Can it be schizophrenia if it's your own voice you hear?

I should tell the shrink.

I want to tell her, but I don't want her thinking I'm a total nut job as well as being a depressed recluse. I'm not fucking crazy; I mean, I'm sane enough to recognise that I shouldn't take advice from or heed the bleak ramblings that spout forth from the dark hollows of my mind.

CHAPTER 64

Stand up, sit down, go out, come back in, stand up, sit down, stand up, sit down, go out …

The prosecutor is good. By that I mean he is sadistically dismantling my character piece by fucking piece until all that's left of me is a billion tiny fragments scattered all over the courtroom floor. When the clerk opens the door to allow the jury to exit for yet another adjournment the subsequent draft swoops through the room and lifts another few particles of my discarded being and they waft towards the departing group like drunken butterflies.

Gone.

Paul Young doesn't even get it as he sings 'Every time you go away you take a piece of me with you.'

Throughout the trial more and more of my essence escapes by riding the thermals caused by the opening and closing of doors. I want to rush out of my seat and salvage the remaining scraps before I'm reduced to a single speck of me.

GET ON WITH IT!
Okay, okay. I'm doing it …

The prosecutor was awesome. Not for me, obviously. I hated that prick with all the passion I could muster. This smug fucker was fighting Danny Foster's cause like it was his only reason for living.

Where the hell did the Fosters get this guy anyway? HOW did the Fosters get this guy?

The family was notoriously skint. As kids they were so impoverished that the Foster siblings' only method for survival was beating the living shit out of anyone that moved before stealing their victim's money or items of clothing that they thought would look better worn by them. Yet here was Mr Smart Arse, the Diego Maradona of the legal world representing Danny?

What the fuck happened there?

Without meaning to offend her (but clearly doing so) I raised there concerns with my QC who dismissively advised that the Advocate Depute is paid for by the State and *NOT* the Fosters.

I think she thought I was questioning her appointment in a roundabout way.

That wasn't what I was getting at!

Sorry Hen!

The prosecutor was a frightening character. He appeared to be in a permanently foul mood. Perhaps this was because I was only being tried for culpable homicide and not murder? As there were no witnesses to the event and I had admitted from the start that I had inflicted the fatal blow this made the prosecutor's job very easy indeed. At least that's how it appeared to me. I'd already done the hard part for him. All he had to do was focus his energy on convincing the jury that I was guilty. He didn't give a fuck about trivial matters such as the truth. His brief was simple, convict James Steel for the death of (delete as appropriate) my Son/Brother/Father/Partner/Friend and you will be handsomely rewarded.

For him this case was the equivalent of making Einstein find the exit in a maze designed for children. He resented me for denying him the opportunity of unleashing his exquisite legal brain for the masses to behold.

Plus, he was probably getting paid by the hour so like a dishonest tradesman he huffed and puffed and oohh'd and ahhh'd, convincing everyone in the room (except the judge who's more than likely witnessed this kind of behaviour on numerous occasions) that this case was a tricky one and would take days of meticulous planning on his behalf to ensure no stone was left unturned and that justice would be served.

Is that right? Well, when you put it like that, good sir, and can I just say thank you very much for explaining it to me using The Layman's vernacular, you might as well add an extra couple of zeros to your Bill. No, no, I insist.

DING DING, ROUND ONE!

He started with a few gentle jabs to get a feel for me, to find out what I was made of. There was no point in going for the knockout blow in the first round. His supporters had come here to see a mauling, oh yes. But they wouldn't stand for a quick one, oh no. They wanted to see their hero complete his repertoire.

By the time the bell went to signal the end of round one I was hurting. I was weary.

Through his thrusts and jabs the prosecutor had skilfully opened me up and presented a violent alcoholic to the bloodthirsty crowd.

They sat enthralled as he regaled them with his own take on the events that happened. The jury were handed a sheet of paper containing all the abusive texts and the dates on which Danny sent them to me.

His QC argued that they were *ONLY* threats. Threats that were only issued after the images of Debs were published online. Threats that were never meant to be fulfilled, threats that were made to make me feel as uncomfortable as Deborah Smith was made to feel. Danny Foster merely did what any caring, loving partner would have done when put in that horrible situation.

I looked over at the majority male jury and could see a few nods of agreement from some of them, as if they were saying 'Yeah, quite right. If that was me and somebody had done that to my other half I'd do exactly the same. Perhaps more.'

Shit.

Please don't fall for that trick.

How was my version of events to be plausible when I'd consumed umpteen pints and multiple whiskies that evening, he argued?

The ruddy nosed barkeep from The Cross Keys confirmed the fact that I had ordered six pints and six whiskies in a very short space of time on the night in question.

Haud the bus!

Danny's QC, the eminent Thomas Mayer-Winstanley, is telling the jury that I'm a piss head who can't recall the facts accurately but they've to believe the tale of some raging steamboat barman who had been drinking since opening time on the night in question?

Where's the justice?

At most I had four pints and four whiskies.

Anything I said or didn't say was turned against me and he made me look like a complete fool who was capable of much more than killing someone.

Manipulation.

Pure and simple.

He was destroying me up there.

Guilty.

I'm going down for this.

For effect he reiterated the fact that on the night in question I had taken part in a marathon drinking session and, having recently purchased more intoxicating liquor to stew in, I approached an innocent man whom I had been in disagreement with and after a heated altercation knowingly struck the decisive blow.

Work the body, work the body, punch, jab, jab!

On hearing the bell, the prosecutor skipped back to his corner like a triumphant matador.

I slumped further whilst trying to catch my breath. My coach, a wiry QC named Sadie Palmerston, tried her best to offer me words of encouragement. "You're doing well out there, but you need to keep your guard up."

Inexplicably her pep talk failed to inspire me.

DING DING, ROUND TWO!

I could still hear the distant echo of the bell as the prosecutor sprung from his stool and thundered towards me. He lost no time in dulling my senses with a couple of rapid crosses to the face followed by a jarring uppercut which resulted in me biting clean through my tongue.

I could taste the salty metallic juice as it flowed freely from my crumpled mouth.

Jab, jab, cross, cross, jab.

My right eye had closed completely due to the swelling and the only thing I could hear in my left ear was a high-pitched ringing noise which I sadly mistook for the bell that would put an end to this senseless slaughter.

I was still able to hear his lyrical waxing of Danny Foster though.

"A leader of men, a hero who despite having experienced horrendous hardship as a child showed tremendous tenacity to overcome his difficult beginnings and rise up the ranks within the Great British Army. He served this country with pride and distinction whilst on various tours of duty. Daniel witnessed some horrific sights as one must when engaged in the patriotic act of defending one's Queen and Country.

"God save the Queen.

"But Daniel did not bring his work home with him. The gruesome images that he witnessed were permanently seared into his brain but due to his courage and strength of character he never allowed those memories to manifest themselves under the cowardly banner of Post Traumatic Stress

Disorder.

"For Daniel was better than that.

"What occurred on the battlefield, remained on the battlefield. Daniel was a soldier, a disciplined disciple, a faithful servant who represented these Great British Isles with valour. Daniel was a liberating lantern of light delivering emancipation to the dingy downtrodden dictatorships he encountered. He was a fighter until the bitter end, and it was with this trait, this strength, this ingrained need for supplying salvation to the unprotected that he was able to inflict the injuries sustained by the accused.

"Alas, by disarming and subduing his perpetrator, as Daniel had been trained to do, and by gathering strength from thoughts of this violent intoxicated nuisance inflicting further damage to his devoted partner and unborn child if he escaped his clutches, brave Daniel Foster neglected the life-threatening wound upon his carotid artery.

"Let's make one thing clear, ladies and gentlemen. Daniel Foster, by applying the knowledge he gained through his exceptional military training, could have survived the wound that killed him, IF and only if he had acted swiftly. But, by engaging in a fracas with the accused, Daniel selflessly sacrificed his own life to ensure his partner and unborn child's safety."

Objection.

The referee, much to his annoyance, reluctantly agreed with my agonised protest that one of the prosecutor's punches had strayed marginally below the belt line. The ring side judges also appeared to take umbrage at my cynical attempts to distract the prosecutor from his exquisite display and frantically scribbled something on their score cards.

DING!

The prosecutor attempted a sort of 'Ali shuffle' as he made his way back to his corner, much to the delight of the whooping crowd.

I'm exhausted.

I dinnae ken how much more of this I can take.

"You're still doing okay out there but you need to move your head more, keep your chin in," Sadie advised as she smeared Vaseline into my blood-splattered brow.

"That's the best you've got? Years of coaching and it boils down to that? Duck and fucking dive?"

"It's the best form of defence, it makes you harder to hit," she replied despondently whilst wafting smelling salts under my smashed nose.

"Aye it's done me proud so far, eh?"

DING DING, ROUND THREE!

"Oh shit!" we both groaned.

Hook, hook, cross, jab, jab, jab, jab, hook.

It was more of the same old vitriolic banter served up by Thomas as he asked the jury why a stupid junkie bass player would feel the need to bring a knife to a fist fight?

For intimidation?

To even the score?

Or because he was a cowardy cowardy custard who couldn't stand the thought of being defeated by an ex-servant of Her Majesty's Great British Army in a good old-fashioned square go?

He's probably a socialist too!

Bloody cheating, lefty bastard!

Out of the corner of my half-shut eye I could make out frantic scribbling on notepads from the jury.

No no no no no …

DING!

Sadie was as animated as I'd seen her as I gulped for air and flopped about on my stool like a seal pup having a seizure. She slapped my face and shook her clenched fist whilst attempting to stem the flow of blood that spewed from a deep cut above my left eye. Through the tiny range of vision I still had, I could detect that she was deeply concerned about the damage and its implications to any further involvement in this fight. But, to her credit, or her training, she refused to abandon me and carried on working to the best of her ability. Little beads of sweat plunged from her creased forehead and caressed mine. They merged with the expanding volume of sticky fluids that seemed to be permanently residing there. Sadie was clearly bawling instructions for the benefit of my cauliflower ears to ingest and relay onto my bedraggled brain but the squatter-like inflammation that obstructed her vocal vibrations from being manufactured into coherent sentences severely disabled me as I was to enter the fourth round.

Pummelled into a state of paralysis.

Try as I might, the guttural groaning that tumbled from my mouth was misconstrued by my QC as she insisted that I continue with my plight.

What I was actually trying to convey was ...

"See that wee white thing lying there?"

"What wee white thing?"

"That wee white thing there ... no, over there, behind the spit bucket ..."

"What this? Oh yes, the towel?"

"Aye, the towel. Gonnae go and fling it into the ring to save us from suffering any more pain and humiliation."

"What? You want us to simply give up and throw away any chance we have? Denying the crowd a chance to see the ultimate comeback? Have you not seen Rocky? I can't believe I'm hearing this, especially from you, the so-called Champion Of The Underdog. Come on, where's your fighting spirit? It's not over until the final bell, we've still got the opportunity to deliver that knockout blow, one shot, that's all we need, you can do this."

I attempted a smile of appreciation which resulted in my gum shield sliding from my slavering crevice and onto the dirty canvas. Like a claw machine at the penny arcade, I struggled to pick it up.

"On second thoughts, you have a wee seat here and catch your breath and I'll take a shot in the ring."

And with a gleam in her eye Sadie bound through the ropes whilst throwing fierce mock punches.

DING DING, ROUND FOUR!

"Your honour I'd like to bring Deborah Smith to the stand."

I was shook from my temporary concussion by her name being mentioned out loud.

A door to the side of the courtroom creaked open and from the gloom she stepped forth and made her way up to the witness box. I couldn't take my eyes off her. This was the first time they'd gazed upon her in such a long time. In that briefest of walks I couldn't get over how strange she appeared with that bulging belly of hers.

She must be due soon?

She looks tired.

Oh and I wonder why that would that be, eh?

I looked into her dark tired eyes for the first time since … my mind frantically searched for an image.

Must've been that argument you had with Foster doon the pub afore the tour started.

Sigh.

Having scanned the court room briefly from her perch, her eyes fluttered down upon my own for a fraction of a second.

I'm so sorry Debs.

She cannae even bare to look at you.

What a mess.

Stricken by the fact that Debs couldn't maintain eye contact I allowed myself to become lost in self-loathing brought about by the terrible decisions I'd made in life.

"I know it must be difficult, Deborah, but can you please tell the courtroom of the last conversation you had with Daniel?" Sadie asked.

Oh come on Sadie, I dinnae need to hear this. You're meant to be on my side.

"Well um, it was Christmas Eve … I was preparing the vegetables for Christmas dinner when Danny came through to the kitchen to tell me he was going out," Deborah recalled.

"Approximately what time was this?" Sadie countered.

"Um I can't be sure for definite but I'd say around half past nine … "

"In the evening?"

"Yes. There was a film starting at 10 p.m. that we'd planned on watching together and when he came through to tell me he was going out I thought it strange that he'd miss the start of the film. He wouldn't tell me where he was going or why, so we started arguing. I told him he was being selfish for ruining the evening we had planned. He started shouting that he was doing it for me …" Debbie closed her eyes and bowed her head.

"You're doing well, carry on," soothed Sadie.

"I started shouting 'doing what for me?' He said that if I must know he'd received a phone call to tell him where Jimmy was."

"By Jimmy he meant Jimmy Steel, yes?" Sadie interjected.

"Yes."

"Did Daniel say where that was?"

"No. I asked him to leave things be, to forget about Jimmy so we could enjoy Christmas Eve together."

"Tell the courtroom what happened after that."

"Daniel was agitated and angry. He was shouting and swearing and when I tried to stop him leaving the house, he forced me against the wall and grabbed me by the throat. He told me that it was all my fault and that as per usual he'd have to clean up everybody's mess," Debbie claimed, and she looked visibly upset at the recollection.

What the fuck?

That bastard!

"What do you think he meant by that, Deborah?"

Deb's eyes left Sadie's and came to rest on my own wearied peepers, and I flinched as they connected.

"He told me what he meant. He said I was too soft, and he was going to sort out my ex-boyfriend for all the pain he'd caused me." Her eyes never left mine.

"By ex-boyfriend you mean Jimmy Steel, correct?"

"Correct."

"And do you remember Daniel's exact words on the night in question?" Sadie pressed again as Debbie's stare shifted to hers.

"Yes. He said, 'I'm going to kill that bastard for what he's done to you.'"

"Just so we can be clear, who was Daniel referring to when he told you that he was going to kill that bastard?"

"Jimmy."

"Jimmy Steel?"

"Yes."

"No more questions."

My head spun from Debbie's testimony. Numerous questions and statements fired through my brain.

That was unexpected.

Nice one Debs.

He WAS trying to kill you.

She must be a wreck.

That'll have evened out the scorecards, eh?

Dinnae get too cocky.

She protected me?

Maybe she still has feelings for me?
Oh for fuck's sake!

Sadie briefly returned to my corner to reapply some dressings to my beleaguered character.

There was hardly a hair out of place on her.

She looked amazing.

She was amazing.

She had performed with such grace out in the ring.

Grace?

I think I love you, Sadie.

After swiftly applying epinephrine to my reopened wounds, she bounded back into the centre of the ring for her big finale.

* Legal disclaimer – The following speeches from both defence and prosecution are subject to my limited recall (of which I have almost zero because I was a shambling, nervous wreck throughout the whole trial and could barely concentrate on anything that was being said) so I have used some artistic licence to portray their closing statements in a way that fits my own agenda but I'm quite confident that had I been concentrating, then these words would closely resemble what was actually said even though they didn't happen in the exact order below. (Defence goes last.)

Names have obviously been changed to protect the privacy of individuals.

Also, no punches were actually thrown in the courtroom.

It's an analogy.

Some might call it creative writing.

Ladies and Gentlemen of the Jury I ask you, no … I implore you not to be swayed by Thomas Mayer-Winstanley's somewhat biased retelling of events. True, he possesses a certain charisma that separates the mundane from the downright bloody fantastic and yes he is also in possession of a charm that makes you want to cling onto every word he utters. A charm which is so powerful that not only do you *want* to hold onto those words, you *need* to grasp them as if your future existence depended upon it. And yes, Ladies and Gentlemen, I am well aware of the fact that he cuts a dashing figure whilst swathed in his black robes and I admit that the harsh, lifeless grey wool of his courtroom wig juxtaposed with the smooth, auburn tones of his multiple foreign holiday skin indicates vitality, which is of course necessary in the context of the longevity of the human species.

What the hell is this, Sadie?

What I am trying to say, Ladies and Gentlemen of the Jury, is that this man does indeed have all the attributes that one would find desirable to be displayed as an example for the continuation of the human race should we ever find ourselves in a situation where we are compelled to flee the planet and start all over again due to apocalyptic instances. But *all* human beings are flawed, even the great ones. Let he or she who is without sin cast the first stone. Even this wonderful man with whom I do battle, suffers from a major blemish in his otherwise righteous persona. I speak of a terrible affliction which affects all people burdened with power. Ladies and Gentlemen, I speak of an illness known as the overinflated ego and unfortunately this poor fellow has it bad. Due to his illness, 'truth' is nothing but a hindrance, an obstacle he must overcome in order to satisfy his ego's voracious appetite. 'Justice' is deemed worthy only on his own terms. But truth and justice must prevail. They must, for the continued evolution of our species … the truth is this … Jimmy Steel did what he had to do to defend himself against an UNPROVOKED, highly trained warrior.

Would you view his supposed crime differently if he had used another instrument to halt the brutal assault?

A brick perhaps?

Or is it down to the fact that Jimmy used a knife?

A knife that he only carried to repel such an attack as the one he was subjected to?

The truth is Jimmy Steel did not mean to kill Daniel Foster … Jimmy didn't even mean to hurt him badly.

Jimmy didn't *want* to hurt him at all.

But he *HAD* to inflict enough damage upon Daniel Foster so that Daniel would cease his assault and allow Jimmy to flee to safety.

Jimmy Steel is a lover. He is not a fighter.

Yes, he is guilty of making mistakes, but who here among us today isn't?

It is only by making mistakes that we learn and grow as individuals.

Yes, Jimmy ruined his relationship with Deborah and he's told me on so many occasions that if he had a time machine he would jump in without hesitation and set the dials to go back and undo the mess that he has made so that he could still be with her.

In love.

But Jimmy is not Dr Emmett Brown and therefore does not have a time machine and so he is forced to live with his greatest mistake every day.

And that hurts him.

I mean it really fucking hurts him.

Jimmy is not a violent man. He is just a man who was in the wrong place at the wrong time on that terrible night.

Ladies and Gentlemen … Jimmy Steel is an innocent man.

Right on cue, Billy Joel burst into the courtroom, microphone in hand and belted out the chorus to his classic song.

I rose from my seat and vaulted the barrier to join him in song.

Probably due to the emotion I was feeling, my vocal cords struggled to match his high pitch, so I was forced to come down a couple of keys until our voices entwined in a beautiful harmony.

"I aaaaaaaaaaaaaaaam an innocent maaaaaaaaaaaaaaan oh yes I am …

an innocent man."

CRACK!

My beautiful harmony with Billy Joel was cut short by a fierce right to my left cheekbone.

Ow!

Is this guy even wearing the regulation gloves?

The prosecutor was having none of this showman-like emotional bullshit. If anyone was going to pluck on heart strings whilst summing up it would be him.

He countered swiftly with another tirade of anecdotes which made Sadie's statement seem weak and feeble, therefore banishing any thoughts the judges may have had of amending their score card in my favour.

This feeble man (arm stretched, finger pointing at me) carried forth by a poisoned mind loves nothing more than violence and destruction. It's what makes him tick. Through some perversion he feels it adds verve to his mediocre existence.

But the simple fact is this, my little bunch of fanatics … oh by the way, head juror, have you done something different with your hair today? It really frames your features and makes those eyes sparkle, I love it, you look glorious

... this deplorable man who slouches in his chair and forces us exalted mortals to breathe the venomous vapours that hiss from his deceitful pours, LIVES for destruction. With the precision and skill of a master sculpture he delicately constructed relationships, friendships, interests, and hobbies thanks to years of calculating strokes. He even had the audacity to take a few steps back, enabling him to better admire his handy work. Only when he was satisfied did he then set about destroying his creations with all the force of a builders wrecking ball.

First! He hypnotised the impressionable Deborah Smith with false charm and tales of fame and fortune. The young Deborah sacrificed her own well-laid plans on his promise of an eternal, loving, and devoted relationship. A promise which he never intended to keep. Continuously back tracking on his word on the subject of raising a family together, and furious that he was not going to get things his own way, James Steel lit the fuse that would raise their relationship of seven years to the ground, encasing Deborah in a dusty cloud of disillusion, despair, and regret.

BOOM!

Secondly! Gaining little satisfaction from the resultant blast and still in possession of a considerable amount of TNT, he swiftly proceeded to wreck his employment prospects. Spending six years slowly garnering employees' and customers' respect and trust, it would take him merely minutes to dismantle the charade that he was a thoughtful, loyal and hardworking individual.

BOOM!

The switch had been flicked.

But still he demanded more.

He NEEDED more.

Thirdly! As a member of the band Champions Of The Underdog, which included two of his best friends, James Steel along with Ian Hughes and Joseph Serevi embarked on a tour which they hoped would enable them to fulfil their dreams of obtaining musical stardom and critical acclaim. Sadly for that innocent pair they had a rat in their pack and they failed to smell it. Incensed at his perceived lack of input into the band's revised direction, James Steel concocted a tale that would not only obliterate the band's loyal fan base but exterminate the band itself. A band that he 'dedicated' over 20 years of his life to. He assisted in their propulsion to the outer fringes of fame only to decide that he would wipe out any chance of future success they may have had.

BOOM!

This specimen who is displayed before us, Ladies and Gentlemen, is a selfish coward who revels in the pain and discomfort of others brought about by his own hand. Having his appetite whetted but not satiated by these initial vulgar acts he then hatched plans for his big finale. The act to end all acts. The curtain closer if you will. An act that had taken him a lifetime to achieve and would shockingly conclude with the loss of an innocent man's life as well as his metaphorical own. As preposterous as it may seem to you and my good self, Ladies and Gentlemen, there is no denying the fact that James Steel draws courage from the absurd notion that what he may create he may also destroy and it is this need for destruction which drives the man, pleasures the man, satisfies the man.

I can imagine the accused as a small child deriving much joy from patiently building his Lego bricks piece by piece to emerge as a three-dimensional reconstruction of the image that projected itself from the one-dimensional paper instructions he held in his hands. That joy, however, would slink in comparison to the ecstatic feeling that pumped through his veins as he kicked and tore at the structure he had spent hours creating.

It is difficult to understand the workings of an evil mind, Ladies and Gentlemen, and I urge you to not even try. All that I urge you good people to do is look deep within yourselves. Go on, do it now. Let all of us do it now. Let's spend some quality time within the silence of our own sanctuary and listen out for that little voice of reason. That voice of truth. That voice of justice. That little voice of humanity that's within each and every one of us. Close your eyes. Can you hear it? Can you? Yes? It whispers softly. Still the ignorant chatter of your gullible minds, Ladies and Gentlemen, and allow it to penetrate your thoughts. It's becoming louder. Louder. Much louder until all you can hear, all you can feel is truth and justice, yes? Truth and justice, can you hear it with me? Can you? You can? All right, then say it with me now, truth and justice, truth and justice, yes that's it, truth and justice, truth and justice, all together now, truth and justice. Come on, clap your hands. That's it. Okay just the women, yes that's beautiful. Now only the men. Keep in time with the rhythm, truth and justice, truth and justice, come on stamp your feet. Let's hear it. I feel it, oh Lord I feel it. Can you feel it too? As God is my witness, I can feel it. I can believe it. I do believe it. Believe in me. Believe in the power of me. When I say that God is my witness, I truly mean that, Ladies and Gentlemen, or so help me God. Believe in the power of truth and justice, believe in the power of God the Almighty, believe in me. I am the truth, I am justice, I am the light. Come on now, feel it, clap your hands, even you, the lanky boy at the back who affirmed, I want to feel you, I want to relate to you.

DING! DING! DING! DING! DING!

The referee thrust his body between my broken form and that of the prosecutor to signal the end of the fight. The prosecutor, pumped into a frenzy through adrenaline and hatred, was still trying to sneak in a few cheeky punches even though this contest was over.

The referee had seen enough carnage inflicted and pushed my attacker back towards his corner whilst Mayer-Winstanley held his arms aloft in victory.

I had never felt so much pain in my life.

So much abuse.

So much humiliation.

Too many lies.

Every part of my being ached.

My brain reeled.

My soul clawed at my innards like a lion ripping apart its prey whilst attempting to flee the fleshy confinements of my doomed body.

The immaculate Sadie who was far more confident than me had her arms aloft and was prancing around the ring goading the opposition.

My QC regained her composure and returned to raise me from my corner so that I could stand in the ring to hear the inevitable outcome.

I leaned on her for support and twice she had to grab my lightweight frame to stop me from falling over.

CHAPTER 65

"Laydeeeeeez and Jennelmen, yoooooooo have just witnessed four rounds of ssssssssssspectacular physical jousting!"

"Ladies and Gentlemen of the jury, have you reached a verdict?"
"Yes."

"Live from the MGM Grand we go to the scorecards. Randy Mickleson scores it 118-112, Chuck Mamzic 116-114 and Dale Ulrich 118-112 …"

"On the charge relating to culpable homicide, how do you find the accused?"

"… all three to the winner by yoooooooonanimous deeeeeeecision …"

"We the jury find the accused …"

Crazy as it may sound, I was actually calm during the announcement.

It was as if my mind had finally decided to stop the war with itself and accept the inevitable.

A warm blanket of comforting peace descended upon my fragile emotions, instantly transcending me towards Zen-like fulfilment.

There are no bad experiences.

Or good experiences.

There is only experience itself.

No right or wrong.

No love or hate.

No good or bad.

I gratefully received the soothing rapture that was bestowed upon me.

I've made my peace.

Do not let your heart be troubled.

"Aaaaaaaaaaaaaaaaaaand new champion of the wooooooooooooooorld …"

"Not guilty."

"Jimmy Fuuuuuuuuuuuuuuucking Steel!"

I sunk to my knees and wept.

Bleak thoughts of a future I'd thankfully never have to endure screamed as they were thrust from my mind.

Thank you.

Oh thank you.

Sadie tapped me on the back, and I arose to hug the utter shite out of her.

I squeezed her as tightly as I could despite her efforts to quell me.

"Thank you so much, thank you, thank you, thank you," I repeatedly bleated into her ear.

"You're a free man again," she smiled.

I turned to the gallery to see my parents, but my attention was grabbed by the scene that was occurring to their left.

Stevie Foster, on hearing the result, had made his way to the front of the gallery and was now being restrained by a couple of the G4S guards as he bellowed "You're a fucking dead man, Steel!" Spittle flew from his raging mouth as he fought and gesticulated with the security team.

Sadie, upon seeing the fracas, ushered me from the court room but I stupidly looked back just in time for me to see and hear Stevie Foster scream, "I'm coming for you, boy, I'll fucking kill you!"

He looks like he means it too.

No shit! He's clearly insane.

CHAPTER 66

It's a hellish notion, the thought of incarceration.

I'd already suffered through a sneak preview of my potential fate and being brutally honest I cannot say that I would have survived had I been forced to return there to serve a sentence.

I exited the courtroom to a couple of photographer's flashes and a random reporter's question, but I took no heed.

My mind was awash with adrenalin-fuelled crescendos yet the moment I surfed that glorious wave my brain inexplicably rolled my board so that I was driven deep beneath the waves of my own ecstasy and forced to toil within the drowning images of what ifs and maybes.

Gasp!

Splutter!

"Welcome home, Jimmy."

My spinning thoughts were brought to an abrupt halt as the taxi door opened and I was greeted by my parents who stood open armed.

She called you Jimmy?

I stepped from the cab and noticed a slight twinge in my back as I did so.

Getting old, son.

But that mattered not a jot as I embraced my mother and father as if for the first time in a millennium.

"By Christ it's fucking great to be home," I announced as I wrapped my arms around the two of them.

"James!" Mum scolded. "You're not in prison now, spare me that language," and she laughed.

She actually laughed.

"Sorry, Mum."

It didn't matter.

Not anymore.

I was lost in that triangular huddle.

Comforted.

The smells, touch, sounds.

"I'm sorry, folks …"

It was all too much.

"You've nothing to be sorry for, son," whispered my dad and I broke down for the umpteenth time in such a short time.

CHAPTER 67

I would love to say that I slept like a baby upon returning to my parent's house, safely contained within the nurturing boundaries of my hometown for the first time in months.

But that would be a lie.

The hastily assorted items that were presented to me as they ushered me into my old bedroom clearly represented the fact that my parents thought I'd be going down for quite some time. Or perhaps they were just trying to be nice and thought I'd like my old room back?

I was fine in the spare room.

Where the hell did they get this shit?

Where the hell is not the question.

How the fuck can you still buy a rickety camp bed from the 1960s?

I probably wouldn't have slept much had it been upon a memory foam king-sized mattress due to the internal chatter that racked my conscience.

However, a foosty, springy, creaky, actually-worse-than-prison-issue sleeping apparatus made sure that I got next to zero hours kip on my first night of freedom.

With every turn of my guilt-racked body I crept between tortured slumber and squeaking reality.

Will there ever be peace?

"Good morning, son," my mother cooed as I rubbed my eyes upon opening the kitchen door.

"Morning," I croaked. "What time is it?"

"It's just gone ten, did you sleep well?"

"Eh? Aye? No' bad thanks," I replied as my brain registered and then drowsily processed the fact that my dad had saw fit to enquire about how I'd slept for the first time in my life.

Despite being confused but pleasantly surprised by his questioning I had to lie that I'd slept like a baby and that it was great to be back home.

Gee but it's great to be back home.

Home is where I want to be.

"Do you still listen to PopMaster?" my mum asked, smiling as she turned from shovelling what looked like eggs around a smoking pan.

"Eh yeah, when I can."

"Well you sit yourself down and I'll be over with some breakfast and we can all play together like we did that time when Clare was over. We went up to that caravan park at Embo. Do you remember, James? Clare had just come home from New Zealand with Jonathan and told us they were getting married and …"

It really didn't bother me.

Trivialities, much like sibling rivalries, were for the focused of mind but by the habitual look she clocked upon my befuddled coupon she tenderly drifted from the days of old.

"Yeah I remember that, Mum. That was a really nice spot."

No it wisnae, it pished wi rain and that pair showed you up in front o' Clare at every turn.

Clare did everything she could to discourage it, it wasn't her fault.

Jonathan was a right wanker though.

Aye he was a bit.

"Ken Bruce is back from a week's holiday, it's always better when he's reading out the questions, isn't that right, William?" Mum looked to Dad for confirmation.

Due to the horrendously similar but weirdly new situation I burst out laughing and shook my head. My dad looked at me for a second and promptly let out a chortle of his own.

We ate our breakfast in a silence that wasn't comfortable but at the same time not as uncomfortable as it used to be. Chewing and gentle slurping of tea was quietly diffused with polite nodding and occasional smiling interrupted with sporadically shouted PopMaster answers such as …

"Alison Moyet."

"1984."

and

"Oh what's his name again, the wee French boy …?"

"F.R. David?"

"That's it."

Fuck this is creepy!

But nice.

And that's how it was for two whole days.

I was stuck in a perpetual unworldly faze where my parents were uncharacteristically pleasant to me whilst I stumbled about in a stupor agonising over whether I was an evil murderer or a misunderstood, underachieving wordsmith.

Or mibbe just a useless cunt?

I couldn't stop thinking about Debs. Seeing her for the first time in too long in that unnatural horrific situation turned me inside out.

Still want tae shag her though, eh?

Fuck off.

I obsessed about how differently things could've been if only I'd done this or that or hadn't …

Killed the cunt?

I've really screwed things up. Not just my own life but I've really ruined things for a lot of people.

Mum and Dad, Debbie and her unborn child. Danny Foster's mum, Stevie Foster, Bobby and Mel. Sid, Molly. The list could go on if I really wanted it to.

To distract myself from people, from noise, or just from being alive, I took a walk up to the old reservoir. You followed a wee pathway at the edge of town that took you up and over a hill. At the top of the hill if you looked back you were rewarded with a spectacular panorama of the whole town. A gentle walk through the woods brought you out at a clearing and once you climbed the padlocked gate the reservoir and all its sights and smells awaited you.

We used to come up here as kids during the summer holidays and it was a place of comfort.

I'd caught tadpoles up here, chased dragonflies, ridden my bike, smoked cigarettes, swam, kissed lassies, drank cider, fingered a lassie, smoked weed, and got half a blow job.

This combination of nature and memory helped define my youth.

Fuck I'm old.

Spring was in full bloom.

The beautiful white noise of my favourite time of year was lost on my senses.

I'm empty.

Save for a shriek, I mumble.

Grabbed by evil,

I check my conscience, remembering who I am.

Will I be free from this pain?

I long for the day.

Happiness is a state of mind,

yet mine is only in a state.

I get irate, impatiently waiting, always waiting.

For nothing to arrive.

The water's reflection sparkled with pond life.

DO IT!

A dragonfly hovered nearby and then shot off in fright as I made to wipe the snot from my nose.

GO ON, DO IT!

All around me new life was beginning.

Shoots, leaves, larvae.

Even the light had improved.

FUCKING DO IT!

Shimmering eyes returned my stare.

Would the weight of my own sorrow be enough to tie me down?

I closed my eyes.

The human body is a remarkable piece of engineering, and its spirit is almost unbreakable. The body and brain can suffer terrible traumas, yet it can continue to survive. The body can cope with the loss of limbs. It can continue to operate with the loss of hearing and sight. It can also continue to survive despite the loss of loved ones. Throughout the centuries the human being has been faced with war, famine, drought, disease, and all the hardships they deliver.

Yet we continue to survive.

I asked myself is there anything we cannot deal with?

I searched for Debs and her unborn child.

Danny's mother.

I looked at my own life. The loss of my reputation, my dignity.

I struggled despite these cruelties to survive.

There is one element that the human spirit needs to have to continue its fight for survival. Without it the spirit is easily crushed, and survival is over.

Hope.

We all need something to strive for, something to live for, and far too often in this cruel world that something is quite simply, hope. Hope that all the wrongdoings, all the evils, all the injustices, all the heartaches will cease. Hope that you will meet 'the one', that you will be wealthy, and that you will be happy.

Hope simply for hope's sake.

But I have now lost all hope.

Without it there is no hope.

What is the point of my tragic existence?

How am I to cope, without hope?

Why should I continue to survive when there is nothing to survive for?

No family, no friends, no legacy, no nothing.

No hope.

CHAPTER 68

"JIMMY?!"

The air cracked.

"Jimmy?"

Snapped from my pondering, I turned to see Bobby sprinting through the wild flowers towards me.

"What the hell are you doing, man?" he shouted as he grabbed me from the water's edge.

"Just thinking ..."

"For fuck's sake, come here," Bobby wrapped me in his arms and damn near squashed out the little bit of life that was left in me.

"Thinking? Dinnae be thinking that, man. That's no' the way. Come on."

"No, no, I wasnae gonnae do that," I stammered, suddenly embarrassed by the turn of events.

"Jesus Christ, man. That's no' the answer," he soothed.

"I wasnae gonnae do it ... I was just ..."

"Mon, sit here."

"I've had enough, Bobby. It's too much," and I wept in his arms. "I've caused so much pain, I didn't mean to kill him. Debs and her bairn and ... "

Bobby held me as I howled with grief.

So much loss.

GUILT.

"Your Mum phoned me, she was in such a state saying you'd gone out and weren't yourself and that she was worried sick."

Mum?

Aye she kens you better than any cunt and tae think you thought she didn't even care?

"I'm sorry, Bobby. I wasn't really gonnae do it. It's no' even that deep in there ..."

"You silly bastard," Bobby laughed.

CHAPTER 69

After speaking to my mother on the phone and assuring her that I wasn't going to drown myself in a reservoir that had seen water levels depleted to a record low, rendering the task near impossible (thanks global warming), I bade a shameful retreat to Bobby and Mel's house where I was introduced to the newest member of the family whilst being treated in a similar fashion whilst crashing on their couch.

Bobby insisted that I stayed with Mel and him for a few days to help 'assimilate' me back into civilian life.

I can honestly say that if by 'civilian life' they meant watching them cleaning the arse of a never-ending shite bomb whilst constantly engaging in meaningless baby talk I think I'd rather go back to prison thank you very much.

JOKE!

After a pleasant breakfast of porridge with dried figs accompanied by the sounds and visuals of a baby self-imploding, my mother called to tell me that she was arranging a dinner at home to be attended by my good self and a few select others to celebrate my release from prison/commencement of what's left of my pishy life.

I was initially sceptical/anxious about this plan as I didn't want to draw unnecessary attention to myself but having listened to Bobby and Mel's argument about a lifelong friend stitching them up and leaving them cold and lonely on a Glasgow street as plans of fame and riches went down the swanny and that I was not to be such a self-obsessed selfish prick and allow my parents to do something nice etcetera etcetera, I reluctantly agreed.

It's nice to be nice.

It was a pleasant evening as the McGee household and myself slowly strolled through town to my parent's house. This was the first time that I had actually walked the main streets since my release due to fear of confrontation from locals and the obsessive notion that I may fall prey to Stevie Foster. I met a couple of the older custodians whom I was on nodding terms with and who had stopped to tell me that they were glad I was a free man because 'that

Foster boy was a bloody nuisance.'

The Foster's reign of terror could only have lasted a couple of years and it was nearly 25 years since Danny had left to join the army, but the townsfolk here had long memories and were an unforgiving mob.

Buoyed by their support I walked the remaining few streets with my head held a little higher than it had been in a good while.

I almost saw the skyline.

My parent's house came into view as we turned into their cosy little cul de sac and my stomach turned a little.

I'd spent the first 18 years of my life in this idyllic urban bungalow but strangely felt no attachment to it. Not that I'd ever been one for sentimentality and had felt the old heart strings tugging every time the place came within sight, but I'd thought I'd at least feel something. Well, something other than the dreadful feeling that hit me now. I mean, I've got some amazing memories of the place but … och I don't know. After all that's happened and what with my parents putting on this wee shindig in my honour, I'd envisaged it feeling great returning here. (I know it's only been a couple of days since I last stayed here but that doesn't count. Allow me my self-indulgent triumphant return to a place where I don't belong.)

I could see the net curtain twitching and as we approached the newly chipped driveway the front door was flung inwards as my mother blurted "Where have you been? The guests have already arrived." She looked ashen and as stressed as a lifelong resident can appear whilst having to (and I'm only guessing) engage in small talk with fellow lifelong residents.

That's the beauty of this place, or maybe it's simply the beauty of my parents. Or perhaps it's the beauty of all once affluent towns countrywide. I'm talking about that scenario whereby every inhabitant pretends that they're living a life of perpetual bliss and that bad things only happen to bad people or those weak enough to succumb to life's trivialities and when actually faced with a little bit of trauma they have no idea how to cope in front of the people they've been misleading their entire life.

Think Facebook before Facebook was even a thing.

It's better to be honest from the start.

New life lesson number one.

"Sorry, Mrs Steel. It's totally our fault, just as we were leaving the wee one needed changed again and ach you know what it's like?" Bobby interrupted like the big hero that he is.

"Oh and is this the wee one?" The bleak accusing mood suddenly lifted from my mother's face as she spied Mel and Bobby's distraction.

Perhaps maternal instinct kicks in a generation later?

I left Mel, Bobby, and baby Rachel to get better acquainted with Mum as I made my way indoors.

The first person I was greeted by as I made my way down the hall was our old neighbour Bob Noble who had just exited the bathroom and was shaking drips from his hands when he clocked me.

"Here he is … FREEEEEEDOM!"

It's amazing what a wee bit of sunshine and house-measured alcohol can do to a normally quiet and unassuming man.

I was almost rugby tackled by his elderly embrace.

"What a result, son. Glad to see you're a free man. Never in doubt, never in doubt. I telt your old man there was nae reason to worry. Never in doubt."

"Eh cheers, Bob," I acknowledged as he slapped my back.

"Thon Foster boy was trouble from the start, and I ken he didnae have it easy but that's nae excuse, nae excuse."

"Aye thanks for your support, Bob. Cheers for coming, how's Morven getting on?" I asked as way of a distraction.

"She's doing really well, son. Really well. Just been promoted in fact, the first women to manage—"

"That's brilliant, I need to catch up with her at some point, listen I better go and mingle and that …" I shrugged off his wrinkly embrace before I was bored into submission about his daughter's wondrous exploits.

"James?"

"Mr Crawford?"

Jesus Christ, I thought you were deid.

Having rid myself of Bob's clutches I hastily turned into the kitchen and smacked square into the ghost of my old primary school headmaster.

"You're looking well, James, considering your stramash," he announced, overemphasising the R's as he always did, making it sound like stRRRRRRamash.

I hadn't seen him in nearly 30 years.

He looks exactly the same.

Whit fucking Dorian Gray type shit is this cunt up tae?!

Maybe he went grey at 20?

"Aye, Mr Crawford, eh, you know, self-preservation …"

"Good for you, James. So what are your plans now?"

I can't quite believe that the man who taught me in primary seven is standing before me now looking exactly as he did all those years ago and I don't know whether to praise him or fear him.

He's still got that horrible yellow tobacco-stained streak under his nose and lip from that pipe he smoked.

Dae ye think it was just tobacco in that pipe?

Try as I might to answer I'm suddenly transformed into the 11-year-old kid he taught.

"Eh dunno, Mr Crawford. Maybe do the band thing again … eh …"

"Hmm," he pondered whilst stroking his nicotine-stained beard the way he always did. "You were always good at creative writing, what about channelling your energy in that direction?"

"JIMBO?" A voice called out from beyond.

"Eh, aye good idea, Mr Crawford. Listen I'd better crack on, there's Malcolm Jordan shouting on me. We'll get a proper catch up soon though. Good to see you."

"JIMBO?"

FOR FUCK'S SAKE!

Is this some sort of horrific trip down memory lane?

Nae doobt they've slung the entire occupants o' yer ninth birthday party intae the shitiest time machine going and this is the result o' this pure and utter waste o' fucking time!

At least they're trying.

"Jimbo? How long has it been?"

The fact that you're still calling me Jimbo suggests it's been at least a while, eh?

CUNT!

For those of you not in the know, 'Jimbo' was a terrible children's cartoon from the late 1980s with an awful theme tune that reverberated around your brain like a dentist's drill. It was the type of awful theme tune that would have had you running in fear for your own safety if your name happened to be Jim or Jimmy. Thankfully the reality of every kid yelling Jimbo at me was brought to an abrupt halt by the hands of its perpetrator.

Malcolm Jordan.

Fucking moron!

I must've been about nine when Jimbo and the Jet-Set first aired on Children's BBC and due to my obsession with kicking a ball about after school completely missed the momentous moment.

Malcolm, however, had not.

The next morning as Sid (as he wasn't then known) and me and our regular bunch of pals walked to school we were rudely interrupted by a high-pitched whining noise.

Turning to our left we all witnessed Malcolm Jordan (who was always a little bit special) sprinting towards us, arms splayed and pointing at me, screaming, "Jimbo, Jimbo, Jimbo," until he spluttered whilst in crescendo and tripped and fell in dog shit.

This unfortunate turn of events saw Malcolm and not me renamed "Jimbo."

For some obscure reason despite finding himself now named Jimbo he still referred to me as Jimbo.

Which always pissed me right off.

"Malcolm, long time no see."

"Jimbo? How are your pal?"

Mungy Malcolm.

Shut up.

"I'm good, Malcolm. How are you?"

"I'm doing good, Jimbo. That's crazy what happened to you and Danny Foster though eh?"

"Aye," I rubbed my face in exasperation.

"You killing Danny Foster? I wish I'd had a pound on that. What odds do you think you'd've got back in first year of that happening?"

I exhaled air and shrugged my shoulders as one must do having been asked a weak rhetorical question.

"Probably like a thousand to one," Malcolm declared thoughtfully and raised his eyebrows and nodded at me in expectation of the mathematics registering in my brain.

"Aye probably," I sighed.

"Wish I'd had a pound on that."

"Why? So you could've spent the entire winnings on Monster Munch you stupid—"

"JAMES?" my mother hollered from afar.

"Coming."

I about turned, leaving Malcolm confused and open mouthed and fled from the kitchen.

There was no need for that.

I charged down the hall feeling angry at myself for treating Malcolm that way and pissed off at my parents for inviting all these people whom I didn't even know and yet was expected to feel humbled by their show of solidarity.

I could hear my mother's laughter echoing from the dining room as I made my way towards her.

"Oh what are you like, Ian?" she chuckled as I stuck my head through the door.

"What is it?" I enquired, but as she turned to face me I knew what it was. Or rather who it was as he popped his head out and displayed that glaiket grin of his.

"There's somebody here to see you," and my mother smiled as if I would be pleased to see her special guest.

"Jimmy?" Sid shouted as he bound towards me with open, arms awaiting my embrace.

"What the fuck do you want?" I replied as he gathered me up in an over exuberant hug.

"James?" my mother scolded. "Ian's come all the way up from London to see you, where are your manners?"

"Yeah, Jimmy. Where are your manners?" Sid mocked into my ear as he withdrew from my limp frame to smile before me.

"I'll let you two catch up and then you can come and join us for some snacks and wine, okay, Ian?"

"Sounds magic, Mrs Steel."

Mum closed the door behind her, leaving me trapped in the dining room with Sid.

Old emotions of love and respect and adulation no longer hung around my being. The current lodgers were disgust, loathing, and contempt.

They made themselves comfortable as I continued to glare at him coldly.

"It's good to see you, man."

"Is it?" I replied flatly.

"Aye, aye it is. So how you been?" Sid couldn't maintain eye contact with me so took off on a lap of the dining room, tapping the backs of chairs and scrutinising a painting on the wall as he awaited my reply.

"Oh tremendous."

"Good, good."

"Look, what the fuck do you want, Sid?" I seethed, whilst attempting to hold back my anger at this pathetic excuse for a human being.

"Why are you so angry at *ME*, eh?" moaned Sid.

I just stood and smirked at his response and remained silent so I could hear his rehearsed speech about how it was him who should be pissed off.

Come on, Sid, regale us all.

"If anybody should be angry here it's me." He even had the audacity to thumb his chest just to add that wee bit of emphasis to his puny rant.

Oh boy this is going to be better than I thought.

I pulled out a chair so I could enjoy this one in straight-backed comfort, but my actions seemed to confuse Sid and caused him to fluff his lines.

"Please continue," I offered sarcastically.

"You fucked it for us, Jimmy," and Sid pointed at me in disgust as he took off on another half lap of the dining room before turning to face me again and continue with his spiel. "You humiliated me. But no' just me, you humiliated Bobby and Molly too. To fuck it up for me is one thing but to ruin it for those two is just sad. You fucked everything I'd worked for, everything I'd built. Years and years of toil ruined because of you so dinnae be gieing me your pish about how sad you are that I didn't come and visit you in the jail."

Clap Clap Clap Clap Clap.

"Outstanding," I whooped and rose from my chair to give him a standing ovation.

"What the hell are you doing?" Sid asked, bewildered.

"Is that why you think I'm pissed off? Oh boo hoo my pal wouldn't come and see me in prison," I raised my hands to my eyes for effect. "Fuck off you twat, you're not that important. I'm angry because you've got the nerve to turn up here at my parents' house demanding a reconciliation after all you've done."

"After all I've done? What have I done? You're the one who ruined my reputation," Sid raged as he stomped round the table to face me.

"You still don't know? You just don't get it, do you, Sid? You don't think that wee incident with you putting those stupid videos on the internet had anything to do with this, no?"

"What? That was just a bit of fun, a laugh."

"Oh aye it was hilarious. Debs was humiliated, Danny Foster took it upon himself to almost kill me for it and we all know how that one turned out, eh?" I fumed.

"Oh so it's my fault that you killed Foster? Aye that's right, Jimmy, I mind telling you to tool yoursell up and stab the cunt tae death, eh? Are you aff your heid?"

"No, if anything I've never been more at peace, Sid. You see, being locked up gives you plenty time to think. Time to get to know yourself and I mean really get to know yourself, what makes you tick. The things that you need in your life and the things that you don't. It makes you think about the people you need in your life and about the people who are holding you back. Excess baggage so to speak."

"Look, Jimmy, I know it couldn't have been easy in there, but it was only temporary, I mean, you're out now. Time to start again, eh?" Sid shuffled backwards as he stalled for time to come up with a new strategy.

"Aye you're right, time to start again. A clean slate if you will," and I forced a smile.

"Aye forgiveness and all that, eh? I mean, it wasn't easy coming back here, I still had a lot of anger inside, hatred almost. But I thought no. I've got to be the bigger man, everybody deserves a shot at redemption, a clean slate like you say," Sid soothed. He smiled at me, but the smile was more a smile of self-satisfaction at a corny half-arsed speech than of warmth towards an old friend.

Sid still didn't get it.

He never will.

When you are so self-obsessed and ego-driven it's too much of an effort to extract your head from the tight clutches of your arsehole and smell reality.

I returned his smile and sighed.

"So, Sid, what the fuck do you want?"

At this his pupils dilated and his whole manner changed into a seething ball of energy.

He pulled out a chair and sat down.

"It's not so much what *I* want, Jimmy. It's what *WE* want," he thrust his hand out for me to join him in sitting at the table.

Here we go again.

I looked down upon him as he again gestured frantically with his hand as if to say will you please take a seat promptly as what I'm about to tell you will blow your tiny mind.

I sat down.

My arse cheeks had barely touched the soft upholstery when Sid sprung from his seat and launched into his latest and greatest bargaining plea as if the past year was merely a bad dream.

"It's what we want, Jimmy my boy. And it's what the fans want."

I laughed and shook my head in disbelief at the sheer audacity of the man in front of me.

Sid, however, thought my laughter signalled delight at his revelation and carried on with even more excitement.

"It's back on, Jimmy. I mean this time it's really on," he beamed as he gripped the back of his chair and gave it a wee shake.

His enthusiasm was infectious like it always was and it was hard not to get excited by the look of utter delight on his wee face.

"What's back on?"

As if I didn't know.

"Us. The band. Champions Of The Underdog."

"How? I put an end to that."

This ought to be good

"Not entirely, Jimmy. Although you really did try your hardest to fuck that one up for me, eh? And that open letter was just downright nasty." Sid had to actually shake his head to rid himself of the memory before continuing. "I'm digressing, it turns out the fans want us back. My phone's no' stopped ringing these past few months and I'm still trying to sift through all the emails, it's mental."

"So why all the sudden interest now when before there was like … none?"

Take that, ya cunt!

Sid winced at my remark but regained his composure well enough to continue without showing the true hurt that it had caused.

"It's not that there wasn't any interest before or that, it's just all about timing, Jimmy."

Oh the poor wee man's floundering at your nasty remark!

Better ease it up a bit for effect.

"No you're right, Sid, it is all about biding your time. The right place at the right time and all that, eh?"

"Exactly, mate. Exactly."

The wee hatch that separated the dining room from the kitchen was abruptly flung open and my mother's smiling face filled the vacant space.

"Are you two boys behaving in there?"

Whit the fuck? Whit's she daein' poking her nosey puss in here, get yersell tae fuck ye auld boot!

"Yes."

"Aye, Mrs Steel, all good."

"We're starting to serve up the food through here, so you'd better be quick and get some before it's all gone." And she promptly closed the hatch as quickly as she had opened it.

"Please continue," I added to break the spell of confusion that had entered the room.

"Eh … so … aye, about the time that you were … you know … awaiting trial and that … I started to get a couple of phone calls from agents and events teams just asking about the band and if we could play for them and I told them that the band was no more, we'd split up … and I thought no more about it you know … the band's fucked, crashed and burned, time for me to move on."

I nodded in agreement just to show Sid that I was still interested in his long-winded story.

Just ask me.

"Anyway I start getting these emails from this TV company in America saying they're interested in our story and that they want us to perform over there and I'm still like, no way, it's no' happening we're done, as sad as that is, it's just no' happening."

"Go figure," I add for validity.

"Aye so I'm down in London thinking what the hell am I gonnae do with my life now, everything I've worked for has been ruined. But there's nae use in greetin' about it though, you ken?"

How very stoic, Sid.

"So I'm just carrying on and trying to get my life in order but these phone calls and emails are coming in thick and fast, these folks are really persistent you know and they're all saying look, you need to get this band back together, there's a huge market out there waiting for you. I mean I'm getting calls and emails from Australia, New Zealand, Canada … did I mention America? Aye? I even took a call from a TV company in Germany. Germany? But I'm like nah it cannae happen, stop pestering me, we've split up and anyway, even if I did want it to happen, our bass player's in the jail for murder—"

"Culpable homicide," I interjected.

"Eh?"

"I didn't murder him, it was self-defence. *He* tried to kill *me*. I just defended myself, so the charge was culpable homicide. There's a huge difference."

"Aye, aye …" Sid's befuddled coupon looked like he'd just been asked to divide the square root of 13 by the circumference of a giraffe's nutsack so he shook his head again to allow him to continue with his tale. "Anyway I thought, right, when Jimmy gets off with this, which I knew you would by the way, cause Foster was a fucking psycho and naebody in their right mind would send you doon for that, so I'm thinking aye, they are right. There is still a market out there for us, you know? People do want to hear us and hear our story. So, when Jimmy gets out we need to get the band back together. I mean, it's no' as if the music industry is full of bands with a mental back story like oors, eh?"

Fuckin' hell that was torture!

"So what kind of offers have you had?" I asked, suddenly intrigued by this so-called new wave of interest.

Sid, upon hearing my interest, returned to his seat and was now hopping from left cheek to right cheek on his chair, the boy couldn't contain himself. His face would have imploded if I'd denied him this one.

"Oh, mate, you're no' gonnae believe the offers I've had. Mental by the way, absolutely mental. Last week I spoke to the head of VH1 who wants to do a documentary on us. Fucking VH1, Jimmy. There's been ABC, the BBC, fucking TCP, everyone wants a piece of us, man, and I mean everyone. They're talking about interviews, podcasts, tours, record re-releases, shit they even want to put us out on vinyl. Vinyl for fuck's sake. I've got management companies begging to represent us, this shit has got real, man."

Sid should seriously consider a career in sales. His enthusiasm knows no bounds. You cannot help but get swept up in his rhetoric. It's not just the wild hand gestures and knowing winks or even the theatrical nods of the head he thrusts in your direction, it's the fact that he genuinely believes in every word that comes out of his filthy, lying, self-obsessed mouth.

It really is a sight to behold.

I think I might almost be sold.

You've got nothing to lose.

"I suppose when you really think about it, about us, Champions Of The Underdog, our story is pretty unusual," I pondered whilst stroking my chin for effect.

Sid nodded keenly.

"Childhood friends form a band," I continued. "There's a wee flirtation with fame from the outset which is ruined due to a terrible performance," I looked over to see Sid grinning excitedly at my retelling of events. "Unperturbed, the band endure two decades of pubs and clubs until they decide that social media platforms aren't the way forward in a time when thousands of bands find that they actually are the way forward and instead embark on a gruelling tour of more pubs and glorified clubs countrywide instead of county wide."

"Hang on a minute," Sid protested as the smile vanished from his face.

"No let me finish, Sid. This is where the story gets good. You've got the classic tale of a spurned lover and his love rival who was a notorious bad guy. There's seething jealousy bubbling at the surface and when you throw in sex tape revelations, that festering pot bubbles over."

"Piss off," he seethed as he stood to rise.

"No I'm serious, Sid. This is the story, fucking VH1, man," I swept his admonished face aside with a sit-down motion and continued with my voice over style ramble. "With a record deal in the bag, the triumphant band performed a soon-to-be-forgotten concert to bemused guests whilst the moody bassist revealed that he'd staged the whole thing and brought about an abrupt and quite frankly disappointing end to a band that nobody outside of Fife had heard of or even cared about."

"Wait a minute," Sid complained.

"No, Sid, listen. They're right, our story has to be told, it has to be exaggerated for effect … the two love rivals meet, the hero soldier is finally pitted against the drunken bass guitarist and one of them is slain. Ridiculous as it may seem, the trained killer is actually killed by the treacherous bassist who then goes free only to meet up with his old pals to reform some rubbish band that nobody has heard of until now but thanks to the internet is suddenly trending and everybody wants a piece. Desire. Lust. Revenge. Hatred. Death. Fuck me, you've got all the right ingredients for a bloody good film there, Sid."

"No, no that's no' the way we're selling it, it's about the tunes, it's always been about the music," Sid countered.

"Oh aye I mean we'll get to that but that's no' why these folks have come sniffing around though, is it? I mean, they'd have been here already if that was the case, eh? The music?"

I watched his expression shift from confusion to realisation.

A bit like the poker player who suddenly sees that their winning hand has in fact been humped by the turn of the river card.

"Maybe, aye, probably," he shrugged.

"I just find it strange that suddenly the whole world is interested in a band that was going nowhere and had split up yet is now the number one topic for the online music community?"

"Well it's like you say, our story is unique and it's no' every band that's been around for the amount of time we have and ..."

It was sad seeing my oldest friend flounder like this, grasping at anything he could to make me buy his sorry tale.

"The 90s bands are in huge demand now, Jimmy. They're massive, even the shite ones. It's like how when we were teenagers and thought the 60s were cool, kids these days cannae get enough of the 90s and we're a 90s band, 1994 eh? Mind, when we started? 1994?"

"Aye I suppose we were. Look, what is it you want from me, just tell me straight up."

I'd prolonged his agony and seeing him waffle now was just time consuming and infuriating.

"Will you come back and join the band? Our story needs to be told; the people need to hear us."

"Have you spoken to Bobby?" I asked.

"What?"

"Have you asked Bobby?"

"No. I've no' even seen Bobby yet, I only flew in this morning, but Bobby'll be cool. If you say you're back in then he'll be there nae bother, it's no' like last time, there is a deal for us and that's guaranteed by the way. I fucking swear it."

"What about Molly? How's she getting on?" I asked, genuinely interested in how she was doing.

"Aye Molly's good and she's up for it as long as she gets to come on board full time and I've agreed to that so I guess it's up to you, Mr Steel," Sid raised his left eyebrow to reiterate his fact.

"What about money? How would that be split?" I inquired.

"Four ways man. Obviously, I'd get mair of the royalties but that's to be expected, eh?"

"I suppose so, look I'd need time to think about it, it's a big ask. Fuck it was only last week that I was contemplating a large stretch and reforming the band couldn't have been further from my thoughts. Shit, being honest, I was gutted that you didn't even come to see me. I was really toiling and to have you, my best pal, not even show face … that was tough."

Stop it ye're makin' me greet!

"I know, mate. But being honest I was still mad at the way you'd treated me, treated us as a band. Everything we'd worked for you destroyed. Looking back, I should have been the bigger man, but I couldn't do it, Jimmy. I was still too raw. But I'm here now as your friend. Fuck, your oldest friend, and I'm asking you to put aside the past, think of the good times and imagine what can be."

"I'll think about it," and I stroked my chin again for good measure.

"That's all I ask of you, mate," Sid pouted and stroked my arm for affirmation.

"Okay I've thought about it and my answer is no."

"Whit?!" howled Sid.

"I said no. You're full of shit and you always have been."

"Are you fucking serious?"

"Yes. I'm deadly serious when I say I have got no interest in reforming your shitey band."

Sid threw his chair back and loomed over me.

"We've got the chance to make millions here and be huge fucking stars and you're saying no? Are you fucking mental?"

The kitchen hatch pinged open again and my mother, God bless her little cotton socks, upon hearing raised voices stuck her head into the gap to announce, "There's only a couple of egg and ham sandwiches and sausage rolls left so you'd better be—" Sid raced over to slam the hatch shut, aborting my mother's snack inventory.

"You'll never change," Sid spat at me. "There was me stupid enough tae think that a wee bit time spent inside would sort ye oot but naw, you're still the wee selfish prick you always were."

"Look, Sid, nae hard feelings," I pacified. "You're a cunt, always have been, it just took me a wee while to see it."

Sid threw a chair to the ground and rushed around the bereft dining room table to grab me by the throat.

"Why do you always fuck things up for me, eh?" he screamed in my face as he pinned me to the wall, sending historical portraits of my sister crashing to the ground.

"I don't, you always fuck them up yourself," I wanted to reply but my vocal cords were compressed so I simply omitted a hissing noise as he choked the life out of me.

"Sid?!"

"You better gie me my fucking money, Jimmy. You still owe me—"

"Get aff him—"

"Jimmy?"

"Are you okay, son?"

Crash, bang, wallop!

May or may not have been the last things that I heard as the life blood was squashed from me.

I realised I was not yet for the netherworld as a dozen or so eyes from my past gazed upon my gasping, flopping body.

"Water?" I uttered and in response a carafe of liquid was shoved down my throat, making me gag and splutter.

"Don't worry, son. He'll not be back here again."

I looked up at my mother through watery eyes and couldn't share her noble affirmation.

I was propped up and sat upon a chair, the very chair that minutes before I had sat and paid witness to a tale that was so epic it was almost worth a choking.

"Quite the week you've had, eh, son? Would you like a sausage roll?" Bob Noble offered as he thrust a flaky monstrosity into my reddened face.

"No thanks, Bob. I think I'd rather go for a pint."

CHAPTER 70

"This is not good," Bobby kept repeating to himself as Mel, Rachel, and myself retreated from my parents' house.

"Are you sure you're okay, Jimmy?" Mel asked on a five-minute repeat cycle.

"I'm fine, are *you* sure you're okay with me crashing at yours?" I replied.

"What the hell did Sid think he was going to achieve?" Bobby butted in, still speaking to himself. "Jeezo this is too much, I spoke to him a couple of months ago telling him to relax. To take stock and that everything would work out just fine and now this? I dinnae think I can take much more of this hassle."

"Yeah it all went a bit mental in there. Good to see Sid's not changed though. eh? Thanks for helping get him off me, mate."

"It took three of us to drag him from you, I've never seen him so mad," Bobby replied.

"I'm really sorry that you guys have been dragged into my mess once again, if it's too much for you I can just stay with my folks, it's nae bother."

"No it's fine, Jimmy. Besides, I think Rachel likes you. You can repay us by baby-sitting tomorrow night so Bobby and me can go out for dinner, I think we need a wee break."

"A wee break?" Bobby queried, exasperated. "I think we need a year off."

The last half mile to Bobby and Mel's cottage was walked in silence and it should have felt like a treat. It was on the outskirts of town and the white noise decreased with every step we took, shaking off the memory of yesteryear but the screaming of Sid was still within my ear.

"Good morning, bubba," I overenthusiastically waved at the baby in the highchair as she sat staring at me whilst choking a banana to death.

"I dinnae think she likes me."

"Why not, Jimmy?" Mel responded without looking up from sifting through a pile of baby clothes.

"She just keeps staring at me with that psycho glare. Like she sees straight through me."

"She's probably filling her nappy, don't worry about it. I think she does like you and even if she doesn't, you're still babysitting tonight."

"There's nowhere else I'd rather be on a Friday night, Mel."

The babysitting gig was easy and it was the least I could do to help out two great friends who had been nothing but supportive of me.

Besides the babysitting evening, I spent another couple of baby-filled days with Bobby and Mel as I tried to adjust to the never-ending curve balls of modern life.

It's just called life, there's nae fucking curve balls involved.

I was sat out the back of their cottage on a nice sunny morning having just changed my first nappy when I got the call. I was delighted with myself, I didn't boak too much and the nappy stayed on when I held her up in triumph.

At first I'd thought the vibrations were rumblings in the newly changed nappy but the annoying tune told me it was a phone call.

The caller ID told me that it was my parents.

"Hello?"

"James, it's Dad, you'll need to come over, someone's thrown a brick through the living room window and painted graffiti on the house."

"What?" My mind raced. "Are you and Mum all right? Nobody got hurt?"

"No we're both fine. We were out when it happened, we've just arrived home to find this mess, there was a note attached to the brick …"

I knew straight away who the culprit was so my dad didn't have go any further.

"… for you."

But he did anyway.

"Okay I'll be straight over. Have you called the police?"

"Yes they're on the way. They'll want to speak to you because, well, you know …" And my dad tailed off as he tried to spare my feelings.

"Yeah, yeah that's fine, I'm leaving Bobby's now, so I'll see you shortly."

I blew a long sigh of despair from my cheeks.

"Everything a'right, mate?" Bobby asked, concerned.

"Eh no. No' really. Stevie Foster's chucked a brick through my parent's living room windae and spray painted a message on the front of their hoose."

"Shit," Bobby replied in disbelief. "That's terrible. Are your folks a'right?"

"Aye I think so, they were out when it happened. Look, I'll have to go, mate. I'll see you later."

"Aye, aye, nae bother. Mel shouldn't be much longer with the car, if you want to wait I can drop you off?"

"No it's fine, I need to go now."

"Right, well just gies a shout if you need a hand with anything."

"Thanks."

As soon as I was clear of Bobby's front door, I sprinted down the road. My head was spinning. I'd forgotten all about the threat of Stevie Foster thanks to Sid's little outburst but this confirmed that he hadn't forgotten about me.

After ten minutes of constant running and struggling to draw breath, I jumped on a bus. I sat upstairs and thought I saw Stevie Foster driving every car that passed us. I saw him in every pedestrian that crossed the road.

Keep calm, it was just a warning, nobody has come to any harm.

Aye yet. Ye ken fine well that you're next. He's relentless, he'll no stop until you're deid.

No, keep calm, everything will be okay.

Will it fuck. You think Danny Foster gave you a rough ride? This boy'll no stop until he's tortured ye tae death.

Oh fuck.

Feeling claustrophobic, I disembarked the bus and carried on with running the remaining mile.

I saw the spray-painted remark before I'd even entered the driveway such was the size of the lettering. It brought me to an abrupt halt, and I simply stared at it as I caught my breath.

Like a teenager's crass tag in bright red paint it read JIMMY STEEL DEAD MAN.

I was quite surprised that he'd actually spelt everything correctly.

That wasn't going to be easy to remove from the harled wall.

Shaking rogue thoughts from my mind, I moved to go inside but the door was locked.

Wise move folks.

I could see my mother's form peeking out through the net curtains as I rang the doorbell.

"How you folks doing?" I asked upon entering.

"Your mother's a wee bitty shaken up but we'll survive," my dad responded sullenly.

"Aye, a'right, Mum?" I asked as I caught sight of my mother clutching a cup of tea as if her life depended on. "Where's this note?"

"We got a bit of a fright and that message scrawled on the front of the house is a blooming eyesore … the note's on the coffee table there," she pointed to the folded note lying next to a half brick.

"Don't worry about that I'm sure the paint will come off with a power hose," I lied as I picked up the scrap of paper and unfolded it.

YOU'RE STILL IN MY THOUGHTS JIMMY I'LL SEE YOU SOON X X

This is not good.

Not good? This is fucking terrible. He's coming for you.

"You know who did this, James? That boy is a menace," my mum sighed.

"Everything will be fine, Mum. Don't worry about it. He's just trying to get to me," I lied again.

"Get to *you*? He's getting to all of us," she blasted.

The police arrived shortly afterwards and took statements. Despite my parents and me telling the police who was responsible for this, the two officers remained non-committal, stating that they couldn't make any arrests at this stage but would send a patrol car around periodically for prevention purposes whilst they made further enquiries.

A local glazier appeared an hour later to size up the job and fit a nice piece of chipboard which, alongside the spray-painted message, left my parent's house looking like one of the vacated town centre shops.

My parents failed to see this poignant point of view and simply sighed and retreated back indoors.

The next couple of days were fraught with yet more anxiety. My mind was transported back to the tour when I was besieged by the nauseating feelings of doom which only an impending beating can bring. Except this time it was worse. A beating would actually be good, I could take that. Stevie Foster meant business. He wasn't in the game of simply dishing out beatings. Especially to someone who was responsible for the death of his brother.

I couldn't risk anything happening to Bobby, Mel, or the wee one so staying with them was out of the question. I phoned Bobby to update him on the situation and got him to drop off what little belongings I had left at his house.

I couldn't risk my folks' well-being either. Or the house that they'd spent decades upgrading with toil and love.

I had to get out of town.

Again.

You need tae get oot the fucking country mair like. Stevie Foster is gonnae kill ye!

Since my release from prison, I'd barely drank alcohol, but on the second night after the bricking incident I raided my dad's booze cupboard. I needed a release, but more importantly I needed some ideas, a plan of what to do next.

And so, like a teenage drinker, I poured Cointreau, Cinzano, and Bell's whisky into a pint glass and threw in some cranberry juice to disguise the taste.

It tasted pretty horrific, but I could feel the alcohol quickly making its way through my blood stream as it numbed my senses and kick started my brain into action.

Donald's still down in London, it's a big place, I could go there for a while. I'm sure he'd put me up for a couple of nights.

And then whit? Have ye seen the prices o' rent doon there?

Aye I know but I'm sure I could sort something out.

Whit wi' £50 in yer hipper and a guid luck message? Piss off!

Lorna Ferguson's still doon in Birmingham, she'd put me up for a few days.

How? Cause you got aff wi' her twenty year ago and she'll still be fond o' the memory? Get a haud o' yersell, she's married wi' kids noo.

Shite.

Ronnie Laing?

Inverness? No far enough!

Lyndsay Cooper?

Did she no' marry an Italian boy? Lives oot near Naples noo? You cannae speak Italian, nae use!

Kev Wilson then.

New York? Now we're getting somewhere, Stevie wouldnae go that far but ye'd only get a couple o' months on a visa!

I'm no planning on emigrating.

Well ye cannae come back here anytime soon. So ye piss aff for a year or two and come back once ye think the heat's died doon and yer feeling aw smug wi yersell, hiya Maw, hiya Bobby, look at me strolling doon ma auld street in dear auld Caledonia when BLAM! There he comes oot o' naewhere and smashes intae ye wi' his works van! Deid! Taken oot the game! Naw, naw, ye need tae think lang term!

New Zealand? I could go out and see Clare, she'd put me up. Aye that would be rare, I've never been out there before and I dinnae think I'll need a visa, it's perfect.

Clare? Aye, sure it'd be rare tae see her again but putting up wi' that wanker o' a husband o' hers? Nae chance. Anyway, New Zealand's the other side o' the world, you want tae be invisible for a wee while, no fucking non-existent!

I'm fucked then, I'll just have to go on the run and see where that takes me.

Shh, wid ye let me think. I almost had it there. Whit's his name, mind the wee skinny cunt that was in yer geography class? Aw fuck, ye ken, had the greasy hair and wide nostrils? Laughed like a dug's toy being stood on?

Struan Donnelly?

Fucking Struan Donnelly! Stupit name as well! He's oot in Ibiza or wan o those places running a pub, he'll put ye up. It's perfect!

How? I've not spoken to him in decades, how's that perfect? Eh a'right Struan? Jimmy Steel here, Aye from school, no I know we were never pals and haven't spoken apart from the occasional a'right in the passing but I'm right up shit creek at the minute and if it wouldn't be too much trouble can I come and stay with you please?

Message the cunt on Facebook, yer mates on that. Lure him in wi' some wee remarks aboot how it's been too long and ye'll be in the area soon. Nae bother.

Struan Donnelly? Unbelievable.

As unbelievable as it may seem, I was shit out of options.

Or any better options.

I purchased a tin of Brasso and with an old rag started rubbing the smelly paste into my neck to give it a nice golden shine.

Oh Christ.

CHAPTER 71

Fearing for my life and the wellbeing of my family and friends, I did what any desperate person would do and reached out to an old acquaintance through the medium of Facebook.

As we were already 'friends' on the social media platform, I cut straight to the chase and kicked off proceedings with some small talk about my current situation (minus the bit about Stevie Foster plotting revenge) and how desperate I was in need of a holiday after all the shenanigans.

To be honest I wasn't expecting much in way of response.

Why should I?

Apart from the occasional 'likes' to a few of his online posts I had had no correspondence with him.

But to my pleasant surprise I received a direct message just a couple of hours later informing me that he'd heard the news about Danny Foster and the subsequent court case and that it was great to hear from me and to give him a call (private number duly supplied).

Fucking Struan Donnelly eh? Telt ye! Fucking wee legend!

I couldn't have wished for a better reply.

I didn't even feel nervous when typing in his phone number. Nor did I feel ashamed or desperate when the oversees dialling tone rung in my ear.

"Jimmy? How's it going? Long time no' see, mate."

Mate? I barely know you but thanks very much.

"I'm a'right, Struan. All things considered …"

"Yeah no wonder, I couldn't believe it when I heard the news. Danny Foster? Crazy. He was a prick though so good on you."

We chatted for about ten minutes like long lost pals, it was great. Nothing like the conversation I'd expected to have. Due to the ease I felt whilst chatting, I opened up to him about needing a change of scenery and a chance to clear my head whilst steering clear of the Stevie Foster situation.

He was so nice and understanding.

I think I love you, Struan.

"So, can you pull a pint?" he asked.

"Well I've drank plenty so I should be able to," I laughed.

"Perfect. Well you know I own this bar in Ibiza?"

"Eh aye," I answered, trying not to sound too jealous.

"So one of my bar staff quit the other night and I've been doing interviews all morning and I've been getting all the usual young English tossers coming over for the season and to be brutally honest, Jimmy, I just can't be dealing with all their shite any more, you know? I'm getting too old for their pishy patter."

"Aye, kids, eh?"

"Yeah, the scene's changed completely. Look I'll cut to the chase, Jimmy, I need new bar staff and you want a break from Fife so why don't we do each other a favour? Help each other out."

"Eh, aye that sounds cool like …"

"Brilliant, I'll be honest, the wages aren't great but the crazy season's about to start so you'll get tips and it's free digs. I even throw in a lunch before you start the shift. Not literally though ha ha ha ha."

"Tremendous, Struan. I'll away and book my flight now."

"Nice one, Jimmy, message me with the arrival time and I'll meet you at the airport."

"Fantastic. Cheers, pal."

My head was spinning from this turn of events. I couldn't believe my luck. I'd managed to find an escape, nail down a job, secure a place to stay, and all in the sunshine too.

Spawny Bastard!

CHAPTER 72

I booked my flight as soon as I'd finished my call with Struan. I felt like a teenager booking their first holiday without the parents.

Refreshed, invigorated, fucking ecstatic.

My flight left Edinburgh in two days' time and although not cheap (thanks overdraft) I couldn't wait to get away from Fife.

I broke the news to my parents over breakfast.

It was scrambled eggs again.

"It's for the best, Mum, I cannae put you folks through any more torture, you've endured enough and where does it stop, eh? A brick through the windae at first but the next time it could be a petrol bomb. I'm no' having that."

"So what is it you'll be doing out there?" Mum asked.

"Ach it's … I'll be running a tour company, you know, taking Brits up into the mountains and showing them the scenery and that."

I couldn't tell them I was working in a bar as they just wouldn't understand. Hell, I couldn't even tell them I was going to Ibiza, not because it was party central but because I didn't want them inadvertently blurting out to Mr and Mrs So and So my whereabouts.

This town has no secrets.

I told them I was going to Portugal instead.

Close enough.

"Oh well at least you'll get some sunshine, that'll be nice," she added.

"Aye it will be, Mum. I'll not be gone forever, I just need some time to gather my thoughts after everything that's happened and … well to let things die down here for a bit. Once I return, I'll probably go back to college and get a decent job and settle down, you know. Everything will be fine."

I had no plans whatsoever, but I knew that they would need to hear this bullshit for their own peace of mind.

Still trying tae please these two at your age? Fucking disgrace!

"Well what's meant for you will not pass you by," my dad chipped in as my mother nodded in agreement.

Have they been smoking weed? Whit hippy type bullshit is that? Aye, cause you were meant tae stab some cunt tae death and then go tae the jail for a while afore finally restoring your karma wi' a wee stint selling alcopops tae steaming kids in Spain eh? Whit's meant for ye? Utter pish!

They're only trying to help.

Still not wanting to jeopardise Bobby and his family by showing my face at his house, I phoned him to tell him my plans.

He agreed that it was the best thing for me to do in the current climate and hoped that it would all blow over soon so that I could continue my life with a sense of normality in the near future.

I was gutted to be leaving so soon after my release.

It felt amazing being reacquainted with everyone again.

Family, friends, old colleagues.

I felt that I was just getting to know them better, understand them even.

Old feelings were returning to the pit of my burning, nauseous stomach for the first time in years and I was frightened by the thought that leaving these people, this place behind would result in these feelings becoming lost forever.

I have to go though.

CHAPTER 73

I'd like to say that I had a lump in my throat as the plane took off and headed for the Balearic Island of Ibiza, but that wouldn't be true.

I felt a slight twinge as I gazed down upon the peninsula of Fife and briefly took in the coastal towns and the Lomond Hills, but my main feeling was one of relief.

Relief that I would be free from the anxiety of an impending brutal, violent death at the hands of a grieving psychopath.

Relief that I would be free from the incessant burden of being a disappointment in the eyes of my parents.

Relief that I would be easing the mind of a lifelong friend whose only priority besides that of his family's safety and well being was that of my own.

Relief that I was free from the clutches and all the mental torture that went with being friends with a megalomaniac.

As my mind scanned images of memories, the peace was shattered by an image that had once filled me with bliss.

Debs.

My heart sank as I thought of her predicament.

My predicament.

Our predicament.

Brought about by so many wrong turnings.

If only.

A thousand what ifs.

If only I'd …

What's the point?

What's meant for you will no' pass you by, eh?

Pish!

"Jimmy?"

I turned around in the busy arrivals hall of Ibiza airport to see Struan pointing at me and giving me the thumbs up as he approached.

"How are you doing, man?" I asked cheerily upon seeing his beaming expression.

"Good to see you, mate. Been a while, eh?" he replied and swept me up in a big hug.

I'd probably only said a handful of words in my entire life to this man before our telephone conversation but here he was grinning away like a Cheshire cat and hugging me like a long-lost brother.

"Welcome to Ibiza, mate. You're going to love it."

"I hope so, Struan. Mind you, it cannae be any worse than where I've come from, eh?"

"Well at least the sun shines here. Right, give me your bag and we'll go and get a taxi."

We strode out of the terminal and I smiled as the warm air and bright sunshine engulfed me.

Here we go!

I didn't get much of a chance to drink in the scenery en-route to my digs as Struan kept me occupied by giving me a condensed version of the near 20 years he'd spent on the island.

Left school, worked in the family business for two years, took a holiday here with a couple of colleagues, found out that nobody cares about your schooling or nickname or history whilst they're off their tits on ecstasy, discovered dancing, discovered ecstasy, discovered his people. Quit his job in Fife, moved out here, worked in bars, saved up, got a loan, bought a bar, made some money, bought two bars, made more money, got a suntan, found a girl, fell in love, married girl, had kids, sold bars in centre of town, and bought nice big villa and bar on outskirts of town, picked up Jimmy Steel at airport.

The taxi dropped us off at Struan's villa and my jealousy grew with every room we entered as he gave me the tour and when he finally showed me the back garden complete with private pool and barbecue area it was then that I decided I wanted to punch him in the face for making fantastic life decisions.

After a whirlwind introduction to the wife and kids, another taxi arrived to whisk us off to his bar.

"I wish I'd made friends with you in school, man. You're a right guid cunt," I slurred as I gulped another beer at my new office.

"Nah, you guys were too cool for me back then," Struan smiled.

"Fuck off. We were only playing at being cool. Well, Bobby and me were.

We didn't have a clue; we were just trying to survive."

"Aye it was pretty brutal, eh? I'm just glad I'm not a kid these days. You think we had it bad back then? Shit, I'd be destroyed if I was a bairn now, other kids filming me being slapped about? No thank you."

"Aye when you put it like that, I suppose our childhood was idyllic."

"Idyllic ha ha ha ha."

We rolled about the table in laughter and regaled each other with stories from yesteryear as well as stories from the not-so-distant past. Despite his slightly tipsy disposition, Struan did not pry nor judge.

Fucking top man this cunt, eh?

The drinking and merry making continued into the night as we listened to some young guy clumsily plucking his way through his repertoire of puke-inducing covers on a beat-up guitar.

"Christ this boy's fucking terrible, Struan. Where the hell did you get him from? He's scaring all the punters away."

"It's the wife's cousin," he stared at me straight faced and looked slightly miffed at my insult.

"Did I say terrible? I meant fucking brilliant. Really good."

Struan burst out laughing upon seeing the serious look upon my own coupon, much to my relief.

"Aye he's no' the best but he brings in a few of his friends to watch and they all have a beer so it almost pays to have him on. If you think you can do better, you're more than welcome to have a spot of your own up there?"

"Whit? Really?"

"Aye of course, belt out a few of those famous songs from the Champions. You're almost famous, you'd draw a decent crowd."

"Aye, that's a great idea, Struan. I could definitely do that; I've got loads of songs I could do."

"Of course you'd need to be really good to pull it off though, I mean you're no Sid, are you?" Struan smirked at me when he saw the fury blazing behind my drunken eyes.

"Dinnae even go there," I sneered.

Then he burst out laughing as my lips puckered like a cat's arsehole.

"I'm only joking, you'll be great. Once you're comfortable with the shifts you can get up there on your night off and depending on how it goes we can work out some sort of extra payment, okay?"

"Aye that would be fantastic, mate. Look I really cannae thank you enough, Struan. You've been absolutely first class; I really appreciate everything you've done for me."

"Save your thanks until you've completed your first week, it can get quite mental once the holiday season is in full swing."

"I'm looking forward to it already."

"Right, lets finish the night with a whisky. Rosie, bring us a bottle of Johnnie Walker over please."

I watched through glazed eyes as Rosie the barkeep put a bottle of Johnnie Walker Black Label in front of us with two glasses. Struan unscrewed the top and steadily poured two large measures. He offered me one then raised the other.

"To the future," he proclaimed.

"To the future," I replied, "and to new friendship."

"Slainte Mhath!"

We toasted each other with every refill and having drained the bottle we reluctantly called it a night.

I was very drunk but in a nice way. Buoyed by the opportunities that I'd been given and with the thought of performing my own songs on stage, albeit a tiny one in a bar on the outskirts of a town in Ibiza, I drifted off to a peaceful, delightful sleep.

"This is going to be great," I whispered to myself as I closed my eyes and I truly believed it.

CHAPTER 74

Referring to my time spent on remand in prison, I'd previously written that time flies when you're having fun and I can now honestly say that time does indeed fly when you're enjoying yourself.

And oh how I've enjoyed myself.

So much so that, as I write this, I've worked out that I have now spent 378 consecutive days on this idyllic island.

I am now officially in my forties too. It wasn't as painful as it is made out to be, it's more a state of mind and my mind is no longer in a state.

When I was told by the visiting shrink in prison that writing my thoughts and feelings down and telling my side of the story would be cathartic, I didn't believe her.

Even when I had started compiling my memories onto paper it still caused me a hellish amount of pain and anxiety and I couldn't see the point in her exercise.

I'd write down anything that came to mind and in any order.

Initially all that I'd produce was a frantic jumble of aggressive reflection but as the weeks went on and I showed the psychiatrist my efforts, I began to open up more and remember more and through her kind words and praise I began to enjoy it.

I actually looked forward to writing. Sometimes it was all that kept me going when I was stuck in that cell day after day with no end in sight. No way of knowing if I'd actually be released or not. Frantically trying to appease the negative thoughts of long-term incarceration.

Since my release I hadn't looked at the notes, poems, or stories that I'd written. I'd brought them back to my parents' house and stuffed them in a carrier bag inside a drawer.

This action was probably a metaphor for my way of dealing with life.

Besides, I had more important things to think about, such as what the hell am I going to do with the rest of my life?

I hadn't even begun to get to grips with that question when Stevie Foster decided to vandalise my parent's house and I decided to get the fuck out of dodge ASAP.

The completion of some hastily formed diatribes housed in a carrier bag at the back of a sock drawer was probably the last thing on my mind as I sat in seat 32F whilst the aeroplane thundered down the tarmac at Edinburgh Airport, bound for Ibiza.

It was also the last thing on my mind when I landed and met Struan.

It would be way down my list of priorities when I started work shortly afterwards.

In fact, all pressing issues were put to one side as I started my new career as a barman.

I'd at least had some great practice in spending thousands of hours (albeit from a different perspective) in bars and pubs and being in a band for years meant that I was accustomed to the late nights/irregular sleeping pattern combination.

You could almost say I was born to do this gig.

And I would almost agree with you.

Almost, except for the part where I am stone cold sober and everyone else is completely out of their face.

Now in normal circumstances I would have partaken (as the other bartenders often do) in drinking alongside the customers whilst serving them their drinks. But having had ample time to reflect I came to the conclusion that it was normal circumstances which were partly to blame for my demise.

I may not be guilty of murder or even culpable homicide, but I sure as fuck am guilty of making some piss poor decisions in my lifetime.

Getting the sack for being steaming on the job, a job that was kindly offered to you by someone who doesn't really know you and who also offered you a lifeline by giving you the job in the first place, would surely be up there with one of the worst decisions I have made.

So, to save another sliding doors style fuck up, I abstained.

And it was hellish.

But only for the first three or four months.

I didn't think I was going to make it. I wasn't even sure how long I was going to be out here. I was so thankful at being given this opportunity at such short notice that I was happy to go along with the old wait and see what happens and had no plans for the future.

That all changed in the third week of my employment.

Struan had been good enough to be up front and tell me that the wages were poor (they are) but that I'd receive free accommodation (I do, 1 star rating on trip advisor at best) and that the job would be crazy busy when the high season started (fucking mental) but I'd also get tips (don't play leapfrog with a unicorn mate ha ha ha!), however, I wasn't fully prepared for a million pissed up teenagers from Essex shouting "Oi sweaty?" at me and demanding multiple rounds of Jagerbombs and other shots of a similar ilk.

I was already a bit miffed at receiving my first pay check of 200 euros cash (I now see why you own a plush villa, Struan) and was three hours into a pulsating Friday evening shift when the shit started to hit the fan. One lad had just ordered 20 shots and after I had finished pouring them and was ringing it up on the till, I turned around to see that the lad and his friends had tanned all the shots and legged it from the bar without paying.

Guess who would have to cover that cost?

As our wages were so poor, I basically worked for free that night after covering the cost of the drinks that had been stolen.

Over the course of the next few hours, I had the remains of two drinks thrown in my face by angry punters who accused me of serving other people before them, I had lit cigarettes flung at me and a launched beer bottle narrowly missed my head as it smashed off the wall behind me.

The final straw was towards the end of the night when a couple of drunk lads ordered ten shots. After the earlier incident I had become very wary when serving large numbers of drinks but seeing as every person in the place was ordering double figures of drinks I soon eased up. I wasn't sure if these two were from the group who had legged it earlier in the night, but I kept my eye on them and sure enough when I asked for the money, they both downed their last shots and turned to bolt from the bar.

"Ah, fuck this," I sighed and vaulted the bar, booting empty bottles and glasses as I did so.

One of the two deviants had clearly been more affected by the night's intake of alcohol as he hadn't even reached the door by the time I bundled him to the floor.

"Right ya wee prick, gies your money," I raged as I grabbed him by the throat and held my clenched fist out ready to strike him.

"Sorry, sorry mate," he mumbled as he raked in his pockets and pulled out a bundle of notes to hold in front of his face.

Just as I was about to reach for the money, the door swung open and the other deviant lurched back through and aimed a kick at my head. Luckily for me the alcohol had also had an effect on this guy's judgement as his ferocious kick swooshed passed my left ear by a good yard or two and even luckier for me was that this full swing without contact momentum brought his left leg way beyond his own ear, causing his standing leg to also lift from the ground.

Gravity did the rest.

I snatched the money from the first drunkard and then flung/escorted him through the door and then quickly did the same with the second one whilst shouting in my angriest Scottish roar, "If I ever catch you wee pricks in here again, you're fucking dead a'right?"

Thankfully, due to the remaining punters being as sozzled as the would-be thieves, nobody had batted an eyelid at the aforementioned stramash. I counted the money that I had removed from the thief and it more than covered his bar bill but still left me short from the earlier incident.

After the place was closed for the night, myself and the three other staff members shared a much needed drink as we tidied up.

"I dinnae think I can do this anymore. It's fucking mental, hundreds of steaming kids just being wee cunts …"

Rosie, Martina, and Kristoff all looked at each other whilst smirking.

"You'll get used to it, Jeemy," Martina replied.

"I doubt it. So does that happen a lot then? Folk legging it before they've paid?"

The other three looked at each other and smiled before Kristoff replied, "They do if you give them the drinks before you charge them," and then they all fell about themselves laughing and comparing my exploits in jumping over the bar to "A rubbish Indiana Jones" and "An arthritic James Bond."

Pricks!

"How long does this high season last?" I dared to ask as their laughter dried up.

"About the end of September."

"For fuck's sake," I groaned. "We're no' even in June yet."

Martina was right, I have gotten used to it.

I've not had another runner since. Primarily because I heeded their advice and take the money before handing over the goods.

The banter is actually good fun, getting called 'Sweaty' and 'Grandad' used to piss me off, but most things do when you're feeling down.

And this time last year I was really down.

Saddled with all the guilt of killing a man and leaving a child without a father, a mother without a son, and a woman without her partner alongside the trauma and stress of a spell in prison and subsequent court case, I felt I was dealing with it all reasonably well.

I think the Stevie Foster incident was the straw that broke the camel's back, however.

After a month in Ibiza, I was really struggling.

Due to working late nights and it being very warm during the day, I couldn't sleep properly and my mood was deteriorating to the point that my co-workers had spoken to Struan and he'd come to speak with me.

It wasn't the kind, caring Struan who met me on arrival and showed me a night on the tiles but the shrewd, profiteering businessman that he'd become that I spoke with. Or more accurately, who spoke to me and told me that if I didn't sort myself out, I'd be replaced pretty quickly.

I felt that he was very harsh and if not for the fact that I had nowhere else to go at such short notice, I would've told him to stick his lousy job firmly up his arse.

Being desperate though and with limited options I meekly agreed with his appraisal and promised to buck up my ideas.

I got back in touch with the psychiatrist I'd seen whilst in prison and she kindly agreed to do half hour phone sessions for a nominal fee.

The fact that I was actively seeking her out to help me shows how much I've changed as a person.

Through her weekly sessions and by curtailing my drinking and smoking habits, my mental health improved to the point that by the end of my second month in Ibiza I was going for a run every day.

This in itself doesn't sound like much but besides the odd kick about at 5-a-side football, I hadn't done any serious running since I was a teenager.

By my third month I was running 5k every day and joining my co-worker Rosie at a weekly yoga session.

Throw in a healthy diet of organic vegetables purchased at the weekly market and I'd become quite the little new-age wanker I'd always detested.

Yoga?

Running?

Organic vegetables?

Nae bevy?

Nae fags?

Nae drugs?

Prick!

Aye, but I feel magic.

My shrink asked me if I was still writing my thoughts and feelings down

"No."

So she told me to carry on as before, continue to let it all out.

I phoned my mum and asked her to send me the bag in the sock drawer.

"It's in a plastic bag, in the drawer. No, the bottom drawer, there's nothing else in there so it cannae be hard to find. Right, don't look at the contents, just wrap it up and post it out to me. Whit?! No there's nothing incriminating in it, I'm hardly gonnae get you to send drugs out to me, am I? It's stuff I wrote in prison. Just some stuff, notes, poems, look can you just post it out to me please? Thank you."

The postie duly obliged and, when it arrived, I read it with my afternoon coffee.

It was clear when I started to read the jumble that spewed forth from its encasement that I was dealing with the ramblings of a troubled mind. However, when I sifted through the rants and the mumblings, old memories came flooding back. The great times Sid, Bobby, and I had spent together. but also the painful times too.

The shrink had said that it would be cathartic to write it all down but what I hadn't banked on was how cathartic reading it would be.

I laughed.

I cried.

I remembered.

Although it wasn't written with any sense of order, I was quite taken by how good it was.

I'd surprised myself.

I mean, I'd always had dreams of becoming a fiction writer and the short stories I'd written were all decent enough but this was different.

This was raw.

This was angry.

This was brutal.

This was true.

As melancholic as the words on paper made me feel, it strangely ignited a long smouldering flame within.

That flame slowly grew and with it hope and excitement.

After six months in Ibiza, and with the high season finally over, I had gotten into a great routine. As soon as we'd finished for the night, I'd run 10k along the beach and through the sleepy streets. After a six hour sleep, I'd awake at 11 a.m. and go for a swim then have eggs and coffee for breakfast. At midday I'd start writing, recalling all the thrills and spills of our time on the road together. The next five hours would fly by and then it would be time to head downstairs to start my shift.

By the end of month nine on the Island I was two months into an acoustic residency at Struan's bar. It was the quiet season so the acoustic jangling of a 40-year-old ex-bass player were more in keeping with the vibe of the place rather than the happy hardcore of several months previous.

Due to the advertising campaign conducted by Struan (which consisted of action shots from The Champions back catalogue and online propaganda about how huge a band we were), I could draw in a decent crowd of mainly ex-pats who wanted to hear cover songs from the British bands of their youth. I'd happily oblige whilst throwing in a few of my own compositions from time to time just to see if they were paying attention.

Not really.

But that didn't bother me.

I was enjoying myself up there on that wee stage.

As part of the deal I'd cut with Struan, I'd receive a whopping 250 Euros extra for performing two nights a week, bringing my monthly wage packet to 650 Euros.

That sounds like a terrible wage because it is a terrible wage.

But when you factor in free rent, albeit for a tiny bedroom with shared kitchen and bathroom and the fact that I rarely drink and don't smoke any more, the only thing I spend my money on is food so I'm still able to save the majority of my wages every month.

Plus, I've been moonlighting at a bar in the centre of town on my one night off which brings me in another 200 Euros a month.

This won't last long though because as soon as Struan finds out he'll put a stop to it. I'm his resident performer and his only.

I did think about free lancing, but I wouldn't be able to stay at my current digs if I did that and looking at the prices for renting a place, I'd actually be worse off so I'm happy with the current regime.

And why shouldn't I be?

Only last month I received a phone call from Bobby, that in itself wasn't unusual we have a weekly catch up whereby we both end up promising to visit each other soon but never do.

At least I've got an excuse for no' visiting him.

But no' any mair!

Bobby announced that Stevie Foster had been killed in a road accident.

Two tourists had been driving on the wrong side of the road and smashed into Stevie's car head on as they came round a bend. Ironically, the people who caused the crash survived but poor Stevie perished as he wasn't wearing a seat belt at the time.

It was strange news to receive.

I felt glad and sad at the same time, if that is possible.

I'd pretty much forgotten about Stevie and his violent threats. I mean, he had no way of contacting me and he didn't know of my whereabouts, so the threats dried up the minute I left Scotland.

I tried to think about the last time I had seriously thought about him or Danny for that matter.

Months at least, could be nearly a year, eh?

Aye probably.

It would have been a weight off my mind had there been a weight there but through my writing and healthy living I've never been in a more positive frame of mind.

"I guess it'll be me who comes back to see you then, eh?" I said to Bobby. "Although the weather will be shite. It's much nicer out here so you and Mel would be better off coming over."

He didn't bother though.

I took the opportunity to take a fortnight's holiday, the first time off I'd taken since I arrived nearly a year previously and unpaid of course.

I need to join a union.

CHAPTER 75

The sun was actually shining when I stepped off the plane which made me smile.

Ah Springtime in Scotland, I love it!

An icy gust of wind that nearly blew me from the steps as I descended soon wiped that smile from my face.

I wrapped the only jacket I had tightly around my frame.

I need to buy some warmer clothes.

But it was genuinely great to be back home.

Sweet Caledonia.

Bobby picked me up and drove me back across to Fife.

He dropped me off at my parents' house and I surprised them with an appearance. I hadn't told them I was coming so I was unsure what the reception would be like, but they were both pleased to see me and hear all about my adventures in Portugal.

I took them out for dinner and told them where I'd really been and the reason for my deception.

"We can't blame you, son. You had to do it for your own safety, I'm just glad it's all over now and you can come back here and get a proper job," my mother said sympathetically.

"I have got a proper job, Mum. I like it out there and I've got a few things in the pipeline too. Anyway, there's nothing for me here, if it wasn't for you two and Bobby being here, I don't think I'd ever come back."

My parents both looked hurt by this remark, but it was true.

"I can't see any future for me here. I'll still come back and visit you though."

I cannae believe they're making me feel guilty about not coming back here.

It's aw that yoga and organic pish, you've gone saft, hae a drink!

The rest of the evening was a flat affair thanks to my earlier revelation.

"Look why don't you both come out for a wee holiday, see it for yourself. It really is a cracking place and the weather's great too, you'd both love it."

"Och we're too old to be going on those long flights," my mum replied.

"Whit?! The flight's under five hours. Anyway, I thought you were talking about going out to see Clare in New Zealand? That takes over a day to get there."

"We were only thinking about it, I doubt we'll ever get out there."

"Oh well suit yourself, I thought a wee break in the sunshine would do you good, but I guess not."

"Aye well maybe a week would be okay?" my dad interrupted.

"Och it would be far too hot for us out there, you'd never cope with that heat, William," Mum declared.

"I suppose so," my dad reluctantly agreed.

"Not if you came out in winter. Or spring, it's a nice temperature then."

Why are you trying to get them to come out? You know it'll be a nightmare having them over listening to them moaning about the heat and the food.

"We'll see," and they left it at that.

The remaining 13 days in Scotland were thankfully more enjoyable than the first.

I spent most of my time with Bobby, Mel, and baby Rachel but also followed up on a wee lead I had.

I'd been in contact with a number of publishers regarding my first book and having read my synopsis and the first few chapters a couple of firms in Edinburgh were keen to meet me, so I printed off another couple of chapters to let them see my progress.

Having met with both companies and enjoyed their praise, I checked into my hotel room in the city centre so that I could get showered and changed as I had a more important meeting later that afternoon.

After spending six months in Ibiza, I'd finally plucked up the courage to initiate contact with Debbie.

I felt I was in a better position mentally to really express my feelings. Not in any romantic way but to apologise for the way everything had turned out. For all of us.

I wasn't expecting her to reply at all. Then I thought if she did reply, it would only be to tell me where to go. I wouldn't have blamed her if she did.

But she was always the bigger and better person and so she got back in touch. Not only that, she thanked me for taking the time to apologise.

She thanked me.

What an amazing woman.

Don't go there …

If the shoe was on the other foot, I can't say that I would have done the same.

And so we struck up a gentle correspondence, it was very light and formal at first. But as time went on and memories faded and confidence grew, it started to feel like the old days.

The old banter.

I called her one day to just to hear her voice. The conversation was weird at first. Unlike a computer screen there's nowhere to hide when you're on the phone.

There was still a spark there though.

A minute one, granted. But a spark all the same.

I told her I was coming back to Scotland for a few weeks and that it would be good to see her, to catch up properly, but she wasn't too keen on the idea so I tried not to push it. I called her on my second day here and asked again if we could meet.

She agreed.

I felt my heart lurch when she said yes.

Careful, Jimmy, don't go down this road again.

Not long after the incident with Danny, Debs had moved back to her hometown of West Calder to live with her mother.

Her mother Anne had always liked me but when Debbie had told her of the plan to meet with me Anne had not been impressed by the idea.

Thankfully Debs had stuck to her guns, and we'd agreed to meet for coffee in Livingston.

As the train lurched into the station, I was as nervous as I can ever remember being.

I was under no illusion that I'd be able to gather Debs up in a loving embrace and whisk her and her child off to a magical life in Ibiza but that didn't stop my imagination trying to egg me on.

Upon seeing her sat at the table, cradling her child in her arms, my heart did another somersault.

I still love her.

She saw me approach and rose from her chair.

And smiled.

Forever and always that smile.

"Hey you," I called.

"Hello," she replied.

"You're looking well," I commented and leaned in for a hug.

She still smells fantastic.

"I've still not lost this baby weight but I'm getting there. You're looking much better than the last time I saw you."

"That wouldn't be hard though, eh? And you must be wee Dick?" I said, rubbing the wee man's cheek.

"Jimmy!" Debbie scowled.

"Sorry. Wee Richard. I'm just getting him used to it cause that's what he's going to get at school you realise?"

"Very funny."

"He looks just like you, very cute. Here, these are for you and this is for the wee man," I said as I placed some flowers and a soft cuddly toy on the table.

"Aw thanks, they're lovely."

We sat and chatted as if the past two years had never happened, and it was magical.

We still had that connection.

Careful, Jimmy.

Even baby Richard liked me. He was grinning away and trying to talk as I bounced him on my knee when a woman from the next table commented that he was such a lovely baby and was the spit of me.

"Eh he's no' actually mine," I replied whilst awkwardly handing him back to his mother.

I had a weird sense of loss come over me there and then.

I actually wished he was mine.

That they were both mine.

This brought a lump to my throat.

My thoughts were rudely interrupted by the sudden shriek that bellowed from Richard's lungs.

"Right, he's getting cranky, we'll need to get going."

"Yeah of course, sure. Listen I'm still here for another few days, why don't I take you out for dinner, you know just the two of us?"

"I don't know about that, Jimmy. Maybe," she answered whilst stuffing a wriggling infant into its pushchair. "Look we need to go, give me a call, okay?"

"Aye nae bother. Great to see you, Debs," I leaned in for a goodbye hug. "And you too, wee man."

"I'll see you, Jimmy," she replied before gathering up her many belongings and throwing them onto the rack in the buggy.

I watched with an infinite sadness as she waltzed the buggy around the tables and chairs and then out the door and from my view.

I shouldn't have booked that hotel in Edinburgh.

I don't know what I was thinking.

A tiny part, the egotistical part of my brain had envisaged Debs agreeing to come back to my room for an all-night love-making session. Exactly where little Richard was supposed to hang out when this whole lotta shaking was going on, I'm not entirely sure.

I kidded myself on when booking the room that it was simply easier to stay in Edinburgh rather than having to get a train back from Livingston and then change and get another one back to Fife.

It's hardly a mammoth task getting back to Fife from Livingston but that was how I sold it to myself rather than admitting it was for the hopeless fantasy of getting back together with Debs so that the three of us could live happily ever after.

Alone in my hotel room I flicked through the myriad of useless channels on TV all the while thinking about my meeting with Debs.

Do you think it went well?

Aye, I think it went well.

The goodbye could've been better

How do you mean?

Well she could be back here.

Or at least agreed to have dinner with me.

Take it easy.

Change the subject.

To ease the thoughts from my mind and to relieve the boredom I did something that I hadn't done in quite some time. I went out and got drunk.

It didn't take long.

By the third pint I was really feeling it. On my second whisky I was in danger of being asked to leave as I staggered to the toilet like there was a force ten gale blowing through the place.

After a third whisky and with swimming vision I decided to call it a night. On my way out I asked one of the smokers huddled at the door for a cigarette.

Old, drunken habits die hard.

My head was spinning after a few puffs, and it made me feel like puking, so I flicked the poisonous tube to the kerb. I had planned on stopping by an off-licence to purchase a few cans or a bottle of wine for the room but after three pints and three whiskies the only thing I was fit for was my bed.

CHAPTER 76

I awoke the next morning with that all too familiar feeling of a thumping head accompanied by its old sparring partner, the nauseous gut.

I only had a few drinks, I complained to myself.

Aye you're out of practice.

And getting old.

I quickly showered and made my way down to breakfast. After shoving a full Scottish breakfast around my plate and nibbling on a slice of Lorne sausage, I gave in and returned to my room to gather my belongings.

I checked out of the Balmoral Hotel and made the short walk to Waverley Station to catch a train back to Fife.

Well that was a waste of £350!

On the plus side I received a call from one of the publishers whilst on the train. They really liked the extra couple of chapters I gave them and would like to publish my book once it's finished.

Thanks to my back story and the publicity gathered from the court case, they said they'd have no problem doing an initial run of 1,000 copies.

Check me out.

I'm going to be a published author.

I'll get to have my J.R. Hartley moment after all.

I called Debs when I got back to my parents' house. I only had a couple of days left in the country so there was no point in hanging about.

"I don't think it's a good idea, Jimmy," she replied to my offer of dinner then a night on the town.

"How no'? It'll be fun. It doesn't have to lead to anything, Debs," I said, knowing full well that I hoped it would lead to something.

"Look, Jimmy, I'd be lying if I said I didn't want to meet up with you. I've not had a night out in … well since, you know … and I get lonely at times. I love my wee boy to bits, he's the best thing to have happened to me but it's full on and sometimes I wish I could just let my hair down and be with somebody, no strings attached …"

"But you can, Debs. Just you and me, why don't you give it a try?" I pleaded.

"I've had this same conversation with my mum. She said it was a bad idea meeting up with you again. Not for me, more for Richard."

"But how? I'd take care of the wee man."

"It's not that, we had our chance years ago, you had your chance, and you didn't take it."

"Don't I know it; it's been the biggest mistake of my life."

"Richard is my life now, he's all I've got. I can't go backwards, Jimmy. Imagine you and me together and having to explain to him that his real father was killed by you. How do you think that would make him feel? He'd be hurt and confused, and he'd probably end up hating you and resenting me for my choices."

"I didn't kill him, Debs," I sighed heavily. "It was an accident, and you know it. It was self-defence."

"It can't happen, Jimmy, it just can't. As good as it was to see you the other day, and as much as a part of me wants to get close to you again, I just can't do that to Richard. It wouldn't be fair. My mum's right."

"I'm sorry. You're right, it's not fair of me to ask or put you through more grief, I've done enough harm. I just want you to know that I'm here for you whenever you need me. Anything I can do to help you've just got to ask, okay?"

"Thanks, I really appreciate that. Sorry it's got to be like this, I can only do what I think is right for my boy."

"Of course, no need to apologise, Debs. I fully understand, I'm out of order for dragging up old feelings. You take care of yourself and the wee man, okay?"

"Yeah I will do, you look after yourself, Jimmy."

Debs hung up and I lay back on my bed and closed my eyes.

I warned you.

Ach well, chin up.

It was worth a try.

That rejection hurt more than I thought it would and my mood soured.

I wished I was flying back to Ibiza in the morning, but I still had two days to kill in Fife.

I went for a run the next day to help clear my head and ease my woes.

I still couldn't wait to be back on that plane though.

On my last day I had lunch with my folks and then went round to Bobby's for tea and a couple of drinks. I wasn't really in the mood for either meeting, it was more for their benefit, but I was glad that I went.

The rain reappeared in spectacular fashion as I left for the airport.

I wasn't sorry to leave the dreich weather behind.

After saying farewell to my parents, it was onto the sunnier climes of Ibiza.

CHAPTER 77

And now the end is near and so I'll face the final curtain. Except this isn't the end. This is only the beginning.

When I first arrived in Ibiza, I used to ask myself, "Is this the life I saw myself living when we set off on our musical journey all those years ago?"

Hell no.

Is this the life I would have *wanted* to live when we set off on our musical journey all those years ago?

Also no.

And what about a couple of years ago? When the three of us climbed into an old fish van and set off for a six-month tour of Scotland with dreams a plenty, would I have liked to be where I am now?

Again no.

But having withstood a torturous six-month tour to nowhere. Having witnessed a lifelong friendship turn to hatred. Having survived a brutal assault and dealt with the subsequent killing of a lifelong enemy. Having endured months in prison awaiting my fate. Having suffered the defamation of my character and having fled my country to escape murderous threats, would I like to live the life I am living now?

The answer would be a resounding fuck yeah!

That hellish couple of years have made me the man I am today.

Wiser, stronger, and kinder. Kinder not only to other people but also to myself.

I'm more relaxed too. It took a harsh lesson to figure out that it's possible to have a wondrous perspective of life when your shoulders aren't slumped, and your eyes aren't constantly fixed on your feet.

As I look up from my laptop and allow my eyes to readjust to the fading light, I am met with a beautiful sight.

I am currently perched at a table on a rooftop bar overlooking the Mediterranean Sea. The island of Formentera is silhouetted against the setting sun and the temperature is a lovely 20 degrees Celsius.

Later on this evening, I will feast on a freshly prepared seafood salad drenched in the finest extra virgin olive oil and it shall be accompanied with a delicious glass of local wine. After cleaning up I will shower and head down to Struan's Bar to serenade a group of like-minded individuals with a set of my own choosing.

If the set goes well the night may be a long one. If not, well, que sera an' aw that.

Either way I do not mind because all is well in my world.

And why shouldn't it be?

My first book, this book, a book born from dreams that turned into a nightmare is soon to be published.

I'd be lying if I said that this is the type of thing I saw myself writing about.

But it's a start.

Who knows what roads lie beyond this one? Perhaps many, long and winding. Perhaps none. I'll never know unless I start walking.

Ladies and Gentlemen, my name is Jimmy Steel, and this has been my story.

Make of it what you will, after all, it's just a story.

ABOUT THE AUTHOR

Graham W.B. Smith was born and raised in the Kingdom of Fife, Scotland, and can usually be found gazing wistfully upon the peninsula from his home in Edinburgh whilst his partner Jean sighs and shakes her head.

An avid fan of music, comedy, and traversing his beloved nation, Graham decided to combine his three favourite pastimes into one handy bundle of joy for you all to enjoy with his debut novel *Something To Do With Luck?*

His other writing credits include: Demanding Christmas lists, apology letter to next-door neighbour for smashing their greenhouse with a football, tortured attempts at Valentines poetry, hilarious letter to The Sunday Post's reader's page about Mrs Green's hat blowing off on a windy day and then getting stuck up a tree (unpublished).

Graham is also a keen admirer of Scotch whisky or simply whisky as it's often called in Scotland and has been known to partake in a dram or twelve of an evening which probably explains why this book took him so long to complete.

Look out for his second novel which should be hitting the shelves sometime this century (21st).

Printed in Great Britain
by Amazon

23801068R00278